THE
HIGHLANDER'S
FOLLY

THE
HIGHLANDER'S
FOLLY

A Novel of Loch Moigh

Barbara Longley

Montlake
Romance

This is a work of fiction. Names, characters, organizations, places, events, and incidents are either products of the author's imagination or are used fictitiously.

Published by Montlake Romance, Seattle

www.apub.com

Amazon, the Amazon logo, and Montlake Romance are trademarks of Amazon.com, Inc., or its affiliates.

ISBN-13: 9781477821541
ISBN-10: 1477821546

Cover design by Megan Haggerty
Illustrated by Dana Ashton France

Library of Congress Control Number: 2014915563

Printed in the United States of America

To readers of fantasy fiction everywhere:
May you never cease believing in the possibilities.

CHAPTER ONE

Scotland, 1441

Five long years he'd been away, and were it not for the offal covering the shores of Port Leith, he'd drop to his knees and kiss the ground. Hunter covered his destrier's eyes with a cloak and led him down the ship's plank. His stallion snorted and bobbed its head in an attempt to free the reins from his grip. For certes Doireann scented the verdant, sprouting greenery of early spring beyond the borough. The stallion must be as glad as he to be off the malodorous vessel.

Once the others in his small band of traveling knights were gathered about him, Hunter began issuing orders. "Tieren, you and Nevan seek a stable near Haymarket Square. See to purchasing a wagon and a rouncy or two to pull it whilst you're there. Nothing fancy, mind. 'Twill no' do to draw attention."

Tieren nodded. "I've heard the roads are overrun with brigands since the old king's assassination."

"I've heard the rumors as well." Hunter placed his hand briefly upon his most trusted friend's shoulder. "Take care. No' even the streets of Edinburgh are safe."

Tieren shot him a cocky grin. "You've naught to worry about on my account."

A brine-tinged breeze blew in from the sea, carrying with it the odor of dead fish. Combined with the acrid stench of sewage from the city, the smells assaulted Hunter's senses. The port was no better than the hull of the ship. "Gregory, Murray, stay with the lads to guard our belongings. Cecil, come with me." Hunter removed the cloak from his mount's head and swung up into the saddle. "We will secure lodging for the night." He surveyed his men. "We depart at first light on the morrow."

"Och, Hunter. We've just arrived. Can we no' stay at least a se'nnight?" asked Nevan, the youngest in their party. "We've been at sea for nearly a month, and a month without a lass to warm my bed is far too long. I wish to sample all the pleasures Edinburgh has tae offer." He sent him a pleading look. "What was the purpose in winning all that gold and silver if I canna spend a bit of it on debauchery?"

"Wheesht, ye wee lummox!" Murray cuffed Nevan's ears. "Would ye tell all and sundry what we carry? Ye put us needlessly at risk afore we even begin our journey," he hissed beneath his breath.

"Oy! Leave off. The ship's crew ken well enough what we carry. Think you they'll keep it to themselves once they're visiting their favorite haunts and downing one ale after another?" Nevan rubbed his ears and glowered at Murray before turning back to Hunter. "At the very least, we should make our way to the castle. 'Tis discourteous indeed no' to take the time to pay court to our king, and the captain says young James is in residence."

Hunter shook his head. 'Twas not that his rank as a knight was any higher than theirs. In fact, other than Tieren, the rest were of noble blood whilst he was not. Yet shortly after they'd banded together, by tacit agreement the group had begun looking to him to lead them. "James is but a lad of ten. He cares naught whether a group of lowly knights pay him court whilst passing through. Besides, since the murders of the sixth earl of Douglas and his younger brother, I've no wish to make any aware of our presence here. Old Archibald and his sons William and David were close allies and friends to the MacKintosh. Well, I recall them from their frequent visits to Moigh Hall."

"Murdered, ye say? When?" Murray's eyes widened. "I too recall the lads."

"A year past." Hunter lowered his voice, rested his forearm on the pommel of his saddle and leaned forward, glancing at the men who had circled closer. "Lords Crichton and Livingston along with William's great-uncle James conspired to influence the young king and his advisors. The uncles manufactured charges of treason against the new earl and his next in line. William and David were beheaded right here in Edinburgh while our young king looked on, and with the old earl only recently laid to rest. In exchange, the Annandale and Bothwell holdings went to the crown, and William's great-uncle James took the earldom for himself."

"'Twas a year past, you say? How come you by such news?" Nevan raised an eyebrow. "Were you no' abroad and in the field at the time?"

"Aye." Hunter nodded. "My kin sent word through my foster father's aunt. Her husband holds a marquessate near Flanders. I was privy to the intimate details when we visited their donjon on our way to Calais. 'Twas before you rejoined us for the journey home, Nevan. I kept it close until this day."

Hunter cast a commanding look around the circle of knights. "We will no' tarry here. I trow you will find willing lasses enough along the way to Loch Moigh. I propose we take the northerly route and stop in Aberdeenshire. Three days there to rest, purchase supplies and send word of our homecoming to Loch Moigh will suffice, aye?" A chorus of assent followed.

He glanced toward the crenellated wall surrounding the keep where it perched high upon the rock above them, and shuddered. "Though he went about it all wrong, the elder King James had it aright. Scotland must become a united kingdom if we are to survive and prosper. 'Tis been but four years, and already the king's murder has torn Scotland asunder. Our clans do more harm from within than any enemy could from without."

"'Tis the truth, and I for one have nae wish tae remain in Edinburgh any longer than need be," Gregory said, crossing himself. "When shall ye return tae port?"

Hunter glanced at the sun. "'Tis but midmorn. We'll return when the bells chime for None." He turned his horse toward the city's busy roads and nudged him into a trot. Hunter's thoughts roiled with the treachery that had occurred in this very place. These days, the MacKintosh stuck close to home and stayed out of the politics at court as much as possible. For a brief moment, gratitude that he was naught but a landless, untitled knight filled him. Hunter held no power or property to be taken by their greedy young liege— or his *advisors*.

Cecil brought his mount up to flank his. "'Twas the elder King James who knighted you, aye?"

He nodded. "Tieren and Murray as well. 'Twas a personal favor to the earl of Fife for taking part in King James's ransom from the British. 'Tis hard to credit that nearly a score of years has passed since the year he returned to take his rightful place upon Scotland's throne, aye?" He sent his friend a wry smile. "Were it no' for my foster family, neither Tieren nor I would have dared hope to aspire to knighthood. I'm naught but an orphan and have ne'er even met my kin, and Tieren is the son of an alewife from our village at Loch Moigh."

"Who might your clan be?"

"My sire was a MacConnell. He disappeared before I was born, and my mother, a MacKintosh, returned to Loch Moigh to live with my granddam." Disappeared indeed! His poor father had perished when he'd been caught up in the wake of the time-traveling

4

faerie who called herself Madame Giselle. A shudder racked him at the thought.

"Did you never seek out your father's kin?"

"Nay, nor did they trouble themselves to find out what became of me." The bitterness still galled him deeply. Why hadn't his father's clan searched for him when his mother and granddam had passed? Surely his granny had sent word to his kin when his mother passed. For certes he must have had uncles, aunts and grandparents on his father's side.

Cecil barked out a laugh. "Mayhap no' by lineage, but by skill and valor you've more right to knighthood than most." He slapped Hunter's back. "You are undefeated upon the field and in the tourneys, and I for one am much heartened to ride by your side, sir."

"My thanks." Heat suffused his face. He shifted in his saddle and studied their surroundings. Though Murray was also aware of their clan's time-traveling secrets, only Tieren and his foster family kent the way of it with him. Hunter had a trace of *Tuatha Dé Danann* blood running through his veins. He had fae gifts, and one of them was the ability to anticipate the moves of his enemies. 'Twas why none could defeat him in battle or in contests of skill.

Like his foster mother, who had come to him from the future to save his life, he also sensed whether someone spoke truth or falsehood. Other people's emotions were a physical force to him, and it had taken some time before he learned how to shut them out. He kept his abilities well hidden. In these times fraught with superstition and peril, 'twas prudent not to draw too much attention. Prowess in the lists was acceptable; fae abilities were not.

Hunter lowered his voice. "Once we're settled, I want us out of chain mail and into our *feileadh breacans* or tunics and hose. I dinna wish to appear as if we are of noble rank or transporting anything of value through the countryside. Once we're in Aberdeenshire, we'll purchase sacks of grain, foodstuffs and wool to cover the casks and trophies in the wagon. Until then, a tarp will have to suffice."

"'Tis wise, but what of our saddles and tack, not to mention our weapons, tournament tents and banners? None will mistake our gear for that of mere villeins."

Hunter rubbed his hand over the stubble covering his chin. He wanted a bath, a shave and a decent meal this day. He longed for a good night's rest on a pallet that did not heave and shift with the ocean waves. "We can arrange to have those items transported to Castle Inverness with the next merchant caravan heading in that direction. The earl of Fife holds that keep for our king, and once we have our wealth safely stowed at Moigh Hall, 'tis an easy enough journey to Inverness to retrieve them. We can bring a contingent of the earl's men with us."

He searched for a likely inn up one side of the cobbled road and down the other. "As for the weapons, I plan to wear my claymore and daggers hidden under my oldest cloak. I suggest the rest of you do likewise. Our other weapons shall remain out of sight upon the wagon, so they are close to hand should we need them."

A short distance away he spied a sizeable inn that appeared well tended but not overly opulent. "There." He nodded toward the place he had in his sights. "The Dancing Stag," he read the sign aloud. "'Twill do nicely."

Hunter and the men had been on the road since dawn, and each league they traveled brought him closer to home—closer to Sky Elizabeth. She was old enough to wed now, and 'twas well past time for him to return home to claim her before her father married her off to someone else—someone of noble blood.

Aye, he'd gained his fortune in tournaments and hiring out as a mercenary, but would it be enough when he lacked land and a title?

Mayhap he could find a way around those deficits. After all, Sky's mother had come to them from the future with naught in the way of a dowry, land or political connections, yet she and his foster father had wed. Of course, Malcolm was the earl's heir whilst Hunter had no claim to anything.

"Do you smell that?" Nevan rode up beside him. "I swear I smell the roasting fires of Aberdeenshire from here," he said, sniffing the air. "First thing I plan to do once we reach town is to order roasted beef from the very best inn available." He grinned. "That and I'll have freshly baked bread, ale and a willing lass."

One side of Hunter's mouth turned up. "Is that all you think on? Filling your belly and plunging your tarse where it does no' belong? What of your future?" He suspected the lad would give in to gluttony well before he reached thirty.

Nevan snorted. "What future? I am the fourth son of an impoverished baron with no hope of inheriting a title or land. I'll return home to my father's keep and do my duty to my liege lord when called upon to do so. In the meantime, I shall plant my tarse where e'er I find a warm and willing wench."

"You've amassed a small fortune of your own," Hunter said, flashing him a wry look. "Mayhap there is a lady or a rich merchant's daughter with a sizeable dowry who might look favorably upon the fourth son of a baron. Do you no' wish to become a laird in your own right, settle down and raise a family?"

"Nay." Nevan shook his head, disgust plain upon his face. "Stewardship of a holding, a family and a clan are far too much responsibility. I prefer to squander my youth."

Hunter laughed, just as they came to the crest of a steep hill. His eyes widened, then narrowed, and a prickle of unease raised his hackles. Below them, nestled in the valley beside the North Esk River, stood a group of tents, booths and painted wagons like those of the wandering Romany. The scent of roasting meat, spices and ale wafted up the hill toward them. He signaled a halt. Why had he not sensed the presence of so many before this moment?

"Ah, I did detect the scent of roasting meat after all," Nevan said with a grin. "I feared 'twas naught but longing for it that made it so."

Frowning, Hunter spied a familiar sight, a green-and-white-striped tent set toward the far edge near a copse of pine. Memories tugged at his awareness, an old crone whose appearance shifted and changed before his eyes. She'd blown her breath into his ears, restoring his hearing—the hearing that had been lost to him by the same fever that took his mother. Sensing the old crone's otherworldliness, he had feared her.

Madame Giselle, or Áine, as was her true name, was the daughter of the *Tuatha Dé Danann*'s high king. The faerie princess was Hunter's distant kin and the source of his fae abilities. She was also the same faerie responsible for his father's demise. Premonition prickled and skittered over his skin, but of what he could not say.

Tieren rode up to flank him. "What is it?"

He jutted his chin toward the fair below. *"I recognize the green-and-white-striped tent toward the far end."* He used the signing they'd been taught as youths and glanced at his friend. *"'Tis Madame Giselle's."*

"Are you certain?" Tieren signed back as he studied the scene laid out beneath them.

"Aye." He had no need to offer more. Tieren understood him well enough.

"I smell meat and ale." Nevan passed them by, nudging his horse down the hill. "And I intend to fill my belly with both."

"Hold," Hunter commanded. Nevan ignored him.

"What harm could befall us at a village fair?" Cecil rode up beside Hunter, flashing him a puzzled look. Murray followed close behind.

Gregory joined them and peered down at the cluster of tents and wagons below. He shrugged. "Seems harmless enough."

"What village?" Hunter scowled at his companions. "There are none between here and Aberdeenshire. Have you ever heard tell of a fair being held here before, or at this time of year? Crofters are far too busy readying their fields for planting to travel anywhere this early in the season. Sheep are lambing, and the kine are calving. 'Tis no' natural to hold a fair now."

He turned his attention back toward the slope. "Return at once," Hunter called again. Exasperated, he blew out a breath as Nevan continued on, once again defying his command. "All manner of harm can befall us if my suspicions serve."

Gregory grunted. "I for one am beyond hunger for more than camp fare. The scent of roasting fowl has me drooling down the front of me tabard. A brief respite will do us good. We'll do naught but fill our bellies, and then be on our way."

"Aye?" Tieren said. "And what of the wagon, our squires and pages? Shall we risk all for the sake of our appetites? For all we ken, the gathering below might be a band of thieves intending to lure the unwary into their midst. I suggest we give heed to Hunter's warning."

Nevan's lads had already started down the hill after him, their gangly limbs bouncing as they rode upon the bare backs of their trotting palfreys. Hunter's insides twisted. Madame Giselle's presence could not be construed as anything but intentional. *What did she want? Could he avoid her?* Nay. He could not. Already her summons tugged at him, sending fingers of trepidation traipsing down his spine. Surely she'd kept her presence masked from him until 'twas too late to keep his distance.

Mayhap she simply wished to lay eyes upon him. He was her progeny after all, no matter how distant the tie, and no matter how much it galled him that she was responsible for the loss of his father. Besides, he owed her a debt of gratitude. Were it not for her meddling, he would not have survived his youth, nor would he have been blessed with the foster family who had raised him. 'Twas certain she had done what she had for him to atone for the loss of his da.

He glanced toward the stone-arch bridge spanning the Esk. "Move the wagon across the river to the far side of the next rise. Wait for me there. I'll go after Nevan and the lads. If all is well, the rest of you can visit the fair in turns." He met each of their eyes before asking, "Agreed?"

"Aye." Murray turned his horse back to the wagon and ordered the squires to take up their places. Gregory rode to the rear of their small procession as they got the wagon moving again.

"*Are you certain you do not wish me to accompany you? Isn't it you who bids us never to go anywhere alone?*" Tieren signed, reverting again to the private method of communicating Lady True had taught them.

"*Not this time,*" he signed back. "*'Tis folly to go anywhere near the fae.*" Hunter shook his head. "*Best I do so without risking your hide as well. Stay with the wagon.*" He huffed out a breath. "If all goes well, I'll be back within the hour, two at most."

He started down the hill, anxiety tying him into knots. Once he got to the periphery of the fair, tension stretched his nerves taut. He couldn't shake the feeling of wrongness overwhelming him. Though all appeared ordinary enough, he noticed the lack of patrons or villagers. Where were Nevan and his lads?

He scanned his surroundings, vigilant for aught amiss, for any danger lurking in the shadows between the painted wagons. Vendors called to him as he passed, offering their wares. Swarthy men and women, dark-eyed and raven-haired, peered at him, their expressions slightly mocking. Aye, as he'd suspected, this was no ordinary fair. These folk were the wandering Romany, and all kent they were in league with the fae.

The smell of meat pies and roasted fowl caused a rumbling in his stomach, yet he didn't dare partake. The closer he came to the faerie's tent, the slower his pace. The flap of Giselle's tent swung aside, revealing the old crone exactly as he remembered her. Hunter shivered in his boots and fought the urge to turn tail and gallop for the hills.

"Hunter! How fortuitous that our paths should meet thus. I have yearned to lay eyes upon you for far too long, and here you are." Her dark eyes gleamed, and a cunning smile lit her wrinkled face.

Hunter's blood rushed through his veins. His ears rang, and sweat beaded his brow. Though he could not read her like he could ordinary souls, she fair pulsed with power and magic. "Madame Giselle." He made her a slight bow. "I suspect luck had no part in our meeting this day."

She cackled as he dismounted, and dread settled like lead in his gut. Hunter tied Doireann's reins to a low-hanging pine bough and turned to face her. Masking his expression, he did his best to hide the fear and revulsion being in her presence elicited. He wanted no part of the unnatural association he had with the fae. Gladly would he give up the gifts bestowed upon him if it meant severing the ties of kinship that bound them.

"You have naught to fear from me, Grandson."

Was that hurt he spied flashing through her eyes? Despite his best efforts, he couldn't hide his feelings. Why did he think he could? He'd gotten his abilities from her. Surely she'd be aware of everything he felt and thought.

"Come in." She beckoned with a gesture and preceded him into the tent. "I wish only to spend a bit of time with you." She looked at him over her shoulder. "Mayhap I'll tell your fortune whilst you're here."

"Nay." He ducked to enter, his glance darting around the interior. A trunk sat to one side, and fresh rushes covered the hard-packed ground. In the center a roughly hewn table and two chairs had been set. A teapot and two mugs resting next to a deck of cards drew his attention. "I dinna need you to tell my fortune or my future,

Madame Giselle. By my will alone do I forge my future, and by my sweat and blood do I earn my fortune." She cackled again, and his muscles tensed for flight.

"By whose blood? Thanks to me, none can touch you with mere weapons of steel. Because my blood runs through your veins, you have the ability to anticipate how your enemies will strike before the strike occurs." She took a seat at the table. "Are you so certain of what the future holds for you, my lad?"

"Aye."

"Mayhap the path you've set your feet upon leads you astray." She shrugged. "'Tis possible fate has other plans in store."

"I am a knight, and I have made a vow which I intend to keep. Indeed, everything that I have worked toward these five years past has to do with keeping that promise." In fact, he'd spent the whole of his life attempting to live up to the faith and expectations placed upon him by his foster family and clan. Their approval and high esteem meant everything to him. He owed them his life and his loyalty.

"I ken your true identity and what you are." He remained standing, his posture rigid. "I suspect you are aware of the intentions I made clear the day Sky Elizabeth was born. Think you to alter my path or to induce me to renege?" He raised an eyebrow and sent her a pointed look. "I willna. What is it you want from me?"

"Aye. I'm well aware of the vow you made as a mere lad of but five of your mortal years. Sit." She gestured to the chair across from hers. "Have some tea. You are my kin." She canted her head and studied him. "Is it so beyond the realm of possibility that I wish only to spend a bit of time in your company? I have not seen you for far too long. The *Tuatha* have hearts not unlike those of mortals. We too bear affection for our progeny, whether they accept that affection or not."

His eyes widened, and a sliver of guilt wedged its way into his heart. He had intended to thank her for saving his life, and he'd done naught but posture defensively. "My apologies if I have offended you, madam. For certes I have you to thank for my life, and I am grateful." He bowed to her again and sat down.

"Tea?" She filled the two mugs with the steaming contents of the pot, and the scent of herbs and honey wafted up around them in a cloud of steam. She slid one of the mugs toward him.

"My thanks." He took a sip and struggled to come up with something to say. What conversation could he offer that would be of interest to one such as she?

"Hunter, you are a direct descendant of the goddess Danu, as am I. My father is the high king of the *Tuatha Dé Danann* and also your kin. You come from a royal line. Never think yourself *unworthy*." Her tone had taken on a haughty cadence. "'Twas my mortal husband who traveled here from Eire eons ago. He began the MacConnell clan on this land and ruled a vast holding. Time has reduced that proud kingdom to naught, but never forget where you come from."

Did she see what lay in his innermost thoughts and in his heart? He yearned for more than knighthood—a title, land and a strong keep. Only then would his offer for Sky be worthy of acceptance. His mind reeled with Giselle's revelation. He was royalty and descended from the first MacConnell? Was this the source of his yearning and for the ambition thrumming through him? Mayhap, but it served him naught at present, and he needed to keep his wits about him. No matter what she said, he kent well enough the ways of the fae.

"Shall I declare to the world that I am royalty and the descendant of a goddess of old?" He snorted. "Who would believe me, and how would such a claim alter my rank within the society in which I live?" He shook his head. "Nay, I canna, lest I be ostracized, or worse, condemned for a madman and thrown into some deep, dank dungeon to be shackled in irons. I'm grateful for the gifts my lineage has bestowed upon me. Truth be told, 'tis the reason for my success, but I canna make it public. No document of patents from you will aid me. I must make my own way."

"Ah, but you are grateful?"

"You may be certain that I am. Were it no' for your intervention, I would no' be here today. I have you to thank for my family and for my place within the MacKintosh clan."

"Hmm." Her eyes filled with a triumphant glint, and her face creased with amusement. "Then you will not be averse to doing me a small favor in return?"

"Och!" He plowed his fingers through his hair, his position suddenly untenable. "I am no match for you, Madame Giselle. What is it you wish of me?" Apprehension sent his heart racing again.

"Restore balance." She shrugged. "Make right a wrong of old."

"Is that all," he bit out in a dry tone.

She laughed, only this time the sound was less a cackle and more melodious. Tiny bumps rose upon his flesh. "If you please, dinna shift your appearance. I canna abide your true mien. I will admit I fear you in your fae form. 'Tis no' of this world."

"As you wish, my lad." Her smile softened. "I do not want you to fear me. I wish only the best for you, and I hope one day you will see that truth for yourself." Her expression turned pensive as she scrutinized him. "You are so like him—so much like the mortal man I wed. It does my heart good to look upon you."

He squirmed in his chair and gripped his mug with both hands. "The favor?"

"Ah, yes." Her gaze sharpened. "'Tis a small thing, really."

Frustration overwhelmed him. For certes this favor would delay his homecoming or inconvenience him greatly in some unforeseen way. God's blood, he hoped it did not involve time travel! Too well he kent the havoc 'twould wreak upon his well-laid plans. His entire being rebelled at the thought, and mortification burned a path through to his very soul. He had been so easily manipulated, and now he was truly caught up in her machinations. "What must I do to make right this wrong that in no way involved myself in its inception?"

"Ha!" She shook with mirth. "Trust your instincts, Hunter, and leave the rest to me."

"I dinna wish to leave my time, madam. Do I have your assurance that this *favor* involves the present, and no' some distant future or past?"

"Grandson, you must learn to give up your false sense of control. Your fate, no matter how you will it otherwise, is already written in the stars by another's hand." She rose from her place and pointed toward the rear flap of her tent. "Go now, and have faith. You are my kin. You will always hold my deepest affection."

May the saints preserve me! He didn't want her *affection.* Hadn't he learned long ago the trouble such affection had caused his kin—both MacKintosh and MacConnell? He clung to the notion, no matter how false Giselle deemed it, that he did indeed control the course his life would take. Hadn't he proved it these five years past? He rose, and a sickening dizziness overtook him. The world around him flattened, and pressure assaulted him from all sides, pulling and pushing all at the same time. "Nay! Dinna send me—"

"This way."

Giselle shoved him through the rear door of her tent into a rending vortex so powerful he feared he would not survive. For certes he would be torn to bits. God's blood, the pain was enough to make him weep, and the fleeting images and flashing lights racing by made him ill. Trapped in the center of the force hurtling him forward, all he could do was grit his teeth and pray.

Just when he thought he could not bear another second, whatever held him in its grip spat him out, and he landed with a thud. Prostrate on the ground with the tent still at his back, Hunter shook his head to dislodge the disorienting dizziness and fatigue overwhelming him.

The sound of steel against steel fell upon his ears where he lay. *Damnation!* He'd landed in the midst of a battle. He raised his head.

Shock and the need to survive restored his wits in a rush. Spectators ringed the combatants, booing and cheering them on. Some were dressed like he was, and others wore garments not unlike those Lady True wore when hunting. As he regained his feet, Hunter glanced toward the combatants. His vision went red with rage.

A large knight attacked a younger knight half his size and less than half his weight. Still, the lad acquitted himself well against the brute. He must have just earned his spurs, because he could be no more than ten and seven or eight winters. Hunter straightened just as the youth tripped over an exposed tree root and fell flat on his back. The larger knight gave a shout of glee and moved in for the kill.

"Nay," Hunter shouted as instinct took over. With a battle cry, he drew his claymore and lunged forward, blocking the blow meant for the lad. Straddling the youth where he lay on the ground, Hunter engaged the blackguard. "Coward! Knave!" In a flurry of strikes, he beat the man back. "If you wish for a fight, let *me* accommodate you."

"Who are you?" The knight parried his blows easily enough. "What the hell do you think you're doing?"

"Upholding my vow to protect those weaker than myself. As you ought." The familiar sense of anticipation flowed from the knight to him, and he blocked the blows coming at him.

"Wait!" The youth clambered back and leaped to his feet. "Stop!"

But it was too late. He was in the throes of battle lust, and he had no cause to cease that he could see. Hunter attacked, slicing through the knight's chain mail. He drew first blood, leaving a gash across the man's shoulder. His opponent hissed in pain and faltered. Hunter took advantage, sending the man's sword flying out of reach.

Screams erupted from the crowd. Men bearing arms surged forward. Hunter gripped the lad's wrist and dashed toward Giselle's tent. He tossed his charge through the entrance first and dove in after him.

Giselle stood by the tent's opposite exit. "Hurry. Through here." She held the flap aside.

The young knight struggled to get past him toward the rear exit. Once again Hunter gripped his wrist. "That way is no' safe, ye wee fool."

He struggled to free himself from Hunter's grip. "You don't understand. Let me go!"

"Be off," Giselle commanded. "Go before they come through after you."

Hunter's gaze went between the panicked face of the lad and Giselle's imploring look. Indecision seized him. "Call nine-one-one!" The roaring shouts grew closer. "Stop him! Get him!"

The sounds of pursuit spurred him into action. Hunter dashed through the tent's front opening, dragging the lad behind him. Once again the debilitating force took hold, hurling them both through a bone-crushing tunnel that tore at his limbs as it propelled them forward. The ground rushed up to meet them, and the lad let out a cry as they came to a sudden and painful halt.

"We must be away," Hunter shouted, pushing himself to his feet. He helped the youth up and tossed him atop his mount. Hunter snatched Doireann's reins from the tree and swung up behind him. Spurring his destrier into a full gallop, he wended his way through the wagons, booths and tables, heading toward the hills as if chased by the devil himself.

He topped the first rise and urged his horse onward to the bridge across the Esk. They raced over the cobbles, Doireann's steel-shod hooves raising a thunderous clatter. Finally they were upon the slope where his men awaited him on the other side.

"You moron!" The lad wriggled as if he meant to leap from the horse's back in mid-gallop.

"Moron?" He encircled the fool's waist, lest he injure himself trying to get free. "I just saved your life."

"No you didn't." He tried to pry free of Hunter's hold. "I didn't need saving."

About the same time the swell of breasts atop his forearm registered, along with the slender curve of a feminine waist where it met the slight flare of hips, the cap upon his captive's head blew off in the wind. A wealth of silken auburn tresses cascaded down across his chest and arms, and a sweet floral scent filled his nose.

He was a she.

"Bloody hell!" That made the attack against her even more foul. He checked over his shoulder for any signs of pursuit and saw none. Hunter reined his horse to a stop.

She turned to glare daggers at him. "Take me back."

Now that he got a closer look at *her*, he wondered how he could have mistaken those comely features for that of a lad. She had wide-set dark-brown eyes, framed in thick lashes. A sprinkle of freckles covered the bridge of her finely wrought nose and high cheekbones. Her mouth—wide with full, ripe lips—drew into a straight line of displeasure at his perusal.

He stared, disconcerted. "I saved your life. You wish to be returned to the cur who attacked you?" He scowled, taking his arm from around her waist. "Why are you dressed as a knight? You've no business wearing chain mail and spurs. None. What manner of lass are you to wield a broadsword thus?" He dismounted, reaching up to help her down.

She batted his hands away, swung her leg over his mount's back and slid free to land lightly upon her feet. "How is anything about me your business?" She widened her stance and crossed her arms in front of her. "Take me back where you found me right now, or you *will* regret it."

He already regretted it. "Think you to threaten me?" He grunted and pointed at his chest. "I am a blooded knight and undefeated upon the field. What harm can a wee lass such as yourself do to me? You've no right to carry that weapon, much less to wield it. No. Right. Do you no' ken 'tis a crime to impersonate a knight of the realm? You should be—"

She let out a growl of frustration and whipped around so fast he had no time to react. Her booted foot connected with the center of his chest, sending him reeling back. Before he could regain his balance, she crouched low and swung her leg behind his heels to trip him. He went sprawling.

Bloody hell! Somehow she'd managed to wrest the dirk from his belt in the process. With her boot once again planted firmly upon his chest, she pressed the point of *his* dagger against his throat. He seethed. Humiliation and anger fought for dominance within him.

"No *mere* woman can defeat a big, strong knight such as yourself, eh?" Her brown eyes flashed. "Well, score one for the wee lassie."

"I did no' anticipate . . ." Confusion clouded his brain, and he forced himself to focus upon her. She was magnificent. Like the woman warrior Boudicca in the tales of old, the strange lass stood victorious above him with her fiery tresses blowing about her shoulders and her eyes raining angry sparks down upon him. He blinked.

He could read naught from her. He hadn't been able to sense her intent to attack, nor could he feel her emotions—though they were plain enough to read upon her face. "But . . . I saved your life," he muttered.

"For the third time, no you didn't." She stepped back, flipped his dagger in the air and caught it by the tip. She handed it back to him hilt first. "You interrupted an exhibition, a show at a fair. The man I sparred with is my father. He would never harm me." Her eyes grew bright with tears. "You *wounded* him. You hurt my dad! Who asked you to intervene, anyway?"

"Shite." Who indeed? Giselle had asked him to intervene, and he should have kent better. Hunter picked himself up off the ground and sheathed his dirk. Brushing the dirt from his hose and tunic, he avoided direct eye contact with the angry female. He was the cause of her tears.

She ran her fingers through her tresses and stared toward the way they'd come. "On second thought, I don't need you to take me anywhere. We haven't come that far." She gave him her back and started walking.

"Nay!" he bellowed, and for the life of him, he had no idea why he didn't just let her go. She had it aright. They hadn't come all that far, and the way was safe enough—for her anyway. "I will accompany you." He strode over to his destrier and grabbed the reins. "Indeed"—he lengthened his strides to catch up to her—"I must find one of my men at the fair, his page and squire as well. My apologies for misconstruing what I saw, lass. 'Tis my fault, and I will set things aright by returning you into your father's keeping and offering him my most sincere apology."

She shrugged, her indifference toward him clear, and continued on. "Do whatever you want."

Leading Doireann, Hunter took his place beside her, concentrating fully upon gleaning anything he could from her. Naught came to him. Why was she closed to him? He'd never encountered another soul he could not sense. No matter. He had more pressing worries, like how he would deal with Madame Giselle once they were back at her tent. Surely this was all a mistake. Plucking this woman from a mock battle couldn't be the wrong he was meant to set right. "By what name are you called, my lady?"

Sighing, she stopped and peered up at him. "My name is Meghan McGladrey, though I hardly see how it matters to you."

"Hunter of clan MacKintosh," he said, bowing low. "I am at your service, my lady."

Her eyes grew wide. "MacKintosh?"

"Aye. Does the name hold some meaning for you?"

"Where are we right now?" Once again her expression turned to panic.

"Halfway between Edinburgh and Aberdeenshire, at the north branch of the river Esk."

"Oh no. Oh God. All that pressure . . ." She swallowed a few times and turned in a circle, staring at her surroundings. "This is . . . Tell me I'm not . . . This is Scotland? I'm in Scotland?"

"Why do you say it thus?" He frowned. "I took you from the fairgrounds right behind Madame Giselle's tent."

She wrung her hands in a wholly feminine gesture, and her face filled with anguish. "What year is this?" she whispered.

"'Tis the year of our Lord 1441." Realization dawned, but he held his tongue. The foul force he'd endured whilst passing through Giselle's tent could only mean one thing: he'd traveled through time. Hadn't he heard the tales from his kin? He should have recognized the odd garb some of the spectators wore as that from the future, but everything had happened so fast.

For certes he'd become muddled in his thinking when he found Giselle's tent and his destrier exactly where they'd been before the journey. At least he'd returned to his own time just as quickly— a little worse for wear, but intact. And soon Meghan McGladrey would be Madame Giselle's problem. Not his.

She made a growling noise deep in her throat and circled her arms about herself. "We need to hurry. Can we ride?"

"If it pleases you, my lady." He cupped his hands beside Doireann. Without hesitation, she accepted the proffered help and lifted herself easily onto his destrier's broad back. He handed her the reins before swinging up behind her. Once he'd mounted, he reached to take the reins back. Before he could do so, she leaned forward and touched her spurs to his mount's sides, keeping a good seat and the reins deftly in her grasp as the destrier took off at a canter.

Meghan McGladrey wielded a sword like a knight, rode his powerful warhorse with the skill of any man, yet felt and smelled entirely feminine. His senses reeled. She'd had the audacity to lay him out flat, even threatening him with his own dirk, when all he'd done was try to save her from certain death. How was he to reckon the knave was her father? And now she thought to take control of *his* stallion?

Nay, I will not allow it.

He reached around her and took the reins from her hands. Then he spurred the beast—*his beast*—into a full gallop. His actions caused her to fall against him. Her curves pressed against him from chest to groin, and his stallion's rhythmic gait had her derrière rocking against his manhood in a most provocative manner. His blood heated, and lust surged through his veins in a powerful, all-consuming rush.

Bloody hell! Impersonating a knight, no less. How dare she?

He pulled on the bit, slowing Doireann to a jarring trot. The sooner he returned the irksome female to her father the better.

CHAPTER TWO

*I*t'll be OK. It will. Her insides quaking, Meghan repeated the mantra to herself over and over. They would return to the fortune-teller's tent and demand that she be sent back to her own time. Her stomach lurched, and her eyes stung. She'd seen her father bleeding—not an experience she ever wanted to repeat. Was he OK? He had to be.

The scene replayed itself in her mind, and all the horror returned. Her hands trembled, and shock seized her lungs. She and her dad had been sparring as they did every day, only in front of an audience. From the corner of her eye, she'd seen the knight appear out of thin air. Startled, she'd lost her balance, tripping over an exposed root. Everything after that had happened so fast, she'd had no time to react.

What if the faerie refused to send her back? What would she do then? *Don't think like that. It'll be OK.* Her dad and her brothers must be frantic right now. They'd seen her disappear. *Why me?*

Sure, years ago her father had been taken by one of the *Tuatha Dé Danann* from thirteenth-century Ireland to twentieth-century America, ending up on her grandparents' farm. But that didn't explain why or how she'd somehow landed in fifteenth-century

Scotland. Had her father's involvement with time traveling some-how made her more vulnerable to the whims of the fae, or had she just been in the wrong place at the wrong time?

Turning her mind away from her painful thoughts, she studied the unfamiliar landscape surrounding her—rolling, rocky hills as far as she could see, with sparse grass just beginning to show hints of green. She could smell the salt tang on the easterly breeze. The coast must be nearby.

She tightened her knees against the trotting horse's withers. Oh, how she wished for stirrups. With stirrups she could put a little dis-tance between herself and Hunter of clan MacKintosh. *Disturbing.* That was the only way she could describe her reaction to the man who'd hurt her father and yanked her from her time.

Against her will, acute awareness of the way he sheltered her between his beefy arms and thighs thrummed through her. Her heart pounded away in her chest, and heat rose to her face. There was no hiding the effect their bodies rubbing together had on the well-meaning knight. She couldn't fault him. He was a male in his prime, after all, and subject to the laws of physiology. That's all there was to it. She would *not* take his erection personally. Still, what she couldn't account for was the way she responded.

Sure, her would-be rescuer was a gorgeous hunk, with his thick golden-brown hair, serious gray eyes and chiseled, über-masculine features, but she didn't know him from Adam. She sure didn't intend to stick around to get to know him any better either.

"My cap," she cried, spying the bit of dark-green velvet on the ground. "Stop. I want it." Her mother had made it for her, along with the gorgeous suede tunic she wore with the McGladrey crest embroi-dered across the front. Her eyes filled at the thought of her mother, father and brothers. She'd be devastated if she didn't get home right away. Her chest tightened, and she clamped her lips together to keep from sobbing. Brushing at her tears, she focused on her hat.

Hunter didn't slow his horse's gait. The rasp of his claymore leaving its scabbard filled her ears. He kicked the beast into a smooth canter and veered toward the scrap of velvet on the ground. Leaning over, he lifted her cap by the tip of his sword and presented it to her.

"Thanks." She snatched it from the end of his claymore. Tucking the hat into her belt, she kept her eyes on the trail ahead. The fair that Hunter had taken her from lay just over the next hill. Soon she'd be at the fortune-teller's tent, and the faerie would send her home.

They reached the top of the hill and came to a sudden halt. She gasped. Nothing remained of the fair. No tents, tables, wagons or booths. Where were the people, oxen and horses? How was it possible that the bare field edging the river showed no signs of wear? Shock seized her, and she couldn't get enough air into her lungs.

What kind of magic did you have to possess to make an entire fair and all its inhabitants disappear into thin air?

Her entire body trembled, and she forced herself to take in a gulp of air. She didn't want to pass out and fall off the horse. The field wasn't entirely empty. Three bridled horses with reins dangling grazed contentedly where the center of the fair had been a short while ago. "What have you done?" she cried. "What the hell is going on here?" She jabbed her elbow into Hunter's ribs.

"Oof." His breath came out in a huff, and he dropped the reins into her lap. "Against my better judgment, I entered the spider's lair. That is what I have done. Now we are both truly caught up in her sticky web." He slid off the back of his horse. "Come, or stay here with *my* horse," he commanded. "I must see if Nevan and his lads are still about."

Meghan swung her leg over the stallion's back and dismounted. "I'm coming with you." She took the reins and led the horse along behind Hunter. The large dapple-gray destrier nudged her shoulder, and she reached up to give him a scratch behind the ears. The feel

25

of his warmth, his snuffling breaths as he nosed her and the familiar smell of horse reassured her. "He's a gorgeous animal. Does he
have a name?"

"Doireann."

"What does it mean?" She gave the horse's sleek neck a pat, and
then she ran her hand down his forehead to pet his velvety nose.
"He's such a good boy," she crooned, gratified to see the horse's
ears move forward and his large head dip at the sound of her praise.

Hunter glared at her over his shoulder. "Doireann means
'storm,' and he's no' a *good boy*," he imitated her croon, his tone
derisive. "He is a well-trained warhorse. Dinna coddle him as if he
were a pet, lass. Make no mistake; my destrier is a weapon as surely
as the claymore on my back and the dirk at my waist."

"Well, *excuse* me," she snapped. His arrogance stung. "This is a
stupid conversation, and I don't even know why I'm talking to you.
This is all your fault. How am I going to get home? *You* brought me
here against my will, so how are *you* going to fix this?"

"Where is home?" He stopped mid-stride and turned to face
her. "I dread the words you might speak."

"You have good reason to dread." She swallowed the lump forming in her throat. "You took me from the twenty-first century. I live in
Minneapolis, Minnesota, in the good old United States of America,
and I was performing at a Renaissance festival in Shakopee—also in
Minnesota."

He let out a shout and swiped his hands over his face. Turning
away from her, he kicked a stone hard enough to send it careening
down the hill. "Accursed fae! I kent Madame Giselle meant to divert
me from my purpose, and yet I did naught to prevent her meddling." He aimed a baleful scowl her way. "'Tis true, I am to blame,
and therefore duty-bound to see you safely returned to your home.
Once we are at Moigh Hall, I shall send word to Inverness. Madame
Giselle keeps a cottage there for her amusement. She has . . ."

He clamped his mouth shut and bowed his head for a second. The muscles along his jaw twitched. He stared out over the valley where the fair had been and blew out a breath that sounded to her very much like resignation.

"She has ties to our clan. You and I are no' the first to fall prey to her wiles. I will enlist the help of my kin to persuade Madame Giselle to return you to your rightful place and time."

"I've heard that name, but I didn't know Madame Giselle was at our fair," she muttered. "Are you by any chance familiar with Robley MacKintosh?" She gestured for him to start walking again. He did.

"Aye." His tone held no surprise. "He is kin to me."

"And Erin?" Her pulse raced, and goose bumps did the wave over her skin.

"Aye, and Erin, his lady wife, as well. She and my foster mother both came to us from the future. Minnesota is a familiar name to me."

Her heart bounced around in her chest. "I know Erin and Robley. I was sixteen when they came into our lives. That was seven years ago. I know all about Robley's deal with Madame Giselle, and I also know about the faerie warrior who sent Erin back to the twenty-first century," she babbled on, her nerves revved up to full throttle. "After she'd accidentally traveled back to your century, that is."

"Aye?"

She glanced at him and shut up. He wasn't listening and probably didn't care about what she knew. Why would he? Exhausted and still in shock, her brain couldn't take any more. She'd passed the point of overload the minute she'd watched Hunter fight her father for real. Tumbling through the crushing portal through time had been the final blow. Her gaze drifted to the cluster of pine trees where the faerie's tent had stood. "How do you plan to find your guys?"

"My guise?" He shot her a puzzled look. "Why would I need a guise to search yon field?"

"Fellows. Lads. Nevan, I think you called him."

"Och, I dinna ken. Mayhap she put Nevan and his lads to sleep in the field somewhere. I've heard the fae do such when they wish. At any rate, let us fetch his gelding. If you take one side of the glen, I'll take the other. We can make fast work of our search."

"OK," she said, and one side of Hunter's mouth quirked up. A dimple appeared. Her heart did an annoying little *oh-boy-I-am-so-attracted-to-you* Snoopy dance in her chest. *Inappropriate.* She'd just been ripped from her life. How could she possibly be attracted to the man responsible for her current dilemma?

"I've no' heard 'OK' since leaving Moigh Hall. My foster mother oft uses the expression, as does Lady Erin." His expression softened at the mention of the two women. "'Twill be good to be home once again. I've missed my kin, odd though they be."

"Have you been gone long?" If she didn't get back to her own time, she'd miss her family too. A wrenching ache tore a swath through her heart.

"Aye. Five long years." They'd reached the three horses. The destrier stood obediently as Hunter reached for the reins. The two smaller horses moved out of reach. Hunter made no move to go after them. "I dinna think Nevan would mind overmuch if you borrowed his steed. I trow the two palfreys will follow along readily enough." He knotted the reins and put them over the bay's head. Cupping his hands, he motioned for her to mount.

"I'll take the side where the faerie's tent stood," she said, settling herself on the horse.

"As you wish." He peered up at her, his expression contrite. "My sincerest apologies for the disruption I have caused you, my lady. My greatest wish is to set things aright."

Lord help her, he was incredibly appealing when he wasn't being incredibly arrogant. Too many emotions swirled through her. Fear and grief, not to mention the shock the day's events caused to her system. Her unfortunate attraction to Hunter only added confusion to the mix. Being attracted to the man who had taken her from her life and family made no sense at all. She had to get home.

What would her dad do without her there to help him run their fencing club? Who would take over the mixed martial arts and fencing groups she instructed? Her throat tightened. Her chair would be empty at dinnertime. Who would help her mom and grandmother with Sunday dinners? Her sister-in-law didn't enjoy cooking like she did. Besides, she was busy chasing after her niece. Her heart wrenched at the thought of little Allie. Who would play with her as only an aunt could? Plus, she was the one who made sure her grandparents got to the grocery store and to doctor appointments. She nodded, not trusting her voice.

Turning the gelding's head in the direction of the pines, she gave his sides a kick. The destrier went easily from standing into a smooth canter, and despite everything that had happened, she loved having such a well-trained horse at her command.

Her dad had seen to it that all three of his children learned to ride at an early age. They kept horses on her grandparents' farm, and her family had spent as much time as possible there when she and her two brothers were youngsters. Her brothers had learned to joust and perform mock battles on horseback. She'd trained alongside them, but she preferred to ride solely for pleasure. Charging a quintain with a lance or knocking her brothers off their mounts held no thrill for her—being knocked from hers even less.

She surveyed the ground as she went, looking for any sign of the missing knight, his squire and page. Drawn to the place where the faerie's tent had been, she held herself rigid, expecting some residual effect from the portal through time. Bruises and aches from her journey still throbbed. Weary to the bone, only adrenaline kept her going. She slowed her mount and walked him toward the spot where Hunter had kidnapped her.

How was it possible for the faerie's tent to be in two centuries at once? She'd seen Hunter fall through the rear tent flap. The way he'd landed, it looked as if he'd been hurled with a lot of force behind him.

She caught a glimpse of metal near one of the pines and moved closer to investigate. A cry escaped her at the sight of her very own sword on the ground. She slid off the horse and hurried to the place where it lay. Wonder of wonders, her leather scabbard rested on the dirt a short distance away—just as she'd placed it before starting the exhibition. Only then, she'd been on different ground, on a different continent and in the twenty-first century.

Her knees buckled, and she sank to the pine needles on the ground. Her hand shook as she reached for the sword her parents had given her. She wrapped her palm around the tang. The feel of the leather-wrapped steel crossguard and the leather-wrapped grip against her skin set off a wave of misery.

She wanted her mom, dad and grandparents. She wanted her brothers and the safety of home and the comforts of her proper century. Wrenched from everyone who mattered, being separated by time and distance just didn't compute. Her head spun with the effort to wrap her mind around what had happened. Tears filled her eyes again, and desperation welled. The sound of thundering hooves approaching barely registered.

"What is it, lass? What have you found?" Hunter came up behind her.

Forcing herself up off the ground, she brandished her sword in the air for him to see. Then she moved to retrieve the scabbard, sliding the blade inside the silver-tipped leather sheath. Keeping her back to the man responsible for this mess, she wiped her face with the linen sleeve of her shirt. "My sword," she muttered. "I found my weapon here on the ground along with the scabbard—as if I'd left them here and not . . ." Her voice broke, and she took a few deep breaths to gain control. "And not a world and centuries away."

"I am sorry, lass. You canna imagine how very sorry I am."

"You were used, and I can't fault you for trying to do the right thing. Don't beat yourself up over it."

"Beat myself up? I dinna take your meaning." He huffed out a breath. "Never mind. I can find no sign of Nevan or his lads. Let us depart. I dinna like the feel of this place."

"Sure. Let's do that." Grief turned to anger, and nothing steadied her nerves like rage. "We've been set up. You get that, right?"

"Aye. I do indeed *get that*."

"I realize this is not entirely your fault, but I'm pissed, and I don't want to talk to you . . . or even look at you right now." She sniffed and brushed at her tear-streaked cheeks. "I need my space."

"I would like nothing more than to give you your *space*, but 'twould no' be wise under the circumstances. Ride a short distance behind me, and I will endeavor to keep to myself."

"Why me?" she cried as she fumbled to get her scabbard buckled across her chest.

"I dinna ken." He shrugged his broad shoulders. "Madame Giselle said I was to restore balance and right a wrong of old."

"Restore balance?" She frowned. Had the faerie been referring to her father's displacement? If that were the case, shouldn't she have been sent to thirteenth-century Ireland instead of fifteenth-century Scotland? At least in Ireland she had family, and she looked enough like her father that her ancestors might believe her when she told them she was Connor's daughter.

"Aye. I canna begin to divine her purpose in having me take you as I did. My foster mother was sent here from the future to save my life, as Erin was brought here to save hers. Mayhap you are meant to do the same for some poor soul. Who can say?" He pointed to her feet. "Remove those spurs from your boots, lass."

"What?" She glared. "Why should I?"

"Because only a knight may wear spurs, and 'tis unlikely our young King James has bestowed that honor upon you. We are about to ride into a group of true knights of the Scottish realm, and I doubt they will take it well to see a lass in spurs. 'Tis bad enough you're dressed as a man." He held out his hand. "I will return the spurs to you once we reach Moigh Hall. I swear upon my honor."

Though his words took a bite out of her pride, she couldn't fault his reasoning. When in Rome and all that. She unfastened the silver spurs with their Celtic markings and handed them to him. "For your information, I earned these spurs the same way you did. Don't lose them."

He made a disdainful grunting noise deep in his throat and put her spurs in the sporran he wore on his belt. He moved to the gelding's side and once again cupped his hands to help her mount. "Come. Let us depart. My men await."

Heaving her own sigh of resignation, she climbed up on the horse and waited for Hunter to mount Doireann. "Lead the way. No more talking. I have a lot to process," she grumbled. Nodding, he shot her a warm smile, his eyes filled with sympathy. The sight left her breathless and sent her heart racing. *Damn those dimples!*

"As you wish, my lady." He led the way toward the hills, and the ponies soon fell into step behind them, just as Hunter said they would.

True to his word, he kept to himself. She chewed on her bottom lip and tried to pull herself together. For the time being, she was safe. That counted for something. She knew Robley and Erin—another reason to be thankful. Plus, after Erin had been sent to the past, she'd managed to return to the twenty-first century, which meant going home was possible.

When Erin had made the decision to leave the present to return to Robley in the past, she'd shared with Meghan's family what had happened with Haldor, the faerie warrior who enforced the fae laws. If Madame Giselle wouldn't return Meghan to her time, maybe Haldor would. Surely he'd be willing to take care of another of

Madame Giselle's transgressions. The fae enforcer must be aware that Madame Giselle was at it again. She had options, and that gave her hope.

She stopped gnawing on her bottom lip and threw her shoulders back, just as they rode over the top of the hill and into a group of men and adolescent boys. They gaped at her, mouths and eyes open wide. Meghan lifted her chin. She was descended from Irish nobility, Milesians, in fact, and she wasn't about to show weakness or fear to a bunch of ill-equipped fifteenth-century knights. They weren't even wearing chain mail. Where were *their* spurs? They couldn't be all that successful as knights if they were so poorly outfitted, right?

A tall, well-built, good-looking man with ebony hair and stunning deep-blue eyes detached himself from the group and approached Hunter. "Where are Nevan, Bertrand and Geoffrey?" He had his hand on the hilt of the dagger at his waist. He shot her a curious look. "Who is this lass, and why is she dressed as a squire and carrying a sword?"

"Tieren," Hunter said as he gestured toward her, "this is Lady Meghan of clan McGladrey. My lady, this is Tieren of clan MacKintosh." He pointed to the others. "There you have Sir Gregory, Sir Murray and Sir Cecil. Good knights all, and trustworthy. You are safe with us." He glanced her way and gestured to a boy who stood staring at her with open curiosity. "My page, Allain, is the lad by the wagon. Next to him are Tieren's squire, George, his page, Tristan, and Murray's squire, John."

He went on to introduce the other pages and squires, whose names went in one ear and right out the other. She couldn't take in any more information. She nodded toward the younger boys. The men moved closer, and her mouth went dry. "I'm pleased to meet all of you, though it's going to take me a while to learn your names."

"Why is she riding Nevan's horse?" the knight called Gregory asked, eyeing her with suspicion.

"The fair is gone," Hunter said, his tone once again filled with resignation. "Along with Nevan and the lads. We found their horses grazing in the field, and I reckoned Nevan would no' mind if she rode his gelding."

Tieren's eyes widened. "What do you mean *gone?*"

"'Tis as if it had never been." The muscle in Hunter's clamped jaw twitched again. "No sign remains of the wagons, tables, the Romany or their tents. The ground is bare of any evidence that there was ever aught there. We searched. Nevan and the lads were nowhere to be found."

Gregory made the sign of the cross, and all eyes swung to her. Heat rushed to her face. She knew how superstitious people were during this era. She also knew what they did to people whom they suspected of witchcraft or anything else out of the norm.

"I had nothing to do with it. Hunter believed he was rescuing me from an attack. He nabbed me, and we rode toward this hill. Once I convinced him I hadn't been in any danger, we rode back together. That's when we found everything gone." She met their wary glances. "I swear. I had nothing to do with any of this. All I want is to go home."

The blond knight with slightly bowed legs frowned. Cecil. That's what Hunter had called him. "The lady's speech sounds foreign," he remarked, also placing his hand on the hilt of the dagger at his waist. "Where might she be from?"

Hunter's brow creased. "Och—"

"Gone, ye say? The fair is no more?" Murray pulled at his wiry beard. "How can that be so?"

"'Tis my belief that the fair was naught but an apparition wrought by a faerie," Hunter told them with a sharp look.

"I dinna believe it." Cecil's expression hardened. "'Tis no' possible. We *saw* the wagons, horses and the folk. We beheld the tents and booths with our own eyes and *smelled* the roasting meat."

"Have I ever told you a falsehood in all the time we've traveled and fought side by side?" Hunter snapped. "Go. See for yourself, Cecil, and if you can manage to find Nevan where I could no', I'd be most grateful. I dinna look forward to telling his kin he's been taken by the fae."

Cecil turned to the others. "Who will come with me?"

Gregory crossed himself again and kept his mouth shut.

"I'll guard yer back, Cecil." Murray snatched up his horse's reins. "I've kent Hunter since we were pages together. He's honest tae a fault. If proof is what ye seek, proof is what ye shall have." He swung up on his destrier's back. "I ken ye've all heard the tales at your parents' knees of the fae and their doings. Hunter warned us something was amiss, and Nevan chose no' tae pay him heed." He looked in the direction she and Hunter had just traveled. "Come, Cecil, let us seek proof that Hunter spoke the truth."

Cecil mounted his horse and kicked the mare into a gallop. The two rode away in a reverberation of hoofbeats. Meghan sucked in a fortifying gulp of air and faced those remaining. Her heart thundered in her chest. All that equilibrium she'd talked herself into a while ago fizzled, to be replaced with gnawing fear. "I'm not a faerie, and I had nothing to do with any of this."

"Of course no', my lady." Gregory bowed to her before turning to Hunter. "What will we do with the lass?"

Hunter dismounted. "'Tis no' proper for her to travel unattended by a maid or another lady." His expression turned thoughtful, and he stared her way. "I find myself in need of a squire. I suggest you hide your hair in that cap as you had it when I found you, Meghan. Whilst we are in Aberdeenshire, we'll pass you off as one of the lads. You'll attend me as my squire."

"*Attend* you?" She blinked.

"Aye, as my squire." He studied the chain mail and the coat of arms embroidered upon her tunic. "Your insignia and chain mail will no' suit. Do any of you lads have a plain tunic and an old cloak she might borrow?"

"I do." Allain's face turned bright red as all eyes turned his way. "She's welcome to them, and I do believe my tunic will fit her well enough." The boy went to the wagon and lifted the tarp.

"Why do I have to change?" She surveyed the others, taking note of their plain clothing.

"Your tunic marks you as a lad of noble birth. We dinna wish to draw unwanted attention." Hunter came to her side. "All of us have sent our armor, spurs and gear on ahead of us. Our weapons are hidden under the tarp on yon wagon. We transport a fair amount of gold and silver, so we travel as common folk. These roads are overwrought with brigands and thieves, and we dinna wish to draw their interest."

"Oh." That explained how ill-equipped they appeared. She removed her scabbard and drew her chain mail off over her head. "Makes sense, but I'm keeping my sword."

Hunter snorted, and she shot him a scowl. "If you're pretending to be common folk, why would any of you have squires and pages? Wouldn't that give you away? Besides, since I'm the one who has been wronged here, shouldn't *you* be serving *me*? After all, it was you who—"

"Because we are no' commoners, we are knights. That is why we have squires and pages." Hunter's eyes held a determined glint. "I will see that you are fed, sheltered and protected. Is that no' service enough? In exchange, you will pretend to be my squire for the duration of our journey."

She glared at him. "I don't need your protection."

"Ah, but you do, lass," Hunter quipped, and the others nodded in agreement.

Meghan opened her mouth to give him a piece of her mind, but thought better of it. He was right. Social mores and the culture she'd fallen into here were far different from those in her own time. She fought against the sting burning at the back of her eyes, not to mention the sting to her pride.

"Where did you say you hail from again, my lady?" Tieren asked, looking from her to Hunter and back again.

"She didn't say, nor will she until Cecil and Murray have returned. Cecil is far more likely to accept the truth once he's proven to himself that I did no' tell him false."

She fumed at his domineering ways. "I can speak for myself."

"Aye, I ken as much, but you *will no'* do so."

"What makes you so sure?"

"Because I command it, and I ken best how to protect you whilst you are on Scottish soil." He sent her a pointed look.

"Arrogant much?" she snapped. Snorts and choked laughter erupted around her. Mortification heated her blood, and she comforted herself with the memory of how she'd laid the conceited fifteenth-century knight out on his back and held his own dagger against his throat. Turning away, she studied her surroundings. The sooner they found a faerie willing to send her back home the better.

CHAPTER THREE

Make ready. We will depart the moment Cecil and Murray return," Hunter barked. "I wish to put some distance between us and this place before we camp for the night." His head ached, and he could scarce keep his wits about him—surely the results of his brief sojourn through time. He closed his eyes and rubbed his temples, opening one but a slit to keep Meghan in his sights.

Why could he not sense any of the lass's emotions, and what scheme had Madame Giselle combined upon them both? His heart wrenched at the piteous lost look the lass couldn't hide. Her shoulders slumped, and her mouth drew down at the corners. For truth, she looked as if she might burst into tears at any moment.

He hated when women wept. Their tears drew forth a helplessness and frustration within him that he could not abide. Moving to her side, he fought against the impulse to draw her into his arms. Instead, he widened his stance and crossed his arms in front of him. "No harm shall come to you, my lady. I swear it."

"OK."

Her small nod and grief-stricken expression nearly felled him where he stood. "I meant no offense by suggesting you act as my

38

squire during our journey. 'Tis but an acceptable means to keep you close. Er . . . safe." Heat crept up his neck, and he nearly rolled his eyes. 'Twas her fault he was so tongue-tied. Not knowing what she might be feeling had him off-kilter.

Allain approached and handed her a bundle of wool. She accepted it. "Thank you, Allain. I appreciate your willingness to loan these to me." She smiled at the lad.

"'Tis my pleasure to aid you in any way I can, my lady." His page's face went scarlet again. "I saw," he whispered, glancing from him to Meghan.

"Saw what?" Meghan asked, her brow creased. "What do you mean?"

"'Twas my turn to keep watch over the hill, ye ken? I saw you defeat Sir Hunter." A wide grin split his face. "Well met, my lady. Would you teach me that move? The one you used to land Sir Hunter on his ar . . . er . . . backside?"

"Oh. Sure." Meghan straightened. "I'd love to teach you that move, and I know others. Lots, in fact. I'm a certified mixed martial arts instructor," she said, her voice tinged with pride.

Confusion clouded Allain's expression for a second before he turned to Hunter. "I said naught to the others. You being my master, it seemed disloyal to point out your defeat at the lady's hand."

"My thanks," he replied dryly. "You *do* realize 'twould have been unchivalrous indeed to have used brute force against the fairer sex."

"For certes." Allain's head bobbed as he hurried away.

"Right. Unchivalrous." Meghan's eyes glinted with challenge. "Care for a rematch?"

"Nay." He took the garments from her. "One demonstration of your considerable skill shall suffice." He shook Allain's tunic and cloak vigorously to free them of any vermin that might have taken refuge in the woolen folds. "Be quick about changing, and stow your good tunic and chain mail on the wagon with the rest of our things."

"All right," she murmured. She blinked, and her tone was once more subdued.

"I much prefer your ire, lass." Had he said that aloud? For certes, he had not meant to, but now he was committed. "Moping does you no good, nor does it become you."

"So sorry to disappoint," she hissed, snatching the garments back from his hands. "No thanks to you, I've had a very trying day—what with losing my family, home and century and all. Forgive me for succumbing to a moment or two of self-pity."

"You are forgiven." He grinned in spite of himself. "See that it does no' happen again."

Her eyes narrowed, and her lips pursed. He gave her a slight bow and walked away before she could loosen her tongue to blister his hide and prick his already overburdened conscience further. He strode to the crest of the hill to watch for Cecil and Murray's return. Tieren soon joined him, as he'd hoped he would. He reverted to signing. *"'Tis all Madame Giselle's doing."*

"As you suspected." Tieren nodded. *"What is the faerie up to now?"*

"Time will tell." He shook his head. *"I am unable to read aught from Meghan. She is closed to me,"* he signed. *"I've never encountered the like before."*

"Good." Tieren laughed as he signed back. *"Finally we are on equal footing when it comes to a lass."*

"She's from True and Erin's time." Hunter frowned. *"We are not vying for the lady's favor. She will not be here long. Besides, I am already pledged to Lady Sky Elizabeth."*

Tieren met his frown with a cocky grin. *"As you recall, our Lady True and Lady Erin were only to be with us a short while as well. Yet both are now settled with families of their own. Both have been here for nearly a score of years."* His gaze went to Meghan. *"I'd just as soon not have you as a rival for her affections."* He shot Hunter a wry look. *"I may decide to court her."*

"Court her?" The notion soured his stomach. What could he say? He had no rights in the matter. Stifling a growl, he turned back to his watch over the hills. "Here they come." Murray and Cecil raced toward them. Judging by their haste, Cecil had his proof and wanted to be away as quickly as Hunter did. *"As soon as we're home, I'll send to Inverness for word of Madame Giselle's whereabouts. I'll see that Meghan is returned to her own time as soon as can be arranged."*

"Och, aye?" Tieren said aloud, then switched back to signing. *"Think you the faerie will be swayed by your wishes?"* He laughed again. *"In the meantime, I shall endeavor to persuade Meghan to remain. With me."*

Tieren's words shouldn't have made him angry, but they did. Most likely because he'd already taken it upon himself to protect her. He'd snatched her from her time. 'Twas his responsibility to see to her welfare until she could be returned to her family. Surely 'twas all there was to this anger churning in his gut. *"In what capacity would you have her stay?"*

"Once we return to Moigh Hall, I intend never to leave again. 'Tis certain the earl will grant me a good living as a captain in his garrison. As you ken, I've earned a tidy fortune myself while on the continent. I can well afford a wife, bairns and a comfortable home." His attention strayed to where Meghan stood with her back to them as she changed into the rough tunic. "Och, but she's a braw, bonnie lass, is she no'? 'Twas quite provocative to see her dressed as a squire with a sword strapped across her back," Tieren said aloud.

"Aye, a braw, bonnie lass who wishes to go home to her own place and time."

"We shall see."

Cecil rode into their midst, his face pale and drawn. "Let us leave this place anon." His mare pranced and tossed her head against the tight pull Cecil had on the bit. "Hunter spoke the truth. The fair is no more, nor are there any signs 'twas ever there." His eyes wild, he stared at all of them. "You saw the wagons and such, aye? Mayhap 'tis true they were never there, and the fae bewitched us all."

"We found no sign o' Nevan or the lads." Murray gestured to his squire and page to mount their palfreys. "Let us be off. We can talk more freely once we're well away and camped for the night."

Meghan swung herself up on Nevan's warhorse without aid. Another knightly feat she managed with ease. He shook his head and went for Doireann's reins. "You saw?" he asked Tieren, who walked beside him.

"I did," Tieren whispered. "Who trained her, do you suppose?"

"Her da. I'll tell the tale once we camp."

"I look forward to it. I'll take up the rear."

Tieren veered off for his own mount, and they were soon upon the road again, traveling in silence. Like him, each of them pondered the events of the day. The air was rife with the speculation and fear coursing through the group. Once again the prickle of premonition skittered over his skin. If only he could discern what it meant. If Meghan had been sent here to save some hapless soul's life, he could only hope against hope 'twas not his hide she was meant to protect. Surely he was naught in Giselle's scheme but the means to bring Meghan here.

He glanced back at her from his place at the head of the line. Deep in thought, she worried her bottom lip between her teeth. Beleaguered, he blew out a breath. If he didn't stop her, she'd chew it bloody. "Cecil, take the lead," he commanded, turning Doireann's head. He trotted back to flank her mount. "You will tell me where your thoughts lead you."

"Will I?" She snorted and blinked at him. Her brow rose. "Just because you command something, it's a done deal?"

"For the most part, aye." That he couldn't read her emotions frustrated and puzzled him. She was a mystery, and he did not like mysteries. He preferred having the upper hand and being in control of every situation. 'Twas his natural inclination. Those very same tendencies made him a natural leader. She thwarted him, and that rankled. "I canna help you if I dinna ken where your thoughts are leading you, lass. Tell me now."

"You feel honor bound to direct my thoughts?" Her eyes widened. "Don't bother. That kind of control must take an awful lot of energy on your part, and I don't want to be responsible for exhausting your pea-brain."

"I thank you for your concern, my lady. Humor me nonetheless." Without thought, he placed a finger under her chin. Turning her to face him, he ran his thumb over her lower lip. Ignoring the frisson of excitement touching her caused, he assessed the damage she'd already inflicted. "I fear your lip canna bear much more . . . *thought.*"

She jerked away from his touch. "It's not that big a deal," she said, keeping her voice to barely a whisper. "I was just remembering what you said about entering the spider's lair and her sticky web." She shrugged. "The strands of a spider's web intersect, right? Robley and Erin spent a lot of time with my family. Robley shared a little of your story when he told us about his clan and family. I know Madame Giselle has played a part in all of your lives. I'm just trying to figure out the whys and wherefores of my current situation."

Her expression clouded. "If Giselle meant to restore balance, then I *should* be in thirteenth-century Ireland right now, because that's where and when my dad was taken by the fae."

"Your sire was taken from his time as well?" This tidbit did naught to give him ease. Indeed, it only muddled Giselle's true purpose even further.

"Yeah. It's a long story and not the point." She blew out a breath. "Where do I fit into Giselle's plot? What do you think she has in store for me?" She paused as if gathering herself, and then her sorrowful brown eyes sought his. "Will I be able to go home, do you think?"

The vulnerability and insecurity he glimpsed in her expression turned his insides to porridge. The urge to protect and comfort her surged with such force, he could scarce prevent himself from snatching her from her horse and placing her on his lap. He wanted to hold her. Nay, 'twas far worse—he *needed* to hold her. He gripped the reins in his hands with such force the leather edges bit into his palms.

He might not be able to read her emotions as he did with others, but it mattered not. She wore every one of them upon her comely features. Such an odd mix was she, entirely feminine, lovely, graceful and delicate, yet possessing the skills, courage and strength to rival any well-trained squire.

Guilt, sharp-edged and swift, pierced his heart. Where did this inclination to hold Meghan come from? He was promised to Sky, and had been since the day she was born. He'd held her tiny, wriggling form in his arms and kent in that instant that they were meant for each other. He was as sure of it now as he had been then. Taking himself firmly in hand, he answered, "Och, lass, if I'd had even an inkling of what Giselle had in mind—"

"You would have prevented the whole thing. I get it. Thanks. Just so you know, I don't blame you for what happened."

"Nay? Still, I blame myself. I should have refused to do her any favors." He surveyed their party to assure himself all was well. "If it pleases you, my lady, I'll ride beside you awhile to ensure your bottom lip remains unmolested."

Her sudden burst of laughter went straight through him. Unbidden, the happy sound wrapped itself around his heart and wended its way to his very soul. He basked in the warmth and marveled at the sparkle in her eye—before his sanity returned.

Shaking himself free of the heady sensations, he gathered his defenses, hardened his heart and firmed his resolve. A knight's honor was his most valuable possession, and above all else, he was an honorable man.

By the time they made camp for the night, the weather had turned. Damp chill and a thick fog cloaked the surrounding hills and forest. "Under the circumstances, I believe 'twould be safe enough to build a fire. The fog will mask the smoke, and the heat will be a welcome relief from the cold and damp." Hunter glanced at Meghan where she stood shivering by the wagon.

"Aye. 'Twould be good to sit before a fire this eve." Tieren lifted the wagon's tarp and withdrew a thick woolen blanket. "Come, my lady, rest a bit whilst the lads go about gathering wood." He wrapped the blanket around her shoulders.

"I should help," she protested, glancing his way. "After all, I *am* Hunter's squire."

"No' this time. There are enough hands to gather tinder as it is." Tieren removed the board from its brackets at the end of the wagon and leaned it up against one of the rear wheels. He shoved their gear back far enough to create a place at the end for her to rest. "Sit."

Meghan lifted her brow in question. Hunter nodded. "Do as he bids you, lass. As you said earlier, the day has been trying, to say the least."

She gathered the blanket around herself, and was about to scramble up, when Tieren lifted her by the waist and set her upon the spot he'd cleared for her. Hunter stifled the growl rising in his throat.

Tieren smirked at him. "I'll see to making ready our evening meal, such as it is."

"You do that," Hunter muttered and busied himself collecting stones to ring the fire pit the squires had prepared before they joined the men who were hunting. "Mayhap the others will be successful, and we'll sup on fresh meat this eve." Conscious of Meghan's eyes upon him, he felt overly large and as awkward as a young page under her scrutiny. What was she feeling right now? What did she think of him? Mayhap 'twas his inability to read her that drew him to her so incessantly. Aye, that must be it.

By the time he had a fire going, Murray, Cecil and Gregory returned, bearing a few fat geese they'd already gutted and plucked. The squires followed, carrying a brace of coneys.

"The saints be praised!" Tieren exclaimed. "We shall feast this eve."

The pages, Tristan and Allain, took the catch from the men and made quick work of adding what seasonings they carried, spitting the fowl on green wood, and placing them atop the two branches set into the ground on either side of the fire. George and John worked at dressing the coneys. Once the geese were done, they'd spit the hares and roast them to break their fast on the morrow. The two lads tended to the roasting geese, and the rest of the party gathered to sit near the welcoming warmth of the fire.

"Tell us the tale, Hunter," Tieren said, helping Meghan to sit between them.

He sighed. "You dinna wish to wait until our bellies are full?"

"Nay." Cecil laid down a bit of sheepskin and settled himself upon it. "I would hear it now, if you please."

"All right." Exhaustion made it far more difficult for him to close himself off from his companions' reactions to the day's mysteries. Curiosity, wariness and fear wafted over him. For certes he wished for a reprieve. He needed solitude, a full belly and a good night's rest. "Gregory, keep watch but stand near enough to hear."

"Aye." He called to his squire to take up the watch on the opposite side of camp.

Hunter stared into the flames and wondered how much to reveal. If he kept to the tale and said naught of his ties to the fae, mayhap he wouldn't be forced to lie. "I rode into the fair and began searching for Nevan and the lads. When I came to the green-and-white-striped tent, an old Romany woman stepped out. I thought she might have knowledge of Nevan, so when she bid me enter her tent, I did so. We conversed a bit, and she gave me tea. She asked that I do her a favor, and I felt 'twas my knightly duty to comply."

From there, he related events exactly as they happened, leaving nothing out. "I snatched Meghan and brought her here, believing I was rescuing her from certain death. I was unaware that I'd been sent through time to do so. The two of us discovered the truth as we spoke." He met the eyes of each of the men and lads sitting around the fire. "She is come to us from the distant future. The rest you ken, for we rode straight here upon finding the fair gone."

"Impossible!" Cecil leaped to his feet. An overpowering determination to deny what he kent was the truth flowed from him. "This canna be."

"It's true." Meghan's chin lifted. "I'm from the twenty-first century. My father and I were putting on a sword fighting demonstration at a Renaissance festival when Hunter appeared and snatched me away. It's what we do. My family teaches sword fighting and other skills from your era." She gestured to their surroundings. "Hunter snatched me from what he thought was a fight to the death, and here I am."

"You saw the proof for yourself when you went to see if the fair had indeed disappeared. Why do you doubt me now?" Hunter sent Cecil a look sharp enough to split wood. "What would I gain from making up such an outrageous tale?"

"'Tis sorcery." Cecil paced.

"Aye, for certes, but no' of our doing. Surely you see that," Hunter offered in a placating tone. Cecil's mounting panic and fear assaulted Hunter's senses. "There are none here who are capable of sorcery, as well you ken. I speak naught but the truth."

"Nay?" Cecil's pacing came to a sudden halt, and his suspicious glare fixed upon Meghan. Distrust and malice cloaked him in a thick cloud. "What do you ken about *that lass* in truth?" He pointed an accusing finger at her. "Mayhap she's fae and wishes to steal our souls whilst we sleep."

"I'm not!" Meghan cried, jumping to her feet. "I told you. I was just minding my own business when Hunter popped out of that tent and grabbed me. Everything that has happened today has been totally against my will." She sucked in a breath. "Besides, why would I want to steal anybody's soul? Not that I could," she muttered. "Because I can't."

"Why, to make it all the easier to take our gold and silver, of course." Cecil's hands fisted at his sides. "'Tis naught but sorcery, and I will no' consort with the fae." Spittle flew from his mouth as he ranted and paced. "Heresy, I tell you!" he shouted, pointing at Meghan again. "I say we bind her and leave her here in the wood. Let her own kind take her back. We dinna want her with us." He stopped and drew his sword. "Be gone, witch, and may God have mercy upon your black soul."

"First she's fae and now she's a witch? Here now, Cecil, you're spewing nonsense." Tieren was the next to rise to his feet. He shoved Meghan behind him. "Have you lost your wits?"

"Humph. She has already bewitched you, sir." Cecil waved his sword in front of him. "Do ye no' see it is so?"

"Enough." Hunter got up and relieved Cecil of his claymore. "Be reasonable. Sit down. Once you've filled your belly with a hot meal, things will look better."

"Once she is gone from us, things will look better." Cecil glared. "*You* brought her into our midst. *You* must force her away."

"I will do no such thing." He caught Gregory's frantic movements from the corner of his eye. "Och, cease with crossing yourself, Gregory. 'Tis causing my head to pound worse than it already does." He stuck the point of Cecil's sword into the dirt. Massaging his temples, he tried once more to restore reason. "By all that is holy, I swear to you—neither I nor Meghan had aught to do with what happened this day, and for the last time, she is no' fae." He sent a pointed look around the circle of men. "She's Irish."

Strangled hysteria-tinged laughter broke free from Meghan. He quelled it with a stern look. "'Tis true, is it no', lass?"

"It's true. Not even a little bit faerie." She crossed her heart and held up her hand in some sort of salute. "Scout's honor. I'm one hundred percent Irish."

"'Tis just as bad," Cecil cried, but once again he took his place by the fire. "Were it no' for the fact that I've lived in close quarters with you for nigh on four years, Hunter, I would take my leave anon. 'Tis true you have never led me false in the past. For that alone, I have no reason to doubt things went just as you say they did." He cast Meghan a dark glance. "Still—"

"You have my word, Cecil. Let us sup together and say no more about bewitchings and such." Hunter handed him back his sword and settled himself once again. "Smells good, lads. Do we have any wine left?"

"Aye." Allain rushed to do his bidding. "I'll fetch it from the wagon."

His heart and temples pounding, Hunter did his best to behave as if all were well, even though he now had a new worry. He signed to Tieren, *"We must guard Meghan carefully this night. I sense Cecil's hatred and fear. I worry he might try to slit her throat as we sleep."*

"Done," Tieren signed back.

"I will no' have it." Cecil leaped back up and launched into a fresh complaint. "I like it no' when you two speak with your hands. You share secrets." He narrowed his eyes at them. "Do you plot some treachery against me?"

"'Tis naught but the language of the deaf I learned as a bairn. You ken I lost my hearing for a time as a young lad." Hunter shook his head. "'Tis habit is all. I was just asking Tieren to take the first watch." Partly true, at least. They would both be on guard through the night. "No treachery involved."

Hunter awoke with a start. *Shite!* He'd failed to stay awake as he'd intended. He checked to see that Meghan and Tieren were well. Once assured of their safety, he stilled himself. Listening with both his ears and his senses, he cast about for the source of his unease. Did he hear the sound of horses in the distance? Turning toward the warm glow of the fire, he spied Murray staring into the flames whilst tugging at his beard—a sure sign his friend wrestled with troubling thoughts. Rising quietly, he went to join him.

"Cecil and Gregory have left us," Murray said in a low tone.

"Aye?" Hunter sat down beside him. "Och, it could have been worse. I feared Cecil would attempt some nefarious deed as we slept."

"I let them go without an argument. They took only what belonged tae them, and their lads went with them."

"Humph. We are down to the same number we set out with from Moigh Hall when we left for the continent with naught but our gear and ambition." Not enough. Not nearly enough, considering what they carried and how they traveled. "In what direction did they go?"

"Back toward Edinburgh, though I dinna believe they mean tae stay tae that course. There are, after all, many roads they could take along the way." Murray shifted and rolled his shoulders. "As ye ken, Cecil's family seat is in Dumfriesshire. Mayhap that is where he means tae go. Should I ha' awakened you as they gathered their things?"

"Nay. Given Cecil's bent, 'tis best they are gone from us, though I fear 'twill no' be the last we hear from either of them. Their armor and gear is on the way to Inverness as we speak." He shook his head. "I'm grateful they took only what belonged to them. I thought Gregory at least would remain, though I reckoned Cecil had some plot in mind."

"'Tis nearly dawn," Murray said, studying the eastern horizon. "Mayhap 'twould be wise tae get an early start."

"Aye." He rose and gave Murray's shoulder a squeeze. "Where is young John?"

"My squire keeps watch upon yon hill. Let us wake the others. John can take his rest upon the wagon, since the load is considerably lighter now." Murray stood and stretched. "Cecil and Gregory took one of Nevan's palfreys for a packhorse, and I allowed them tae do so without protest. I want no bad blood between us lest they return with bloodshed on their minds."

"Fair enough. I'll see to waking everyone. Put out the fire and recall John to camp. We'll be off in a trice."

"This is my fault, isn't it?" Meghan came up behind them, still wrapped in her blanket. "I heard you talking." She tugged the wool tighter around her shoulders and looked to him. Her lovely brown eyes were large and filled with worry. "I'm sorry."

His insides knotted, and his heart took a tumble. "Nay. 'Tis no more your fault than mine. Madame Giselle is responsible, and since we now have naught but the company of my clansmen and the lads whose clans have long been allied with ours, we might speak more freely." He reached out and tucked an errant strand of her silken hair behind her ear. Why could he not resist the urge to touch her? "Go on. See to your needs whilst we keep watch. Once we break our fast, we'll depart."

It took considerably longer than a trice to get everyone up, fed and moving, and once again Meghan's expression said much about her state of mind. Distress turned the corners of her mouth down and creased her brow. Tieren hovered close to her, and for that Hunter was glad—at least he told himself 'twas so. "Let us be off," he grumbled his order. "By the saints, I canna fathom what is taking you lads so long this morn."

Neither the squires nor the pages answered, but a flurry of activity ensued. "George, you will drive the wagon, and once John is rested, he can take over. You may then take your turn to rest. Mayhap we can travel longer this day if you lads all take turns thus. Fix a lead for the palfreys."

They were down to three pages and two squires, not counting Meghan. It should have taken half the time to pack up and begin their journey. Unease pricked at him. The sooner they reached Aberdeenshire the better. He would send word to Moigh Hall and request a guard be sent to accompany them. Aye, that's what he'd do. They'd wait in the comfort of an inn he'd oft stayed in with his foster father and uncles. Once he had word that their guard was close, their small band would set out to meet them. A good plan. Once again he had things well in hand.

Hunter glanced at the dark, low-hanging clouds and shivered. The weather had grown worse since the day past when Cecil and Gregory had departed. 'Twould soon rain, and they'd be forced to travel on through the mud whilst wet and miserable. There were no inns between here and Aberdeenshire.

At least his lads had readied themselves for travel much quicker this morn; Meghan as well. All were as anxious as he to see the safety of Aberdeenshire's gates. He swung up on Doireann's back and started for the road, trusting the rest would follow. The creaking of the wagon wheels assured him he'd assumed correctly.

Hunter kept a careful watch upon the way ahead, scanning the edge of the fog-shrouded forest along to his left for any sign of danger. Naught but the sea and rocky cliffs lay to the east, and none could approach undetected from that direction. He set a goodly pace and prayed they'd encounter no trouble along the way. The closer they came to town, the thicker the thieves. God willing, they'd reach town just past Prime this very day.

They traveled on in silence. Tieren took up the rear, and Murray guarded their middle. Meghan's mount was directly behind his, flanked by Allain on one side with Tristan and Harold, Murray's page, on the other. John would likely sleep on the wagon until midday again today, since he'd had last watch. George took his place, reins in hand, behind the rouncies pulling their belongings along the muddy, rutted track stretching before them.

'Twas the best they could do, and their two squires were close enough to earning their spurs that they could enter into battle and manage well enough. After all, they'd been trained by Tieren, Murray and himself, all MacKintosh knights and the best in the realm.

By late morn the rain began to fall in earnest. Still they slogged on, and the collective glumness of his cluster of weary travelers weighed heavily upon him. 'Twas cold enough that huffing out a breath caused a cloud of steam. He kept his focus on the way ahead and hunkered down under his wet cloak. They'd been traveling for hours when they reached a menacing stretch of road with forest on either side. At least the rain had eased some.

Hunter sent his senses into the shadowy depths of the woodland stretching before them, not liking at all what came back. Nefarious intent rolled in waves from the darkness, chilling his blood far more than the weather ever could. He halted and signed for silence. Fog obscured the way, making it impossible to see beyond the edges of the tree line on either side. He concentrated in an attempt to locate the source of the evil lying in wait, grateful that their own presence upon the road was as equally obscured.

"What is it?" Meghan whispered, coming up beside him. She too stared toward the forest.

He whispered back, "These woods are teeming with a thieving lot of brigands and murderers."

With a quick intake of breath, her head whipped around, and her eyes grew large. "How can you possibly know that?"

"I am a seasoned warrior and have developed instincts about

such things." *Partly true.* "Look to your mount's ears, lass, and to Doireann's. Their senses are far more acute than ours." Indeed, Doireann's ears pricked forward, flattened back and pricked forward again as if seeking the source of danger he surely felt. Meghan's gelding did the same, lifting his front hooves in mincing steps. Murray and Tieren soon joined them.

"I dinna like what I'm sensing ahead," Hunter said, giving the two knights a meaningful look. "We've only the three of us for defense. If we enter the forest, we are sure to meet with trouble, and 'tis certain we are far outnumbered."

"We've John and George to defend the wagon," Murray whispered. "And our pages have weapons as well."

"I can fight," Meghan said, looking to each of them in turn.

She'd tucked her sodden hair beneath her equally sodden cap. She shivered under her cloak, and her cheeks and the tip of her nose were ruddy from the cold. Yet not once had she complained or shirked her share of the duties when they camped. His admiration for her grew with each passing day. "Nay, lass. I willna allow you to do so."

"But you saw," she hissed between her teeth, her eyes flashing indignation. "You know I can handle a sword as well as you can."

He wiped the rain from his face and clenched his jaw. "Do you recall when you found your weapon upon the ground?"

"Of course I do."

"When you swung it about above your head, think you I did no' notice the bluntness of the edges? 'Tis for naught but show. It matters no' how well you wield the thing. You could no' slice an apple with that blade, much less separate a man's head from his shoulders."

All of the color leached from her face. "Oh. Right." She chewed her lower lip for a second. "You have spares on the wagon, don't you? I could—"

"Aye, there are spares upon the wagon, but the lads will need them, and our other weapons outweigh you by two or three stones at least," Tieren told her, his tone filled with feigned regret. "You could no' heft a war club adequately, my lady."

"I'm good with daggers, and throwing them would keep me a distance away from our enemies," she argued. "I can help. I want to help. Don't you carry a whetstone or two? I could sharpen my sword right now."

"And if our enemies carry crossbows? Would ye have us sit like fat geese in the middle of this quagmire of a road whilst ye make ready yer sword for battle, lass?" Murray huffed, shaking his head. "'Twill no' be long afore the outlaws sense our presence just as we've discovered theirs."

Hunter couldn't help but be impressed by her courage, and by the fact that she viewed their enemies as hers as well. Any other lass would have gladly scampered off to some safe hiding place until he and his knights had vanquished the threat. "Have you ever killed a man, Meghan?"

"No." She glared at him. "Of course not."

"As I thought." He blew out a breath before turning to her. "If it pleases you, I would rather today no' be the day you make your first kill. 'Tis a messy business." He searched the outer edge of the forest. A barely discernible path ran along to their left. Clearly theirs would not be the first group of travelers to circumvent the brigands hiding in the thick trees.

"As quietly as we can, let us move the wagon off the road and into the brush. We'll unload everything to carry ourselves from here on in. See yon path along the edge of the forest?" He pointed to the trail. "That is our way."

"Aye," Tieren agreed. "The extra palfreys we can use as decoys. Let us divide the contents of our casks between the bedrolls, sporrans and satchels. We'll place the empties upon the palfreys' backs along with some of our gear. We can cover their loads with the tarp, which we can cut into three pieces easily enough."

"'Tis a sound plan, Tieren," Hunter said. "We must each carry our own weapons. Meghan will take the food, waterskins and blankets."

She shot him a disgruntled look. He shook his head. "Dinna argue, lass. I'm doing my best to protect you."

"I don't need your—"

"'Twould be prudent to have her sword sharpened by a black-smith in Aberdeenshire," Tieren interjected. "Whether or no' she ever joins us in battle, I would feel better knowing she could defend herself if need be."

Meghan flashed Tieren a grateful smile. "Thank you. I agree. Let's have my sword sharpened." Then she turned a glare his way. "In the meantime, give me a bunch of daggers just in case."

"I'll see it done, my lady," Tieren said. "We've several to hand."

Hunter bit his tongue. Tieren received beatific smiles and grati-tude, while she gave him naught but defiance and cheek. Did the woman not recognize that *he* was her champion? Did she not under-stand and appreciate his attempts to keep her safe? Ah, but hadn't he also been the fool to take her away from all she held dear? He stifled the groan rising in his throat and turned to oversee the wagon being moved off the road.

Together they made quick work of redistributing their goods. "We'll use signing until we can see the gates of Aberdeenshire." Hunter accompanied his words with the signs.

Meghan's expression suffused with frustration. "Even though I recognize ASL, I don't know how to sign."

"Just stay where we put you, and follow along as quietly as you are able," he whispered close to her ear. "Mayhap I can begin to teach you once we're safe."

"Or I can," Tieren said, inserting himself between the two of them.

Hunter reached out with his senses to get a read on him, but Tieren had long ago learned how to mask his true feelings. All he could glean was a distracting jumble. Was Tieren serious about claiming Meghan? "Aye, or you can." Hunter let the matter go and took up the lead, well aware that Meghan's gaze once again followed him. Mayhap he was as much a puzzle to her as she was to him.

He signaled for the group to follow as quietly as possible, and they started out for the path leading around the outskirts of the forest. They'd tied bits of canvas over their horses' hooves to muffle the sound, and they rode with only rope halters lest the jingle of bits and curb straps alert any to their whereabouts.

Like wraiths they crept along at a snail's pace through most of the afternoon. By his reckoning, they had little more than a league to go before clearing the wood and gaining sight of Aberdeenshire's gates. Though the prickling dread still rode him hard, a fervent hope ignited that they'd managed to outwit the fiends lying in wait.

He led them around the next bend, and the fine hairs on his forearms and at the back of his neck stood on end mere seconds before he spied six rough-looking villains, two on horseback, all blocking their way. They held broadswords and axes. Their malice slammed into him like a war club. "Shite."

Tieren, Murray, George and John rode ahead to join him. He flashed them an incredulous look. "If you are all with me, who watches our rear?"

"Meghan, Allain, Tristan and Harold." Murray spared him a glance.

"Shite."

"You've already said that," Murray remarked while drawing his sword.

"Aye, well it bears repeating." He looked to Tieren. "Go back and guard her."

"'Twould be an honor." Tieren bowed his head briefly and turned his warhorse on its hind legs. He cantered back and dismounted, positioning himself at the end of the line facing the way they had just come with his sword drawn. Hunter issued orders to the lads to herd the horses into a tight knot and hobble them so they couldn't bolt.

Once he was assured Meghan, the palfreys and the lads were protected, Hunter turned back to face the brigands before them. "May God protect and give us strength this day," he prayed.

"We're knights, lad." Murray frowned. "They're naught but poorly trained vagabonds."

"One could hope, but I fear otherwise. In these perilous times, 'tis just as likely they're well-trained knights whose laird fell upon hard times and had to let them go." Hunter drew his claymore. "They are hungry and desperate, and that makes them all the more dangerous. All we ken for certain is that they are without honor. Outlaws. Keep your eyes open for aught coming from the tree line.

"Stay here until I give you word that our way is clear," he called back to Tieren and the rest. "Guard the horses and each other." With those parting words, he prepared himself for the fight ahead. "Loch Moigh! Touch no' the cat but with gloves!" He shouted his clan's call to battle at the top of his lungs and spurred his horse forward, his weapon at the ready.

CHAPTER FOUR

Meghan's insides quivered and shook like Aunt Betty's lime Jell-O salad straight from the mold. She heard men grunting with effort, the *thunk* of blows parried and steel ringing against steel. Swallowing convulsively, she strained to see what was going on ahead, but the fog was too thick. This fight was not an exhibition, and her life depended upon the outcome. Her stomach roiled. She was going to be sick.

"Keep your eyes to the tree line, lass, and keep your dirks at the ready," Tieren whispered, turning her around and placing her behind the horses. "Stay put. Any danger to us will come from the woods."

She nodded, took one of the borrowed daggers from her belt and began flipping it in the air end-over-end. A nervous habit. Allain and the other two pages, Tristan and Harold, moved into strategically spaced positions around the livestock. Closest to her, Allain held his sword in front of him, gripping the handle in both hands with white-knuckled tenacity. All three of the boys had gone pale and still.

Oh my God, they're just children, barely preteens if even that.

She drew in a deep breath through her nose and blew it out slowly through her mouth. *Flip, flip, flip*—she tossed the dagger in

59

her right hand. *Thump, thump, thump* pounded her heart against her rib cage. She gasped at the sound of breaking brush to her right. Two men on foot charged out from the trees. One held a large, heavy-looking club; the other brandished a rusty axe. Both men were filthy, ragged and fierce.

Tieren strode forward and engaged the man with the club. The one with the axe headed straight for Allain. Hunter's page trembled, but stood his ground, ready to defend himself and their horses. The other two boys inched closer to help him, but they wouldn't get to him in time. Besides, none of them would be a match for the enormous thug.

A streak of wetness darkened Allain's hose as his bladder let loose. Rage exploded within her at the injustice. Meghan stepped out from her place beside the horses. "Hey," she shouted. "Pick on somebody your own size, asshole!"

The thief's gaze shifted her way. His eyes traveled over her, and he snarled, dismissing her as a threat. He turned back to Allain, kicking the kid's sword from his hands far too easily. Allain raised his arms to cover his head. The brute hefted his axe to deliver the killing blow. Meghan snapped. She could *not* let this creep kill Allain! Instinct took over, and her focus narrowed to the bully's most vulnerable spot—his bare neck. Flipping her dagger in the air once more, she caught it by the blade and hurled it through the air with all the force she could muster.

The thug staggered back and clutched at the knife protruding from his throat. Eyes filled with hatred and shock turned her way as he pulled the blade out by the hilt. He threw it to the ground and stalked toward her with his axe raised. A gurgling sound emitted from the wound, and frothy blood spilled down his chest to stain his tunic. She must've severed an artery.

She stepped back, unable to take her eyes off of the thick red stream spurting down his front with each pulse of his heart. Less than a yard away, he dropped the axe and fell to his knees. Then he toppled over face-first on the ground. A pool of crimson stained the mud beneath him.

All the air left her lungs at once. Spots danced before her eyes, and she collapsed to her hands and knees. Crawling away from the corpse, tears dripped from her cheeks to the ground, and the awful taste of bile rose to her throat. She shut her eyes tight in an effort to block out what had just happened, but the image was as real with her eyes closed as it was with them open—and the memory every bit as terrifying.

I killed a man.

Her gut lurched. She sucked in huge gulps of air and concentrated on breathing, on the feel of the wet ground beneath her palms and knees. She focused on anything other than the gruesome images flashing through her mind.

Strong hands lifted her to her feet. Alarm lit her nerves on fire, and she tensed to fight. Her eyes flew open. Hunter had her. All the fight left her with a whoosh of air from her lungs.

"Are ye hurt, lass?" His voice came out a gruff rasp, and he gripped her arms so tightly he'd leave bruises. His worry-filled gaze traveled over every inch of her.

"No." She shook her head, and a tear slipped down her cheek. Next thing she knew, she found herself crushed against his broad chest, his strong arms banding around her with such force that all the energy she had left was squeezed right out of her. Good thing he held her up, because she couldn't have stood on her own to save her life.

Aunt Betty's Jell-O had nothing on her. She shook uncontrollably. Placing her palms on Hunter's chest, she closed her eyes again and rested her cheek against the wet wool of his tunic. Somehow, finding his heart pounding as rapidly as hers gave her comfort.

"You should ha' seen it, Sir Hunter," Tristan cried. "The lass popped out from behind the rouncies and felled the man with a single toss of her wee dirk."

"Aye," Allain squeaked and cleared his throat. "Do ye ken what she said to him afore she smote him dead?"

"Nay. What did she say?" Hunter asked, his voice hoarse. He rocked her back and forth in a soothing motion.

"She told him to pick on someone his own size," Allain answered, his tone filled with incredulous awe. "His own size, sir, and she's nae bigger than I! Then she had the ballocks tae call him an *asshole*."

· Hunter grunted and cradled her head against his chest. She heard him swallow a few times. Her heart rate slowed a bit, but the shakes still gripped her. She was safe. Somehow she'd managed to live through the ordeal, thanks to a lifetime of training at her father's knee.

Lord, how she wanted her dad right now, and her mom. Hell, she wanted to go upstairs to her own bedroom—after a long, scalding hot bath, that is—crawl into her bed and sleep for a week. In clean sheets and wearing her favorite flannel jammies. She hiccupped against Hunter's chest.

"She saved Allain's life, and that's the truth," Harold said. "Here, my lady." He nudged her shoulder. "I cleaned the dirk for ye."

"Keep it." She burrowed closer to Hunter and gripped handfuls of his tunic. "It's not mine anyway."

"'Tis now," Allain crowed. "A war trophy, my lady, tae recall the deed. Mayhap I'll compose a ballad for ye, in honor of yer bravery."

She groaned, gagged and slipped her arms around Hunter's waist.

Hunter stiffened. He removed her arms from around him and stepped away. "I'll take the dagger for now, lad. We must be off. Open your eyes, Meghan. 'Tis over and done."

Wait. Who'd flipped his switch? Why had he shifted from caring, comforting protector to brusque commander? She wasn't finished with being comforted. Not by a long shot. "I prefer to keep them closed."

"Aye, but 'tis far more difficult to see where you're going that way." He made a grunting sound deep in his throat. "Allain, the rain has caused a small burn to run from the wood yonder. Clean yourself up, lad, and be quick about it. Tristan, Harold, help me remove the hobbles and take the canvas from the horses' hooves. We won't need to muffle our passing any longer. The enemy has been routed and vanquished."

Oh Lord. She'd vanquished one of them herself. "You were right. Killing is a messy business," she muttered. "I don't ever want to have to do that again." She opened her eyes but kept her gaze on the path ahead. "Where are Tieren and Murray?" Her heart pounded again, and panic stole her breath. "John and George aren't . . . Tell me everyone is OK."

"Everyone is indeed OK. The others are ensuring our way ahead is clear." Hunter unfastened the nearest horse's hobbles. "We dinna have much farther to go. Once we're in Aberdeenshire, we will remain there until my kin sends a guard to escort us the rest of the way. You will be safe."

"Safe? In fifteenth-century Scotland?" She snorted. "You've got to be kidding me. I've read a book or three about your century, and there's nothing *safe* about it."

"And yet, have you no' insisted more than once that you have no need of my protection?" He met her gaze, his steel-gray eyes deadly serious.

"Touché." Heat surged to her cheeks. "I'm beginning to see that we all need each other's protection." She hiccupped again and reached for the gelding's reins with a shaky hand.

"Aye. 'Tis the way of it." Hunter moved to her side and cupped his hands. "I ken you are able to mount on your own, but accept my aid all the same."

"Gladly." She placed her muddy boot in his palms and hoisted herself onto the horse's back. "My legs are like rubber bands right now anyway."

"I dinna ken what rubber bands are, but I've oft felt what you are feeling now, Beag Curaidh. A good hot meal and a day or two's rest, and I trow you will recover well enough." He patted her leg, leaving a muddy handprint behind. He smiled up at her, his expression filled with understanding.

She frowned. "What does *beg coo-ree* mean?"

"'Tis but a sobriquet to honor your bravery. It means 'wee warrior.'"

"Oh." She blinked back the tears filling her eyes again. "I don't think I was brave, Hunter. Everything just kind of happened at once, and I acted on instinct."

He smiled at her again, and a flush of heat suffused her insides. "Will I be able to bathe in Aberdeenshire and clean these clothes maybe?"

"Aye."

"Good." Grief and a bone-deep weariness overtook her. She wanted to put her arms around the horse's neck and fall asleep on his back for the rest of the trip. Could she do that? Too bad they'd abandoned the wagon. "Does this horse have a name?"

"Aye. Nevan called him Mìlidh, which means 'champion.' He's a fine destrier."

"He is." She patted the bay's neck. "But Milly? Where I come from, that's a girl's name." The gelding tossed his head as if she'd insulted him.

"Och, but you are no' there. You are here, and here 'tis a strong name for a horse that has proven himself in battle more than once."

"Point taken." She yawned, and her mouth opened so wide, it made a popping sound. Tristan and Harold finished removing the canvas from the hooves of their ponies. Allain returned from the brush wearing a kilt of plain brown wool. His hose were dripping wet. He wrung them out and rolled them before stowing them with the rest of his things. Still babbling on about the battle, the younger boys mounted and took their places in line. Meghan scrubbed both hands over her face in an effort to wake herself up. Man, what would she give for a mocha latte about now, with extra whipped cream and chocolate shavings on top. She sighed heavily.

"Are you able to ride, lass?" Hunter wiped his muddy hands on a patch of wet grass before swinging up on Doireann.

"To tell the truth, I don't know how long I'll last." She glanced at him. "I'm still adjusting to all the changes." The constant dampness, the cold, traveling and the tension from the last few days had definitely taken a toll. "Seems like I've been tired ever since I got here."

"Why did you no' tell me? You could have rested upon the wagon as we traveled."

She lifted her chin. "I can handle it."

He drew his mount up beside her. "You *must* give up this ridiculous notion that you possess a man's strength and stamina." He reached over and snatched her off her horse like she weighed nothing. Settling her in front of him with his arm around her waist, he called over his shoulder, "Allain, take her mount's reins and lead him. You"—he gave her a shake—"rest."

Too tired to argue, she opted for the easiest retort. "You are *so* arrogant."

"Aye, but I've earned the right to be thus, and the sooner you accept that I am your superior in every way, the better we'll get along. Sleep now, and hold your tongue whilst you're at it."

"*Superior?*" Her eyes widened, and she straightened away from him. "Bring it, buddy. I demand a rematch. Anytime. Anywhere." She twisted around to glare at him, stunned to find his eyes twinkling with amusement and one corner of his mouth twitching up. Her insides melted, and she studied him for several seconds before settling back against his chest. "You're teasing me. Why would you do that?"

"To divert your troubled thoughts." His arm tightened around her waist.

"Oh." She nodded. "Sleep *and* hold my tongue at the same time, eh? I'll give that a try."

"Do," he commanded. Leaning close, he whispered, "You ken I was raised by a twenty-first-century lass and a twenty-first-century foster cousin, aye? Both have proven themselves a man's equal in every way. You've been through much these past few days. Take your rest now, whilst I watch your back. 'Tis the MacKintosh way."

His breath against her neck and the way he held her sent shivers of pleasure coursing through her center. But the moment she stopped talking, the horror of what she'd done came flooding back. She preferred talking to the pictures in her head. "What happened to your last squire?"

"Randolph caught his thigh upon a rusty scrap of iron whilst on the ship carrying us home. The wound festered, and he grew feverish. My squire perished at sea."

What was she doing in this place where life was so utterly fragile? She shuddered. "I'm sorry."

"As am I. He was a good lad and would've been knighted this summer. I dinna look forward to sending word to his kin. Randolph was a Sutherland. They're close allies to the MacKintosh." He gave her another slight shake. "Did I no' just tell you to rest, Beag Curaidh?"

"Yep. You did." With another huge yawn, she snuggled against him. Despite how wet and cold they both were, a luxurious warmth spread where her back pressed against his chest. The contact and the heat lulled and soothed her. She felt protected, cherished. Sleep took her away from the damp chill, the never-ending mud and the day's trauma. For right now, she was safe in Hunter's arms.

"Meghan." Hunter's deep voice penetrated her sleep. "We're in Aberdeenshire. A meal and a bed await us within."

She yawned and straightened. They were on a cobbled street with charming stone cottages crowding either side and the North Sea sparkling to the east. Before her stood an impressive two-story inn built with a massive timber frame and some sort of material like the stucco familiar to her from the twenty-first century.

Hunter slid off Doireann and reached up to help her dismount. She set her pride aside and placed her hands on his broad shoulders. He lifted her to the ground, and their bodies touched for an instant, setting off a host of whirligigs inside her. All too quickly he stepped away and began issuing orders. Already she missed being sheltered in his arms.

"Once the horses are unloaded, Allain, Tristan and Harold, take the horses to the stables in back," Hunter said, untying the packs fastened to one of the ponies. He hoisted the load to the cobbles. "The rest of us will transport our belongings inside. Wait here, and I'll see what is available in the way of lodging."

He disappeared into the inn, and Meghan helped with the unloading. Oh, how she looked forward to sleeping under a roof. What were inns like in the fifteenth century, anyway? For the past week she'd been sleeping on the ground between Tieren and Hunter and surrounded by snoring, farting males. Was it possible she might have some privacy while they were here?

"How do you fare, my lady?" Tieren asked, his tone low. "Though we will no' be addressing you as 'lady' for the foreseeable future, aye?" He grinned.

She smiled back. "Other than being weary to the bone, I'm fine. It'll be nice to be dry and warm for a change, won't it?"

"Och, aye." He took the bundle of blankets from her hands and set them on top of the casks already on the ground. "The lads sang your praises all the way here. Allain has sworn to become your champion once he's earned his spurs. I am greatly indebted to you."

She shrugged. "I only did what any of you would've done."

"Aye, but 'twas my duty, no' yours. I was charged with protecting you, and I feared the worst when I saw that miscreant approaching you with his axe raised. You saved Allain's life and defended yourself as well as any warrior. You truly are a braw and canny lass. 'Tis a blessing indeed that you have come to us." His expression turned somber. "I hate to think what would have befallen Allain had you no' been so handy with a dirk."

"I've secured two private chambers for the duration of our stay," Hunter said, appearing at her side. "Let us take these things inside lest prying eyes take note." He covered one of the small trunks with a leather satchel and lifted it. "Come, lads," he said, his eyes resting on her for a second, "the sooner we are settled, the sooner we can sit by a warm fire with tankards of ale and a fine hot supper."

With a quick backward glance toward the sea, she inhaled the cool, salt-tinged air and followed her crew inside. Hunter led them up the stairs and down the dim hallway lit only by the daylight coming through a single window at the end. He opened the first of two doors. "Squires and pages here." He motioned for George and John to come forward. "We have the room next door."

Meghan followed the squires. Hunter took her by the arm and tugged her toward the second door.

"Nay, *lad*," he said. "I want you close where I can look after you."

"Aye, here where *we* can look after you," Tieren added, his tone firm. "What shall we call *him*?" He winked at her.

"'Tis up to *him*." Hunter shot her a questioning look.

"Kevin." Her throat tightened, and a tidal wave of homesickness washed over her. "It's my oldest brother's name. Call me Kevin."

"Come, Kevin." Tieren gestured for her to enter. "Let us put these things away and go to our supper."

Curious, she surveyed the interior. The room resembled a dormitory, with six wooden bed frames strung with rope. Thin wool mattresses were rolled at the end of each bed, and all of the beds were pushed up against the walls, leaving the interior space open. At least it had a fireplace. Not lit, but kindling, split logs and peat bricks stood ready to heat the room. Pegs lined the walls, and the men were already hanging their wet cloaks up to dry. She stood where she was, her hands full of their camp food and waterskins and her damp clothing chafing her skin. Which cot should she take?

"You will sleep here, Kevin." Hunter pointed to the cot between the one he had chosen and the one where Tieren had dropped the bundle of blankets.

"I guess a room to myself is out of the question," she grumbled, approaching her assigned spot.

"Ye've slept amongst us for three nights without complaint." Murray's brow lowered. "What objection can ye have now to such an arrangement? Ha' we no' looked after ye well enough fer yer liking . . . Kevin?"

"You have looked after me very well, and I'm grateful." She sighed. "I don't object to the arrangement. It's just that I could use a little privacy." She wanted a bath, and she really needed some alone time. She dropped her stuff on the narrow cot before her.

"There are no such chambers to be had in our inns." Tieren shot her a sympathetic look. "Oft times more than one family or group of travelers share a chamber such as this, and for those who canna afford a chamber, the corridor serves well enough for a night's rest. See you how the center of this chamber is open? That is where servants and guards take their rest when a noble travels with his retinue. At least we're out of the elements, and the Boar's Head Inn has a reputation for being well tended and safe. The innkeeper boasts of a fine cook as well." He rubbed his stomach. "I'm starving, and I've a powerful thirst. Hang up your cloak, Kevin, and we'll sup in the hall below. When we retire for the eve, we'll have a fine fire in yon hearth. I trow we will all sleep well within these walls."

Once their things were stowed, she trudged downstairs with the rest of the pages and squires to the great hall that served as the dining room and pub. Large timbers stretched to the ceiling, supporting equally broad crossbeams. The wood-plank floor had been strewn with fresh straw. They were given the largest table by the hearth, and soon food and tankards of strong dark ale appeared before them. Her stomach growled, and she dug in.

The innkeeper hadn't lied. The lamb stew was thick, rich and delicious. Meghan stared into the pewter tankard before her and yawned. The warmth from the roaring fire behind her dried her clothing, and for the first time in days her body temperature rose to normal. Full, warm and drowsy, she only half listened to the conversation going on around her.

"Kevin, ye look as if ye mean tae sleep sitting up, lad." Murray chuckled. "Send yer squire off tae his rest, Hunter, afore his face lands in his supper."

"Aye, off to bed with you, lad," Hunter ordered, his expression warm.

"Thanks," she mumbled, rising from her place. "Good night. See you in the morning." Her limbs heavy with fatigue, she climbed the stairs and dragged her sorry butt down the corridor to their room. Heading straight for her assigned cot, she pushed the day's events to the far recesses of her weary brain.

She unrolled the mattress, checking it for bedbugs. Then she grabbed one of the wool blankets from their pile. Perching on the edge of her assigned cot, she tugged off her muddy boots and her borrowed tunic. She hung the tunic on one of the wooden posts on the bed frame, lay down and pulled the blanket up to her chin. *Ah, blessed sleep.* Yawning once more, she dozed off with the image of Hunter's dimpled smile firmly fixed in her mind.

Coming to with a jolt, Meghan awoke covered in a cold sweat. Her hand trembling, she ran her fingers through her hair. She blinked, and the nightmare came back to her in a rush.

"Wheesht, Beag Curaidh. You're safe, lass," Hunter murmured. He ran his hand up and down her back. "'Tis naught but a dream."

"I . . . I was dreaming about . . ."

"I ken well enough what haunts your sleep." He rose. "Come with me," he said in a quiet tone. "We dinna want to wake the others."

Still trembling, she stood. Hunter took the blanket from her cot and wrapped it around her shoulders and turned her toward the door. He ran his hands up and down her arms as he propelled her out of the chamber. The familiar sound of the men's snores followed them into the dimly lit corridor. A few tall candles on pewter stands had been lit, casting scant light to play along the walls. Hunter stopped at the stairway and sank down to sit on the top step. He gestured for her to join him.

Placing her hand on his shoulder for balance, she lowered herself beside him. "I had a nightmare."

"Night *mare*?" He cast her a sideways glance. "Though I dinna ken the reference, I take your meaning well enough. You were crying out in your sleep."

"A nightmare, one word, is a bad dream." A chill ran down her spine, and she pulled the blanket tighter.

"Ah, we call them 'night-hags.' After the day we've had, I can imagine the dreams plaguing you. 'Tis only natural." He put his arm around her shoulders and drew her close. "Och, I've had my share of night-hags as well."

"What are your bad dreams about? Battles you've fought?"

He shrugged his broad shoulders. "At times, aye, but when I was but a lad, I oft dreamt of my ma and my granny leaving me. Ma died of a fever when I was still a bairn of but three winters, and my granny passed the following spring."

71

His voice carried a load of hurt, and her heart broke for him. "I'm so sorry."

"Hmm." He seemed to draw into himself. Lost in his own thoughts, he stroked her arm absently.

"Do you remember your mother and grandmother?"

"I do." He sighed. "My ma had soft gray eyes and gentle hands. She mourned for my da. I recall her sadness most of all. My granny was the clan's wisewoman and midwife, yet she could do naught to save her daughter from the fever that took her."

The grief in his voice wrenched at her heart. "What happened to you after they died?"

"'Twas frightening and confusing." He huffed out a breath. "Hellish. I'd lost my hearing to the same fever that took my ma, and no family would take me in because of my defect. If it had been any other clan, 'tis certain I would no' have lasted through that first winter." A shudder wracked him, and she felt it to her very bones.

"The earl and his kin are more compassionate than most." He hung his head, his voice barely audible. "Instead of driving me off, they allowed me to sleep in the great hall or in the stables. I begged for scraps to fill my belly and survived as best I could. Eventually the earl had his stable master give me odd jobs to do. I believe 'twas his intent to provide me with some means to support myself once I'd grown, and for that I am most grateful."

"I can't imagine how terrifying that must have been. No little kid should be alone like that, especially at such a young age." Meghan laid her head on his shoulder and took his large callused hand in hers. "I'm glad you survived." She wanted to wrap him up in her arms and hug the hurt and loneliness away.

"'Twas long ago." He grunted. "'Tis you who needed comfort this night, lass. You were crying out in your sleep." He nudged her knee with his. "'Tis only natural to suffer bad dreams after a battle.

The horror of what befell you today will fade with time." He cast her a sideways glance. "Do you wish to speak of it? 'Twill help if you do."

She shook her head. "What is there to say? If I hadn't done what I did, that man would have killed Allain before Tieren got to him. I just . . . I never expected . . ."

"You handled yourself well this day, Beag Curaidh, and I'm proud to count you as an ally."

She blinked several times, and her heart flipped at his praise. "Thanks. Even though *you're* the one who took me from my time, I'm glad you're my ally too."

He chuckled, stood and stretched. "Are you ready to go back to your rest?"

"I guess." She wanted to stay right where they were, sharing secrets, savoring their growing closeness a little longer.

Hunter offered her a hand up. "Should the bad dreams trouble you again, I'll be there to wake you. Dinna fash. I'll look after you, Meghan."

She placed her hand in his. "I'll look after you too."

Meghan had slept on and off for two full days since arriving at the inn in Aberdeen, and she finally felt human again. She combed her damp hair while sitting cross-legged on the floor in front of the fire burning in the hearth. After three days of traveling, and this her third day at the inn, she decided nothing compared to being clean, warm and under a roof.

Her stomach rumbled. OK, food was also on her top-ten list. A knock on the door sent adrenaline surging through her veins. Since her brush with death, every little sound affected her that way and probably would for a while. "Who's there?"

"'Tis me, Allain. I'm sent to fetch you for supper. Sir Hunter says 'tis well past time you left this chamber."

Her jaw tightened, imagining what else Hunter had to say about her self-indulgent recovery time. She rose, cinched the belt over the itchy, too-large, borrowed woolen hose and Allain's now clean tunic before snatching her hat from the chair. "Just a sec," she called, while tucking her clean hair into the warm, dry velvet. The crew, as she now called the band of boys and men she traveled with, had been kind enough to give her a few hours of privacy to bathe in one of the two rooms they'd secured, while they did the same in the other room. She should've known the bath was a message that her time lounging around was at an end.

Somehow Hunter had procured a comb for her, and he'd had her borrowed clothing cleaned. She'd kept her tights and underthings to wash herself. The modern-day garments might cause questions, not to mention the fact that fifteenth-century squires did *not* wear Victoria's Secret panties and bras. Thank heavens they'd dried quickly by the heat from the hearth. She opened the door, and Allain gave her the once-over.

"Aye, ye'll pass as a lad well enough if none look too closely, and they willna, since yer naught but a lowly squire now." He shot her a grin and led the way along the hall to the stairs descending to the great room.

Still awed by the fact that she stood in an actual fifteenth-century structure—a sturdy, well-appointed building at that—she scanned the room. The inn did a good business, and tonight the place was filled to capacity. Did the Boar's Head still stand in her time? Maybe once she was home, she'd take a trip to Aberdeen just to see.

"Dinna forget yer a lad now," Allain whispered. "We canna call you Lady Meghan whilst we're here, ye ken."

"I won't forget. I'm Kevin now." The image of her older brother flashed through her mind, and grief pinched her heart.

"'Tis a good name ye chose, my l—er, Kevin." His cheeks colored. "Look you there." He pointed. "We've the same large table by the fire we've had each night. The innkeeper kens the MacKintosh clan well. Hunter's foster da is the earl of Fife's heir. 'Tis why we have the best rooms and the best table in the hall," he said, his tone boastful.

Meghan's eyes widened. "Who is the man sitting at the end of the table?"

"'Tis the sheriff." Allain wove his way through the crowded room, and she followed.

Tieren began to rise when he saw her. Hunter placed his hand on Tieren's shoulder and pushed him back down. Knights didn't stand in the presence of squires. She smiled at Tieren just the same. He never ordered her around or teased her like Hunter did. Speak of the devil . . . Hunter had also bathed and shaved. Damn, he cleaned up well. Her knees went a little weak, and the memory of being held securely in his arms sent delicious tendrils of heat spiraling around inside her.

Tieren scooted over to make room for her between himself and the squires seated on the bench beside him. "You must be hungry, lad."

"Aye," Allain said, taking up a pewter pitcher of ale and filling a goblet. "I could hear Kevin's belly rumbling all the way down the stairs." He handed her the ale and winked.

Hunter leaned forward to peer at her. "Are you feeling better now, lad?"

"Aye," she muttered as Allain placed a pewter platter piled with root vegetables, cabbage and slices of what looked like beef before her. Whatever it was, the steaming aromatic meal was smothered in thick gravy and smelled divine. Tristan handed her a chunk of bread and a slab of cheese. "My thanks," she said, keeping her voice low, trying to blend in.

"Your sword has been sharpened by the local smithy," Tieren told her. "He was quite impressed with the weapon."

"Oh?" Her eyes widened. "Thanks for taking care of that for me." Of course her sword was amazing. Her dad had it made for her, and he'd only hire the best swordsmith available for a weapon to be used by one of his children. Her heart gave a painful wrench. Before now, she'd never known a day without her parents' presence in her life. Never had she suffered a moment's doubt that she was loved. The loss of that security left her staggering for a foothold in a foreign landscape, and she didn't like the feeling at all.

"'Twas my pleasure."

Settling into her meal, she kept an ear on the conversation going on between the men and the sheriff, curious about how such things as slain thieves and brigands were handled in this era.

The sheriff hoisted his tankard and poured the remaining contents down his throat. He set it down with a resounding thud and rose to his feet. "Och, 'tis one band o' scoundrels I no longer have tae worry about. My thanks, sirs. 'Tis good tae have ye back upon Scottish soil. Give my regards tae the earl once ye've reached Moigh Hall." He gave them a slight bow. "I'm afraid yer wagon is gone, but my men took care o' the corpses." He barked out a laugh. "What remained o' their carcasses, that is. The carrion feeders lightened our load considerably by the time we got tae them." Still chuckling, he headed toward the door, stopping here and there to chat with other patrons.

Meghan dropped her eating dagger and covered her mouth. The food she'd just swallowed threatened to come back up her throat.

"Here now, take a drink." Tieren lifted her ale and wrapped her fingers around the pewter. "Dinna let his crude speech spoil your appetite. Turn your mind to something else, like the good company surrounding you." Warmth and concern filled his eyes.

He'd also bathed and shaved, and she couldn't help noticing how good-looking he was as well. Still, he didn't send her heart racing or weaken her knees the way Hunter did. "Thanks." She sipped the ale. "Mmm, it's fortifying all right."

She peered into the goblet. Thick, bitter and strong would be a better description, but her crew seemed to like it, so she'd best learn to enjoy it too. "You're right. The company is superb, the food good, and I am hungry. Just give me a minute."

"Mayhap a game of dice will distract you." John drew a leather pouch from his sporran.

"Aye," George added, his voice eager. "I'll play, and for certes the other lads will join us."

"You go ahead. I don't know how to play," Meghan said. "I'll watch while I eat. That will distract me enough, and by the time I'm finished, I'll have the game figured out."

"'Tis certain you will." Tieren's eyes heated as his gaze roamed over her face, settling on her lips. "None can doubt your cleverness." He leaned in and whispered, "Or fail to notice your beauty."

How much ale had he consumed? He shouldn't be looking at her like that, and she sure wasn't going to look back. "I . . . um . . ."

The front doors of the inn were thrown wide, and an intimidating group of well-armed knights in kilts and chain mail strode through. She gasped, shot up and called out, "Robley!" She stepped over the bench, ready to run to him, overjoyed to see his familiar face.

Tieren caught her by the wrist. "Dinna draw attention, *Kevin*," he hissed. "He'll come to us anon."

Hunter rose, left their table and met Robley halfway to the door. The two embraced, slapping each other's backs. "How is it you come to be here this eve?" Hunter asked, leading him to their table.

"Let us sit before I tell the tale." Robley gripped Hunter's shoulder. His gaze flickering toward Meghan in surprise, he strode toward their table. His men trailed him, staring pointedly at the group sitting nearest to their table. The occupants got the message and moved away, taking their ale and food with them. John, George and the pages began moving to the recently vacated table. Meghan rose with them. Since she was a squire, shouldn't she follow them to the kids' table?

Again Tieren tugged at her wrist. "Stay. I ken Robley will want to speak with you, aye?"

Her eyes burned. She blinked and nodded. Robley had aged. Silver streaked his tawny blond hair at the temples. The laugh lines around his eyes had deepened, but his bright-blue gaze and ready smile were so familiar her heart ached. Seeing him brought back memories of dinners at her house with him, Erin and her family. Another surge of homesickness hit her, and she sank back down on the bench.

Robley inserted himself between her and Tieren. He wrapped his arm around her shoulders and gave her a fierce hug, whispering in her ear, "By the saints, what are you doing here, Meghan McGladrey?"

All of the stress from the past week came flooding back. She buried her face against his shoulder, unable to speak past the lump in her throat.

"Och, though 'tis been some time since you've laid eyes upon *him*, dinna squeeze Kevin overmuch," Hunter cajoled. "He's recently recovered from a stomach ailment, and I'd hate to see his supper end up all over your chain mail."

Robley let her go, his brow furrowed in confusion. "What the bloody hell is going on?"

"First, how is it that you are here so soon?" Hunter leaned forward, placing his forearms on the table. "We sent a messenger but three days past, and he would no' have reached Loch Moigh until today or mayhap on the morrow."

"I've been making my regular rounds of our holdings." Robley rubbed his face with both hands, weariness drawing his features tight. "We were traveling home from Castle Inverness when we intercepted your messenger where the two roads meet. He asked if he could join us since we were going in the same direction. Once we learned where he was headed and why, he gave us your missive and we made for Aberdeenshire straightaway. *We* are your guard."

He grinned, both dimples making an appearance. "I sent your messenger on to Meikle Geddes with a new missive. Erin, our bairns and my parents will travel to Moigh Hall. They'll inform our clan of your homecoming, and we'll have a fine feast to celebrate once we're home."

"You have children?" Meghan's brow shot up.

"Aye." He grinned. "Erin and I have three sturdy lads and one wee, bonnie lass. Our oldest is ten and four, and the youngest, our Hannah Rose, is but five years this summer."

"But . . . how is that possible? It's only been seven years since you were . . ." She frowned.

"Nay, 'tis been a little more than ten and five years since last I visited with your family," he whispered. "We land in time wherever the fae choose to place us, and the future and past exist simultaneously." Robley straightened and grinned. "At least that is what Haldor told my wife, so it must be so. 'Tis good to see you, lads. I ken your families will rejoice to have you home and safe. Where is Randolph, and how did you come by"—he canted his head toward her—"young Kevin here?"

"Whilst you were in Inverness, did you happen to hear whether or no' Madame Giselle was about?" Hunter asked.

"Ah." Robley's eyes filled with understanding. "I canna say, for I had no reason to inquire as to her whereabouts." He shifted on the bench. "I make a point of it to stay well out of her way."

"We met with her halfway between Edinburgh and Aberdeenshire." Hunter's eyes touched on Meghan for a second, before he launched into the edited version of their story, including their encounter with the thieves.

"'Tis likely Madame Giselle's whereabouts will remain elusive until whatever it is she's conspired against the two of you has come to fruition," Robley muttered, a speculative glint filling his eyes as he looked from her to Hunter. "Of that you can be certain."

A shiver slid down her spine at the mention of the faerie's name. How would they find her? "What about Haldor? Do you have a way to reach him?"

Robley snorted. "Nay, lass, but mayhap between Erin, True and Hunter a way can be found to set things aright. In the meantime, you have a home with us. Erin and I will act as your godparents and guardians for as long as you have need of our protection. 'Tis the least I can do for Connor and Katherine. I consider them kin to me and mine."

"Thank you." Gratitude surged through her. She had a place to stay and people who cared about her. Things could be so much worse. The events of the past week swirled through her mind, and for the thousandth time, she relived the moment she'd thrown that dagger. She leaned close to Robley and whispered, "I killed a man." She swallowed against the tightness constricting her throat. "I . . . I had to."

His eyes filled with concern. "We'll talk later when we have some privacy. Dinna worry overmuch, lass. I'm certain you did what needed to be done. 'Tis a good thing your father trained you as he did. There's no sin or cause for shame in defending yourself and those to whom you are pledged to protect." A pensive expression suffused his features. "Mayhap Connor feared the day would come when one of his children might suffer the same fate as he, and that is why he trained you thus."

"The thought crossed my mind," she muttered. "It's just as likely he trained us up the way he did because that's all he knew how to do. All things considered, it's kind of amazing he managed to carve out a niche for himself the way he has." She'd always known her father was an extraordinary man, and her present situation made it all the more apparent. He'd only been sixteen when he'd followed the faerie who accidently hurled him to the future. Had Giselle been that faerie? Her father hadn't even spoken the same language as her grandparents. It must have been terrifying for him. She sucked in a deep breath, trying to ease the ache in her heart.

"Robley," Hunter said. "Might we depart on the morrow, or do you wish to rest a day or two before making the journey?"

The innkeeper approached and placed several more pewter tankards on the table along with a fresh pitcher of ale. Robley poured himself a tankard and requested meals for himself and the six warriors traveling with him. Once the innkeeper departed, Robley turned to Hunter. "We'll leave at daybreak. I've no wish to linger. I dinna like to be away from my family for too long, and 'tis already a fortnight since I left Meikle Geddes."

Drat. She'd be on the cold, muddy road again tomorrow. "How long will it take us to reach Loch Moigh from here?"

"Depending upon the conditions of the road and the weather, three or four days." Robley yawned. "Have you any space to spare? The innkeeper says there are no more chambers to be had this eve, and I require a cot."

"Aye, Uncle Rob," Hunter told him. "Your men can bed down with our squires and pages. We've two cots left in our chamber, and you're more than welcome to one of them."

"I'm pretending to be a squire," Meghan whispered to Robley.

"Och, aye?" His brow rose. "Whose?"

"Hunter's, since he's the one who *brought* me here, and he's currently without one."

"Hmm." Rob sent Hunter a meaningful stare. "Well, I'll be taking care of you for the remainder of our journey to Loch Moigh, lass. I'm a married man with bairns of my own. 'Tis only proper. Wouldn't you agree, lad?" he asked Hunter, his tone firm.

"For certes," Hunter said. "There's no need to keep her gender a secret any longer then. My thanks."

Meghan wasn't sure she was all that glad to be handed off into Robley's keeping. She'd felt safe and cherished in Hunter's arms. He'd watched out for her every step of the way since rescuing her from what he'd believed was a brutal attack. He'd soothed her when the nightmares came, and as much as she hated to admit it, she'd miss being under his protection. As domineering as he was, at his core he'd proven himself honorable, caring and compassionate.

She sneaked a glance at Hunter, only to find him staring back at her, his expression befuddled. Her insides fluttered. There was no denying the obvious—she wasn't the only one feeling the growing attraction between them. She just couldn't decide if it was a good thing or not.

It hadn't escaped her notice that Giselle's meddling had led to more than one love story. In fact, as far as she could tell, all of her meddling had led to romance. Most likely Giselle had been the faerie who had taken her father from his century. Her dad and mom, True and Malcolm, Robley and Erin—could the faerie have brought her and Hunter together for a reason?

She didn't want to think about it right now. Taking another fortifying sip of her ale, she pretended that every nerve she owned wasn't standing at attention because the gorgeous hunk who had brought her into his world continued to stare at her.

CHAPTER FIVE

Hunter glanced at the sky as the sun peeked through the clouds for a brief instant. 'Twas near None, and he'd be home by Vespers this very eve. Confound it, where was the excitement and anticipation he *should* be feeling? Instead, an edgy restlessness had taken hold. Mayhap 'twas due to his eagerness to set foot once again upon the island, and he'd lost all tolerance for travel. Aye, that must be it. After five years away, he longed for the comforts of home, and 'twould be a long time before he set foot off MacKintosh land again.

His gaze strayed to where Meghan rode ahead of him. Hunter had ceded his place at the front of the line to his Robley, along with all responsibility for the lass. Robley and Meghan were chattering on about her kin and what had transpired since Rob and Erin had left her time. What the devil was a "business degree," and how would such a thing be of any use to her here?

"Are you well, Hunter?" Murray asked, riding up beside him.

"Of course I'm well," he snapped. "Why wouldn't I be?"

"Och, ye look as if—"

"As if what?" Hunter glared him into silence.

"I meant no offense." Murray shrugged. "'Tis only polite tae inquire after a friend's welfare, aye?"

"I beg your pardon, Murray." Hunter blew out a heavy breath, sensing only curiosity and concern from his friend. "I'm weary of the road and eager to be home is all."

His glance drifted once again to Meghan. She no longer followed his every move with her eyes. All of her attention had shifted to Robley. Memories of having her nestled in front of him on the way to Aberdeenshire flooded his senses. He'd never forget the way her curves had fit so perfectly against him, or the way she'd finally entrusted herself into his keeping that day. Nor would he soon forget how she'd saved Allain's life, putting her own at risk. His poor heart had seized when he saw her on the ground but an arm's length away from the blackguard bleeding out onto the ground. Meghan was a rare lass, and if Tieren managed to win her heart, he'd be a lucky man indeed.

He forced himself to stop staring at her. Soon he'd be with Sky Elizabeth, and he could begin courting her in earnest. Needing a distraction, he turned his attention to Murray. "Will you stay with us awhile, or do you mean to go to your father's keep straightaway?" Murray's mother was a cousin of the earl's and his sire a baron whose lands bordered theirs to the south.

"I'll leave for home after a night's rest in Moigh Hall. My father sent word months ago that he has need of me. Our borders and crofters are being harried. There are far too many outlaws roaming the countryside, thieving what they can from smaller holdings such as ours."

Hunter clasped Murray's shoulder briefly. "Should you have need of our aid, dinna hesitate to send word."

"I will, and my thanks. Should you have need of me, I'll come tae lend a hand as well."

"Aye, I ken as much. 'Tis good we live so near to one another." His gaze strayed once more to Meghan. Late afternoon sun broke through the clouds again, lighting her hair until strands of it shone like polished copper. His breath caught, and his blood heated. *Lust.* 'Twas naught but lust for the only female within leagues of him, and Lady Meghan deserved better than his basest inclinations. Clenching his jaw, he forced himself to turn away.

What would Sky look like now that she was fully grown? Even at ten and three she'd shown promise of becoming a great beauty. He recalled the day he'd taken his leave. Her tears and the chaste kiss she'd placed upon his cheek had traveled with him throughout the continent. His lady had thick lustrous hair a deep, rich brown, and her eyes were like her mother's—the color of a storm-tossed sea. Aye, he was meant to be with her—meant to be with a Scottish lass born in his own century. No time-traveling foreigner would do for him.

Home and clan were all that mattered.

Movement caught his eye, and he spied a lone rider approaching at a gallop. Hunter nudged Doireann into a trot, bringing him up to Meghan's unprotected side. "Who is it, do you think?" he asked Robley, keeping his attention fixed ahead.

"I recognize him. 'Tis a guard from our garrison at Meikle Geddes." Robley spurred his mount into a canter. The rest of their party followed suit.

"What is it, Broderick?" Robley reined his mount to a stop.

The guard dismounted. His horse's lungs heaved, and its sides were lathered and soaked with sweat. "Milord, I bring ye dire news from home."

"Tell me."

"'Tis your father. We were setting out for Loch Moigh this morn when he collapsed. Your mother sent me tae find ye. She bids ye ride for home with haste." Broderick peered up at Rob, his expression somber. "He's no' expected tae last through the night, milord. 'Tis sorry I am tae be carrying such sad news this day."

"My thanks." Rob gestured for two of his men to join him. "Can you keep up with us, Meghan?"

"Yes, if I can borrow a saddle." Meghan twisted around to face the riders behind her.

"She's welcome to travel on to Loch Moigh with us," Hunter said, dismayed to hear his foster uncle was so gravely ill.

"Nay." Robley shook his head. "You"—he gestured toward one of his men—"trade mounts with Lady McGladrey, and be quick about it."

The guard rode forward and dismounted, and Meghan did the same. She quickly adjusted the stirrups before mounting again. Hunter opened his mouth to argue, but she gave him a slight shake of her head. He capitulated, already missing her company.

He'd grown accustomed to her presence. And somewhere along the trail, the fact that he wasn't constantly barraged by her emotions had shifted from confounding to comforting. He didn't have to make an effort to close off his abilities from her. She provided him with a respite from the constant flow of emotions churning around him.

"I'll leave you with four men," Rob told him. "Meghan and two of my guards will return to Meikle Geddes with me. Tell the earl what has happened."

"We sent word already," Broderick said. "Along with the missive you sent earlier. The earl is likely on his way tae Meikle Geddes as we speak. My horse is all but done in. By yer leave, milord, I'll travel on tae Moigh Hall with the rest and return to Meikle Geddes on the morrow."

"Of course." Robley glanced at Meghan. "Let us be off." He spurred his horse into a gallop, and Meghan followed with the two guards close behind.

Admiration for the way she rode the powerful warhorse—for the way she met every challenge thrown her way—swamped him. Hunter's gut clenched. She would be out of sight and out of his reach. What if she needed him? More than once after their encounter with the thieves he'd had to comfort her when the nightmares haunted her dreams. He'd brought her here; he needed to see to her safety. After all, she was . . . *his*? *Nay.* Raking his fingers through his hair, he groaned.

Tieren cleared his throat. Hunter turned to find him and Murray staring at him. Their blatant speculation about what ailed him grated upon his nerves. "'Tis all Madame Giselle's doing," he muttered. "Let us be off. We'll keep the pace slow until Broderick's destrier has cooled down sufficiently."

"My thanks." Broderick surveyed his men, and then he looked to Hunter. "Who might ye be, if ye dinna mind me askin'?"

"I am Sir Hunter, Malcolm and Lady True's foster son. This is Sir Tieren and Sir Murray."

"Ah." Broderick swung back up on his horse's back. "Yer names are oft mentioned at Moigh Hall. Where is yer armor and gear? Why do ye ride bareback? We heard naught but tales of victory whilst ye were away, good sirs."

"'Tis a long story," Tieren told him. "And I for one dinna care to share it until we are within the safety of the curtain walls of Moigh Hall."

"Aye." Once again Hunter took his place at the head of the line. "The sooner we reach home the better." News of Robley's father weighed heavily upon his heart. 'Twould be a melancholy homecoming indeed. Robert and Lady Rosemary had always treated him as if he were truly their kin, and he had great affection for them both. 'Twas Robert who'd taught him much of what he'd learned about horses. Doireann had been one of the stallions his foster uncle had bred, and the two of them had trained the destrier together.

He gave the command to set forth, and the lads moved on in silence, each to his own thoughts. His were filled with memories of home. His earliest years had been chaotic, filled with grief, fear and desperation. The revulsion and pity thrown his way had almost crushed him.

Then Lady True had come into his life. His eyes stung, and his chest tightened. 'Twas her love that had brought him back from the brink of despair. He and his foster mother shared their own unique way of communicating, and soon he'd be reunited with her. Soon he'd be surrounded by his foster family. He'd take his place beside Sky Elizabeth, and all would be well.

Home at last. Despite the grim news about Robert, Hunter grinned so wide his cheeks ached. The village herald sounded two tones on the horn to signal their arrival just as Hunter handed Doireann over to the stable master. Once all their belongings were unloaded from the horses, Hunter strode toward the shore, trailed by Tieren and Murray. Their squires and pages busied themselves with transferring their belongings onto the ferry. "Good eve to you, Monroe. Have you the job of ferry master now?"

"Welcome home, Sir Hunter." He bobbed his head. "Aye, I'm ferry master now. Me da passed two summers past."

"Och, I'm sorry to hear it. Arlen was a good man." He stepped onto the wooden deck. "How are the rest of your kin?"

"All are well, sir." Monroe freed the ferry from its moorings and started the vessel across the lake toward the island. "We've a visitor on the isle—a knight who claims he traveled the continent with ye."

"Have you his name?" Hunter shot him a questioning look.

"Aye. Lord Cecil of Dumfriesshire is what I'm told."

"What is it he seeks?" Hunter's gut roiled. Cecil had intended to do Meghan harm. His presence at Moigh Hall did not sit well with him.

"That I canna say," Monroe said with a shrug.

"Shall I leave yet this eve for Meikle Geddes to warn Robley?" Tieren signed.

He shook his head. *"Your presence would be missed, and we dinna want Cecil looking for her any farther afield than Moigh Hall. She is safe enough. Let us wait to see what he has to say."* Cecil, a Cunningham and nephew to the earl of Glencairn, must have traveled to his father's keep before setting out for Moigh Hall. What of Gregory? He glanced Monroe's way. "Did he come alone, or is he accompanied by another knight?"

"Nay, he has a squire, two pages and four guardsmen with him. No other knights."

"Humph. He's a long way from home." The Cunninghams were a Lowland clan whose holdings were far too close to the *Sassenach* border for his liking. Hunter looked to the shoreline where a small crowd had gathered, bringing the grin back to his face. He searched for Sky. Mayhap she was hidden by those in front. She'd always been petite like her mother. Sending his senses forward, he detected no hint of her presence. His smile faltered.

He caught sight of Malcolm, who towered over the rest. Lady True stood by his side with two wee lasses clasping the skirt of her gown. His heart melted. Blinking against the mist in his eyes, he waited impatiently as Monroe brought the ferry to shore. He leaped onto the island and soon found himself in his da's fierce hug.

"Och, I've missed you, son," Malcolm said, his voice breaking. He drew back and studied him. "You've filled out—matured."

A small lass launched herself at him, wrapping her thin arms around his waist. Hunter patted the ginger-haired child clinging to him. "Tell me this is no' wee Helen."

"Aye." She grinned up at him, her brilliant blue eyes twinkling. "'Tis me, Hunter. All grown up."

He laughed. "Well no' quite *all* grown up, I trow." He lifted her into his arms and swung her around, reveling in the sound of her giggles and the feel of her arms around his neck. Setting her back down, he turned to his foster mother. "Lady True . . . Ma . . ." He swallowed against the tightness banding his throat and opened his arms, unable to say another word.

A gangly, brown-eyed lass hid behind True's skirts, peeking up at him with a wary expression. His ma walked into his embrace. The little one followed, still clinging to her mother's gown. Hunter closed his eyes and sucked in a huge breath. He sent his second mother wave after wave of love and happiness, and the same came back to him tenfold.

"Hunter," she sobbed against his shoulder. "Welcome home."

"I've missed you," he murmured. Letting go of her, he crouched down to peer into his foster sister's curious gaze. "You must be Sarah. You were but two when I left. I dinna expect you remember me, but I'm kin to you."

Her face drew into an expression of deep concentration, and he laughed as her childish energy tangled with his. Her curiosity tickled his senses. "Och, we've another—"

True shushed him, just as Cecil nudged his way through the crowd. Hunter rose and hugged his foster mother once more. "Where are the boys . . . and Sky?"

"Sky is visiting her aunt Elaine and uncle Dylan, and the twins are fostering with the earl of Sutherland," Malcolm answered, stepping closer. "We've sent word, but 'twill be a se'nnight at least before we can expect them."

Hunter's heart plummeted. He'd been traveling for what seemed like months to get home. He'd waited years to be with Sky, and now he'd have to wait yet another se'nnight or more? His jaw clenched, and his hands curled into fists. Since setting foot upon Scottish soil, nothing had gone as he'd planned or envisioned, beginning with his unwelcome encounter with Madame Giselle. Nothing.

Frustration tore at him. Was it too late to find someone in the lists yet this eve? He wanted to strike out at something—to vent the pent-up restlessness and frustration. Taking a few calming breaths, he struggled to gain control over his emotions.

"Thomas went to Meikle Geddes with my parents," Malcolm continued, clapping him on the back. "Our lad has always had a special bond with his great-uncle Robert, and he was sorely grieved when news of his uncle's collapse reached us—as were we all." Malcolm gestured toward Cecil. "And here's your friend come all the way from Dumfriesshire to see you, lad."

Hunter sensed the warning emanating from Malcolm and True.

"Be careful, Hunter," True's voice whispered through his mind, though she kept a smile firmly fixed upon her face. *"I can't put my finger on what it is about him that bothers me, but I'm certain he's hiding something. He speaks the truth, but I sense there's more to his presence than meets the eye."*

"There is much I must tell you." He sent her an image of Madame Giselle before turning to Cecil. "What brings you to Moigh Hall, Sir Cecil?" Tieren and Murray came up to stand beside him.

"Aye, especially after taking yer leave from us as ye did, sneaking off in the wee hours without so much as a by-your-leave," Murray huffed out.

Anger flared from Cecil, but he quickly tamped it down and bowed low. "I came to offer my apologies. 'Twas wrong of me to act as I did. As I said before, during our years together on the continent none of you has given me reason to doubt your word. I was fearful the night we came across that accursed fair. I've given the matter a great deal of thought since, and I realize that I acted irrationally and in a most unchivalrous manner. I wish to make amends." He straightened and scanned the shoreline. "Where is Lady McGladrey? I owe her an apology as well, for I wronged her most grievously with my foul accusations."

The last part of his speech felt . . . off. Hunter scrutinized the man. He sensed Cecil spoke truly. He did wish to apologize, yet like his ma had said, something murky lay hidden beneath his words. Ambiguity clouded the man's intentions. "My uncle and his lady wife are acting as her guardians until we can find a way to return her to her family."

Intense interest pulsed from Cecil, and an avaricious glint filled his eyes. "*Is* there a way to accomplish such a feat?"

His desire for personal gain came through quite clearly, and Hunter relaxed. 'Twas likely Cecil's desire had naught to do with Meghan, and everything to do with finding a way to profit from traveling through time's portal, or by forming some sort of association with the *Tuatha Dé Danann*. *Foolishness.* "No' that we ken."

Cecil's expression sharpened with cunning. "Then how will you go about finding a way?"

"I've no' given it much thought. Mayhap we can discuss it on the morrow. Right now I wish for naught but a hot bath, a meal and time with my family." He put his arm around his two foster sisters' shoulders and turned them toward Moigh Hall. "As you ken, we've recently received distressing news regarding my uncle's health."

"Och, of course." Cecil bowed again. "Shall I see you in the lists on the morrow?"

"For certes. Your apology is most welcome, Cecil. I would no' miss the opportunity to train with you once again." Hunter clasped Cecil's forearm briefly. "Until then, I must bid you good eve." Watching the man's retreating form, he hoped he'd not misread him. Cecil was foolish indeed if he thought dealing with the fae or traveling through time would bring him aught but trouble.

"Who is Lady Meghan? What was Cecil talking about?" Malcolm rested his hand on Hunter's shoulder, his tone low. "He did no' share with us his reasons for seeking you out, but said only that he wished to speak with you. I would like to have your impressions about him, lad."

"Once I've eaten, bathed and changed out of these mud-encrusted garments, let us meet in the ladies' solar," Hunter said. "I wish to tell you what befell us on our journey before I share my thoughts about our guest."

True disentangled his younger sisters from him and shooed them on ahead of them. "Of course. I'll see to it that a meal is prepared and brought to you in your chamber. We've put you in your old room. Will that be OK?"

He hugged her close to his side. "I'd like nothing better. That chamber holds many a fond memory for me."

"John, George and the lads have seen to stowing everything in the earl's solar," Tieren said, coming up beside him again. "We're off to seek our rest. The lads and I will eat with the garrison. We'll meet you in the lists at daybreak."

"On the morrow then," Hunter answered. "Allain," he called to his page. "I have no need of you this night, but I will expect you to see you in the lists at dawn."

"Aye, Sir Hunter," Allain called back over his shoulder as he hurried to catch up with Tristan and Harold.

"I regret that we are no' celebrating your homecoming with a grand feast as we'd like to have planned," Malcolm said, "but with Uncle Robert so gravely ill, and with Sky and the twins far from home, 'twould no' seem fitting."

"We'll have that welcoming feast once everyone is home," True promised, giving his waist a squeeze. "I'll have one of the nursemaids look after the girls tonight. Let's spend some family time together, and you can tell us all about your adventures."

He snorted. "Madame Giselle is at it again."

"So I gathered." True's expression grew pensive, and she looked toward the west where the setting sun cast tendrils of orange, azure and gold across the horizon.

"I dinna suppose you've had a vision of what is to come," he asked, a spark of hope igniting in his chest.

"Nope. Not a one, which means whatever is coming can't be too bad. If something or someone were to threaten you, I'm certain one of us"—she canted her head toward her daughters—"would've sensed something."

"Och, aye? I kent the bairns had gifts. That much was clear from the moment of their birth, but I did no' imagine they would have visions."

"Yes, and with the twins being gifted as well, poor Thomas is the only normal one in the lot." True sighed.

"Nay," Malcolm protested. "I'm no' gifted in the least, so Thomas is no' the only *normal one in the lot.*"

"Do not ever doubt that you have an overabundance of *giftedness,* my love." True laughed and sent her husband an affectionate look. "Just because your gifts have nothing to do with the fae doesn't make you any more normal than the rest of us."

"Humph." Malcolm's mouth quirked up.

Warmth and contentment washed through Hunter, replacing the frustration of not finding Sky where he'd expected her to be— where she ought to be. "How is Sky Elizabeth? Did she ken I was coming home before she left to visit Elaine and Dylan? I sent word."

"Nay, lad," Malcolm answered. "Elaine, Dylan and their brood were here for a visit, and Sky departed with them a few days before we received the news of your return. Dinna fash. Once she learns of your homecoming, 'tis certain she'll return as quickly as possible."

A few hours later, bathed, fed and wearing a fresh plaid and a clean linen shirt, Hunter entered the ladies' solar. He suffered a pang that only Malcolm and True were present. He longed to see everyone. Sadness and regret gripped him. If only he'd set out for home a se'nnight earlier, he would have arrived home before Robert fell ill.

"Here, lad." Malcolm handed him an earthenware goblet filled with wine. "Have a seat by the hearth next to your ma, and tell us about this Meghan lass."

"My thanks." He accepted the goblet and took his place on the cushioned bench next to True. "Do you remember Uncle Robley and Aunt Erin mentioning the McGladreys from his sojourn to the twenty-first century?"

"Did they mention them?" True tilted her head as if trying to remember. "The name sounds familiar, but I don't remember what was said."

"Connor McGladrey befriended Robley. Connor too was taken from his time. He's from thirteenth-century Ireland, and Meghan is his daughter."

"Och, aye?" Malcolm handed True a goblet of wine, then took the seat opposite where Hunter and True sat.

He nodded. "'Tis why Robley took her to Meikle Geddes with him, and why he's determined to assume guardianship over her. Robley feels it's the least he can do for Connor, whom he still regards as a close friend."

"How came you by the lass?"

"Madame Giselle," True answered, patting Hunter's forearm. "You'd best tell us the entire story, my boy. Maybe we can tease out a few clues as you go along."

"'Tis my hope, Ma." Hunter told them everything that had happened from the moment his band of knights came over the rise to find the fair, to Cecil's accusations and hasty departure. "As far as my impressions of Cecil go, I believe he means to profit from Meghan's situation somehow. Mayhap he still believes she will lead him to the fae, or that she is fae herself, and he wishes to form some sort of alliance. He seeks to gain something; that much is clear to me. Like you, I sense something lies hidden beneath his simple claim to make amends."

"'Tis best we keep an eye on him then," Malcolm said.

"Aye." Then he told them what had happened upon the road to Aberdeenshire. "Meghan has had a difficult time of it since I took her from her father. I need to find a way to send her home. If I can discover Madame Giselle's whereabouts, would you write her a message? I can present your letter as I speak with her on Meghan's behalf."

"Of course, but you know it won't do any good. The *Tuatha Dé Danann* live by a different code of ethics, and we don't factor into their decision-making process." True's expression filled with sympathy. "I haven't spoken to her since the three of us went to see her in Inverness, and that was almost eighteen years ago."

"What am I to do?" Hunter scrubbed his face with both hands. "I'm to blame for snatching her from her life. 'Tis my responsibility to see her safely home."

"Wait and see, dearest." True ran her hand over his shoulder and sniffed. "I'm so glad you're home, Hunter. I worried about you all the time, and we've all missed you so much."

"I've missed you all as well." He clasped his ma's hand in his. "I dinna think wee Sarah remembers me at all."

"Probably not. You haven't even met Hannah Rose, Rob and Erin's youngest." She smiled. "Now that you're home, you and the little ones can become acquainted."

"Aye, Hannah's a sweet lass," Malcolm added. "'Tis good that our bairns have their cousins nearby. They've formed close bonds that will serve them well in the years to come."

Puzzling over what Madame Giselle's intentions might be where he and Meghan were concerned, Hunter nodded. His mind drifted to other things, like the way Meghan's hair shone in the sunlight, and the way her eyes flashed when she had her boot planted upon his chest.

He yawned. "Och, I'm looking forward to sleeping in my own bed this night. I'm near to falling asleep where I sit." He stood and stretched. "'Tis truth I accomplished what I set out to do. I've earned my fortune, and now I'm home to stay."

"'Tis good tidings indeed, lad." Malcolm rose. "Do you recall the day I wed your foster mother?"

"How could I forget." He snorted. "I slept through the entire thing whilst I was supposed to be her guard."

"Aye, that you did." Malcolm chuckled. "You've come a long way since that day, and I could no' be more proud were you my own flesh and blood. We'll speak of your future plans once things settle a bit."

Nodding, Hunter swallowed against the sudden constriction in his throat. Did they remember the vow he'd made the day Sky was born? How would he broach the subject with his foster father? Gently bred daughters of noble blood were meant to enhance a lord's standing, bringing more land, wealth and allies to the clan. What did he have to offer? Casks of gold and silver, aye, but the MacKintosh had always possessed wealth enough.

He couldn't think on it now. He yawned again, and his eyes burned with weariness. In a se'nnight or so, once Sky was home, he'd share his hopes with Malcolm. How would his foster father react? Leaning down, he kissed True's cheek. "Good eve to you both. God willing, I'll see you on the morrow."

"God willing, you'll see me in the lists at dawn." Malcolm grinned, his eyes alight with challenge.

Hunter laughed, and his heart filled with gladness. Malcolm's hair was now threaded with silver, and the creases around his eyes and mouth had deepened, yet he stood every bit as straight and radiated vitality. "I look forward to the challenge."

Sweat trickled down Hunter's face, and his muscles strained. He'd already spent a goodly amount of time sparring with Malcolm and now Cecil. 'Twas exactly what he needed. Raising his broadsword and grinning, he blocked his opponent's strike. "'Tis good to be training whilst standing upon Scottish soil again, aye?"

Cecil grinned back. He met Hunter's strike and went on the offensive, initiating a flurry of blows against him. "For certes," he huffed out, "and 'tis good to hone our skills. We had little enough chance to do so whilst journeying through the land."

Hunter detected only truth at present. He allowed Cecil's offensive strike to send him back a few paces—as he always did. 'Twas best that he let those around him underestimate his abilities, lest they suspect he held some sort of unnatural edge over them. "Och, I cry pax." He stepped away and thrust the tip of his claymore into the dirt. "Have you had enough?"

A burst of triumph flashed from Cecil. "Aye, if you have."

"I'm starving. Let us go take our midday meal, and we can discuss what is to be done about Lady McGladrey." He fixed a neutral expression upon his face, wanting to draw the other knight's true purpose to light. He gestured for Allain to come take his broadsword. "I've no idea how to return her to her kin, but I believe 'tis best to begin by searching for the Romany's whereabouts."

"The wanderers?" Cecil reached for his scabbard and sheathed his claymore. He handed his weapon to one of his pages before heading toward the keep. "What do you hope to gain from them?"

"I thought mayhap they'd have knowledge of the fortune-teller I visited. I suspect 'twas she who schemed to lead us to the fair. I canna help but believe she is fae, and that she used a spell to hide her true nature from me." No reason not to be as honest as possible. Madame Giselle could certainly take care of herself, and he saw no harm in putting Cecil on her trail. "Though I ken no' the reasons why she would do such a thing. What think you?" They reached the keep, and Hunter let Cecil precede him into the great hall.

"Mayhap 'tis true. I'd like to help if I may. I owe it to Lady Meghan after the churlish way I behaved toward her." Cecil's expression clouded with feigned regret. "'Tis the least I can do."

Cecil reeked of insincerity and selfishness. Anger bit at Hunter. What was the man about, and how did it involve Meghan? "Your aid would be most appreciated. If you wish, you can be the one to treat with the fortune-teller once we find her. I'd just as soon no' face her again."

Cecil lit up like a torch at the prospect. Again a flare of triumph surged from him. "'Twould be an honor," he crowed. "Come, let us break bread together, and we can discuss our stratagem."

Two blasts of the village horn rent the air, and to Hunter's ear the tone sounded mournful. "Och, I fear 'tis news of my uncle. If you will forgive me, I must wash and change. I'll be wanted on the mainland." Hunter tore off a chunk of bread and grabbed a slice of ham from the trestle table.

"Of course." Cecil nodded. "We will speak of this another time. I'd like to accompany the party leaving for the mainland. I too wish to pay my respects."

"For certes. I'll see you at the ferry landing anon." Hunter made a slight bow and took the stairs to the second floor. A short while later, clean and dressed in fresh garments, he made his way to the shore to find a group waiting for his arrival, including Cecil, Tieren and Murray.

"Oh good," True said, hurrying to his side. Her eyes were puffy and red, and they filled with tears as she spoke. "I was about to send someone to find you. We received word early this morning that Robert passed during the night. The funeral procession will begin very soon. We need to be there."

"'Tis grievous news indeed." He took True's arm and helped her onto the ferry. Then he returned to shore and scooped up his foster sisters. A nursemaid followed, clucking and fussing for him to be careful with her wee charges.

"Come, Monroe, let us depart," Hunter said, taking his place amongst the others already aboard. He set the lasses down and took their hands. The ferry master poled the vessel from shore and aimed it toward the mainland, just as a wagon appeared on the crest of the hill. Hunter's heart pounded. Despite the sadness of the occasion, he couldn't wait to lay eyes upon his kin once more—and Meghan. What would his clan make of her, especially garbed as a squire as was her habit?

The ferry did not move nearly fast enough to suit him. He fixed his gaze upon the riders slowly wending their way down the hill behind the wagon. Impatient, he handed his sisters off to True. He took up a pole to help push the ferry across the loch. "Let us make haste, Monroe. Tieren," he said, "will you take up the other pole?"

"Aye," Tieren said, moving toward the corner opposite his.

With the three of them toiling together, the shore quickly grew closer. Once they hit land, Hunter leaped to shore. Tieren tossed him one of the mooring ropes before jumping to shore with the other. Together they pulled the ferry into its landing. He helped the women onto solid ground, and they moved as a group to the village square. Malcolm met them there. He took True into his arms. His foster father and mother wept openly, their foreheads pressed together.

A memory from long ago sprang to his mind. The first time his foster mother had a vision and lay so still in her bed, he'd feared she was dying—like his ma and his granddam. He'd cried then, and Malcolm had assured him then that even the strongest and bravest warriors wept sometimes. Tears filled his eyes and spilled down his cheeks. Not just for the loss of his foster uncle, but for his real mother. Though hazy now, her image still played through his memory now and then. He wept for his granny, who had loved and cared for him after his mother's passing, and he wept for the sire he'd never met.

The wagon approached. Robert's remains had been sewn into his burial shroud and lay in the wooden coffin in the back of the wagon being led by Father Paul, their priest. Father Paul halted the procession when it reached them at the edge of the village. "As kin, you must take your places in line now." He spoke softly. The priest turned to Rosemary and the rest of the family riding behind. "Dismount and leave your horses with the stable hands. We'll walk to the kirk from here as is proper."

Lady Lydia and the earl of Fife, William, supported Rosemary between them. Robley, Erin and their bairns followed, along with Robley's brother Liam, his lady wife and their offspring. Hunter caught sight of Meghan and promptly lost the ability to breathe. She wore a blue velvet gown that accentuated her lithe figure. Why had he supposed she'd still be garbed as a squire? Of course Erin and his aunts had seen to it that she dressed as a proper lady. Her hair had been done up in a coil of braids, accentuating her loveliness. The way she moved, the way she held herself could only be described as regal.

She walked toward him, her hips swaying in a most enticing manner, and her hands folded demurely before her. His mouth went as dry as wheat chaff, and his knees could scarce hold him upright. His eyes narrowed. Why hadn't he noticed the way she walked before today?

Tieren and the other men lining the road stood a little straighter. Their blatant interest and desire clogged his senses. *Bloody hell!* He wanted to cover her from head to toe in plain brown wool. What had become of the old cloak Allain had given her?

"Lady Meghan." Cecil stepped into her path and bowed low. "Please accept my most humble apology for the grievous insults I cast upon you. I have been so distraught with remorse that I hastened here from Dumfriesshire as soon as I was able."

Meghan's eyes widened with surprise. "Um . . . sure." She stepped around Cecil and came to stand before Hunter. "I'm so sorry about your uncle's passing. How are you?"

Her luminous brown eyes met his, and his heart ceased beating for an instant. The caring and sympathy filling her expression caused his eyes to fill with tears again. *Damnation.* He did not want her to see him in such a state. Then she walked right into his arms, and all his worries fled. Closing his eyes, he held her close, resting his soul in the blessed comfort of her embrace. By the saints, he'd missed her.

"Dinna forget when and where you are, Meg," Robley admonished.

Hunter winced at the scolding tone, and heat rose to his face. Meghan was blameless. 'Twas he who had forgotten himself. She left his arms. Feeling the loss most acutely, he cleared his throat, sucked in a deep, fortifying breath and straightened. "Uncle Robley, I am so sorry. Your father will be sorely missed by all. I will miss him."

"My thanks," he said, his voice gruff. "Come, you two. Let us take up our places in line. Meghan, you will walk with Erin and our bairns. We've a funeral mass to attend."

CHAPTER SIX

Meghan stepped out of Hunter's arms. She didn't want to, but Robley's voice had that *disapproving father* tone to it, and she'd already suffered through enough of his lectures about fifteenth-century comportment. *Young ladies of noble birth must guard their reputations well, and as long as Erin and I are acting as your godparents, you'd best take heed.* That's what he said, among other things, like how young ladies didn't walk around with broadswords strapped to their backs.

The Robley she remembered had been much more adventurous, irreverent and free-thinking. He'd been eager to trade his destrier in for a Harley Davidson motorcycle, for crying out loud. Sighing, she glanced at Hunter. His eyes met hers, and she couldn't bear to see the grief filling them. It was all she could do to keep from wrapping her arms around him again. Lord, she'd missed him.

"Sorry," she said. "My fault. Where I come from, no one would think anything of it when two friends hug. Especially under circumstances like these."

"Och, but we discussed this, Meg." Robley ushered her back to the line forming behind the funeral wagon.

"Yep. We sure did," she said, peering over her shoulder at Hunter once more before taking her place in line. She caught Cecil staring at her then, and her skin crawled. Why was he here? She didn't believe his apology was all that sincere. Did he still want to harm her?

Tieren caught her eye and nodded. He placed his hand on the dagger at his waist and inched his way closer to Cecil. She let out the breath she hadn't realized she'd been holding and nodded back, sending him a look of gratitude. Tieren would watch out for her, and that was a good thing, because Robley hadn't allowed her to wear her sword or carry any daggers to the funeral.

Erin leaned close to her. "I apologize for my husband's over-protectiveness. He can't help himself. I think overprotectiveness is hardwired into the MacKintosh male's DNA."

Meghan stifled her smile. This was a funeral procession. "No matter how over the top Robley is, I do appreciate his concern. I'm grateful to the both of you for taking me in."

"We're glad to have you. Do you have any idea how nice it is to speak in twenty-first-century vernacular without getting odd looks? I've been where you are. Robley and I both take our roles as your guardian seriously." She looped her arm through Meghan's. "Are you OK? For a minute there, you looked frightened."

"I'm fine now. Tieren made it clear he's keeping an eye on things for me. Cecil is here. He's the man standing in front of Tieren." She nodded her head in the knight's direction. "He's the one I told you about, the guy who accused me of being a faerie or a witch."

"Oh." Erin frowned. "What's he doing here?"

"Who knows?" She huffed out a breath.

Erin patted her arm. "Don't worry. There's not a MacKintosh man here who wouldn't leap at the chance to protect you."

Her brow rose, and she glanced at Erin. "You think so?"

"I know so." Erin patted her arm again. "Two in particular."

Robley sent them another disapproving look, and Meghan decided now was not the time to question Erin further. Erin had plenty to deal with, and Meghan had already pestered her enough in the past two days about her choice to return to Rob's century. She'd listened raptly when Erin had described what life had been like for her since. Erin and Robley were happy. Their love and respect for each other was plain to see. Erin had told her that, although she missed her family, she'd never regretted her choice.

At the far end of town, they came to a lovely stone church complete with a small bell tower. On a hill beside the church a grave had been prepared in the center of the village cemetery. Four warriors transported the coffin into the church, and the family followed. A few benches took up the front of the nave. For the nobility, no doubt.

Robert's remains were carried to the transept and placed upon a dais. Father Paul led the earl and his family to the front seats, before he continued on to prepare the altar for the funeral mass. Meghan followed Erin and her children to the spot reserved for Robley's family. Liam, Mairen, their son and daughters followed. She hadn't been introduced to Hunter's foster parents yet. There hadn't been time. Meghan studied them. It was hard to imagine leaving your place in time forever, but True and Erin had both done so. She had a million questions she wanted to ask Lady True, since she'd already grilled Erin on the subject.

The knights stood directly behind the benches, and all of her awareness centered on Hunter. Would it be bad manners to turn around and smile at him? Probably. She glanced sideways at Rob. She didn't want to risk another stern look from her newly appointed, hover-ready godfather.

Villagers filed in to fill the rest of the available space, and soon the mass began. In Latin. Her mind wandered, filled mostly with thoughts of the tall, broad-shouldered knight behind her.

By late afternoon, Meghan found herself with the MacKintosh family in the ladies' solar. Hunter reunited with his family with fierce hugs, backslaps and happy tears, while the younger children chased each other around the room, and older cousins caught up with each other. Little Hannah, Rob and Erin's youngest daughter, stared at Hunter, her large blue eyes filled with fascination and her thumb planted firmly in her cherubic mouth. Meghan couldn't blame her, since she had to fight the urge to stare at him herself.

Standing in a corner of the room apart from the MacKintosh, she couldn't help feeling like the outsider she was. A pang of longing for her family brought a sting to her eyes. What were they doing right now? Probably trying to find a way to bring her back home.

Servants came and went, bearing extra chairs, wine and food. More servants appeared to hustle the children to the nursery. Mairen and Liam followed, claiming they were exhausted.

Her palms sweaty, Meghan moved closer to Erin and sat beside her on the cushioned bench. True took the place on Erin's other side.

"Malcolm, True." Robley gestured toward her. "This is Lady Meghan McGladrey. Her kin were of great help to me whilst I visited the twenty-first century. I trow Hunter has told you how she came to us?"

"Aye, he did," Malcolm said. "Rest assured you are welcome here, lass."

"As I told you at Meikle Geddes, you have our protection, Meghan," William added. "We are most grateful to you for the aid you provided to us these past two days."

"I was happy to help." She hadn't done much, other than keep all the children in line when needed and fetch things or servants as directed. Still, it helped her to have jobs to do.

True reached around Erin and patted Meghan's hand. "You

have a home with us. Erin and I understand what it's like to be so suddenly displaced."

"I'm grateful," she said, squirming a bit. "I want to be useful while I'm here. The boys I traveled with are interested in learning mixed martial arts. Would it be all right if I taught them? I'm a certified instructor." Robley frowned, his features turning all fatherly again.

"Rob, you know my father approved. He's the one who taught me everything I know about weaponry, and I taught mixed martial arts at our fencing club." Disappointment knotted her stomach. What was she supposed to do all day? Embroider? She'd never even threaded a needle.

"Meghan is quite skilled," Hunter said. "'Twould be of great value to us if we learned the uh . . . mixed . . . arts."

"Martial arts." She shot him a grateful look. "It's a combination of several combat disciplines including judo, kickboxing, karate, wrestling and boxing." Blank stares met her words.

Erin snorted. "Welcome to the fifteenth century, Meg. Besides me and True, not a soul in this room has a clue what you just said."

"Oh. Right." She twisted the velvet of her surcot in her hands. "I can teach any who want to learn how to defend themselves using a variety of hand-to-hand fighting techniques. I'm no good at the gently bred lady stuff, but I *am* good at teaching mixed martial arts. It's what I've always done." Lost. She felt lost in this time, with no purpose and without the cultural or social skills to fit in.

"She's not *gifted*," Erin said, glancing at True. "Not even a little bit."

"What?" Meghan blinked in indignation. "I have plenty of gifts."

"Of course you do, my dear," Lydia placated. "I find you very gifted indeed."

"You haven't spoken to her about this, Hunter?" True's gaze flew to Hunter. "Given the circumstances, I would have thought you'd explain a few things to her at least."

"Nay, I have said naught." Color crept up his neck. "After all she's gone through, I thought it best no' to speak of it. I did no' wish to burden her further."

"Burden me further?" Meghan frowned. "I don't understand."

Rosemary stood up. "Meghan, you were most helpful to us at Meikle Geddes during this very trying time, and I am gladdened by your presence. Mayhap teaching the lads how better to defend our clan is what you were sent here to do. Have you considered that, Robley?" She arched a brow at her son.

"Nay," he replied. "Mother, why do you no' sit?"

"I'm tired, and grief weighs heavily upon my heart. I will leave you all to continue this discussion without me. I wish to retire to my chamber."

"I shall accompany you," Lydia said, following Rosemary to the door. "William, my love, once Rosemary is settled, I too shall retire to our chamber. These past few days have been trying indeed." She smiled warmly Meghan's way. "Whatever the reason, Meg, I too am glad to have you with us."

Meghan's heart swelled with gratitude. Even though she'd dropped into their lives at a difficult time, everyone she'd met had been nothing but kind to her. "Thank you. If there's anything I can do to help, please let me know."

"We will, lass." Lydia touched her shoulder in passing. "Good eve to you all."

Once the two women had departed, Meghan turned to Hunter. "What is this giftedness you didn't tell me about?"

The color rose higher to his face, and he wouldn't make eye contact. "Lady True, Lady Erin and I have fae blood running through our veins. We possess . . . certain abilities because of it, as do some of their bairns."

"Such as?" Meghan looked from Hunter to the two women sitting with her.

"I can tell whether or not someone is telling the truth, and occasionally, when the clan is in danger, I have visions about things to come," True told her. "Erin has healing abilities, and she can sense things about a person's physical well-being."

"I too can discern truth from lie," Hunter said. He studied the floor, or his boots. She couldn't tell which. "I am able to read emotions and intent as well."

"You see," Erin said, "True and I were brought to this clan specifically because of the connection we have to the fae and because of our abilities. Which is why we're all puzzled about your sudden appearance. Madame Giselle has orchestrated our lives in such a way that our gifts have impacted the entire clan in a positive way. True saved Hunter's life, and I saved hers. So . . ."

"So we're all wondering why Giselle brought you to us," True added.

"Giselle said something to Hunter about restoring balance and righting a wrong of old. My father was taken from thirteenth-century Ireland. Maybe it's a take one forward, take one back kind of deal? Who knows?" Meghan's head spun, especially when it came to Hunter's abilities to sense emotion. Mortification burned through her. Had he picked up on some of the X-rated thoughts she'd had about him? "All this time you've been able to read me like a book?" She scowled at Hunter. "And you said nothing? I would have appreciated a *heads-up*."

"Nay, lass. I get naught from you." He shook his head and met her gaze. "You are completely closed to me. I've ne'er encountered your like before, and 'tis a mystery I've yet to solve."

"Really?" True's eyes widened. "You didn't mention that either."

"I'd prefer that you stop trying to solve that little mystery," Meghan said, glancing at Erin and True. "What about you two? Can you read me?" The two women shared a look before nodding. "Great."

"We can't read your mind, Meghan. I can tell whether or not you're healthy, and True can tell when you're trying to hide something." Erin shrugged. "Stuff like that. For the most part, unless someone wants me to do a reading, I turn it off. I won't invade your privacy and neither will True."

"Oh." Still ruffled by the whole notion, she changed the subject. "Laird, do you have any objections to my teaching the squires and pages hand-to-hand combat? It'll give me something to do until we can figure out a way to send me home."

"Och, we've grown accustomed to the extraordinary over the years." William smiled at his daughter-in-law and Erin. "Nay, I've no objections. You may begin on the morrow. Have we sent a messenger to Castle Inverness to alert them to send word should Madame Giselle return to her cottage?"

"Aye, and I also have several men out scouring the countryside in search of the Romany we encountered. If we can locate the band of wanderers, we may find Giselle is with them still." Hunter met her eyes. "Cecil has offered his aid."

"I don't trust him." Meghan's eyes widened. "First he accused me of being a faerie, and then he accused me of being a witch. Why is he even here?"

"We dinna trust him either, lass," Malcolm said in a soothing tone. "'Tis best that we keep him close. Hunter senses he seeks some sort of personal gain where you're concerned. We suspect you are the sole reason for his sudden appearance here at Moigh Hall."

She swallowed her rising panic. "Cecil demanded that Hunter take me into the woods, tie me up and leave me behind for the faeries. He, Gregory, their pages and squires snuck off in the middle of the night just to get away from me. And now he turns up here and thinks he can get something from me? What on earth do I have that he wants? All I own is my sword and the clothing I wore the day Hunter brought me to this century."

"Mayhap he believes you are fae, and he's reconsidered the ramifications of his hasty actions. Mayhap he wishes to form some sort of alliance with the fae through you." Hunter's eyes took on a determined glint. "I willna let any harm come to you, Beag Curaidh. You have my word. I will protect you with my life if need be. In the meantime, avoid any circumstance where you might find yourself alone with him."

Hunter came to stand before her. "Come, let me show you to the lists whilst there is still light. If you are to begin training on the morrow, you'll want to ken where to find us."

"I'll join you." Robley rose from his place.

"Robley, I think we'd better go check on Hannah and the boys. Losing their grandfather has been traumatic for them, and they need our reassurance before they go to sleep," Erin said. "Our bairns need you more than Meghan does right now."

"Humph." Robley's brow furrowed. "All right. I suppose 'tis safe enough. Remember all I told you, Meg."

A flush heated her face.

True laughed. "She's a grown woman, Rob, and a *wee warrior* besides. Stop acting like a mother hen clucking after her chick."

"Her da would no' forgive me if I let aught—"

"God's blood! I will be right beside her," Hunter said, raking a hand through his hair.

"Aye, I ken as much." Robley glared at him. "Young, gently bred ladies—"

"Oh stop." Erin snorted. "You didn't give a rat's behind about *comportment* when I came here with you. In fact, I remember a few times when—"

"Wheesht, *mo anam*. 'Tis precisely why I worry over her now."

"Come, Meghan." Hunter opened the door. "Let us walk to the lists. You have naught to worry about, Rob. Her virtue is safe with me."

Dang, not exactly the words she longed to hear. "All right. Lead the way." Meghan followed him out of the solar and down the corridor. She had to jog to keep up with his long strides. "Where's the fire?"

He stopped and looked at her in confusion. "I suspect 'tis in the hearth where it belongs. Why would you ask such a thing?"

"To get your attention." She lifted her chin. "Why are we in such a hurry?"

He peered down the hall in both directions, then stepped closer. "What was revealed about me in the solar . . ." His jaw tightened. "I'll tell you all once we're outside these walls." He took her elbow and led her toward the stairs. "'Tis no' something I wish to share where there might be anyone lurking about, hoping to hear a juicy tidbit of gossip to spread."

She'd been scared to death when Cecil accused her of being a witch. Maybe Hunter had good reason to keep his abilities to himself. "All right. You can trust me. You know that, right? I've got your back." He grinned at her, his eyes filled with warmth and amusement. Her insides melted.

"You are a mystery to me in more ways than one, Beag Curaidh. 'Twas I who took you from your place and time, and yet you bear me no ill will."

"Wasn't your fault." They reached the great hall, and he continued to lead her toward the large double doors to the outside. He let go of her arm to swing them wide, and she preceded him out into the cool spring evening and down the stairs to the inner bailey. The sun cast long shadows, turning their silhouettes disproportionately tall and stretched thin as they made their way to the northern side of Moigh Hall.

"Aye, 'twas entirely my fault. I ken Giselle well enough. I should have refused her."

"If you had, I'm sure she would've found another way to toss me into your era. Maybe Rosemary is right, and I'm meant to teach all of you another way to fight."

He grunted and took her arm again. A large open field lay before her, with sparse patches of grass sprouting here and there through the sandy soil. A quintain and jousting rail had been set on the far edge closest to the lake, and wooden benches hugged the stone wall of the keep. The lists were empty.

"The quintain reminds me." She picked up a stick and crouched. "We'll need a couple of punching bags for the martial arts training." Drawing in the dirt, she illustrated what was needed. "They're like quintains, only they don't swivel around on their frames. Plus, the bags have to be longer, preferably made of leather and weighted, so that we can kick them at about chest height." She glanced up to find Hunter studying her drawing. "What do you think?"

"Och, I see." He rubbed his chin. "To practice what you did to me the day we met?"

"Exactly."

"I'll see it done. 'Twill take but a few days to install them." He studied the lists and pointed toward an empty spot across from the quintain. "Mayhap over there?"

"Perfect. That's where I'll train then." She rose, dropped the stick and dusted off her hands.

"Would you care to sit, my lady?" he asked, gesturing toward the benches. "We need to talk."

"OK." Her breath hitching, she headed for the nearest bench and sank down.

Hunter paced before her. "Besides Tieren and my foster family, none ken that I have fae *gifts*."

She nodded, realized he wasn't looking at her and said, "I understand. You have good reasons to keep it to yourself."

"Aye." He sat next to her. "I'm sorry I did no' tell you before today. 'Tis a difficult thing to trust another with such damning information. Given the circumstances though, you've a right to the truth." He took a deep breath and let it out slowly. "Giselle is kin to me. I get my fae abilities from her."

Her brow rose. "Oh."

He got up to pace some more, and his jaw muscles twitched away. "I wish that it were not thus, and if there were some way I could rid myself of that part of me, I would."

She frowned. "Why?"

"'Tis unnatural," he bit out, his expression tight.

"Is it? I don't see it that way. Aren't the fae as real as any other living creature on God's green earth? They exist in this world; therefore, they can't be anything but *natural*. You're a fine man, Hunter, and you use your gifts for good. Right?"

He shrugged and stared out over the bare field.

"Have you ever used them to hurt or manipulate anyone?"

"Nay. 'Twould be dishonorable to do such a thing." He glanced at her for a second and then away. "I have used them to profit though, and that must be a sin. I use my abilities to prevail against my enemies and to win at contests of skill and strength." His Adam's apple bobbed a couple of times. "I oft ask myself what I did to deserve such a trial. I am plagued with guilt over the advantages I possess. The fortune I earned in tournaments . . . can I truly claim it as mine? Would I have won anything at all had I no' been able to anticipate the intent of my opponents?"

"I'm sure you would have," she told him in a firm tone. "Even with the ability to anticipate your opponent's moves, you'd still have to possess superior skill to win. You need to lighten up; stop being so hard on yourself."

"Lighten up?" He huffed out a breath and sat back down. "You find me corpulent?"

"I was referring to your mood. There's nothing unnatural about you or your abilities. It's just unfortunate that you live in an age so rife with superstitious fears. If you lived in my era, you wouldn't perceive your gifts as cause for guilt and recrimination. I don't see a problem where your abilities are concerned. I see them as advantageous." She shifted around to face him. "They are a part of who you are, but they aren't the sum total. How you act on it is the key. You've chosen the right path, and I for one am glad to know you."

"Sum total?" He chuckled. "Och, lass, I've no' shared this with another soul, no' even Tieren. I should no' be laying my worries at your feet. You've enough to concern yourself with at present."

"There you go into hard-on-yourself territory again." She grinned and pushed at his shoulder. "I'm glad you shared with me, but it does lead to other questions."

"Such as?" He looked askance at her.

"Why do you suppose your extrasensory perceptions don't work with me?" Should she tell him exactly how relieved she was that he couldn't get a handle on what she felt at any given time? Nope.

Hunter scrubbed both hands over his face. "I dinna ken, but 'tis restful, and I find I'm gladdened by the lack. With you, I imagine myself to be like any other lad, and I find I quite like being ordinary." He shot her a wry look. "Have you any notion what 'tis like to be constantly inundated by emotions emanating from all and sundry?"

"That would be tough to handle."

"Aye, *tough to handle* indeed."

Hunter reached for her hand and clasped it in his. His callused skin against hers played havoc with her nerves. Her pulse shot off the charts, and her mouth went dry. She could hardly breathe for fear she'd break the spell of intimacy cocooning them. She bit her lip. She could really fall for him—she already *had* fallen for him a little bit. What was he feeling for her right now? She thanked whatever powers that be that she was the one person he couldn't read.

He squeezed her hand, rose and tugged her up to standing. "Come, my lady." He let go of her. "I'd best return you to the keep lest your overly protective guardian comes looking for us."

"I suppose." She smoothed her gown, straightening the outer surcot so it draped just right. Hunter put his hands on her shoulders and turned her to face him. He leaned toward her, and she closed her eyes, sure she was about to be kissed. His unique masculine scent intoxicated her, and she was close enough to feel the heat radiating from him. Her heart danced around in her chest, and a wave of desire weakened her knees. He placed a chaste peck on her forehead and stepped back.

Dammit. She had to bite her tongue to keep the groan of frustration from escaping from her all too dry mouth. Without thinking, she placed her palms on his cheeks, raised herself up on tiptoes and planted her mouth on his.

He stiffened, pulled back and stared at her with a scowl. She stopped breathing and stared back. His gaze roamed over her face, fixed on her mouth, and the next thing she knew, she was crushed against his chest, and his tongue was doing a delicious sweep around hers. *Yes.*

She kissed him back, circling his neck with her arms and letting go of all control. Every part of her throbbed and fluttered. This was a kiss of epic proportions, and she didn't want it to end. Ever.

He broke the kiss, put his hands on her shoulders and set her away from him. His breaths were labored, heavy. He closed his eyes and clenched his jaw. Again she forgot how to breathe. Was she about to be rejected, or was his reaction just that of a fifteenth-century knight who'd transgressed the boundaries of propriety?

"I . . ." He plowed both hands through his thick hair, hair she longed to run her fingers through. "I should no' have done that. My apologies."

An apology? Disappointment and hurt chased the lust right out of her. "I'm the one who kissed you, Hunter. I guess *I'm* the one who should apologize."

"Nay. Robley gave you into my keeping this eve, and I am responsible." He took a couple of deep breaths. "Let us no' dwell on it overmuch." He placed his hand on her elbow again and guided her toward the inner bailey. "My thanks for your willing ear this eve, Beag Curaidh. You have *lightened me up* exceedingly well."

Great. He wanted to pretend their kiss hadn't happened. Her pride shredded like wet tissue paper. Had she been mistaken about their mutual attraction? Her heart still pounded with a mixture of arousal and embarrassment. Fine. She could suck it up as well as anybody. She could pretend kissing him hadn't been amazing. "You're welcome. I'm here for you if you should ever need to talk about anything."

"And I hope you will come to me as well if aught troubles you. Snatching you from your father's side has been a boon to me, lass. I hope I can find a way to repay you for your generous nature. Tell me about your family. You must miss them, aye?"

"I do," she murmured, her eyes stinging again. "I have two older brothers, Kevin and Aaron. My mom is a pediatrician, and Kevin is a physician's assistant. He's married, and I have a niece named Allison. We call her Allie." She sighed. "She's so cute. I'm teaching her how to play lords and ladies with her Barbie and Ken dolls."

"I see."

She grinned. "Do you really?"

"Nay, but it pleases me to hear you speak of it." He gave her a lopsided grin. "'Tis certain you have many suitors at home, lass. Was there anyone in particular?"

"I dated plenty, but . . ." She shrugged. "Keep in mind, my dad . . ." A grin broke free as memories flooded through her. "Well, you can take the man out of the thirteenth century, but you can't take the thirteenth century out of the man."

"I dinna ken your meaning."

"Imagine, if you will, a young man from the twenty-first century coming to pick me up for an evening out being greeted by a knight from your era. One of the first things my dad did, after intimidating my date with glares, wide stances and crossed arms, was to invite the hapless soul into his man cave."

"Man cave?" Puzzlement filled Hunter's eyes.

"His chamber in the lower level of our home . . . the place where he kept all of his swords, daggers and war clubs on display."

Hunter chuckled. "Ah, I begin to see how that might put a damper on your date's enthusiasm. Robley has told me how much men have weakened from our time to yours. 'Tis difficult to imagine."

"That's not entirely true." She cast him a glance. "There are men and women warriors in our age who are every bit as powerful as you are. Soldiers, professional athletes, boxers . . . all kinds. Keep in mind Robley was with us for a very limited time, and the circle of people he met while there was small."

"Och, for certes you have it aright. You yourself are a fine example of just such a warrior."

She nodded, and her heart rate and breathing came down a few notches. She could do this. She could carry on a normal conversation as if she hadn't just made a pass at him and been rejected.

"It's nice to talk about my family." She glanced at him. "My brother Aaron is an accountant and still single. My dad owns a fencing club, and it really bothered him at first that neither of my brothers wanted to go into business with him on a full-time basis. They both fence, fight with broadswords and joust though. Occasionally they'll do exhibitions with us at the Renaissance fairs." She took a deep, calming breath before continuing.

"I am the only one of the three of us who works for the family business, and I love it. I love working with my dad and performing at the fairs. I have big plans for . . . for . . ." Her throat closed up, and her eyes filled. Too much. After the way Hunter had put her aside, missing her family was the last Jenga block to be pulled out before her entire tower collapsed. What if she never got back home? She stopped walking. What if she never saw her family again for as long as she lived?

"Och." Hunter drew her into his arms, confusing her further. "Dinna fash, Beag Curaidh." He rocked her back and forth while she cried against his linen shirt. "No matter what it takes, I will convince Madame Giselle to send you back to your home. After all, she is my granddam many generations past. I shall become like a thistle pricking at her skin until she relents."

"What ails you, Lady Meghan?" Tieren strode across the bailey to join them. "What has Hunter done now to make you weep so?"

Hunter stiffened and stepped away from her. "I took her from her time and place," he bit out. "Is that no' enough to make her weep?"

"He didn't do anything." She'd been the one who had kissed him first, and she really couldn't bear the way he always stiffened and pulled away. "I'm just homesick is all." She wiped the tears from her cheeks and sniffed. "I miss my family, and it just got to me."

Tieren took her hand in his and placed it in the crook of his elbow. "Let me escort you to the keep, my lady. I vow to do my best to turn your mind to happier thoughts."

Hunter grunted. Scowling, he took the place on her other side. What was he scowling and grunting about now? Her head ached, and she wanted to escape to her chamber. Hunter had sworn to find a way to get her home, and home is where she belonged. She didn't even want to imagine never seeing her folks again. What must they be going through about now? It broke her heart to think of the pain her disappearance must be causing them, not to mention the chasm it caused in her own heart.

"I hear you plan to begin training with the lads," Tieren said.

"Where did you hear that?" She shot him a look of surprise. "We just talked about it a little while ago."

"I overheard Robley speak of it to George in the great hall. He's to inform the other lads." He winked at her. "I would learn this hand-to-hand combat as well, if it pleases you."

"Sure. The more the merrier."

Hunter let go of another grunt as they climbed the steps to the doors of the keep. "I will escort her from here." He removed her arm from Tieren's. "Rest well, for I plan to give you a sound thrashing in the lists at daybreak."

Tieren's mouth quirked up. He bowed low. "Good eve to you, my lady. I look forward to training with you." He straightened and flashed Hunter a wry grin. "As always, you are welcome to *try* to defeat me." He turned and hurried down the steps. With a backward wave, he crossed the bailey and headed for the portcullis.

"Can he?" she asked.

"Can he what?" Hunter opened the doors and ushered her through.

"Defeat you."

"Aye, he can. Over the years Tieren has managed to find a way to confound my abilities. Were it no' for him, I would no' be nearly as skilled as I've had to become. Remind me to tell you how he and I came to be friends."

"How about now?"

"Nay. I've things to do before I retire, and your guardians will be wanting to see that you're safely tucked away in your chamber for the evening. Where have they put you?"

"I'm in the turret next to the room Erin and Robley always stay in when they're here."

"Do you find it to your liking?"

"It's wonderful." The round chamber with its small hearth, feather bed, medieval tapestries and murder holes made her feel like a princess.

He placed a hand at the small of her back and moved her closer to the wall, taking up a protective position on the outside as they mounted the narrow stone stairway leading to the living quarters. "Do you still suffer bad dreams, lass?"

"I've had a few, yes." The image of the man she'd killed flashed through her mind. Regret stole her breath, and she was sure she'd dream about that day for a long time to come.

"I'm sorry I canna be there to wake you from them."

Me too. The thought of his being in bed with her sent her heart racing, and a spool of heat unwound in her center. Ah, but did he mean it the way she wanted to take it? Probably not. "I'm fine. Robley and Erin are right next door if I need them."

They reached the hallway, and awkwardness overtook her. She didn't know what to do with her hands. How would she get past the fact that she'd been the one to kiss him, not the other way around? Confusion and longing swirled around in her brain. She stiffened her spine. Hunter was determined to send her home. She wanted to go home. So why had she tried to start something with him? She shook her head. What a mess.

"What is it, lass?"

"Hmm?" She looked up to find him scrutinizing her, his expression a little too sharp for her comfort. "I was just thinking about . . . my situation. A lot has happened in the last couple of weeks. I'm still playing catch-up."

"Catch-up?" He arched an eyebrow. "I see. I found it most gratifying to speak with you this eve, and my worries have lightened indeed. Dinna fash about . . ." He waved a hand in the air. "These things happen. 'Tis why young ladies of gentle birth should always be chaperoned, so that young men like me dinna take advantage and steal kisses." He tucked a loose strand of her hair behind her ear and peered into her eyes.

"You didn't steal a kiss. I did."

"Nay, your forget the first kiss upon your brow."

His tender smile had her aching for another round of his mouth on hers. "Your chivalry is showing."

"Mayhap you have it aright." His eyes lit with amusement. "I would have your promise that you'll come to me should aught trouble you."

"I will." She nodded. "I promise."

"Good. Sleep well, lass." With that he turned around and hurried back down the stairs.

"OK. You too," she called after him. Dang it. What would Robley do if Hunter told him about the way she'd thrown herself at him? Her guardian would probably throw a fifteenth-century fit and lock her in her turret chamber. Sighing, she turned toward her room, eager for a little privacy to sort through her feelings about this disastrous evening.

"Good eve to you, my lady," a voice said behind her.

Meghan spun around, her muscles tensed for battle. "Cecil. What are you doing here?"

"Like you, I am a guest," he said in an offended tone. "I share a small chamber with my pages and squire on the next floor up." He gestured down the hall in the opposite direction from where she was heading. "I am of noble blood, lass. Did you expect they'd have me sleep on the floor in the great hall whilst there are chambers to be had?"

"Of course not. I'm sorry." *Avoid any circumstance where you might find yourself alone with him.* That's what Hunter had said, and here she was—alone with the man who had demanded she be abandoned in the woods. "I was just startled. I didn't hear you come up behind me."

"Mayhap 'tis because I didn't come up the stairs. I've just come down them." His expression turned contrite. "Have you truly forgiven me for the foul accusations I made toward you?"

"I have, but it doesn't mean I trust you." She inched away. He followed.

"Then let me endeavor to prove myself worthy of your trust, my lady. Accept my pledge to protect and aid you however I might." He placed his hand over his heart. "I swear to search for the faerie who snatched you from your home until she is found."

And then what? He didn't say anything about seeing her safely home, only that he'd find Giselle. Hunter was right. Cecil wanted to sidle up to her to get to the fae, or he believed she was the current faerie in residence. "Thanks. Good night, Cecil."

She didn't give him a chance to say any more and hurried to her room. Once she reached the chamber, she put herself behind the closed door as fast as possible and dropped the bar into the brackets on either side to lock it. As long as Cecil thought he could benefit from being nice to her, he would act accordingly. Somehow that didn't give her much comfort.

Tomorrow she'd be back in her tunic, hose and chain mail with her sword hanging down her back. Now *that* would make her feel a whole lot better, and if Robley gave her grief about it, she'd just challenge him to settle their differences in the lists.

Meghan surveyed her pupils, all standing in a neat line in front of the two newly constructed frames holding the leather punching bags. As the rest of the men training in the lists, her trainees wore plain brown woolen kilts and saffron shirts, allowing for a great deal of freedom in movement.

She strode from one end to the other as they practiced the drills she'd taught them. The drills would eventually enable them to effectively block any blows coming their way, and in the five days she'd been working with them, she was seeing great progress. Of course, fifteenth-century Scottish men were used to training and had been doing so since they were just little kids. She squinted against the morning sun and corrected Allain's posture.

"All right. Listen up." They were ready to move on to the next demonstration. "Today we're going to begin the kickboxing phase of our training." She gestured toward the punching bags. "Watch as I demonstrate a simple kick; then I'll have each of you give it a try." She approached one of the punching bags, curled her fists next to her chest, aligned her side to the target and sent a swift high kick to the center of the weighted leather, snapping her leg back as quickly as she'd kicked. The impact made a nice smacking sound and sent the leather swinging. Grinning, she turned to face her line of pupils.

Furtive glances bounced down the line, and the younger boys shuffled their feet. Puzzled by their reaction, she stepped closer. "Come on. Who wants to be first?"

"Uh, my lady . . ." Allain, her staunchest supporter, murmured. "Mayhap this would be best saved for another day."

"Oh, come on." She set her hands on her hips and scowled. "It's not *that* hard." Tieren and Hunter made snorting sounds. She glared them into silence. "Will no one volunteer?" She stared at each one. "I'm disappointed."

"I will volunteer, my lady." George stepped forward, a cocky grin on his face.

"Good. All of you circle around and watch me demonstrate once more." Again a flurry of glances back and forth mystified her. Shaking it off, she demonstrated with another swift kick to the leather. "You want to be slightly sideways with your balance on the outside leg." She backed up. "Go ahead, George."

"Aye, *go ahead*, George," Tristan taunted. "*Show* the lady how high you can kick."

George aligned himself to the punching bag, curled his hands to his chest as she had done and looked expectantly her way.

"Go ahead." She touched a spot on the leather. "Aim here."

Smothered laughter and gasps erupted. Tristan and Allain's faces were both bright red, and Tieren shook his head and rolled his eyes.

"Och, enough." Hunter strode forward, but it was too late.

George kicked. His kilt hiked up, and she got a flash of bare butt and . . .

"Oh cripes! That was . . . that was just *wrong*," she cried, slapping her hands over her eyes. "Not at all acceptable." Laughter erupted, and she aimed a scathing look at George between her fingers. He smirked and strutted back to his place in line.

"From this day forward, you will all train in hose and tunics," she snapped. "Got it?"

"The lads are used to training in the lists with only other men about." Hunter arched his brow at her. "What did you think they wore under their *feileadh breacans*?"

"I don't know." She lowered her hands from her eyes. "Biking shorts? Briefs? A sumo wrestler's *mawashi* thingie?" She'd figured the males in kilts bound things up with strips of linen or something. Hadn't she read that somewhere? "My dad and brothers wore biking shorts under their kilts, and I just figured—"

"Och, well, I ken naught about the things you speak of, but I suspect we've none of those garments to hand." He snorted. "Have we?"

"Course not. I didn't think of that." Just then the village horn rent the air with two blasts.

"We will continue on the morrow," Hunter commanded, aiming a pointed look at the boys. "George, another jape such as this one, and you will suffer my wrath. Do you take my meaning?"

"Aye, Sir Hunter. My apologies, Lady Meghan." He shot her a sheepish look. "I forget sometimes that you are no' . . . I mean, you're our trainer, and . . ."

"And you see me as one of the boys?" She grinned. "I'm honored."

"Dinna forget in future that she is a lady first and foremost." Hunter scowled at the boys until they squirmed. "I must see who is come. Until later, my lady."

"OK." How could she have been so unaware of her trainees' dressing habits, especially here in the lists where it was usually all male? Her students didn't have any idea what martial arts involved, so they wouldn't have given what they wore a single thought. Kilts wouldn't work for the flips either.

Tieren approached her as Hunter took off for the ferry landing at a jog. The younger lads moved on to swordplay or followed Hunter.

Tieren smiled. "May I escort you to the landing?"

"Sure. Two tones means clan members have arrived, right?" She picked up her scabbard and strapped her sword to her back.

"Aye." He placed his hand at the small of her back, and they made their way toward the ferry landing. "'Tis a fine day. Mayhap you'd enjoy a ride through the hills after the noonday meal? I'd be most happy to accompany you."

"That would be nice. I'd love to see the surrounding hills." Two boys, maybe sixteen or seventeen, leapt from the ferry and wrapped themselves around Hunter. "Are those the twins I've been hearing about? Migizi and Bizhiw?"

"Aye, though they prefer to be called David and Owain of late."

They reached the shore just as a young woman stepped off the ferry. Delicate, ultrafeminine and drop-dead gorgeous, she wore her hair in a long braid down her back. Her large hazel eyes were fixed on Hunter. He disentangled himself from the twins and took her hands in his. Their foreheads touching, the two murmured to each other, and tears streaked down the woman's cheeks.

"Who is she?" Meghan asked, trying like hell to keep the jealousy out of her tone.

"'Tis Sky Elizabeth, Hunter's foster sister."

"Ah." Relief washed through her in a rush.

"She's the reason Hunter journeyed to the continent to earn his fortune."

"Huh?" She tore her gaze away from the intimate reunion and shot Tieren a questioning look.

"Aye. On the day Sky was born, Hunter pledged himself to her. He believes being in possession of a fortune will persuade Malcolm to grant him Sky's hand in marriage despite his lack of a title or land."

"*Oh.*" Her stomach dropped, along with her heart and every other major organ. Of course. Hunter was already in love with someone else. Judging by the way the two lovebirds were cozying up together, obviously Sky felt the same. A lump the size of an apple lodged itself in her throat. *Great.* The happy couple turned her way, along with the twins.

"Meghan, this is David," Hunter said, shoving the boy's shoulder. "And this rapscallion is his twin brother, Owain," he added, tousling the other boy's hair. "I trow they'll be joining us for your mixed martial arts training." He arched his brow and looked from one boy to the other.

"I've no notion what you speak of, Hunter, but if you say we should, then we will," David said with grin. Owain nodded, a look of adoration suffusing his face as he looked at Hunter.

Taking Sky Elizabeth's hand in his, he drew her forward. "Sky Elizabeth, I'd like to introduce you to Lady Meghan McGladrey. She is our guest at Moigh Hall."

Sky took in Meghan's attire, her eyes widening slightly. "'Tis lovely to make your acquaintance, Lady Meghan. From whence do you come?"

"Your mother and I come from the same place and time," she said, trying hard not to let her jealousy show. She wore hose, a tunic and chain mail, still dusty and sweaty from her training session. Sky was the perfect picture of elegance in her medieval gown. Meghan couldn't compete with this paragon of fifteenth-century grace, beauty and proper *comportment.*

What the hell was she doing here, and how would she get back home? She hadn't asked Erin yet if she had a way to contact her fae relative, and doing so just moved to the top of her list of priorities.

"I see," Sky replied, her eyes growing wider still. "I look forward to hearing more about your journey, but first I must recover from my own." She smiled, and her eyes filled with intense concentration as she scrutinized Meghan. "Welcome to Moigh Hall. 'Tis my hope that we will become great friends."

Yay. She was being read by yet another *gifted* person. "Thanks, I'm looking forward to getting to know you too." So not true, but what was she supposed to say? *I dislike you intensely because Hunter is in love with you?* She needed to get away so she could lick her wounds and regroup.

"Sky, Migizi, Bizhiw," True called as she hurried toward them, her arms outstretched.

The rest of the MacKintosh family converged upon the landing, and Meghan slipped away, desperate for privacy. She needed to get control of her gyrating emotions before she could face anyone. She had no right to be jealous, and no real reason for this achy heartbreak tearing her to pieces. Hunter had never done a single thing to lead her to believe she meant anything to him.

Sure, he'd protected her, looked after her, but it was because he saw himself as responsible for taking her from her century. This was not her time, home or family. *Concentrate on getting home.* The twenty-first century was where she belonged, and this whole situation should be pissing her off, not breaking her heart. Madame Giselle had made some kind of cosmic error. Her presence in the fifteenth century was nothing more than a miscalculation on the part of the faerie. After all, she had no fae genes or gifts, and no real reason for being here.

"Lady Meghan, wait." Tieren strode toward her.

Stifling a groan, she stopped. "What is it?"

He frowned, canted his head and studied her. "Is aught amiss, lass?"

"Yep." Her hands fisted at her sides. "There's plenty *amiss.* I don't belong in this time or in this place. I want to go home." She turned away from his scrutiny. "Now if you'll excuse me, I'd like to . . ." *Go cry into my pillow and hide out for the rest of the day.*

"What about our ride?"

"Oh right." She swallowed the bitter mass clogging her throat. "I'll catch you later."

"Catch me later?" He chuckled. "Och, lass, I fear I'm already caught."

CHAPTER SEVEN

The moment Hunter laid eyes upon Sky Elizabeth, all the familiar warmth and affection he held for her welled in his chest. Although, his heart didn't pound at the sight of her, nor did he have to resist the urge to drag her into his arms and ravish her; 'twas only because of their long familiarity. They'd been raised together, after all.

Sky represented all he held dear: home, kin, that elusive sense of belonging and security. Aye. All his dreams would come to fruition through his union with Sky. Finally he would have a family to call his own. With Sky and their bairns to protect and cherish, he'd belong to the MacKintosh clan in truth.

While his foster parents gathered around Sky and the twins, Hunter's eyes slid to Meghan. Her hands were fisted at her sides, and she hurried toward the keep with her head bowed. What troubled her? His heart lurched. He should go after her. The moment he took a step in the direction of the keep, Tieren clasped him by the shoulder.

"Let her be," he commanded.

Hunter shot him a sharp look. "Do you ken what vexes her?"

"You dinna?" Tieren's expression turned incredulous.

"If I did, I would no' ask," he snapped. "You spoke with her a moment ago, aye? What did she say?"

"If Meg wishes to tell you aught, she will." Tieren's eyes followed Meghan's retreating form. "It serves me best no' to enlighten you."

"You speak in riddles." Hunter focused his energy. Envy, desire, determination and frustration pulsed from his friend. Tieren's intentions toward Meghan were serious. His emotions were those of a hot-blooded male in the throes of pursuit and uncertain of the outcome. Hunter's gut knotted, and he had to fight the urge to demand Tieren meet him in the lists. He wanted nothing more than to pound the desire for Meghan out of his friend.

"Cease, Hunter." Tieren's emotions muddled into an indecipherable buzz. "Have I no' told you oft enough? My thoughts and feelings are my own and no' yours for the taking."

"Aye, you have." Heat rose to his face. "'Tis habit."

With a slight shrug, Tieren dismissed the topic. "Have you spoken to Malcolm about your intentions toward his daughter yet?"

"Nay, what with all that has occurred this past se'nnight, I wanted to wait until Sky and the twins were home." He looked toward his foster family. They'd started out for the keep, and he set out to follow. "I will speak with him on the morrow, or mayhap later today should I find him unoccupied."

"Good. I plan to speak with Robley myself this very day," Tieren said, matching his stride to Hunter's.

"About what?" Hunter stopped walking. *Meghan?* Tieren had hinted at his intentions, but declaring himself to her guardian—not something he wished to hear.

"My future." Tieren jutted out his chin. "I expect Malcolm will place you in command of his garrison now that Angus is ready to be pensioned off. I had thought to ask him to make me a captain here at Moigh Hall, but I've decided to see about a post at Meikle Geddes instead. I'm going to ask Robley for Meghan's hand." He straightened. "'Tis doubtful she'll return to her own time, and I want her."

Possessiveness gripped Hunter, sending his blood rushing through his veins and hazing his vision. "You canna have her." The words were out of his mouth before he realized he intended to say them. Everything in him rebelled at the thought of another man touching her, making her his.

"Nay?" Tieren widened his stance and crossed his arms in front of him. "Think *you* to gainsay me? By what right?"

"She wants to return to her life in the twenty-first century, Tieren. I mean to find a way to see that she does." Hunter thrust out his chest, meeting the unspoken challenge. Truth be told, he did want Meghan—and had since the day she stood victorious above him with her boot planted firmly upon his chest.

"Think you I will no' achieve that end now that I've set my mind to it?" Hunter arched an eyebrow and assumed his most intimidating glare. Aye, his passion for Meghan consumed him, disturbed his sleep and played havoc with his fortitude. But she was not for him. He'd laid out the course of his life long ago, and he meant to follow his chosen path to the end of his days. "I took her from her father. By rights, 'tis my responsibility to see her safely returned into his keeping."

"I will no' be swayed by whatever false notions you hold." Tieren took a step closer. "Robley has assumed guardianship over her, and Meghan has accepted him in that role." Tieren returned Hunter's glare with his own. "You canna always have things your way, Hunter."

"*My way?*" Taken aback, Hunter's eyes widened.

Tieren speared him with a look of pure exasperation. "Aye, your way. *You* were taken in by the earl's household. I was no'. 'Tis you whose praises are sung relentlessly, and you to whom others look to for leadership." He poked a finger at Hunter's chest. "I am every bit as skilled. More so for I dinna have fae blood running through my veins to aid me. 'Tis well past time I stepped out from under your shadow to cast my own."

"What?" He raked his fingers through his hair. "*You* have had every advantage I had as a lad. We were fostered together and brought up in the ways of knighthood by the same men." His chest tightened, and he could scarce draw breath. "The only reason Malcolm and True did no' take you into their household was because you still had your ma, and she had need of you in the village. *I* had no one."

A roiling cloud of dark emotion surrounded Tieren. He shook his head, turned on his heel and strode toward the keep. Did his friend truly believe he always had things his way? How long had Tieren felt overshadowed? Guilt bit a swath out of his hide, but then he recalled how, when he was but four, Tieren and the other village lads had thrown stones at him during the harvest. 'Twas Malcolm who had intervened, forcing him and Tieren to serve the clan together during the harvest. After soundly thrashing Tieren that day, the two had gone on to become friends. The guilt dissipated, replaced by a soul-deep hurt and the familiar ache of isolation and betrayal.

Mayhap Tieren was not the friend he believed him to be. Shaken to the core, he struggled to gather his wits about him. *My way indeed.* No matter. 'Twas but one more reason to stay true to his path. After the noonday meal, he'd seek out Malcolm. Hunter turned toward the keep, his mind set.

Unbidden, the image of Meghan hurrying away with her head bowed and her hands fisted came to him. He didn't like seeing her thus. When she was upset, he could think of naught else but coaxing a smile from her. The need to hold her until all was set right overwhelmed his senses.

Her image filling his mind led to other memories, like the way she'd kissed him when he'd shown her the way to the lists. Having Meghan in his arms had nearly swept his legs out from under him.

Her kiss had tasted so sweet, and her feminine curves had fit against him as if she'd been formed solely for his pleasure.

Meghan lit a fire within him that smoldered and flared with a life of its own, and he grew hard just thinking of her. Her unique sweet scent, the silky feel of her hair against his skin and the way she moved stirred him like no other. Steering his mind away from his lust, he sucked in a deep breath and let it out slowly. Resolute, he strode toward the keep to join his foster family in the solar.

Hadn't Malcolm and William told him oft enough that passion burned hot but did no' last? 'Twas common ground, like-mindedness, abiding love and respect that carried a husband and wife through the trials sure to arise in their marriage. Malcolm had instructed him thusly, so it must be true. What did he and Meghan have in common? Naught. They were from different worlds. Hadn't she said she did no' ken how to act as a gently bred lady?

Ah, but I am not a noble. Do I need a gently bred lady as my wife?

He shook off his conflicting emotions. Madame Giselle's assertion that he must give up his false sense of control was naught but meddlesome nonsense, and he would prove her wrong. Or rather—he would prove that *he* was right. Control over his destiny was all he had, and he clung to it with both hands.

The noonday meal came and went, and 'twas late afternoon before Hunter caught sight of his foster father crossing the inner bailey. He hurried toward him. "Malcolm, might I have a word?"

"Aye." He waited for Hunter to reach him. "I'm heading to the mainland to check on a new foal. Walk with me to the ferry."

"Nay." His mouth went dry. "I had hoped to speak with you in the privacy of the earl's solar. Will you be free to meet with me after seeing to the foal?" His heart crawled up his throat. What if Malcolm refused him out of hand? Surely he'd want Sky wed to an earl, or a baron at the very least. Hunter cursed the circumstance of his birth.

Malcolm studied him for a moment. "I can check on the foal another time. Come, lad. Let us have our talk. 'Tis overdue, is it no'?"

"Aye." His future on a precipice, Hunter walked with the man who'd raised him. He could not have chosen a better father. Malcolm's character was beyond reproach, and he'd taught Hunter to be a leader in the very best sense of the word. Silently he followed Malcolm, gratitude and love filling him. They reached the solar door. Malcolm opened it and gestured for Hunter to precede him.

As a lad, he'd been taught the mysteries of life in this very chamber, sitting at the same scarred oaken table that faced him now. He'd listened raptly to his da and the earl's lessons about what it meant to be a man. Swallowing against the constriction in his throat, he turned his thoughts to the discussion to come.

Malcolm took a seat in the earl's chair. "Sit, lad."

Gratefully he sank into the seat on the opposite side of the table.

"You ken Angus wishes to be pensioned off, and your homecoming at this time is most fortuitous. I want you to take over as commander of our defense here at Moigh Hall." He raised his brow in question. "If it pleases you, that is."

"It does." Hunter straightened. "I'll speak with Angus yet this day. Might you consider keeping him on for a bit? I'd like to have the benefit of his experience and training while making the transition."

"'Tis wise to do so," Malcolm said. "I have no objections to such an arrangement."

"I . . . I am grateful to you." Hunter cleared his throat, trying to dislodge the lump so he could speak. "Words aren't enough to—"

"Nonsense. You've earned the post." Malcolm leaned back in his chair and studied him. "When first you became my foster son, I told your ma you'd grow to be a fine man and an asset to our clan." One side of his mouth quirked up. "As usual, I was right."

A strangled laugh broke free from Hunter, and he relaxed. "There's another matter I wish to speak to you about." He took a breath for courage. "Do you recall the vow I made the day Sky was born?"

"I do." Malcolm's eyes glinted with amusement. "Our Helen has made similar vows. First she insisted she would marry her grandsire, and then she declared she would marry me." He propped his elbows on the surface of the table. "You were a lad of but five, Hunter. 'Tis common for bairns to say such things. Now that I have raised you and six more, I can attest to this. We dinna—"

"The vow I made means every bit as much to me now as it did then." Hunter gripped the arms of the chair. "I am asking for your permission to court her. I am asking that I might make my intentions clear to Sky."

Malcolm's brow furrowed, and his jaw clenched.

"I ken I have no title and no land, but Sky holds land as part of her dowry, does she no'? Marrying me will keep it in the family. I have earned a small fortune with which to support her, and—"

"Hunter." Malcolm grew solemn. "You were too young to understand or be aware of all that occurred when True and I wed." He sighed and scrubbed his hands over his face. "When the earl returned from London, he brought with him a contract for marriage he'd arranged between myself and the earl of Mar's daughter. I broke that contract."

He met Hunter's eyes, his mouth set in a straight line. "As you can imagine, hard feelings sprang up between our clan and theirs. To rectify the situation, we suggested a union between Sky Elizabeth and the earl of Mar's oldest grandson. The earl of Mar is a powerful ally, and in these times, such alliances take on greater significance. His grandson will inherit the title eventually. I will no' lie to you, lad—I would prefer my daughter, all of my daughters, wed men who will inherit. 'Tis what is best for our clan."

Hunter's heart pounded so hard his ears rang. His world, all his carefully laid plans began to crumble. "Is this what Sky wants?"

Malcolm shifted in his chair. "I have no' asked her."

Hunter sensed the ambiguity filling his foster father. He latched onto the uncertainty and regret emanating from Malcolm. "And if she objects?"

"Humph." Malcolm's expression softened. "I canna force her, and well you ken I willna stand in the way of my daughter's happiness. Have you spoken to Sky about this?"

"Nay. I thought it best to speak with you first as is proper."

"Hunter . . . are you certain this is what you truly want?"

"I am." He lifted his chin and met Malcolm's stare. "Why do you ask?"

Malcolm shrugged. "You dinna lack for determination, and none can doubt your honor or your word, but what of Meghan?"

"What of her?" His stomach and heart tangled into a hard knot. "I will see that she is returned to her home as I have sworn."

"Aye, lad. I ken you have vowed to do so, but—"

"Have Sky and the earl of Mar's grandson met?"

"Of course," Malcolm said, rising from his place. "Sky and Oliver have met on several occasions during the summer gatherings. Talk to her, lad. Discover what is in her heart, and then we shall meet again."

His hopes soared. *If* Sky wanted him, he still had a chance. "My thanks, Malcolm. I will speak with her at the earliest opportunity."

"Good. In the meantime, a celebratory feast is planned for three days hence. 'Tis good to have all of us gathered together, aye?" Malcolm came around the table and placed his hand on Hunter's shoulder, giving it a squeeze. "Go. Find Angus. He kens you are to replace him, and he will be honored to learn you wish to train under him."

"I will." Hunter rose and clasped Malcolm's forearm. "You willna regret granting me this post, Da. I swear it."

Malcolm laughed. "For certes, you make more vows than your three brothers combined."

"Mayhap." Heat surged to his face. "But I keep them."

Hunter pulled his still damp hair back and fastened it into a queue with a piece of leather. Bathed and dressed in his *feileadh breacans* and a crisp linen shirt, he looked forward to the feast about to begin. Angus had kept him busy these past three days, and he'd not had a single chance to speak with Sky. He'd inspected the curtain walls, the armory, rosters and schedules, while familiarizing himself with the members of the earl's garrison. Angus had introduced him as the clan's new commander, and he had spent every waking hour learning his new responsibilities. He hadn't even had the time to join Meghan's mixed martial arts training, but he'd noticed Tieren in her ranks each and every day. Tension banded his chest, and he forced himself to relax. He and Tieren hadn't spoken since the day of Sky's return.

He uttered a curse under his breath. Now that he and Tieren were estranged, he didn't ken who he could trust to protect his back—and all the tension betwixt him and his childhood friend had to do with a lass. 'Twas best that he keep his distance from Meghan. He would talk with Sky this eve, and all would be settled. The feeling that his life was fast unraveling would disappear. Aye. He needed to focus on the future stretching before him, and he was eager to take the first step upon his chosen path.

With that thought, he left his chamber and came face-to-face with Meghan. "Good eve to you, Lady Meghan." He bowed and fixed a polite expression upon his face, hiding the breathlessness seeing her caused. Could she hear how hard his heart pounded? For certes the sound reverberated loudly enough inside his skull to chase out any ability to think.

She wore a gown of pale green. 'Twas the exact shade of the thistles growing in the meadows, and it suited her well. The fabric draped over her lithe form, accentuating each and every curve. Her

138

lustrous hair hung in a braid that began at the crown of her head and reached her shoulders. Ribbons had been woven into the strands. He ached to unravel the arrangement so he could run his fingers through her soft tresses. He clasped his hands behind his back.

"Good evening," she murmured, color rising to her cheeks. She moved around him and hurried down the hall toward the stairs without another word.

He scowled. Had he offended her in some way, or had Tieren said something to turn her against him? All his good intentions to keep his distance vanished, and he wanted nothing more than to go after her. Voices behind him drew his attention, and he turned to find Robley and Erin.

"Lad," Robley said, slapping his back, "do you find your new position as garrison commander to your liking?"

"I do indeed. Good eve to you both," he said, bowing to Erin. "I'm fortunate to have Angus to aid me as I learn my new responsibilities." The three of them moved toward the stairs to the great hall and met Cecil at the landing.

Cecil turned to him. "Any word yet on the fortune-teller's whereabouts?"

"Nay. No' a word," he said. "You will hear of it the same time I do should a message arrive."

Cecil walked before him as they started down the stairs. "There will be dancing after the feast, aye?"

"Aye," Robley said. "My brother, Lady True and I will provide the music."

"I look forward to it." Cecil rubbed his hands together. "I have heard Lady True is quite gifted when it comes to the harp."

"She is, and my foster uncles are every bit as good with bodhran and pipes," Hunter boasted.

Cecil glanced over his shoulder at Hunter. "Where did you say your foster mother hails from?"

Tension arced through him, and he focused upon Cecil. Curiosity, yes, but also suspicion and cunning motivated the man's query. "I have said naught on the subject, since this is the first you've asked of it." Erin placed her hand upon Hunter's shoulder.

Robley grunted. "My lady wife and True are from a land unfamiliar to most, though the Norse oft travel to their shores for trade. 'Tis a vast land lying due west across the Atlantic Ocean."

"Och, aye?" Cecil's eyes widened, and speculation ran rampant from him. "How did you come here, my lady?"

"My husband has an insatiable thirst for adventure and knowledge," Erin answered in an easy tone, though Hunter sensed her unease. "He traveled to my land. We met by chance at a fair, and he persuaded me to become his wife. I made the journey home with him."

"And Lady True?" Cecil asked. "Did Malcolm also make the journey to your land?"

"Nay. My foster mother is descended from royalty," Hunter told him. "Her father and mother were murdered, and her kin thought it best to send her abroad for her safety. They intended to sail to France, but their ship got caught in a storm and the captain was forced to change course. Lady True's party took shelter in Port Leith and decided to travel cross-country to London instead of continuing on to France."

How easily the story his foster family had concocted to explain True's origins fell from his lips. "They were waylaid by brigands who thought to hold her for ransom. Malcolm and his men happened upon them whilst traveling home from the earl of Douglas's holding. My foster father rescued Lady True and brought her to Loch Moigh. They too fell in love and wed, and she has remained here ever since."

"Ah, I see." Speculation and doubt pulsed from Cecil. "A land across the Atlantic, you say?"

"Aye, 'tis called America," Robley added, catching Hunter's eye with a wink. "If you wish, I can share with you the route I took. Mayhap you'll want to make the journey for yourself."

"Nay." Cecil shook his head. "I've no wish to leave Scotia, as I have just recently returned."

They reached the great hall, and Cecil's attention shifted. "If you'll excuse me, I wish to pay my respects to Lady Meghan."

Hunter's gut roiled as the man's lascivious attention fixed upon her. In fact, she drew every man's eye. How could she not? She radiated innate grace and confidence, and her beauty was beyond compare. He stifled the rising growl and forced his attention elsewhere. If anyone was to win Meghan's hand, he hoped 'twould be Tieren. At least then she'd remain close to Robley and Erin, and that eased his mind.

He sought Sky in the throng of family and clan milling about. He found her near the hearth, chatting with her cousins. His palms sweating, he strode toward her. Her eyes met his, and a welcoming warmth filled her expression.

"You look lovely this eve, Lady Sky." He bowed before her. Her burgundy gown of velvet set off the chestnut of her lustrous hair and made her eyes look more brown.

"Hunter," she said, holding out her hands to clasp his, "'tis good to see you. Angus has kept you from us these few days past, has he no'?"

"He has. There is much to learn before command falls solely to me." He greeted the cousins surrounding her, and asked her, "Might I have a word with you in private?"

"Of course." A slight frown caused a wrinkle to form between her eyebrows. "Is aught amiss?"

"Nay," he said, offering her his arm. "Let us take a stroll in the inner bailey before we sup." The doors to the keep had been set open, letting in the fresh air whilst the hall was filled with so many of their clan. "If it pleases you, my lady."

Her brow rose, and she concentrated, sending her senses to read him. "*My lady?* Why so formal, Sir Hunter? Am I no' still kin to you?"

"Come," he said, leading her toward the door. "I wish to speak to you of a matter close to my heart."

Color filled her cheeks, and the frown returned. He forced himself to be calm, lest she sense the turmoil churning his insides to pulp. The sunlight tarried later and later each day as summer grew nearer, and this was an exceptionally fine evening. He guided her farther away from any who might overhear. Sky seemed lost in her own thoughts beside him. He placed his hand over hers where it rested upon his forearm. "I spoke with your father recently."

"*Our* father."

"Nay, lass. I am but a fosterling. You and I share no bloodline of kinship. We are no' related." She stopped walking, and he sensed her confusion. "You ken the vow I made the day you were born, aye?"

"How could I no'?" She chuckled, but the sound held more nervousness than humor. "The tale has been told oft enough all the years we were growing up. Dinna feel you are bound by such a—"

"I want to be bound to you, Sky." He turned to face her. "I have asked Malcolm's permission to court you. I wish for your hand in marriage."

She gasped and studied the ground. "Let us walk in the direction of the keep."

"If that is what you wish." His heart plummeted. "What are your thoughts, my lady? Is the thought of a life with me as your husband so distasteful to you? Do you care naught for me?"

"Of course I care for you," she exclaimed. "You are my beloved elder brother. We played together as bairns, and 'twas you who always took my side in scraps with other children. 'Twas you who always protected me from hurt. Hunter, you hold a special place in my heart and always will, but—"

"Can you no' turn that love for me into that of a wife for her husband?" He searched his mind for some way to convince her of the rightness of their troth. "Think on it, Sky. 'Tis all I ask. We would remain here, and you would stay close to your parents. That would please you, aye?" They reached the broad stairs leading into the great hall, and desperation set its claws deep into his chest. "Will you consider the matter at least?"

"Hunter . . ." She twisted her hands together and gazed toward the great hall as if she wished she were within rather than strolling the bailey with him.

"Is it my lack of a title and land that troubles you?"

"Nay. You ken it is no'." Anger sparked her tone. "You are my brother. I . . . I am no' certain I could ever see you as aught else."

An angry shout arose behind them, and Hunter sought its source. Two men shoved each other, whilst others attempted to separate the two combatants. The altercation was over almost as soon as it began. He turned back to Sky, only to find her gone. *Damnation.*

He'd handled things poorly, been too blunt, and now he'd frightened her off. Words of love, flattery and wooing were what was needed, and he had no experience with such nonsense. His jaw clenched, and he kicked at the ground beneath his boot.

"What's the matter, Hunter?" Meghan's voice sent his heart racing. "Did you have a fight with your girlfriend?"

"*Girl friend?*" He whipped around. "I dinna ken what you mean. Indeed, where you are concerned, there is much I dinna understand."

"Don't mind me," she huffed. "I just came outside for a breath of Cecil-free air. He's suddenly developed a case of static-clinginess where I'm concerned. I don't like it at all."

"Humph." Her nearness weakened his knees and stole his breath. He did not like the feeling at all.

"So, did you?"

"Did I what?" He scowled at her.

"Did you and your *betrothed* have a fight?"

"Sky Elizabeth is no' my betrothed." Not yet, but he hadn't given up hope. He'd have to go about it differently, but she had admitted she cared for him. That was a start. "And nay. We did no' have a *fight*. Unlike you, she does no' train in the lists with a claymore and war club."

"She's not your fiancée?" She canted her head and crossed her arms in front of her. "The day Sky and the twins arrived, Tieren told me you two were pledged. I assumed—"

"Tieren told you, eh?" he said with a snarl, frustration twisting his innards.

"Do you want to talk about whatever it is that has your boxers in a twist?"

"I dinna suppose you could at least *try* to speak in a manner that I might understand." Despite his foul mood, a grin tugged at the corners of his mouth. "Do I want to ken what *boxers* might be?"

"Probably not." She rolled her eyes at him. "Have you the need to unburden your sorry self of whatever it is that ails you this eve, Sir Hunter?"

A laugh broke free, and he could no longer hold on to his scowl. "'Tis naught."

"Hmm." She scrutinized him. "Methinks it is aught."

He arched an eyebrow at her, but he couldn't prevent another grin from breaking free. "Tieren told you a half-truth, and he did so to serve himself."

"Oh?" Her brow creased, and the teasing tone disappeared. "How so?"

"The day Sky Elizabeth was born, I vowed to wed her. There is no contract or betrothal between us, and her father wishes her to marry the grandson of an earl—her equal in rank." His jaw tightened.

"Malcolm said the choice is hers, and he willna stand in the way of her happiness. This is the first I have spoken to her of my wishes."

"How old were you when you made this vow?"

"It matters no' how old I was." He scowled. "I meant it then, and I mean it now."

"OK. Just asking." She shrugged. "I take it your discussion with Sky didn't go so well."

He shot her a wry look. "Nay, it did no' go well at all."

"What now?"

"I must learn how to woo the lass." Was that disappointment he glimpsed in her eyes before she averted her gaze? Or hurt? His heart wrenched at the sight.

"Well." Meghan turned and set her foot upon the stairs to the great hall. "Good luck with that."

He couldn't prevent himself from watching the way her hips swayed as she climbed the steps. What an arse he was. He hadn't even bothered to ask how she fared. He hadn't looked after her welfare in days, and what had she said about Cecil? He'd best be about his duty toward her. At least he could keep Cecil at bay.

In the meantime, he'd plot ways to win Sky. Such a thing could not be any more difficult than planning battle strategy, and he'd never suffered defeat in battle. He was not about to be defeated now.

CHAPTER EIGHT

H er heart aching, Meghan strode back into the great hall. *Damn this stupid attraction to Hunter.* Her ultimate goal was to get home. But man, his answer to her *what now* question about Sky really stung.

Hunter must be blind not to notice she cared about him. After all, she'd been the one to kiss him, not the other way around. Or maybe he was just incredibly insensitive, and telling her he intended to find a way to woo Sky was his way of letting her know she was barking up the wrong Scottish pine.

"My lady." David, the oldest of True's twins, came to her side. "May I escort you to the dais?" He held out his arm for her. "'Tis near time to take our seats."

"Yes, thank you." She hooked her arm through his, grateful for the distraction. "Did Robley put you up to this?"

"Nay, my da." Color rose to his cheeks. "He says I must practice my courtly manners as oft as possible." He steered her around a man who backed up without looking first. "Owain and I shall be called upon to make an appearance at court soon. We are to be knighted by autumn next."

"Are you looking forward to going to court?"

"No' in the least," he huffed. "'Tis a nest of vipers, I'm told. I'm heir to an earldom though, and I canna shirk my responsibilities." He threw back his shoulders a bit at that statement. "I'm to share a trencher with you this eve, my lady. Owain will take the chair to your right." He shot her a sheepish look. "*That* request did come from Robley. He's quite protective of you."

She laughed. "That's putting it mildly."

"He means well." He helped her up to the raised platform where the earl's table stood. "We are to sit here," he said, pulling out the chair at the corner for her. His attention went to the stairs. "Ah, here comes my grandsire now." Affection and amusement filled his tone. "Grandda likes to make an entrance, you ken."

William and his wife descended the stairs in a regal manner, trailed by Lady Rosemary and Sky. A pang of jealousy squeezed Meghan's heart at the sight of Malcolm's oldest daughter. She did her best to ignore it, focusing instead on the milling crowd as they began to move as one. Everyone scrambled to find a place at the plank-and-barrel tables filling the hall. Tieren caught her eye and winked. She smiled in return. Even though she'd only known him for a short while, she'd already come to rely on his support and friendship.

Tieren took a spot in front of the dais where the other knights sat, and the earl's family began taking their places at the high table. Owain, all gangly limbs and affable nature, made his way to her end.

David's stomach growled. "Och, I'm so hungry," he grumbled. "My pardon, Lady Meghan."

"No need to apologize. I'm hungry too."

"My lady." Owain bowed to her before taking his place. "'Tis an honor to be your table companion this eve."

"You must be practicing your courtly manners too." She snorted. "Robley ordered you to sit with me, didn't he?"

"Aye, for certes," he said with a grin. "But I would gladly have done so even without his command. I have questions about our training."

Hunter strode toward the dais, and her breath caught. Lord, she loved the way he moved. He exuded dominance, confidence and masculine prowess to the extreme. Tonight he wore his golden-brown hair tied back, and it made his strong features even more prominent. His sexy gray eyes met hers, and one side of his mouth quirked up as he took in the twins sitting on either side of her. She bit her lip and tried to squelch the flutter-fest going on inside her.

The chair beside David remained empty. Would Hunter take it? She hoped so. *No, don't think like that.* He didn't want her; he wanted Sky, and it didn't do her any good to spend any more time with him than necessary. In fact, she'd been avoiding him since their last conversation.

Glancing down the length of the table, she noticed Sky had taken the spot between Lady Rosemary and True. *Hmm. Had she done that on purpose? Was Sky avoiding Hunter too?* What difference did it make? It would only strengthen his determination to learn how to woo the lass. *Gag.*

Cecil had his eye on the empty chair beside David as he made his way toward the dais. *Oh yay.* Pages began filling goblets with wine or ale, and servants carried platters of steaming food into the hall from the kitchen. She kept her attention fixed on the twins. "What are your questions about martial arts, Owain?" *Do not look at the empty chair. Do not make eye contact with Cecil.*

"How long did it take you to master your skills in the mixed martial arts?" Owain's voice rang with enthusiasm.

"Years. I started taking karate when I was seven or eight, and I switched to mixed martial arts once I turned fifteen."

"Och, that long?"

"You're doing really well." Meghan gave his shoulder a playful punch. "Be patient."

"Aye, but who will continue the training once you return home?" He frowned. "I find I quite enjoy the martial arts. I dinna wish to cease the training."

"Take advantage of what Meghan has to offer for as long as she's with us, lad." Hunter slid into the empty place next to David. "But dinna neglect the rest of your training."

His deep voice rumbled, sending pleasurable shock waves through her. "He's right. I kept up with improving my skills with the sword and quintain while I learned martial arts." A healthy dose of relief flooded through her. At least she didn't have to try and make nice with Cecil. Risking a peek the visiting knight's way, she caught his disgruntled look as he took the seat at the opposite end of the table.

The earl stood and pounded the handle of his dagger on the table. Voices stilled, and all eyes turned toward him. "Our good Father Paul has been called away to Castle Rait, and so it falls to me to lead us in giving thanks for the bounty before us this eve.

"'Tis true we have much to be thankful for"—William's voice reverberated through the hall—"kin and clan, good health and food to fill our bellies. We are gathered together to celebrate . . . and to remember those who have gone on before us. I ken well we are all gladdened by Hunter's safe return and heartened by his appointment as commander of our garrison, aye?" William raised his goblet and nodded toward Hunter. Cheers erupted, and the earl waited until the sound subsided before continuing. "Let us no' forget his predecessor. We are deeply grateful to Angus for his many years of loyal service to our clan. We have been most fortunate indeed to have one so skilled and canny to lead our warriors in keeping our clan safe." He nodded to Angus as another swell of cheers rose, and the warriors pounded their fists on the table.

William held up his hand, and the noise stopped. "'Tis good to have the twins and Sky Elizabeth home as well, though our hearts are heavy with grief for the loss of my dear brother, Robert. May he rest in peace."

The earl bowed his head, clasped his wife's hand on his right side and his son Malcolm's to his left. He paused, waiting as the clan did likewise. Owain and David took her hands, and a lump formed in her throat. Her family held hands and said grace during their family dinners after church. Her mom and dad had always insisted the entire family gather on Sundays no matter what. Sometimes they'd go to her grandparents' farm, and other times her grandparents would join them in town. Making an effort to gather together at least once a week had kept them close, and she remembered how hard it had been on all of them when her brothers were away at college. What was her family doing right now?

"Let us give thanks to God for all that he has bestowed upon us and pray for the souls of those we've lost," William said, his voice breaking. "We sup this night in the good company of our clan, kin and friends. May it always be thus. Amen." Amens filled the hall, and hands were released.

David's stomach growled again. "Finally," he muttered, carving into the roasted leg of lamb in front of them. He loaded their shared trencher with chunks of the savory meat. "What would you prefer, my lady?" He gestured toward the various loaves of bread and vegetables.

"A little of everything, thanks." She cut off a bit of the lamb and popped it into her mouth, savoring the tender morsel. "Moigh Hall has an excellent cook."

"Aye." Hunter leaned around David to catch her eye. "Though the cuisine in France and Spain had much to commend it, I sorely missed the food from home whilst traveling abroad."

Hunter's comments elicited eager questions from the twins about his adventures while traveling, and Meghan relaxed. As the conversation went on around her, she couldn't help noticing the deep affection shared between Hunter and the twins.

The feast continued until everyone had eaten their fill, and then the servants began clearing the tables. The men sitting below the dais, including Tieren, took the plank-and-barrel tables down and cleared the hall for dancing. Robley and his brother Liam moved to one of the hearths and took up the bodhran and pipes leaning against the wall. A young woman appeared with a small harp and handed the instrument to True. Chairs were put in place for the three musicians, and they conferred with each other with heads bowed.

Meghan stepped down from the dais and found an unobtrusive place to stand. Dancing had never been in her repertoire, and she wished to be an observer, not a participant. Clan members formed lines, and soon a lively reel began. She couldn't prevent her foot from tapping, and the crowd's enthusiasm brought a smile to her face.

Tieren came to stand by her side. "Why are you no' dancing, Meghan?"

"Why aren't you?" she teased.

"I did no' see you amongst the lasses queuing up for the reel." He cocked an eyebrow. "Will you no' join me in the next set?"

"I don't know the steps." She watched the dancers making their intricate turns, switching partners as they did. "I'm not much of a dancer."

"I find that difficult to credit, since you are so light upon your feet in the lists. 'Tis no' difficult, and you are a clever lass." He placed his hand at her elbow as the reel came to an end. "Come. None will notice a misstep or two on your part."

"I don't know . . ." she hedged.

"A stroll in the bailey then? 'Tis still daylight, and there will be many about, catching a breath of fresh air."

She caught a glimpse of Hunter, holding his hand out to Sky for the next dance. Her chest tightened, making it a little harder to breathe. "Sure. A stroll would be nice."

Tieren led her around the outer edge of the great hall. She could feel Hunter's eyes following her all the way to the doors. What was it about the man that made her so tuned in to him? Risking a surreptitious glance, she found him scowling at her, even as he led Sky to her place in the circle for the next dance. She scowled right back. Once she and Tieren were outside, she heaved a sigh.

"'Tis a lovely evening," he murmured close to her ear. "Is it no'?"

"It is." She inhaled the fresh spring air, detecting the telltale scents of human habitation along with the tang of pine and yew. "And so quiet." The sky to the west held the deepening hues of the coming sunset, and the air carried a hint of the chill to come.

"Quiet?" His brow furrowed. "Can you no' hear the noise from within the keep?"

"Of course I can, but where I'm from, we'd also be hearing airplanes overhead and freeway traffic. Sometimes," she said, squeezing his arm, "far too often, in fact, we'd also hear sirens from fire engines or police cars. You and I would be walking down a street crowded with apartment buildings, people and houses. We'd be on a sidewalk next to a busy road or in a city park."

"Fire engines and police cars? Och, I've no notion of such things." Tieren placed his warm hand over hers. "Will you tell me about them?"

"I forget when and where I am sometimes." She snorted. The next ten minutes she spent trying to describe twenty-first-century city life in a way he could wrap his fifteenth-century mind around. Tieren made incredulous noises, his attention riveted on her every word. Several other couples strolled the inner bailey, and a few groups of older clan members talked and laughed together.

"'Tis difficult to fathom flying through the air or riding in a wagon no' drawn by oxen or rouncies." He shook his head. "The constant noise you speak of must be difficult to accustom yourself to, aye?"

"Not really. After a while, you don't even notice." She peered into his brilliant blue eyes. "Have you ever considered visiting the future like Robley did?"

"Nay, but if you ask me to follow you to your time, I will," he said, his voice low and earnest.

Her eyes widened. "You would?"

"Aye, lass." He stopped walking and took her hands in his. "Have you considered the possibility that you might no' find a way to return to your time?"

"No." Her eyes stung, and she studied the ground beneath her feet. "I don't want to think about that possibility."

"I have. Lady True was no' able to return, and Erin made the choice to be with her husband. Indeed, I've given the matter a great deal of thought." He cleared his throat. "Did Robley mention that I have asked him for your hand in marriage?"

"Um . . . no." A shock of adrenaline hit her bloodstream. "He didn't mention it."

"He agreed 'twould be a good match, and he prefers that you wed within our clan so that you might remain close to him and his lady wife. He has pledged a generous dowry on your behalf and granted me permission to court you, with the stipulation that the decision is entirely yours to make."

Stunned, she had no idea how to react and didn't know where to look. The last thing she wanted to do was to hurt or embarrass him, and that kept her from tugging her hands out of his.

"I'm no' the only man to approach your guardian for that purpose." He grunted. "Cecil has also asked, as well as a few of our higher-ranked warriors."

"Cecil?" She shuddered. "I don't understand why anyone would want me. I don't have any social or political ties, and by fifteenth-century standards I'm like a spinster or something." She sent him a questioning look. "Aren't I? I'm already twenty-three. That's old by your standards."

"Och, but you are no' from this era. Being as close to Hunter and his foster family as I am, I've been privy to the truth of Lady True and Lady Erin's origins. They have explained how those from your century live much longer. You and I are of like age, and I dinna think of you as anything but youthful."

Tieren held her arms out and let his gaze wander over her from head to toe. "Truly? You canna imagine anyone desiring to make you theirs? You are lovely, Meghan, and you possess great strength, skill and wit. Political ties mean naught to me when compared to your many fine qualities. I would be a lucky man indeed to have you by my side. I trow more men will seek Rob's approval if you dinna choose a husband soon."

He stepped closer and peered intently into her eyes. "As far as Cecil is concerned, dinna fash, *mùirninn*. I willna let him anywhere near you."

"Thank you." She averted her gaze. Heat flooded her face. "He makes me uneasy, and I still think he's up to something."

"You are no' alone in your suspicions." He placed a finger under her chin and brought her eyes back to his. "Robley has granted me a place in his garrison as a captain, and once the position of commander over Castle Rait's guard becomes available, he has promised 'twill be mine if I wish it. 'Tis a good living, and I possess a small fortune of my own. As my wife, you would want for nothing. I can provide for you and our bairns. Should you accept me, I swear upon my honor as a knight that I will do all within my power to see you are happy and safe." He searched her face. "What say you, lass? Could you find a place for me in your heart?"

"Oh, Tieren, you already have a place in my heart." Her pulse raced, and her mouth went dry. "You've become very important to me, and I value our friendship." She swallowed the lump clogging her throat. "I'm honored by your proposal, but I—"

"Dinna think I have no' noticed the way you look at Hunter." He tightened his hold on her hands. "'Twould be best for all if you accept that he has pledged himself elsewhere, lass. Given time, 'tis my fervent hope that you might look upon me the way you now look upon him."

Ouch. She tugged her hands back and moved out of his reach. Wrapping her arms around herself, she paced. "We don't know what the future holds. I have no idea why I've been brought to your century. How I look at Hunter doesn't really matter, because I could be returned to my time tomorrow, next week or next month. You are such a good man, Tieren. I am grateful to you on so many levels, but I . . . I don't know what to say."

"For the present, say naught." He placed his hands on her shoulders to stop her pacing. "All I ask is that you consider my suit. I swear you will no' be alone or unprotected should you find you canna return to your time." He drew her close and wrapped his arms around her. His heart pounded beneath her palms, and her own heart gave an answering wrench.

His piercing blue eyes were a stunning contrast to the darkness of his hair. No doubt about it; he was extraordinarily good-looking, and she was certain women everywhere swooned over him. But his touch didn't cause the spiraling heat Hunter's did, and the wrenching sensation in her heart had more to do with empathy than passion.

"I want you, Meghan McGladrey," he whispered. "And if you wish it, I shall return to your century to be with you." He cradled her face in his large, callused hands and brushed his lips across hers. His eyes roamed over her face, pausing at her mouth and then rising to her eyes. "Surely your father would find a place for me in his fencing club, aye? He did so for Robley, did he no'?"

She nodded, both touched and alarmed by his declaration—and his kiss. "I consider you a friend, Tieren. I'm grateful to you for the way you look out for me, and I hope you know I've got your back as well. I have a lot of respect for you."

A look of resignation and hurt flashed across his handsome face. "'Tis a good place to start." He jutted out his chin. "Many are obliged to marry with far less between them."

She twisted her surcot between her fingers. What if she never did get home? What *would* she do? Was it entirely selfish to consider his offer when she didn't love him? Knowing what she did of their era, she'd have to partner up with someone. Could she accept Tieren when her heart reached for Hunter?

Most marriages in this century had little to do with romantic love, and everything to do with advantageous partnerships. Could she resign herself to such a life? She wanted heart-pounding, knee-weakening, walk-through-fire-for-you love. That's what her mom and dad had. Nothing less would do—nothing less would entice her to stay in a time not her own. *Like I have a choice.*

"Have I mentioned how lovely you look this eve?" His eyes sparkled, and the laugh lines around his eyes creased.

"Thank you," she said, some of the tension easing out of her. She gave him the once-over. "You're looking pretty hot yourself."

"*Hot?*" He chuckled low in his throat. "Though I am uncertain of the meaning, I quite like the implications." He placed his hand at the small of her back. "Come, my lady. Let us return before Robley realizes we're no' within, where he might keep watch over you."

He turned her toward Moigh Hall, and her heart slammed against her rib cage. Hunter stood at the top of the steps, his arms folded across his chest, his stance wide and a glare drawing a bead straight for her. She lifted her chin. *Glare away.* It's not like he'd offered her anything. *Not entirely true or fair.* He'd offered her protection, and he'd vowed to return her into her father's keeping. Both huge.

With Tieren's hand still on the small of her back, she climbed the stairs, her face a mask of neutrality. Not an easy task considering all the air had left her lungs. She faced Hunter's unflinching stare. "Where's Sky?" she quipped in passing.

"She's suffering with a headache and has retired to her chamber," he snapped, edging himself between her and Tieren. "Robley is asking for you, Tieren. You'd best seek him out."

The air grew thick with tension, and Meghan rubbed her temples. "Must be something going around. I have a headache too. I think I'll head upstairs myself."

She hurried away before either one of them could stop her. Life in fifteenth-century Scotland was far more complicated than she was used to. Hunter's behavior made no sense. He couldn't be jealous. Could he? Nah. More than likely he felt protective of her in the same way Robley did. He'd vowed to return her to her home, and he didn't want Tieren messing with his plans.

Meghan roamed around the solar, too restless to sit. She had stopped by the solar to see who might be there before heading for the lists. She really needed to make a point of it to spend more time with the ladies, but she'd always been a tomboy. Most of her friends had been guys while growing up. Probably the result of being the younger sister to two brothers. Plus, she'd spent every waking hour training under her father alongside a multitude of boys her age.

All the ladies were present—except for Sky. The relief she felt was followed by a pang of guilt. Sky hadn't been anything but gracious toward her.

"Where's Sky?" she asked. Erin and True shared a quick look. *Too obvious?* With their abilities, they must've picked up on her jealousy. Mortification heated her face.

"I believe she and her da are visiting with the villagers this morn," Lydia answered. "Is that no' so, True?"

True nodded, focusing her attention on the work in her lap. The women seated around the hearth worked on mending, embroidery or tapestries. The girls, Helen and Sarah, held pieces of linen, practicing their stitches, while Hannah Rose paged through one of the many books True and Erin had made for their children.

"It's been nearly two months since I came to this century. I still have no idea why I'm here, and we aren't any closer to finding Giselle." Meghan stopped to stare out of one of the open windows. The impressive view encompassed the lake, green rolling hills and shadowy mountains in the distance. "I don't suppose you've been able to reach Haldor, have you, Erin?"

"If I had, you'd be the first to know." Erin put the tunic she was mending on her lap. "I've done everything I can think of, including making a sign on vellum and placing it on the table in our chamber. I had hoped Haldor might see it if he took a minute to check up on me." She shook her head. "Sometimes I can sense when he does that, but I haven't felt anything for months."

Meghan turned back to the view outside. "I'm getting antsy."

"What's *antsy*, Mama?" Hannah looked up at Erin from her book. "I don't like ants."

"It means Meghan is feeling restless and agitated." Erin ran her fingers through her daughter's curls. "No ants involved, sweetie."

"Oh." Hannah turned her big baby blues to Meghan. "What's *agitated*?"

"I miss my family and want to go home. That's what it means." Meghan walked over to where Hannah sat beside her mother. She scooped the little girl up and resettled her on her lap. "Do you want me to read this book to you?"

"Nay. I can do it." She snuggled against Meghan's chest and turned back to the first page. "I will read it to you."

"That would be nice." She hugged her close.

"A is for apple," Hannah said proudly. "My mama brought apple seeds with her when she came back for my da." She twisted around to look at Meghan. "We have lots of apple trees at home. I can climb them just as well as my cousin Thomas, and he's older."

"Cool." Meghan tucked the little girl's hair behind her ear. "Keep reading."

Hannah traced the words with her finger. "B is for bairns. C is for cabbage." She glanced over her shoulder at Meghan again, her eyes filled with glee. "And *cool*. D is for da—"

The sound of the village horn interrupted her. "Two tones. What does that mean again?" Meghan asked.

"It means someone from our clan has returned home," True said.

Meghan frowned. "Who is away besides the men Hunter sent to search for Giselle?"

"None that I'm aware of, my dear." Lydia glanced up from her embroidery. "Mayhap you shall have news of Giselle's whereabouts this very day."

"Do you think so?" Meghan stood and put Hannah down. "Any of you want to go with me to the ferry landing?"

"Nay." Rosemary shook her head. "You go, lass, and bring us the news when you are able. We learned long ago 'tis best to bide our time in comfort whilst the tidings make their way to us. News manages to circulate without any effort on our part."

"She's right." Erin grinned. "We'll be here for the rest of the afternoon. If you need us, you know where to find us."

"All right. I'll come back as soon as I can." She opened the door and strode down the corridor. Cecil waited for her at the top of the stairs to the great hall. *Great.* She took a deep breath and tried to unclench her gut.

"My lady," he said with a bow, gesturing for her to precede him. "Mayhap we shall soon have tidings of the Romany's whereabouts."

"I hope so."

They reached the great hall, and he took her elbow. "I am the eldest nephew of the earl of Glencairn, and third in line to inherit the title."

She moved far enough away that he had to let go of her. "Good for you."

"Regrettably, your circumstances will make it quite difficult for you to marry well," he continued, his tone a little sharper. "You possess no land, nor dowry, and though you are descended from a noble line, we canna share your origins. Nonetheless, I am willing—"

Obviously her guardian hadn't made it known that he'd promised a dowry for her, or he meant it only for Tieren. Probably a good thing. "None of that matters, since I plan to do everything I can to get home."

"Mayhap 'twill no' be possible for you to return." They reached the door, and once again he took her arm. Only this time, he gripped her a little harder. "You will be forced to marry if such is the case. Choose me, and your bairns will be of noble blood. Choose elsewhere, and your issue will come to naught."

"I'm not interested." Meghan jerked away. "With your pedigree, I'm certain you can do better. Besides, I'd rather my *issue come to naught* than to live out the rest of my days with the creep who suggested I be bound and left behind in the forest."

"Surely you realize what a shock the events of that day caused me," he hissed. "Consider well before you choose, my lady. You dinna wish to make an enemy of the Glencairns."

"Meghan, Cecil." Hunter jogged up the stairs to meet them. "I was just coming to find you." His sharp glance went from her to Cecil and back again. He took her by the elbow and drew her to his side. "Two of the men I sent to search for Giselle's whereabouts have returned. Once they put their gear away, they will meet us here in the great hall. Would you see to refreshments for the two returning guardsmen, lass? We'll gather at the table anon."

Meghan's insides still churned from her exchange with Cecil, and now her heart leaped to her throat. "Did your men locate Giselle?"

"Aye, but I bid them wait until we are together before they speak of it. Go to the kitchens. We'll hear what they have to say in a trice."

She could be returned home soon. Her eyes met Hunter's, and an overwhelming flood of regret and sadness nearly dropped her to her knees. Stupid knight. *Stupid me!* Yep. She was already half in love with a man who didn't want her, and stuck in a time she didn't belong.

CHAPTER NINE

Once Meghan left the great hall for the kitchen, Hunter focused his senses on the man beside him. Anger and frustration emanated from Cecil. Hunter's hand went instinctively to the dagger at his belt, tensing for battle. He forced himself to calm down, forced his voice into a nonconfrontational tone. "What did you say to Meghan? She seemed distraught."

"I ken no reason why *she* would be distraught. I offered for her." He grunted. "I am her better in every way, yet she refused me. She owns no property, has no political connections and possesses no fortune. The foolish woman should have been pleased that I am willing to wed her despite her desperate circumstances. Lady Meghan needs to learn her place," Cecil snapped. "I intend to teach it to her."

Cecil's rage surged, and Hunter sensed violence in the other man's heart. He forced himself to remain calm. 'Twas best to keep Cecil talking. Mayhap in his anger, he'd reveal more than he intended. "'Tis true." Hunter folded his arms and looked askance at the other knight. "She has naught in the way of land, wealth or political connections, so . . . why do you want her?"

"Hmm?" Cecil seemed to recall himself. His attention shifted fully to Hunter. "She's a comely enough lass, aye? My clan and family have land and fortune enough that I can choose to marry where I will."

"If she said you nay, 'tis best to accept it." Hunter nearly choked on the deceit emanating from the other knight. 'Twas all he could do to keep himself from wrapping his hands around Cecil's neck. "I willna' allow you to molest her in any way nor will any in my clan. She will return to the protection of her father, or we will keep her here under our protection."

"To wed *Tieren*, the son of an alewife? You would oppose me in this?" Cecil glared. "By God, you risk incurring the wrath of the earl of Glencairn *and* clan Cunningham."

"Your uncle's holdings lie far to our south." Hunter shrugged. "Our clan has had no dealings with yours in the past—for good or ill. Do you truly believe your uncle would turn against a clan as powerful as the MacKintosh? Does the earl of Glencairn hold you in such high regard that he'd risk bloodshed over a foreign lass with naught to recommend her, simply because she refused you?"

"'Tis certain you are correct, and my uncle would no' shed blood over a foreigner." Cecil capitulated, his eyes sliding away from Hunter's. "Let us no' quibble over a mere woman. I allowed my emotions to get the better of me is all. Where Lady Meghan is concerned, it happens far too oft for my peace of mind."

Was it *only* injured pride goading Cecil? Were his threats as shallow and empty as his character? Hunter searched for deeper intent, sensing naught but Cecil's struggle to bring himself under control. Now that Meghan had rejected his suit, mayhap their unwanted guest would return to Glencairn. He hoped so. "Aye. We've kent each other far too long to allow a woman to come between us. I trow she will soon be returned to her kin. Let us put all of this behind us."

Tieren and the two returning guardsmen entered the great hall at the same time Meghan returned from the kitchen. "Molly said she'd send servants with food soon. In the meantime, I brought ale." She placed the tray holding an ewer and several tankards on the trestle table.

"Lady Meghan, this is Patrick," Tieren said as he gestured toward one of the guardsmen and then the other, "and this is Bain."

"It's nice to meet you both," Meghan said. The two warriors bowed to her before pulling out one of the short benches to sit at the table. Meghan filled the tankards and passed them around as everyone took a place.

Hunter reached for the mug she held out to him. Their fingers touched, and his heart took flight. By the saints, 'twould be good to send her home at last. His life would return to normal. 'Twas far too unsettling, this havoc she stirred within him. The merest touch, the feel of her skin against his, and his blood rushed. With his need to protect her, his desire to posses her, make her his . . . he could find no peace.

He didn't want these desperate emotions or this all-consuming longing. He didn't want to need anyone. Doing so would surely lead to his ruin—as it had before. He gripped his tankard with both hands, his chest tight. His poor heart would not survive another loss like he'd suffered when his ma and his granny had died.

He forced himself to regain control. He was a knight, after all, and well schooled in self-discipline. Wrestling his errant thoughts into submission, he took a long draught of the ale and turned his attention to the matter at hand.

Meghan settled herself on the bench beside him—close enough that her warmth and proximity drove him to distraction all over again. Aye, once she returned to her own time, he'd be able to purge himself of the effect she had on him. He inhaled her unique sweet scent, taking it in deep to hold forever in his keeping. God help him.

He'd not purge her from his senses so easily. *She* would haunt him all the days of his life. "What news have you to share?"

Patrick leaned in. "We found the wanderers. The old crone you seek still travels with them. Bain and I followed their trail for a handful of days." He rapped his knuckles against the table. "They're heading toward Inverness. 'Tis certain."

"Aye." Bain nodded. "We left them camped by Loch Dún Seilcheig. The Romany wagons stop oft along the way to trade with local villagers. 'Twill take them a se'nnight at least to reach Inverness at their current pace. If we leave at first light on the morrow, we'll arrive in Inverness at the same time they do."

"Inverness is a large and prosperous borough. I suspect the Romany will remain there for some time, and Madame Giselle will once again inhabit her cottage." Hunter glanced at Meghan. "If it pleases you, lass, we'll leave two days hence. I've much to do to prepare for the journey, and arrangements must be made for my absence."

"Angus would be willing to continue on in your stead for a fortnight, aye?" Tieren's brow rose. "Or if you wish to remain at Moigh Hall, I'd be more than happy to escort Lady Meghan to Inverness . . . whilst you remain here."

Hunter snorted. He opened his mouth to retort, only to have Meghan interrupt.

"We can wait two days." She placed her hand on his forearm for a second, the touch singeing his nerves.

"There is safety in numbers," she continued. "I haven't forgotten what happened on the road to Aberdeenshire, and I'd just as soon have Hunter along. He's almost as handy with a broadsword as you are, Tieren."

She praised Tieren? Hunter's jaw clenched so hard he feared cracking one of his back teeth or two. *He'd* been the one to protect her from the start. Hadn't he soothed her when bad dreams haunted her sleep? Hadn't he been the one to procure clean clothing and a comb in an effort to please her? He'd kept her safe, made sure she was fed and provided for, and did she praise *him*?

Nay. She did not.

"'Tis settled." Cecil rubbed his hands together. "I must send word to my kin of my plans to accompany you on your journey to Inverness. I'll have two of my men take the missive this very day. My other two guardsmen will join us."

Hunter sensed naught but the truth and a measure of triumph from the knight. "Do you require the services of your pages? Mayhap send them home with your guards. I dinna plan to bring Allain."

"Aye, I will have the lads travel on to Glencairn ahead of me. The way south is safe enough for any carrying our standard." He glanced at Meghan for an instant. "My armor and gear still remain at Castle Inverness. Once we reach the keep, I shall collect my property and depart for home." He rose from the table and bowed. "I shall see you in the lists on the morrow."

Hunter nodded absently and watched Cecil's back as he departed. Had their guest truly capitulated, or was he more skilled at burying his purpose than he gave him credit?

"Does he *have* to come with us?" Meghan's voice held a plaintive tone. "He threatened me not more than ten minutes ago."

Tieren's expression hardened. "How so?"

Servants arrived with food for Patrick and Bain, and Meghan briefly described what had transpired between her and Cecil.

"I will see that you come to no harm, Meg." Tieren reached across the table and placed his hands over hers. "You have my word."

"Thank you." Color rose to her cheeks.

More than anything, Hunter wanted to rip Tieren's hands from her. He couldn't bear having another man touch her. "I've already spoken with Cecil on the matter." He stood up abruptly, nearly tipping his bench. "His threats are naught but empty words. We are a powerful clan, and the earl of Glencairn will no' want us as enemies." Surveying the great hall, he plowed his fingers through his hair. "We leave two days hence. Tieren, see to choosing six of our best men for the journey. I'll have our cook prepare camp fare for a se'nnight." He started out for the door.

"What should I do?" Meghan glanced up at him.

"Mollify the twins. They will no' be pleased to hear they are soon to lose their martial arts trainer." He made the mistake of looking into her lovely brown eyes. Would his innards ever cease their tumbling at the sight of her? "Inform Robley of our plans, and I suspect the ladies of the keep will want to hear the news as well."

His foster father and Sky had been gone for most of the day and would surely return from the mainland soon. Hunter wanted things settled between him and Sky before he left for Inverness. The more he felt for Meghan, the more determined he became to rid himself of the debilitating affliction. A man so distracted, so besotted, was good for naught. How could he protect his kin and clan whilst his thoughts spun out of control every time he set eyes on her? Aye, he could not allow himself to become so compromised by emotion—or lust. Meghan rendered him weak-kneed and unable to hold on to rational thought.

By the saints, I willna have it!

Hunter strode across the bailey. He'd spoken with Angus, and now he'd plant himself at the ferry landing until Sky returned to the island. On the way toward the portcullis, he passed the lists. The twins, squires and pages all stood in rapt attention before Meghan, and what he heard coming from her sweet mouth brought him to a halt.

"Size does *not* matter," she shouted.

His brow shot up, and he had to keep his jaw from dropping. What the devil did she intend to teach the lads this day? The adolescents, David and Owain included, shifted uncomfortably, and the younger boys sniggered. Hunter changed his direction, drawing nearer to see what she was up to. At least the lads now wore hose and tunics for their training.

The lass had the audacity to grin at the discomfited lads. "You heard me right. Size. Does. Not. Matter. In fact, you can use your opponent's weight and height to your advantage." She faced her charges with her hands on her slender hips. "Who would like to help me demonstrate?" Again they glanced at each other, their consternation clear.

"Come on." She beckoned with her hand. "I promise not to hurt you too badly."

George took the bait and stepped forward. "I volunteer, milady."

"Good. I want you to come at me like you mean to take me down." She moved him into position and stepped several paces away. She noticed Hunter standing nearby and smiled at him.

Hunter folded his arms in front of him and nodded a greeting.

"Don't be shy or worry about me just because I'm a woman, George. You and I have sparred with broadswords enough for you to know that I can take care of myself. Charge me like you mean it."

"Aye, milady." The squire lowered his head and ran at her. At the last moment, she tucked herself into a ball and let his weight settle over her shoulders and back. Then she straightened, using her legs and his weight to send him flying head over heels. George landed on his back with a thud.

The pages cheered, and the twins beamed their approval. "Well met, Beag Curaidh," Hunter called, reveling in the way his words brought a rosy glow to her face. Shaking his head, he continued on toward the portcullis once again. Never had he encountered such a lass, and 'twas likely he never would again.

Late afternoon, and still Sky and Malcolm tarried in the village. Hunter scanned the mainland and paced. Finally he spied movement upon the far shore. His breath left him, and he ceased his pacing. He didn't want to appear as if he'd spent the better part of his day wearing a new path upon the shoreline. Though that's exactly what he'd done. He scrubbed his face with both hands, trying to rid himself of the frustration fogging his mind.

He returned to pacing. If groveling at Sky's feet was what it took to return his life to some semblance of order, so be it. Mayhap if he slammed his head against the boulder before him, he could knock thoughts of Meghan out of his mind. Was such a thing possible? Eyeing the granite protruding from the ground, he pondered the possibilities. Hadn't he heard tell of men who'd suffered wounds to the head losing all memory of who they were?

The ferry approached. Sky and Malcolm stood on the wooden planks, waving a greeting. Hunter waved back, his palms moist and his ears ringing with the rush of his blood. Ever since he'd laid eyes on Meghan McGladrey, the careful foundation upon which he'd built his life had begun to crumble. Bit by bit his dreams proved harder to hold. The curtain walls around his heart had been breached, and now was the time to shore up his defenses.

Sky Elizabeth was his salvation, his refuge. She always had been. His nerves settled as the ferry landed. He reached out a hand to help his lady disembark.

"Good day, Malcolm," he said with a nod toward his foster father. "Sky, might I have a word?" He trapped her small hand in his, lest she take her leave before he had his say.

"Of course, Hunter." She stepped onto the sand and smiled up at him.

"Lad." Malcolm nodded back. "What news? We saw two riders returning."

"Giselle has been found. Two days hence I will set out for Inverness with Meghan, Tieren and six of our soldiers." He led Sky up the slight incline, tucking her hand into the crook of his arm. "You'll be relieved to hear of Cecil's plans."

"Will I?" Malcolm cocked an eyebrow.

"Cecil offered for Meghan. She refused him, and once he's journeyed with us to Inverness to retrieve his armor and gear, he's leaving us for Glencairn."

"'Tis good news indeed." Malcolm chuckled. "And good riddance. Dinna let down your guard, lad. The journey to Inverness will take five days, at the very least three if you ride hard. 'Tis more than enough time for Cecil to contrive some sort of mischief."

"I never let down my guard."

"Good. I will see you at the evening meal then. Dinna stay away from your mother overlong, Sky. She'll want to hear all the gossip from the village."

"I'll seek her out anon, Da." Sky lifted her chin to gaze up at Hunter. "What is it you wish to speak to me about, dear *brother*?"

Had she put emphasis on the word *brother*? Hunter waited until Malcolm was well away before replying. "I am no' your brother, my lady. I am your suitor."

"Nay, dinna say such a thing." She squeezed his arm and smiled sweetly, though she pulsed with anxiety. "You will always be my elder brother. Were you no' there at the day of my birth? Have our father and mother no' claimed you as their own?"

"They fostered me, aye, but . . ." He frowned. "Sky, have you given no thought to my desire to wed you? Are my wishes so insignificant that you canna even spare them a few moments of consideration?"

"I have given it a great deal of thought. We are no' suited. It does no' please me to think that every emotion I carry would be so easily discerned by my husband." She moved away from him and clasped her hands together. "Erin explained to both of us how genetics work.

You and I are both gifted with fae abilities. Would you risk the chance of our bairns being even more fae than the two of us combined? Would you risk the chance of our bairns being even more of an oddity than the both of us?"

He hadn't considered that. The granite boulder he'd studied earlier somehow found a place in the pit of his stomach. "She also said the possibility existed that genes can mix in such a way that none of the fae characteristics will show in a bairn. Thomas is no' gifted."

"Aye, but neither is Da. One out of the six of us is without the curse, Hunter. One out of six, and that is with only one of our parents carrying the fae gene." She shook her head. "Nay. I wish for my sons and daughters to have a greater chance at a normal life than the two of us can offer."

"You too see our abilities as a curse? Why have you said naught about this before now?" They'd taken the well-worn path to a secluded spot on the lakeshore—a spot where lovers oft hid for a few moments of privacy.

"I do see it as a curse." She nodded, her eyes downcast. "You are only recently returned. When would I have spoken to you about such?"

"If I could find a way to rid myself of the fae abilities, I would do so in a trice." He leaned over and picked up a few flat stones, skipping one across the surface of the loch. "I live in fear that I will be discovered. 'Twould lead to suspicion, isolation . . . or worse." He glanced askance at her. "I could no' bear it."

Tossing another stone, he followed the trajectory as it skipped along the surface. "Still, wouldn't we both be better off together? At least then there would be understanding between us. We'd have no need to keep our abilities and heritage a secret from one another, aye?"

"Do you love me, Hunter? Does your heart cease beating for an instant when you behold me?" She stared at him in that intense way she had and awaited his response.

"I do love you, aye." He hadn't lied.

"Granted, as a dear sister, but does the very sight of me set your blood on fire? Do you feel passion for me?"

He couldn't answer. He kent full well she'd recognize the lie as soon as he gave it voice. A lump rose to his throat. "Mayhap in time . . ."

"Nay." She shook her head. "Time will no' make a difference. I mean to marry Oliver, the earl of Mar's grandson. He's a good man, and—"

"The earl's son. In truth, 'tis my lack of land and a title that makes me unsuitable and no' my fae blood. Isn't that so, lass?" He hurled the rest of the stones out over the water to rain down in a flurry of tiny splashes and ripples. "I kent as much."

"How many times must I say it? Your lack of a title or land means naught to me."

Her words rang with truth, but he chose not to pay them heed. "What if I were to perform some service to our king? He might grant me land and a title, albeit none so lofty as an earldom." Desperation tore at him. His dreams were slipping through his fingers like water through a cracked ladle, and he could do naught to stop it. "Then would you consider marrying me?"

"Hunter . . ."

"Will you wed this Oliver fellow out of duty alone? Do you love him? Does *he* steal your breath and send your pulse racing?"

Her lips compressed into a straight line. She too refused to give voice to a lie. A small victory, but a victory nonetheless. "I ken you as well as you ken yourself, lass—as you do me. There can never *be* lies between us, and that is a good basis upon which to build our lives. What will Oliver make of you once he sees you are no' like others? What will he do when he discovers you are part fae?" He cast her a hard look. "When your husband turns from you out of suspicion and fear, what will you do then, lass?"

"Now you resort to cruelty to bend me to your will?" She glared at him. "I thought you cared for me, but I see now you are like every other man—selfish and somehow entitled to trample upon the feelings of a mere woman." She turned on her heel and marched away from him. "Mayhap *I* will find a way to the future. I hear tell the men there are far more enlightened and much less fearful," she called over her shoulder.

"Shite." He leaned down, scooped up a handful of pebbles and flung them out over the loch with all the force he could muster. Once again he'd failed to find the right words to persuade her. Instead of gentleness, sentiment and ardent words, he'd behaved like a petulant lad, resorting to bullying to have his way.

'Twas Meghan who addled his thoughts and had him behaving like a man grasping at straws. Once she was away, he'd go about persuading Sky in a more logical, rational manner. At least he kent Sky hadn't given her heart to the earl of Mar's grandson.

"Just out of curiosity . . ."

He nearly leaped from his skin at the sound of Meghan's voice. Whipping around, he scowled at her. "What are you doing here?"

"I saw a lot of splashing out over the water and came to investigate." She toed the pebbles beneath her boot. "What did the lake ever do to you to deserve such abuse?"

She still wore her hose and tunic. Her hair hung over her shoulder in a tight braid, and once again she called to mind the warrior queen Boudicca. 'Twas not safe to be so near her in this secluded place. Her wide-set eyes, fixed upon him so earnestly, held warmth and concern. How was he supposed to resist her when with every action and word she entranced him? "I beg your pardon?"

"All those rocks being hurled . . ." She gestured toward the loch. "At first I thought maybe some of the boys were trying to outthrow each other, or maybe they were skipping stones." She picked through the pile at her feet, chose a smooth, flat stone and sent it skimming across the surface of the water. "But the way the rocks were coming down, it seemed less like fun and more like an expression of frustration . . . or anger."

"Humph."

"Humph?" She arched a brow. "Use your *words*, Hunter. What's eating at you today?"

He blew out a breath and chose a flat stone at his feet. He sent it skipping, pleased when his throw outdistanced hers. "'Tis frustration."

Meghan picked up a smooth stone, aimed carefully and threw. Her effort outdid his by several hands. He couldn't let *that* happen. Picking up just the right specimen, he judged the weight of it in his hand before putting a bit more muscle into his next toss. "Ha! Beat that if you can, lass."

"Oh." She blinked up at him in feigned innocence. "Are we competing? Because if we are"—she searched the shore—"you don't stand a chance."

"Think you?" he shot back. "Do your best, Beag Curaidh. 'Twill be for naught, for you dinna possess the strength to match mine."

"Of course you'd think it's all about muscle." Her eyes narrowed. "Watch this." She stepped closer to the water's edge, surveyed the loch and shifted the stone from one hand to the other. Finally, she brought her arm back and flung it out over the loch. Six skips, and the stone traveled well beyond his last effort. "See?" She twirled in triumph, her features lit with satisfaction.

He laughed, drew her into his arms and brought his mouth down to hers before he kent what he was about. Her arms circled his waist, and her nearness, her scent, intoxicated him. She returned his kiss, and he was lost. With her warmth and the feel of her curves fitted so sweetly against him, the kiss took on a life of its own, deepening until his rigid control gave way.

He ran his tongue along the seam of her mouth, and she opened for him. He slid his tongue around hers in a mating dance, and a soft moan escaped her. The need to claim her overwhelmed him. Hard, aching—and yes . . . desperate, he backed her into the trunk of the nearest oak and pressed against her. Cradling her face between his palms, he slanted her head to gain better access, delving deeper into the sensuous feast she offered up so sweetly.

Meghan ran her hands over his chest, then over his shoulders to stroke his back. He ran his palms down to her tiny waist to hold her hips, bringing her up against his hardness, cursing the clothing that separated them. Rational thought burned away in a conflagration of desire.

He had to stop this before he took her right here in the copse. Mustering his will, he broke the kiss and rested his forehead against hers, so close they shared the air between them. Every fiber in his being protested. He labored to breathe, and his heart beat against his rib cage in castigation against his restraint.

"Why are you here, Meghan?"

"Do you mean in your century, or . . . ?"

"Nay." Hunter drew a long, steadying breath. "Here in this secluded place . . . with me. 'Tis dangerous to play with fire, lass." A surge of heat and longing shot through him at the swift intake of her breath. He'd never wanted a woman the way he wanted Meghan, and he was certain he never would again. May the saints preserve him, he *prayed* he never would again.

She cleared her throat. "About the same time I noticed the shower of pebbles, I saw Sky heading for the keep. Judging by the look on her face, I figured the two of you had argued again. I thought maybe you could use a friend."

"Aye. We did argue." He couldn't seem to force himself to let go of her. He nuzzled her temple and ran his knuckles over the delicate skin of her cheeks. How was it his wee warrior had such soft skin?

"What is it with you two?" She searched his face. "Do you want to talk about it?"

He closed his eyes. "The lady and I are at an impasse."

"Not too many would take the vow you made as a child seriously. Why do you persist? If you want Sky so badly, why am I pressed up against this tree with your . . . er . . . umm . . ."

He backed away from her and faced the loch. His face burned, and his tarse throbbed. He ached all over with wanting her. "Mayhap 'twould be best if you returned to the keep."

"Oh, I'm sure it would be, but I'm not going to. I want to know what's going on. Clearly Sky doesn't want the same thing you do. Why do you keep it up?"

Keep it up? She couldn't possibly understand the implications of what she'd just said, or the effect her words had on him. "'Tis complicated."

"I'm smart. I don't find complicated things daunting at all." She huffed out a breath. "Maybe it would do you some good to talk it through with an outsider."

"Humph."

"Again . . . use your words, Hunter." She came around to face him. "I'm leaving soon. What harm can there be in spilling your guts to me?"

"Spilling my guts?" One side of his mouth quirked up. "Sounds quite painful."

"You know what I mean." She lifted her chin and crossed her arms in front of her.

Adorable, in a fierce kind of way. He took another calming breath. "Mayhap you have it aright."

"Of course I do."

Her boastful tone brought a smile to his face. "Our clans are patrilineal. I've ne'er met my kin on my father's side. He disappeared before I was born—taken by Giselle into the future I am told, and he perished before the faerie could return him to us. I am a MacConnell through my da, and because of that, I've ne'er truly felt as if . . ." His throat closed up.

"Give me a break." She threw her hands in the air. "Don't tell me you feel like you don't really belong here with the MacKintosh."

He shrugged.

"Hunter, not only do you *belong* to this clan, but you are *adored* by this clan to the point where it's a little bit sickening."

Heat crept up his neck. "Think you?"

"So, let me see if I understand this little drama correctly." She shot him a wry look and wagged her finger at him. "You want to marry Sky, your foster sister, because you think doing so will somehow make you feel like you truly have a place with the MacKintosh—when in reality, you have always *been* a MacKintosh for real." She shook her head. "Besides which, if clan identity comes from the father, your children will be MacConnells anyway, right?"

The way she said it made him feel like a lad of eight or ten. "What do you ken about how I *feel* or what I want?"

"Huh. I believe I've hit the nail on the head, or you wouldn't be as miffed as you are right now. That's called a *defense mechanism*. And by the way—you wear an entire suit of armor comprising the stuff."

"Enough, my lady," he snapped a little too harshly. "You have given me much to think on, and for that I am truly grateful."

"Liar."

He growled low in his throat, outrage grinding his control down to a nub. "'Tis well past time I returned to my duties." He bowed. "I bid you good day."

"Good day to you as well, Sir Hunter. I wish you well in your bogus quest of epic proportions. "

"*Bogus?* Is there even such a word?" He glowered. "By the saints, you can be most trying."

"By the saints, you are as blind as my grandma's thirteen-year-old pug."

Having no idea what she meant, he let her have the last word. Clearly 'twas important to her to do so. Hunter strode across the bailey, rejecting out of hand all she had said. Meghan kent naught of the way of things in his century, and even less of him.

Angus met him at the bottom of the stairs to the keep. "Hunter, a moment of your time?"

"What is it?"

"Two of Sir Cecil's guards and pages left us this day." His brow lowered until his bushy gray eyebrows nearly hid his eyes.

"Aye." Out of the corner of his eye, Hunter caught a glimpse of Meghan as she came in through the portcullis. He wanted to shake her by the shoulders and then kiss her senseless until she could challenge him no further. "Cecil told us he meant to send word to his kin of his plans to travel with us to Inverness, and he's sending the pages home before him."

"The Cunninghams live no' too far from the *Sassenach* border to the south, aye?"

"Aye." Hunter's attention turned to the older man. "Why do you ask?"

"I ask because I happened to be in the village when the Cunninghams took their leave."

"And?" The hairs on the back of his neck stood on end, and he tensed.

"They didn't take the road south, lad." Angus frowned. "They went north."

Hunter searched his mind for a plausible reason why Cecil would send his guards north. "There are crofters to the north, aye? Crofters with daughters who are of marriageable age. Mayhap one of the guards formed an attachment whilst here and wished to pay his respects before departing."

"Mayhap you have it aright." Angus scratched his beard. "Still, 'twould ease my mind a bit if you took more than six men with you."

"I see no need, but I'll increase the number to ten. Will you see to it?"

"Aye. Think you to take an alternative route to the one you shared with Sir Cecil?"

"Nay." He shook his head. "This far from home and on our land, Cecil canna have too many soldiers at his disposal without our being aware of them. Have any of our scouts noticed anything out of the ordinary whilst doing their rounds along the borders?"

"Nay. No' a thing."

"I dinna fathom the reasons why Cecil would conspire against us, yet I canna shake the feeling that some form of treachery is afoot. If he and his handful of guards do mean to cause trouble, I'd just as soon settle the matter once and for all. We will no' turn away from a fight if that's what he seeks."

"You do us credit, lad." Angus slapped his shoulder. "Spoken like a true MacKintosh."

All of his fears and insecurities surged through him in a cold rush. Would Angus say "like a true MacKintosh" if he truly saw Hunter as anything *but* a MacKintosh? *Damnation.* This day could not end fast enough to suit him.

Hunter sharpened his sword on the turning stone wheel in the armory, his mind doing inventory of the things he'd need to pack for the trip. He stopped the wheel and examined his blade. 'Twas as sharp as 'twould ever be. Slipping the claymore into its scabbard, he surveyed the chamber.

On the morrow, he and ten of their best warriors would escort Meghan to Inverness to return her to her time. The notion caused a hollowness within him, and he rubbed his chest to ease the ache. She wanted to go home, and he'd vowed to see that she did. 'Twas for the best. It had to be done.

Redirecting his errant thoughts, Hunter ran through the list of preparations, making sure all was ready for their journey. He'd told Tieren to pass along his instructions not to share any information with Cecil's remaining guardsmen or his squire. All that remained for the evening was to sup with his foster family. He intended to retire early to get a good night's rest. If sleep would come to him, 'twould be a miracle indeed.

The door to the armory creaked open. Hunter looked up to find Tieren standing half in and half out. Angus stood behind him. "What is it?"

The two men entered, closed the door behind them and approached. Tieren spoke first. "We've had a thought or two about the journey to Inverness."

"Aye?" Hunter had always been able to rely upon Tieren's uncanny ability for strategy, and he sorely missed the closeness they'd once shared. He'd wracked his brain for some way around their current estrangement, but 'twas not he who had shown himself a false friend. It did not fall to him to rectify the matter.

Angus continued. "Cecil believes you mean to bring six men with you, and we see no reason to upset whatever plans he might have by showing our hand."

"He may no' have any plans at all. We dinna ken why his guards went north. Did you have anyone follow them?" Hunter straightened a few lances that had slipped down in their rack.

"Nay." Angus shrugged. "Mayhap you have it aright and naught is amiss. All the same, 'tis good to be prepared, aye?"

"What do you suggest?"

Eagerness emanated from Tieren. "What if we leave with only the six we'd planned on from the start? Have two of the additional guards follow at a safe distance behind. Our lads ken well the route we will take."

"Aye," Angus added. "And have the other two depart afore you. Have them stay off the road and scout your way ahead. If Cecil is leading you into an ambush, our warriors will circle back to warn you, and you can wait for the two who watch the way behind to catch up before you proceed."

"'Tis a sound plan," Hunter agreed. "What about the two remaining Cunningham guards who travel with Cecil? If there is aught afoot, I dinna like the idea of having them in our midst. Do we have time to arrange for their disappearance?"

A wolfish grin split Tieren's face. "Aye."

"Good. Have them taken to Meikle Geddes to be held until we ken for certain whether or no' Cecil is up to something."

"Tieren and I will see to it anon." Angus winked. "The Cunningham guardsmen will have a bit more to drink this eve than they planned. There are fishing boats enough lining the shore that we can secret them away in the dark of night." Chuckling, he headed for the door. "I imagine Sir Cecil will put on quite a show when he finds his men have gone missing. Until tomorrow, lads." Angus tipped his head and left the armory.

Tieren shifted, and his discomfort filled the space between the two of them. "I will have my say before we depart for Inverness."

Hunter straightened, bracing himself for more betrayal. "Say what you must."

"Brothers fight oft enough, and envy plagues even the greatest among us from time to time." Tieren stared at him, his eyes filled with determination. "Never doubt my loyalty to you, Hunter. Never doubt I love you like a brother, for that is what you are to me." His face grew ruddy, but his gaze held.

His words were a balm to Hunter's soul. He cleared his throat. "As you are a brother to me."

"Good." Tieren rubbed his hands together. "As your brother and the elder of the two of us, there is more I need to say, and I do so out of caring."

"By the saints, Tieren—"

"Nay, I willna be gainsaid in this." He shook his head. "All of us are blind to our own folly from time to time, and you more so than others. There are those who will take advantage of that blindness to best you." He shrugged. "Even I will do so if the situation warrants."

"How do you mean to *best me*?" His mind reeled. "After declaring your loyalty, you would say such a thing?"

"Aye. If I can, I will prevail when it comes to matters of the heart." He grunted. "Suffice it to say I meant every word I said, little brother. 'Tis no fault of mine you're an idiot. I do you no wrong in this."

"I like it no' when you speak in riddles, and even less when you call me names."

Tieren chuckled. "Dinna let it keep you up this night. We'll both need our wits about us on the morrow." He started for the door. "One more thing. If Meghan finds a way to return home, I intend to go with her."

His pulse raced, and his mouth went dry. "She has agreed to this?"

"I have." He paused upon the threshold. "She gave me no answer, and I did no' press her for one—yet. If she will have me, I *will* follow her to the future."

"What if she canna find a way home?"

"Then I suspect we will have more to fight about in the near future." He shrugged. "But my feelings for her do no' change how I feel about you, nor does it affect my loyalty."

Tieren left, shutting the door a little too forcefully, sending the lances Hunter had just straightened into disarray. Hunter moved to the table where a dozen arrows awaited repair. He picked up two of them and cracked the shafts over his knee. The splintering sound and the bruising force across his thigh eased some of the tension banding his chest.

He had neither the time nor the will to puzzle out what Tieren meant with his cryptic speech about his blindness or besting him. Hadn't Meghan also accused him of blindness? Neither she nor Tieren understood him, and that's all there was to it.

'Twas enough to have peace between him and Tieren. He trusted his friend to guard his back, as he would guard Tieren's—like they'd always done. He prayed he'd not lose Tieren to the future, and the thought that he might never see him or Meghan again plagued him. Loss was the one thing he could not tolerate. He searched the armory for something else to break, and thought better of it. No sense in wasting perfectly good weapons.

He scratched at the stubble on his face. He had just enough time to bathe and shave before supper. Soaking in a tub of hot water would soothe his frayed nerves. Mayhap he'd calm himself enough to face Cecil at table this eve without throttling the man before they set out for Inverness. What was he planning? Did he mean to snatch Meghan away? For certes, she'd wounded his pride with her rejection. Surely Cecil kent better than to incur his wrath.

Life had been so much easier whilst on the continent. All he'd fashed over then was winning the next tournament or fighting the next battle. His path had been clear and his way unimpeded. How he longed for such simplicity once again.

Letting out a growl of frustration, he left the armory and headed for the bathing room. 'Twas well past the hour of None, and by tacit agreement, the ladies did their bathing before Sext, leaving the room clear for the men during the late afternoon. He hoped to find the chamber empty, for he had no wish to speak to anyone.

By the time Hunter made his way to the great hall, he'd managed to regain control over his emotions. He intended to take full advantage of the cook's skill this eve, for 'twould be a se'nnight at least before he had aught but oatcakes and jerky. He took the stairs at a jog, to find the twins awaiting him in the great hall. For certes, their faces bespoke their mood. Both were unhappy. "What is it, lads?"

Owain kept his tone low. "We want to come with you on the morrow."

"Lady Meghan needs our protection." David nodded, his expression grim.

Hunter wrapped an arm around each of them, giving their shoulders a squeeze. "I appreciate your willingness to lend your sword arms, but I doubt your grandsire or your father would grant permission."

"Lady Meghan needs us," Owain protested. "We want to—"

"Have you sensed this?" He scrutinized the two. "Have either of you had a vision of what is to come?"

"No visions," Owain admitted, "just a general sense of impending trouble."

"Nay, lads. You both need to remain here until such time that you return to the Sutherlands to complete your training. Tieren and I will look after her."

Hunter caught sight of Meghan out of the corner of his eye. His breath hitched. She wore the blue gown again, the one that brought out the creaminess of her complexion and the shine in her hair. 'Twas his favorite. "The lady awaits our company, lads, and I am hungry." He aimed them both toward the table. "If you will allow it, I wish to share a trencher with her this eve. I must tell Meghan of a few changes in our plans."

"Hunter . . ." David's mouth turned down. "'Tis our last night with her, whilst you will spend the next se'nnight in her company."

"I have much to do." He let go of them. "I will leave her in your care after we sup."

That seemed to brighten their moods. Sky and her little sisters came down the stairs. Hunter tried to catch her eye. She refused to look his way. He really needed to go about this wooing business in an entirely different manner.

They sat at the trestle table before the hearth, since this was an informal meal with only kin in attendance. Servants carried platters out from the kitchen, and Allain bore a pitcher of ale. The lad's sullen expression brought a smile to Hunter's face. "Are you still sulking because I want you to remain here?"

"Aye, Sir Hunter." Allain began filling the tankards already set at the table. "I should be with you."

"No' this time, lad. Tieren and I prefer that you and Tristan remain here. We dinna have our armor with us and will do well enough without pages and squires underfoot." In truth, he didn't want to put Allain in harm's way again. Losing his squire at sea, and almost losing Allain on the way to Aberdeenshire, had been enough.

"Lady Meghan." Hunter reached her just as she was taking a seat. "If it pleases you, I'd like to share your trencher."

She shot him a questioning look. "All right."

"There are a few changes in our plans for tomorrow, and I'd like to discuss them." Just as Hunter took his place, the village horn sounded one tone. The doors to the great hall swung open, and one of their guards hurried through.

"Three strangers are on their way to the island, Sir Hunter." He came to a halt before the trestle table. "Malcolm is at the landing and bids you remain in the hall to inform the earl. Malcolm and our guards will escort the visitors to the keep."

Hunter could not imagine who it could be. Mayhap messengers from their neighbors. He had sworn to offer aid to Murray should he need it. They were kin though, and that would have been two tones. William appeared at the top of the stairs with Lydia and the rest of the ladies. Hunter glanced at them before turning back to the guardsman. "Do you have any idea who they might be?"

"Nay, Sir Hunter."

"You may take your leave." He gestured to one of the kitchen servants. "Bring three more tankards and a trencher or two. We have guests." Hospitality was freely given in the Highlands, and three guests inside their well-guarded keep were no threat.

"Who comes, lad?" the earl asked, helping his wife to sit.

"I dinna ken, laird. There are three riding the ferry across the loch," Hunter told him. "Malcolm happened to be close enough to the landing that he sent word. He will bring our visitors to us anon."

"Where is Cecil?" Meghan tugged at the sleeve of his shirt, her tone low.

"He's taking his meal with the garrison."

Robley and his family arrived just as the doors to the keep swung open once more. Malcolm strode forward, trailed by the three strangers. One of the three was an elder. His hair and full beard were completely silver, yet he still possessed a vigorous demeanor and erect posture. He was flanked by two younger men. Their scabbards were empty, as were the sheaths at their waists. Their weapons would have been left at the guardhouse at the portcullis.

"Welcome," the earl's voice boomed. "Who might you be, and what brings you to Moigh Hall?"

"My lords." The elder stepped forward and bowed. "I am Edward of clan MacConnell, and these are two of my sons."

Hunter's heart slammed into his ribs. *MacConnell?* He reached for Meghan's hand where it lay on her lap. Gripping it in his, he clung to her as a ship held fast to its moorings.

"Welcome," William said. "What brings you to Moigh Hall?"

Edward's gaze fixed upon the earl. "We seek a MacConnell lad. He'd be about three and twenty now. His mother Joan was a MacKintosh, wedded to Mahon, a MacConnell. Mahon disappeared before his bairn was born, but Joan sent word to me that she had a son. She named him Alastair after his grandsire, the baron DúnConnell. I've heard naught from Joan since." His gaze never left the earl.

Malcolm rested his elbows on the table and clasped his hands together. "What makes you think the lass you speak of came here? MacKintosh holdings are many and stretch the entire river to Inverness."

"'Twas I who escorted her to the village on the mainland so many years ago." Edward's tone was firm. "I and my men looked after and protected her from the moment Mahon disappeared. She came to live with me and my wife for a time, until she insisted upon returning to Loch Moigh to be with her widowed mother. Aideen, I believe her ma was called. Her ma was the village midwife, and Joan wanted to be near her when her time came."

"What would your business be with the man you seek?" Hunter's voice reverberated through the hall. As one, the three MacConnells turned their attention to him.

Edward canted his head, one side of his mouth turning up. "You've your mother's coloring, lad, but in every other way you are the spitting image of your father."

"Impossible." Beads of sweat covered Hunter's forehead, and he couldn't draw enough air to fill his lungs. "My mother was a commoner. She could no' have wed a baron's son."

"Ah, but she did." Sadness cloaked the older man. "My wife and I witnessed their vows. Your father was a friend to me and I to him."

"A friend, you say. Yet you did naught to find out what became of me in three and twenty years? You claim I'm the grandson of baron DúnConnell?" Hunter shook his head. "There sits my father," Hunter bit out, pointing to Malcolm. "*He* raised me." He gestured to his family seated around the table. Their wide gazes darted back and forth between him and Edward as if watching a jousting tournament. "Here are my kin—the *only* kin I have ever kent for the whole of my life."

Caught in a maelstrom of grief and confusion, he wanted to believe he was the baron's heir, and yet he could not. "If what you say is true, why would my mother have taken me from my clan and home?

Why would she have separated me from my birthright?" He tightened his grip on Meghan's hand. She winced but didn't pull away.

"Where is your mother, lad?" Edward's eyes filled with regret. "Has she no' told you the tale?"

"She and my granddam died when I was still a bairn," he said, his voice breaking. "After all these years, I canna fathom why you would come for me now."

Malcolm stepped around the table to stand at Hunter's side. He placed a hand on his shoulder. "Mayhap this is a conversation best held in the privacy of the earl's solar."

"Aye." William gestured to the empty benches. "Sit, lads. Share our supper, and then we'll retire to my solar to sort it all out."

"We would be most grateful for the meal." Edward bowed again.

"If you will excuse me." Hunter shot up, finally letting go of Meghan's sorely abused fingers. "I need to clear my head." Raking both hands through his hair, he strode toward the door. "I'll join you . . . later."

Mayhap once he was outside, he'd be able to draw breath. The rest of the foundation upon which he'd built his life fell into ruin beneath him, leaving him without a foothold upon solid ground.

The grandson of a baron? Nay. 'Twas not possible. Hadn't he hoped and prayed to be more than he was, of noble blood? And yet, the news gave him no pleasure. Instead, it stirred up all the hurt and abandonment he'd suffered as a lad.

Alastair. Did he only imagine hearing his ma and granny calling him by that name? Faint images and even fainter memories swirled around in his head until he no longer recognized who he was.

Why had his clan ignored him for so long, and why did they seek him out now?

CHAPTER TEN

Meghan started to rise from her place at the long trestle table, intending to go after Hunter. She'd never seen him looking so lost or hurt before. It nearly broke her heart. He needed her. Being an outsider, she could lend an ear without judgment.

Malcolm stopped her. "Leave him be, Meg. He'll be back once he's had a chance to think things through."

The MacConnells seated themselves at the table, and Edward sat opposite her. "Would you be Alastair's wife then?"

"Uh . . ."

"His foster father and I named him Hunter." True leaned forward to speak. "By the time we took him in, most of the clan had forgotten his name."

"That he is of noble blood does no' surprise me." Malcolm once again took his place at the table. "He's a fine man, a braw knight and an asset to our clan." He winked at True. "Did I no' say he would be?"

"Several times." True patted his hand. "Malcolm, introduce everyone."

Introductions were made, and food was served, but Meghan had lost her appetite. She couldn't tear her eyes from the doors to the great hall. She didn't need to be gifted to sense that Hunter was hurting. She flexed her hand and shook it out a few times. His vise-like grip had nearly crushed her knuckles.

"Lady Meghan, you must eat." David slipped into the seat beside her.

"Aye, my lady." Owain pushed a trencher closer. "You will need your strength for the journey to Inverness."

"I'm going to miss you two," she murmured, cutting off a piece of meat.

Owain heaped a pile of mashed turnips onto her trencher. "Then dinna leave."

"Aye." Davids eyes flew to hers. "I like it no' that you mean to go on this journey without us. We both sense something amiss, but what awaits you is no' clear. Stay here where my brother and I can protect you." The twins nodded in tandem. "You have a home with the MacKintosh clan, my lady. You always will."

"That is so sweet, but . . . I'll have Tieren, Hunter and MacKintosh guards with me for protection along the way." Her eyes stinging, she shook her head. Memories of what had happened with Allain and the villain who had meant to murder him flooded her mind. She couldn't bear the thought of anything happening to the twins. "I have to try to get back home. My family—"

"Wheesht, my lady," Owain whispered, tilting his head toward their guests.

She nodded, turning again to watch the doors. How long would it take Hunter to cool down?

Once the meal ended, William stood. "To my solar, if it pleases you, Edward."

"It does, though I dinna wish to say aught without young Alastair there. 'Tis him we've come to fetch. He'll want to hear how and why he came to be with his ma's clan and no' his own, aye?"

"He's called Hunter and has been since he was a bairn of but four." Malcolm beckoned to Allain. "Go find your master, lad, and be quick about it. Tell him his presence is required in the laird's solar."

"Aye, my lord." Allain bobbed his head even as he took off at a run.

Hunter's family and the MacConnells made their way to the stairs leading to the floors above, and Meghan's insides knotted. As much as she longed to find out what was going on, she had no business joining them. This was strictly family business, and she wasn't family. She trailed after Robley and Erin, and when they veered right toward the stairs leading to the earl's third-floor solar, she veered left, heading for her turret chamber.

"Wait, Lady Meghan!" Sky's hurried footsteps echoed along the corridor. She grabbed Meghan's arm to stop her. "Hunter will want you there."

The jealousy she always felt around Sky flared, and she tried to squelch it before the younger woman could get a fix on her emotions. "I don't think so." She shook her head. "I'm not—"

"Hunter does no' love me." Exasperation laced Sky's tone as she tugged on Meghan's arm. "Surely *you* of all people ken as much."

"No. I don't." Meghan huffed out a breath. Even if Sky was right, it didn't make any difference. Hunter wouldn't give up on the idea of marrying Sky. Besides, what business was it of hers? She would travel to Inverness, confront Madame Giselle and go home—where she belonged. "This is a personal matter, and I'm not a MacKintosh . . . or a MacConnell."

"Think you none noticed my brother reached for you when he was overwrought?" Sky placed her hands on Meg's shoulders and gave her a shake. "Do you no' ken you've no reason for the animosity you hold toward me? Even if you'd never come to us, I would no' marry Hunter. He is my brother, nothing more. He's just too thickheaded to grasp what the rest of us can see so plainly."

Her brow rose. "Which is?"

"He loves *you*, my lady. I sense it. My mother and Lady Erin sense it. Even wee Hannah Rose can see it is so. With the exception of my *halfwit of a brother*, all of us ken the truth of the matter."

Meghan had to smile at the tone Sky used while calling her foster brother a halfwit. She'd used the same tone when talking about her own brothers. "It doesn't matter. I'm—"

"'Tis obvious you love him as well." Sky rolled her eyes. "God's blood, but the MacKintosh are a stubborn lot, and I trow the McGladreys are as well."

Love him? She couldn't deny it, so she said nothing at all.

Sky took Meghan's hand. "Come, my lady. Hunter needs you. He's always been plagued by doubt when it comes to his place in our clan." She shook her head and sighed. "For all his prowess as a knight, he still carries a great deal of uncertainty within him—and anger. 'Tis a shame, really." She glanced at Meghan over her shoulder. "He is most frightened of the very thing that could rid him of his insecurity."

She couldn't imagine Hunter being afraid of anything. "What would that be?"

"Why, giving his heart, of course." Sky frowned as if she doubted Meghan had the wits to put two and two together. "Hunter is afraid of losing the rigid control he exerts over every aspect of his life. Why else do you think he wants to wed me? For pity's sake, *I'm* his *sister*! 'Tis security and assurance he seeks. Nothing more. He feels no passion for me, nor do I feel aught but sisterly affection for him. I want my brother to be happy. He needs you. 'Tis certain this is why the faerie led him to you."

Her stomach knotted. Could that really be the reason she'd come to this century? Had the faerie brought them together because Hunter needed her? There was no doubt the two of them were drawn to each other. He fought it, while she tried to hide it.

She should have realized everyone would be able to pick up on the attraction she and Hunter shared. At least now she knew for certain she hadn't imagined his part of the equation. Still, what good did it do her? She had a place and a family across time, and the possibility of never seeing them again tore her to pieces. And if she couldn't get home, Hunter might never admit he cared for her. Where would that leave her?

Brokenhearted and alone, that's where. She didn't want to marry Tieren. It wouldn't be right, and the possibility that she might have to just to survive held no appeal. He deserved so much more than she could give him.

"Hunter will join us in the solar anon, and Edward only awaits his presence before beginning. I dinna wish to miss a single word of Edward's tale. Do you no' want to hear it told?"

"Sure."

They reached the solar at the same time Hunter came up the back stairway. One glance at his face, and her heart slid into a downward spiral. He had a haunted look about him. His mouth was drawn into a tight line as his gaze darted from her to Sky and back again. Saying nothing, he opened the door for them.

Sky entered the room first. Meghan followed. A second before she crossed the threshold, Hunter's hand came to rest at the small of her back. Even that slight touch sent a rush of longing through her. She wanted to turn around and wrap him up in her arms. The overwhelming need to comfort him stole her breath. Just as quickly, he took his hand away, leaving her bereft.

Benches from the great hall had been set around the room, and all were seated. Catching her attention, Sky patted the spot beside her where the women were situated. She settled herself next to True and Malcolm's daughter. All the jealousy she'd felt toward Sky melted away. Maybe they could be friends after all.

As if sensing her feelings, Sky nudged her with her shoulder and sent her a warm smile. She smiled back. Of course Sky sensed her emotions. That's what the MacKintosh did—some of them anyway.

Her gaze roamed to Hunter, only to find him staring at her. She nodded, trying to send him reassurance. He gave her a slight nod back.

"We would hear the reasons why Hunter's mother took him from his birthright, and why you seek him now," William said, taking his place at the scarred oak table that served as his desk.

Edward remained standing, his posture proud and straight, and his two sons flanked him. Both of the younger men remained stoic and silent. "I would have your word first, my lords, that naught said this eve shall leave this room. It is imperative."

The earl glanced at Hunter, and then at Malcolm and Robley. They nodded their assent. "Lydia, my dear . . . ?"

"Of course we shall keep it to ourselves, my lord." She arched a single brow at her husband, and a round of feminine head-bobbing ensued.

"What do you ken of your clan, lad?" Edward turned to Hunter, who leaned against the wall.

"I ken naught of the MacConnell clan," he said, the muscles in his jaw twitching away.

Edward sighed, and his expression held regret. "The MacConnell clan once held all of the western seaboard of Scotia. We were a vast and great kingdom." He scratched at his full beard. "Och, this next part you might find . . . difficult to accept. The first MacConnell, our founder, came here from Eire and wed one of the ancient ones, a *Tuatha Dé Danann* princess named Áine."

When that bomb didn't elicit an outcry, Edward gaped around the room. Poor guy. He had no way of knowing nearly half the people in the earl's solar carried faerie genes.

"Go on," Malcolm encouraged.

"The alliance gave us certain advantages, and for centuries we prospered. Our king's progeny carried uncommon . . . abilities, as do many of their direct line to this day." Again he peered around at the faces of those gathered as if gauging their reaction. "In the olden days, before Christianity came to our land, unions forged between the fae and the MacConnells were no' uncommon. Many of our clan carry fae blood, but . . ."

"But?" Hunter sent the man a hard stare.

"But no' our most recent laird, the old baron DúnConnell." Edward's tone held bitterness. "The gifts were strong in your da, and it caused quite a rift between father and son. Your grandsire Alastair was a devout man, hard and unyielding. He looked upon anything having to do with the fae or the old ways with distrust and hatred. He looked upon those possessing fae gifts as heretics. Your da and his father were estranged, and when your da wed your ma, the baron finally had an excuse to banish Mahon from the clan."

"Yet my mother *named* me after him?" Hunter straightened off the wall, his hands fisted at his sides.

"Aye. Joan was a spirited lass." Edward's mouth turned up in a brief smile. "I believe 'twas an act of defiance on her part. She claimed the baron as your grandsire, whilst the baron denied her very existence."

Raking his fingers through his hair, Hunter growled deep in his throat. His eyes narrowed. "You said *was*. The baron *was* a hard man."

"Aye. You have it aright. He has passed." Edward looked around the room, meeting each of the men's eyes in turn. "His eldest and middle sons died years ago. Young Alastair . . . er . . . *Hunter* is the last remaining heir in the baron's direct line. He is our clan's laird and our liege lord, and we've come to bring him home."

Hunter moved to one of the benches and dropped down. He'd gone pale, and emotions played across his face in rapid succession. Disbelief, anger and grief were plain to see. "No' a word have I heard in all these years, and now you tell me . . ." He shook his head. "I'm a baron?"

"At the time, all who loved you thought it best you remain here where the baron's hatred could no' touch you." Edward sent Hunter a pleading look. "None kent how far old Alastair would go in his zealousness to rid the clan of fae influence. I escorted your ma here for her safety. I left you here thinking I'd done the best I could for you."

"There's more." True stood, her face ashen. "You must tell us all."

Edward's gaze flew to her. He studied her intently, understanding dawning in his eyes. "Aye. There's more, my lady. Our holdings are but a small portion of what we once held, but they are rich in resources. We are surrounded on all sides by the MacKenzies, who wish to destroy us and steal what is ours. We've been harried, raided, ambushed and under siege for more than a decade. The baron and his eldest son were both murdered by the accursed MacKenzies. We canna survive without a strong laird to lead us."

Edward nodded toward Hunter. "One of our clan's wisewomen had a foreseeing. 'Tis how I kent Hunter still lived amongst the MacKintosh clan. Young Hunter will rebuild our clan, bring us strength and lead us once more into prosperity."

Meghan's chest filled with pride for Hunter. He was a born leader. She'd recognized that right away, and now he would lead an entire clan. She needed to talk to him, or listen at any rate. She couldn't bear seeing him so torn up.

Malcolm grunted and rubbed his forehead. "This comes as quite a shock. His mother and I have missed him sorely these past five years, and he's just recently come home to us from the continent. Now you tell us he's to return to the MacConnells to fight your battles for you?"

"Aye. 'Tis so. We would ha' come sooner, but . . . first we had an errand to attend to." Edward pulled a folded piece of vellum from his sporran. A blob of dark-red wax with an emblem pressed into it sealed it shut. "Our king has already recognized Hunter's succession." He held it out. "I did no' wish to take any chances. Young Alastair's patents have been drawn and recorded. He has already been granted the title and all of the lands and estates that come with it."

Hunter lunged to his feet and snatched the vellum from Edward.

His hands trembled as he broke the seal, opened it and read. Handing it to Malcolm, he glared at the MacConnells. "If I refuse to accept, is there someone else to—"

"You canna refuse to accept, my lord. Your king has recognized you as the new baron of DúnConnell, and that is who you are." Edward reached again into his sporran, this time drawing forth a signet ring. He handed it to him.

Hunter studied the ring. It held a crest with a bloodred ruby set above it. He dropped it into his sporran. "Baron or no, mayhap I'll leave for the continent." He lifted his chin. "The MacConnells have done naught for me. I see no reason to do aught for them."

"Hunter, you don't mean that." The words left Meghan's mouth before she knew she meant to say them.

"Do I no', my lady?" He turned his bitterness toward her.

Instinct drove her, and she shot off the bench. "If you will excuse us"—she strode to Hunter's side and wrapped her hands around his biceps—"the baron and I need to talk. I need to—"

"Knock some sense into him?" Erin quipped.

"Exactly," she muttered, scowling at him. "A moment of your time, my lord?" The pain she glimpsed in his eyes brought a sting to hers. She needed to get him out of the solar and away from Edward and his sons.

"Go, lad," Malcolm said softly. "We'll speak of this again on the morrow."

Hunter's head snapped up. "We are to leave at daybreak for Inverness."

"Under the circumstances, I think we can wait one more day." Once again she wanted to wrap her arms around him. He was definitely channeling the lost little boy he'd been after his granny died.

Hunter glanced at the MacConnells where they continued to stand, and then his eyes swung to hers. "Aye, let us take a stroll, my lady." He ushered her to the door and into the corridor.

"Where can we find some privacy?"

"To the loch . . . where we skipped stones across the water." He gripped her hand again.

"OK. To the lake." Neither of them spoke as they left the keep. He practically dragged her through the kitchen, ignoring the startled stares of the cook and her helpers. They continued on along the path through the herb garden toward the postern gate.

How could she get through to him? What could she say that would break through the shield of anger he'd wrapped around himself? Once they were through the gate, they followed the path to the same place where he'd nearly kissed her right out of her tunic and tights. Her pulse kicked up, and her breath caught in the middle of her throat.

Sunlight danced along the surface of the lake. Like tiny dazzling creatures from another world, its brilliance skimmed and hopped across the crests of the waves stirred by the breeze. She shielded her eyes against the brightness, wondering what time it was. The days grew longer and longer this far north, and the sun finally disappeared around eleven.

A slight fishy odor hung in the air. Not a bad or rotten smell, just a lake smell. Thick pine boughs sheltered the spot from prying eyes, and a lone oak stood at the edge of the clearing. How many couples had taken advantage of the seclusion for a bit of privacy? What did she have to do to seduce Hunter into . . .

Ack. What was she thinking? "Talk to me," she ordered, turning to face him.

"I dinna ken what to say."

"You're angry."

He began to pace along the shore. "For certes. Would you no' be? Mayhap if things had been different, my ma would no' have died of a fever. I would ha' grown up without a doubt about where I belong or of my rank." He stopped and plowed both hands through his hair. "By the saints, I'm a baron. If I'd remained with my clan or been sent to foster with an allied clan, I would no' have been reduced to beggary." He glared. "Would such no' make you angry?"

"Yep. You have every right to be angry, but it's preventing you from seeing the big picture."

"What *picture* is that, Meghan?" He continued to pace.

"Stop, Hunter." She blocked his path and placed her hands on his chest. "Let go of the anger for just a minute. Try to get past the hurt. You're not thinking clearly."

He grunted.

She wrapped her arms around his waist and laid her cheek against his pounding heart. "The people who loved you did what they did to keep you safe. They did what they thought best. You can't blame Edward or your clan for your mother's death. She may have died anyway, no matter where you were hidden away." She peered into his stormy gray eyes.

"You heard Edward. Your gnarly old granddad was a zealot. If you had remained anywhere near him, you couldn't have kept your fae abilities a secret for long, especially if he'd been looking for them. He banished his own son. I shudder to think what he might've done to you."

His arms tightened around her, and he rested his chin on top of her head. Some of the tension left him. "Edward could have placed me with another sect of the MacConnell clan. There are still MacConnell holdings scattered along the western coast. I should have been raised as a noble, whether or no' my grandsire acknowledged me."

"Yes, you should have, but your mother wanted to come home. Anyway, thanks to True and Malcolm, you kind of were raised as a noble." She placed her hands on either side of his face and drew his gaze down to hers. "You would not be the man you are today if you hadn't gone through what you did as a child. It's your early years that have shaped you and made you the great leader that you are today."

"Humph. You think me a great leader?" He brushed his lips across her forehead.

"Of course I do. Set aside your anger and grief. Think about the people who desperately need your help. Think about the innocent lives you can save. Would you condemn your clansmen, knowing they had nothing to do with the decisions your grandfather made? Do you really want to leave them leaderless and without direction or hope?"

"Nay." One side of his mouth quirked up. "What am I to do about you, Beag Curaidh?"

Her heart bounced around in her chest. "What do you want to do with me?"

"What is right." He drew her closer and nuzzled her temple.

"What might that be?" She held her breath, anticipation and— she had to admit—a smidgeon of dread obliterating her ability to think. What if he asked her to stay? Would she? Could she be happy here knowing she'd never see her family again? How had she managed to find herself straddled between the future and the past?

"I snatched you from your time and from your kin. I have sworn to return you to your place and time." His gaze roamed over her face, uncertainty once again clouding his features. "Have I no' vowed to do so? And yet . . ."

She waited for the rest of the sentence, but he said nothing more. Impatient, she poked his chest. "And yet?"

He shrugged his broad shoulders. "I find myself loath to part with you." He stared into her eyes, his expression one of consternation. "I have come to rely upon your counsel. You alone give me respite from the barrage of emotional jetsam I must endure each day." He cradled her face between his large hands and ran his thumbs over her cheeks. "More than anything, I wish you to come with me to DúnConnell."

Her heart filled to overflowing. He wanted her with him. "As what? What am I to you, Hunter?"

At her question, he stepped back. Tension stiffened his posture, and she felt his withdrawal keenly. His face a mask, once again he hid behind the walls of defense he'd built around himself. Sky was right. Hunter feared giving his heart. She wanted to shake him silly until the ambivalence toward her fell out of the holes in his thinking.

"Why, I would have you train my garrison in the ways of mixed martial arts, of course. You would help me adjust to my new position and act as my topmost advisor." He averted his gaze. "Mayhap I'll put you in command of my garrison. What say you to that?"

"I don't think it would go over very well with the rest of your men." Her hopes skipped and sank like the pebbles they'd tossed into the lake. "You should make Tieren your commander. He's the perfect choice, and you can trust him."

"See how you aid me? If Tieren will accept the position, 'tis done." He turned her toward the path to the keep. "I will do what is honorable and see that you are returned home as I have vowed. How will I get on without my most valued advisor close to hand?"

"What about Sky?"

"Ah, Sky . . ." He grunted again and placed his hands on her shoulders to propel her forward. "We must return to the keep. I wish to speak with the earl and my foster father, and I want you there."

What did "Ah, Sky" mean? Now that he held a much higher rank, did he intend to keep hounding his foster sister until she caved and married him? Probably. Suddenly her heart weighed a ton, and she had a tough time keeping her tears at bay.

A few minutes later, she found herself once again in the earl's solar, only this time, she was the only woman present. Tieren had joined the group, which consisted of Hunter, Malcolm, the earl and Edward. Hunter seated her on a bench nearest the wall, and if the others found anything strange about her being there, they gave no clue. He took a seat beside her.

"I've a favor to ask of you, my lord," Hunter said, facing the earl. "I need soldiers to quell the assault upon my clan. Will you loan me one hundred men?"

"You dinna even have to ask, Hunter," William said. "You have our aid, whatever you may need."

"Rest assured. The MacConnells and the MacKintosh are now closely tied." Malcolm grinned at Edward. "In fact, my wife is a MacConnell, but that is a tale best left for another time. 'Twill take a few days to gather the men. We'll take fifty from Loch Moigh and fifty from Meikle Geddes. I'll send word to some of our smaller holdings to have men from each keep come to us to ensure we are no' compromised whilst so many are away."

Edward shot Meghan a look so filled with gratitude, it brought a flush of heat to her cheeks.

"My heartfelt thanks, my lords. Your aid is most appreciated and welcome."

"Your clan, Hunter?" Tieren's brow furrowed, looking from Edward to Hunter. "What have I missed?"

Hunter arched a brow at Tieren. "I am baron of DúnConnell and laird to clan MacConnell."

Tieren let out a raucous laugh. "How did this come about?"

"I will tell you later. I ken you have accepted a place at Meikle Geddes, but I am hoping you might consider coming with me. Will you accept the post as commander of my garrison, Tieren? I can think of no one more qualified. I want no other guarding me and mine."

Tieren's brow rose, and he glanced at Meghan. "What of Inverness?"

"I see no reason to delay our journey, and I have need of my armor and gear. It appears I'll be shall be using them oft in the foreseeable future."

He turned to Edward. "Once our men are gathered, you and your sons will accompany the MacKintosh soldiers to DúnConnell.

Make haste, and have the men begin patrolling our borders in groups augmented with our garrison. Get word out that we are now allied with the MacKintosh and that the earl of Fife is kin to me. The MacKenzies are no' enemies with the MacKintosh at present, and I trow they will no' wish to become so in future."

"Aye, my lord." Edward gave him a slight bow.

Hunter turned once again to Tieren. "We shall depart for Inverness at daybreak as we planned. I dinna wish to thwart Cecil's plans, whatever they may be. He must be dealt with before I take up my responsibilities at home."

He'd gone from an angry little boy to a decisive commander in a nanosecond, and Meghan reveled in the fact that she'd helped him make the transition. Maybe that's what she'd been sent here to do. Her heart gave a painful squeeze. She was torn between longing for her family and longing to stay with Hunter, and lately, the scale was tipping more in favor of remaining by Hunter's side. Sky had said he needed her, and that's why she'd been brought to him. Why didn't Hunter see it? Frustration banded her chest. Why did he fight so hard against what they felt for each other?

No matter how she felt, in a week or so, Hunter would send her home. She'd leave this place and the people she'd come to care for so much—separated forever through time from the man she loved.

Rubbing her gritty eyes, Meghan surveyed the village. The sun was just beginning to come up, and the air was filled with the sound of birdsong. Man, she missed coffee. She yawned as she fastened her gear to the back of her horse's saddle. What would she give for a nice big thermos filled with medium roast with lots of sugar and cream? Her mouth watered just thinking about it.

All around her, the men she would travel with prepared to leave for Inverness. They'd gathered outside of the stables on the mainland way too early for her liking. The air held the damp chill of early morning, and the sun had just begun to brighten the eastern horizon. She yawned again, and a slight shiver sluiced through her.

"Meghan." Hunter came up beside her. "Did you no' sleep well?"

"No, I didn't." Too many things on her mind had kept her up, like losing the people here, and the possibility she might not be able to go home to the family she'd lost in the future. Plus, when she had slept, she'd dreamed about the villain she'd slain on the way to Aberdeen.

"Are you able to ride?" Hunter placed a hand on her shoulder.

Memories of being sheltered and held on his lap while they traveled filled her mind. If she said she couldn't manage, would he hold her in front of him again? "I'm fine. I just need to wake up." She caught a glimpse of Cecil storming out of the inn. Judging by the way he moved and the look on his face, he wasn't happy. "Here comes trouble."

"Och, I meant to speak to you about this at supper." Hunter kept his eye on the approaching knight. "There have been a few changes in our plans. Mayhap 'tis best if you dinna ken what they are."

"*What* has become of my two guardsmen?" Cecil strode toward her, his face filled with rage.

Meghan looked from him to Hunter, unsure whom he was addressing with the question.

"What mean you by your angry tone, Sir Cecil?" Hunter stepped in front of her. "How can any here ken where your men-at-arms might be? Do we command them?"

"I wouldst address the lady you shield," he bit out. "*She* kens what has become of them."

"Me?" Meghan scowled around Hunter's shoulder. "I've never even talked to them. I had nothing to do with your stupid guards. Why would you think I did?"

"Why indeed?" Cecil snarled. "Did Nevan and his lads no' vanish the very day you appeared?"

"Wait." She blinked. "The other day you wanted to marry me, and now you're accusing me of . . . What are you accusing me of now, anyway? Witchery or being a faerie? I can't keep up."

"Such insolence!" He raised his hand as if he meant to strike her. She stepped out from behind Hunter. Her muscles tensed for battle, she assumed a defensive pose. "Bring it." Hunter grabbed her arm and shoved her behind him again. "Hey," she protested.

"Don't be absurd, Cecil." Tieren joined Hunter, walling her off from the angry knight. "Lady Meghan has no' left the keep or the island for a se'nnight. Before you cast such foul accusations, mayhap ask if any of the villagers have seen your men."

"I have done so, sir." Cecil kept his evil eye on her. "None has aught to say."

"So you surmise a mere lass is at fault?" Hunter grunted. "I trow you may have it aright, and a lass or two are keeping your lads bound to their beds, but 'twas no' this lady."

The MacKintosh warriors laughed, nudging each other with knowing glances as they moved closer to create a circle of protection. Gratitude warmed her heart. "I don't know where your men are, Cecil. I was with Hunter's family last night, and I never saw your guards."

"Do you need to lay eyes upon them to work your spells?" he spat out.

"Here, now," Angus ground out, coming to join the two men protecting her. "I was at the inn yester eve, and I had an ale or two with your guardsmen. They were both well sotted by the time I left to seek my bed. The baron DúnConnell has it aright. Your lads are sleeping it off somewhere—most likely in the arms of a couple of the village lasses."

"The . . . the baron?" Cecil blustered. "What nonsense is this? I see no baron here."

205

"He stands before you, *Sir* Cecil," Tieren said, grabbing Hunter's shoulder. "Hunter has the missive from King James to prove his most recent rise in rank."

"I think it best that you travel from here to your home on your own." Hunter's tone held an edge of menace. "We'll leave word with the stable master of your direction, and your guardsmen will join you once they are roused. You are no' welcome to travel with us this day or any other."

"Och, I . . ." Cecil stammered.

"Lady Meghan is under our protection." Tieren widened his stance. "If you persist with your unfounded aspersions beyond the MacKintosh borders, you will answer to me. I command the soldiers who serve baron DúnConnell. He is my liege lord."

"So you've decided to accept my offer?" Hunter cast Tieren a crooked grin. "My thanks. 'Twill keep you quite occupied."

"Aye, I've decided to take the post, unless—"

"Mayhap you have it aright, and my guards will join us upon the road to Inverness yet this morn. Indeed, I am certain they will," Cecil capitulated. "I've no wish to travel the roads alone, and there is still the matter of my armor and gear. My most sincere apologies, Lady Meghan. Once again I have wronged you."

Her breakfast turned into an indigestible mass in her stomach. She kept her mouth shut. She wasn't about to accept or respond to his *most insincere* apology.

"Nay." Hunter turned to Angus. "Have four of our men escort Sir Cecil as far as the MacKintosh border to our south. When his guards are found, inform them of their master's whereabouts and see that they leave as well. I will have your armor and gear sent to you, Sir Cecil. You have my word."

Relieved, Meghan put her foot in the stirrup and began to hoist herself up into the saddle. Hunter's hands encircled her waist. He lifted her off the ground and placed in the saddle as if she weighed no more than the woolen blankets fastened to the leather behind her. Once she was settled, he placed his hands on either side of her. "You have naught to fear, lass."

She nodded, her gaze connecting with his. Awareness and something deeper flowed between them, and she lost herself in his serious gray eyes. Saying good-bye to Hunter would be the single most difficult thing she'd ever faced in her short life. Blinking back the threat of tears, she fussed with the reins and adjusted her feet in the stirrups. "Let's go."

"Aye." Hunter backed away. "We have wasted enough time. Let us depart. Tieren, take the lead. Meghan, ride behind him, and I will be right behind you." He spared Cecil a glare. "You are no longer welcome on MacKintosh land, nor are you welcome at DúnConnell."

"It matters no'." Cecil took the reins of his horse from the stable lad. He mounted and swung his horse's head around. "'Twill make no difference."

Angus grabbed Cecil's reins and held them fast. Two soldiers hastened to his side. "No' so fast, sir. There is the matter of your *escort* to attend to."

Meghan and her guards took off at a canter, and Hunter rode beside her, not behind her as he'd said. Once they were out of the village, she turned to him. "Where are Cecil's guards?"

"Both of them are ensconced within the dungeon at Meikle Geddes, and there they will remain until Cecil is far from Loch Moigh."

Once they reached the crest of the first hill, Meghan stole a last backward glance at the village. Then she turned to catch a glimpse of the island keep. Sadness tugged at her. She'd miss these good people. Erin, True, Sky and the twins had risen early to eat breakfast with her. She'd said her good-byes to everyone else the night before. Her chest ached, and a tear slid down her cheek. She wiped it away and frowned.

'Twill make no difference. That's what Cecil had said before they left. What did he mean by the remark? She bit her lower lip. Worry niggled at her. Once again she rode into the unknown, with the possibility of danger around each bend. Fifteenth-century Scotland was *not* for the fainthearted, that's for sure.

She adjusted the leather belt of her scabbard where it crossed her chest. Then she checked the three sheathed daggers Robley and Malcolm had given her. The blades now hung from her belt. Two more were hidden away in each of her boots, courtesy of Erin and True. She wore her own leather tunic with the McGladrey crest, and chain mail hung heavy over her shoulders and torso.

She lifted her chin, threw back her shoulders and faced the road ahead. Nobody could accuse her of being faint of heart. No matter what came her way, she'd face it and fight.

CHAPTER ELEVEN

Hunter couldn't tear his eyes from his wee warrior as they rode out of the village. She checked her weapons, touching each sheathed blade to assure herself she was prepared for battle. Hadn't he oft done the same? His heart filled with such tenderness that he ached with it. He ached with wanting her.

Meghan was such a delectable mix of vulnerability, bravery and generosity that the very sight of her elicited every protective instinct he possessed. She thought of herself as a knight, ready and able to defend those in her care. To his way of thinking, Meghan was the ideal of what every Scottish lass should be—strong, yet wholly feminine and as lovely as the gorse blooming in the glens.

She lifted her chin a proud notch and straightened her posture. Another stone in the turret he'd built around his heart broke free. He'd give his life to see her safe. The sudden realization brought a sting to the back of his eyes. The best he could do for Meghan was to see her safely returned to her home. Blinking against the burn, he turned his attention to other matters.

Scanning the sides of the road and the men behind him, he sent his senses out to make certain all was well. Then he turned his mind to everything that had transpired. In a single day his fortunes and rank had changed. His greatest wish had come true. Baron DúnConnell, no less.

Hunter spurred Doireann into a trot, joining Tieren at the front of the line. "We have much to discuss."

"Aye." One side of Tieren's mouth quirked up. "Naming me your commander is bound to create resentment amongst the MacConnell warriors. Surely the present commander will demand the right to challenge me."

"If there is a current commander." Hunter arched a brow. "Does the possibility of a challenge trouble you?"

"Nay. 'Tis best that the matter be settled sooner rather than later. Resentment only grows with time if no' dealt with properly." He shifted in his saddle. "There are likely those who will try to usurp you as well. Mayhap you have cousins who will argue that, since your father was banished from your clan, you have no right to ascension." Tieren's expression turned somber. "Once we have trounced any who wish to test us, 'twill be important for you to hold a fealty ceremony."

Hunter nodded. "Like you, I'd rather see matters settled straightaway. Neither of us ken what we're walking into once we reach my holding. I trow the MacConnells have been fairly decimated by the MacKenzies." He frowned. "Och, Tieren, for a certainty, we ride into peril on every front."

"Dinna fash." Tieren grinned. "Betwixt the two of us, we will turn things 'round, especially with the loan of the earl's men-at-arms." Tieren glanced at him. "I am certain Giselle will not return Meghan to her time. I mean to ask her to come with me to DúnConnell."

"Nothing is certain where Giselle is concerned." Hunter's jaw clenched. "I do not want her embroiled in the danger we face when I take my place as baron. She is better off in her own time with her kin to look after her." He couldn't bear the thought of anything happening to her. He'd rather live without her in his world than put her in harm's way. "Should Giselle agree to send her home, do you still intend to ask Meghan if you can accompany her?" He held his breath. For more reasons than he cared to admit, he dreaded the answer.

"Nay." Tieren huffed out a breath. "Someone has to guard your back, and that onerous task falls to me. The earl and your foster father made it abundantly clear where my responsibilities lie, little brother."

"Onerous, eh?" Hunter said with a frown. "When did Malcolm and the earl speak to you thusly?"

"Shortly after you asked the earl for the loan of his soldiers. After everyone left, they kept me back to discuss the matter at length. I owe them a great debt. Had it no' been for Malcolm's sponsorship, I'd be knee-deep in barley and hops right now. I'd be brewing ale with no hope of rising above my station." He reached out and gave Hunter a friendly shove. "Onerous indeed, for as we've already established, you are oft blind to what is directly before you. You need me."

Meghan rode up between them. She glanced at Tieren, then at Hunter. "What are you talking about?"

"Och, we were discussing what needs doing once we reach DúnConnell." Hunter couldn't help but notice the way her face fell at his words. Why might that be? Her place was in the future where she would be safe. Surely she did not want to stay, not for him. She must have suitors aplenty in her century. She'd marry, have bairns and forget all about him. His heart wrenched at the thought.

How would he fare without his most valued advisor, his respite from emotional onslaught—his . . . *love?* Nay! He would not lose his head or his heart. Men who allowed themselves to be caught up in passion and romantic love were fools, and he was no fool.

"Thank you for sending Cecil away," she said. "I would've been on pins and needles this whole trip if he'd been with us. Now I can enjoy my last few days in Scotland in peace."

She sighed, and the sadness carried upon that single exhalation cleaved his heart in two.

"Leaving our time and Scotland saddens you, my lady?" Tieren winked at her. "If so, my offer for your hand still stands. Come to DúnConnell with me."

Meghan said naught, but her cheeks blossomed with color, and she bit her lip. Once again jealousy and possessiveness trapped Hunter in its iron jaws. Never had he been so at odds. He wanted her for himself, and that bedeviled him more than any enemy he might face. The passion she alone elicited, the soul-deep longing to have her by his side . . . Nay, such wrenching emotions would be his downfall. He had a responsibility to his clan and to his title, and he would not be diverted.

"Of course leaving Scotland upsets me." Meghan sighed again. "Leaving all of you, the earl and his family, never knowing how things turn out for the two of you at DúnConnell . . . It's tearing me up inside, but the thought of never seeing my family again makes me sad too." Her shoulders slumped. "At least in the future I'll be able to look you up in history books. Then I'll know whether or not . . . I'll find out . . ."

"Tell me you dinna doubt the outcome, lass." Tieren laughed. "I'm insulted."

"You are not." She grinned. "You're way too cocky to be insulted."

"'Twill take a good deal of sweat and blood to turn things 'round at DúnConnell, to be sure." Hunter grunted. "If credence can be given to the words of the wisewoman Edward spoke of, the MacConnells will prevail. I will build up our defenses so that none think to trouble us again."

"I wonder what shape your keep is in," Meghan mused. "Do you have any idea how many MacConnells there are, or how many soldiers you have in your service?"

"Nay." Hunter shook his head. "My clan has been without their baron for several months. Before traveling to Loch Moigh, Edward journeyed to Stirling to inform our king of my grandsire's demise and to register my patents with the record keepers. I imagine my holdings are in a sorry state by now."

"I don't know." She tilted her head as if giving the matter a great deal of thought. "If Edward is any indication, I suspect he placed good men in positions of temporary leadership in his absence. I'll bet he's the current commander of your garrison. Did you think to ask him?"

"I did no'." Hunter cast her a wry grin. "I wonder about his sons. Neither of them entered into any of our conversations, but I could no' detect any enmity from them." He turned to Tieren. "If indeed he is the present commander, your challenge may come from one or the other of Edward's sons."

"If you're smart," Meghan said, "you'll form a council of elders, including Edward. That will gain your clan's loyalty and their respect. Plus, the council will help you get to know the lay of the land."

"'Tis sound advice, Beag Curaidh." Hunter gave her a slight bow. "Rest assured I will do as you suggest."

"'Tis a shame we did no' spend time in the lists with Edward's lads," Tieren said. "'Twould have been advantageous to gain some measure of their skill."

Meghan flashed them both a pointed look. "After so many years defending themselves against the MacKenzies, you're going to find the MacConnell soldiers are either a well-oiled fighting machine or in total disarray."

Hunter frowned. "A *well-oiled fighting machine*, like a trebuchet?"

She blew out a breath. "Your soldiers are either going to be a well-trained, tightly coordinated unit, or you're facing a hot mess."

"*Hot mess?*" Tieren's brow rose. "Did you no' say you found me hot? Now I dinna ken whether you praised or maligned me that day."

Meghan laughed, and the sound caused a familiar tumbling sensation in Hunter's chest. 'Twas easy enough to grasp her meaning, and he liked it not at all that she'd told Tieren she viewed him as such. "Am I *hot* as well?" He scowled at her.

She chuckled, touched her mount's sides with her heels and cantered ahead. "Definitely, my lord," she called over her shoulder. "Steamy hot."

Pleased, he smirked at Tieren. "Steamy."

Tieren arched a brow. "Aye, steaming like a fresh pile of—"

"Dinna say it." He spurred his horse into a canter. "You go too far ahead of us, Beag Curaidh," he warned, once again admiring her horsemanship. When the time came, how would he manage to part with her?

Hunter surveyed the spot he'd chosen for their camp. They were close to the shores of Loch Mór, and nestled in the foothills of the Monadhliath Mountains. Well hid, and without Cecil's presence, he worried far less. Still, he would not allow a fire. He saw no reason to tempt fate.

They'd been riding hard for two days, and in two more he and his small band would reach Inverness. "Oatcakes and jerky for supper. I dinna wish to risk a fire."

With quick efficiency, Meghan and the men each did their part to set up camp and unsaddle their mounts. Hunter removed his gear from Doireann's saddle, and then he placed his things where he planned to take his rest. Each night Meghan had slept betwixt him and Tieren, as she had on the journey to Aberdeenshire. Having her so close whilst not being able to make love to her was wreaking havoc upon his mood.

He'd awakened before dawn this morn, facing her with his arms around her and her head nestled against his neck. His tarse had been as hard as stone against her hip, and he'd been thrusting against her.

Good thing she'd been sound asleep—even better that he'd been able to disentangle himself before anyone else noticed. He scrubbed his hands over his face and heaved a sigh.

'Twould be best to sleep a good distance from her for the rest of the journey. He had enough men to stand guard. She didn't need to be sheltered betwixt him and Tieren any longer. Come to think on it, he didn't want Tieren that close to her either. He sighed and returned to unsaddling Doireann.

The spot he'd chosen provided fodder for the horses and a natural enclosure of rocky outcroppings to keep their mounts from wandering. He moved to unload one of the packhorses. "Give the horses a measure of grain this eve. They've earned it, but form a guard to take them to the loch for a drink first."

"I'd like to bathe in the lake if I could," Meghan said. "Would that be possible?"

Tieren came to her side. "Whilst we water the horses, I'll look for a likely spot. We canna let you go anywhere without a guard."

"Fine, so long as I have my privacy," she said.

"A screen of sorts can be fashioned with blankets and branches," Hunter offered. "I expect we'll all want a good wash. Take your turn first, lass."

She nodded and went back to stowing her things and procuring her evening meal. Tieren and two other men led the horses down the path to the loch for a drink. Once the men and horses returned, Tieren picked up a few blankets, rope and a hatchet. "Gather what you need, my lady. I have chosen a place for bathing."

Hunter fought the urge to follow. 'Twould only torment him further to be so close to Meghan whilst she bathed. Would she remove all of her clothing? His groin tightened. Growling low in his throat, he dug into his pack for jerky and a bannock. He settled himself on the ground to eat, keeping his eyes trained upon the path Tieren, Meghan and the two guards had taken to the loch.

He trusted Tieren and his men. He did. Still, the need to guard her himself thrummed through him, turning his bannock to ash in his mouth. His senses alert, he kept an ear cocked in case she should call out.

Ridiculous. A MacKintosh man would never lift a hand against a lady. None would assault her, and he'd best turn his mind to something else.

A twig snapped, and hurried footsteps approached. Hunter's attention returned to the path. Meghan strode into camp. Her expression tight, she clutched her things to her chest. She kept her eyes on the path and headed straight for her place in the circle they'd formed. Tieren followed a short distance behind. His shoulders were curled in, and his head was bowed in defeat. Instead of stopping once he reached their camp, Tieren continued walking in the direction of the horses. Hunter could easily read his friend's hurt and the deep sting of rejection.

Hunter made his way to Meghan's side. "What happened between you and Tieren?" he asked in a low tone.

"Nothing." Fresh color bloomed in her cheeks.

"I can see by your blush that you do no' speak the truth." He leaned closer to peer into her eyes. "Something happened. Tell me."

She fussed with her gear, rearranged her blanket and gave a little shrug. "Tieren asked me again if I would marry him." Her eyes darted to him and away just as quickly. "I told him no, and that I don't love him. It wouldn't be right or fair to him."

"Ah." Hunter nodded. "I see."

She met his gaze, hers searching. "Do you?"

"Aye. 'Tis never pleasant to deliver news we ken will cause hurt. He'll mend, Beag Curaidh. Before long the two of you will once again be easy in each other's company."

"Of course." She went back to laying her sheepskin and blankets as if readying herself to sleep. "You can go now. I'm fine. Tieren is fine."

Her tone carried a bite, and it puzzled him. Clearly she wished for privacy. "Good eve to you, my lady." He bowed and took his leave. In the face of Tieren's pain, he should not feel such relief. He should not, yet he did, and he could do naught to prevent the flare of triumph from igniting within him.

He moved his sleeping blankets to the side of camp directly opposite Meghan's, then set out for the loch. A thorough dunking in the frigid water would do him good.

Your enemies are near! Hunter went from deep sleep to fully alert in a trice. Was it Giselle's voice in his head that woke him? His skin prickled with the warning. Never before had the faerie spoken to him thus, but he suffered not a moment's doubt. Silently he crawled out of his blankets toward Tieren.

The sun had just begun its ascent above the eastern horizon, casting enough light that his friend would be able to read his signing. He poked him, motioning for silence when his commander tensed and woke.

"Wake the men and have them ready their weapons," he signed. *"Bunch blankets and whatever is to hand in our beds to give the appearance we still sleep. Our enemies approach."* Tieren set about his task with quiet precision.

Hunter gave three soft whistled calls of a warbler, a warning to their guards to return to camp. Then he crept to where Meghan slept. He covered her mouth to prevent her from crying out as he shook her. Her eyes grew wide as she startled awake, and he caught her hand as she gripped one of her daggers. She blinked when she recognized him. He motioned for her to be quiet and leaned close to whisper in her ear. "Gather your weapons and head due east. Hide in the hills until I come for you."

"Why?" she whispered back, her eyes clouded with confusion.

"We are about to be ambushed."

"I can help," she hissed. "You know I can fight."

"Aye, I ken well enough you can defend yourself." He couldn't help himself; he drew her into his arms. "I canna bear the thought of . . . of . . . Grant me this request, Beag Curaidh. Hide in the hills where I ken you will be safe." He crushed her to him and inhaled her sweet, clean scent. "I beg this of you."

"All right, Hunter." She stroked his shoulders. "I'll go if it will ease your mind."

"'Twill ease my mind considerably." He blew out a shaky breath and let go of her. "Stuff something under your blankets to give the appearance that you are still there. Load our supplies upon the pack-horses and take them with you. I dinna want the rouncies to run off, nor do I wish to lose our food." She nodded, and he backed away.

He watched to be sure she did as he commanded before readying himself for battle. Once he and his soldiers were prepared, they hid behind the ridge of stone forming a natural enclosure for their camp. Twenty paces from where they had slept but a few moments ago, he and his men hunkered down to watch—and to wait. It didn't take long.

A dozen shadows crept toward their encampment, followed by two men on horseback. One of them wore a tunic emblazoned with a crest—*MacKenzie*. The other man was far too familiar—Cecil.

The enemy snuck into their camp like the dishonorable curs they were. They spread out and positioned themselves above the lumpy forms under the blankets. Just as they reached to pull the blankets back, their swords ready to commit murder, Cecil called out, "Dinna kill the woman. She is mine."

A chill ran down Hunter's spine, and he ground his teeth. He gave the signal to wait. In that moment of chaos, when the enemy discovered they'd stabbed naught but blankets and brush, Hunter gave the war cry. He, Tieren and his six warriors charged over the ridge of stone and into their camp with swords drawn—eight against twelve.

"There," Cecil shouted, pointing at Hunter. "There is the new baron of DúnConnell."

"Kill him," the commander ordered, his voice dispassionate.

Tieren took up his place beside Hunter. Soon the two of them were surrounded. The sounds of battle filled his head, and battle lust thrummed in his veins. The MacKenzies formed a wedge, separating Tieren from him. It took all of Hunter's concentration to defend himself. Rage fueled his blows as he drove his attackers back. He needed to get to Cecil. He longed to drag him from his mount and separate his worthless head from his shoulders.

Awareness coursed through him like a river as another warrior approached from his right. Three against one was one too many. He needed help and gave a shrill whistle. Blocking blow after blow in defense, he couldn't get off any offensive strikes. He sensed the sword rising above his head from the third warrior. The two soldiers before him increased their efforts, distracting him from the death blow to come.

He caught a blur of movement in his periphery. She moved so fast he could scarce believe what he saw. Meghan ran with her sword drawn. She kicked out at the warrior about to deal his deathblow. Her boot connected with his enemy's chest. A grunt, the rush of air, and the warrior was on the ground. Meghan drew her sword from the dead man's chest and came to stand with her back to Hunter's and her bloody blade raised.

"By all that is holy, woman," he snapped. "I told you to hide in the hills until I came for you." Her presence frightened him enough that he forgot his fatigue and made a desperate sweeping arc with his sword. One of his attackers fell, and he turned all of his effort toward the second.

"You're welcome," Meghan huffed just as two more took the place of the slain warriors at their feet. She engaged one of them, her blade flashing out beside his ear.

"Tieren, lads," Hunter called out. "To me!" Fear for Meghan's safety clogged his throat. Where were the MacKintosh men who followed behind them? Now would be a good time for them to appear. He cast a glance about him. His soldiers were fully occupied, and Tieren was hemmed in.

"Shite." Desperate, he sucked in a deep breath and sent a plea to his ancestor. After all, 'twas she whose voice in his head had warned him of the ambush. *"Giselle, Áine . . . Granddam, I need your help. I beg of you—keep Meghan safe."*

He received no answer. No help came to him. Hunter's muscles screamed, and his lungs burned as he deflected the strikes coming at him from all directions. Meghan's sword rang out as she fought, guarding his back. *God, keep her safe!* he prayed. Pounding hoofbeats approached from behind him. A thudding sound, Meghan's moan, and suddenly the place where her warmth had radiated against him went cold.

Panic surged through him. He snatched a second sword off the ground and lunged, attacking mindlessly any soul unfortunate enough to get in his way. Slowly he gained ground, inching ever closer toward the edge of the battle—closer to the horses.

Two more MacKenzies fell. Finally, the battle turned in his favor. He could not walk without stepping over the bodies of their foes, and the air held the coppery scent of blood. Hunter raised his eyes just in time to see Cecil riding over a distant hill, Meghan draped over the betrayer's lap, still as death. Fear such as he'd never before experienced exploded in his chest. "Nay," he cried out.

"Hunter," Tieren shouted. "Go after her. The enemy commander has hied off like the coward that he is. MacKenzie filth, drop your weapons—or die," he commanded.

At his statement, the few remaining MacKenzies ran off in the direction from whence they'd come whilst sneaking into the camp. "Go after the cowards. Tieren, 'tis up to you. I'll no' have a single one of them escape the consequences of their perfidy this day. Once you've routed them all, gather our belongings and return to the road toward Inverness. Make camp by Loch Dún Seilcheig. Meghan and I will rejoin you there." *If he were not too late to save her, that is.*

His chest heaving, he ran toward the place where they'd hidden their horses. Doireann, saddled and ready, tossed his head when he caught sight of Hunter. The battle had excited the destriers, and their eyes showed white around the edges. They pawed the ground, and their ears pricked back and forth at the sound of their masters coming toward them.

Hunter could think of naught else but getting to Meghan. Aye, getting to Meghan and running his sword through Cecil's black heart. He swung up onto his stallion's back and urged him into a gallop in the direction he'd seen Cecil last. Over hills and culverts he sped, heedless of his mount's footing. When he crested the hill where last he'd seen Cecil, he brought Doireann to sudden halt. Searching frantically in every direction, dread lodged itself in his gut. He could find no sign of Cecil or Meghan. The rocky terrain beneath him held no imprint of their passing.

He shouted to the heavens, fear, anger and desperation chasing through him in equal measures. This very morn, Áine had spoken to him in the way he and True oft communicated. Yet the faerie did not answer him earlier when he'd pleaded for her help. Would she answer his pleas now? What choice did he have but to try? His lungs worked like a bellows, and his heart nearly pounded its way out of his chest. He struggled for control.

Opening his mind completely, he centered himself and poured out his energy, pleading for all he was worth, "*Áine, if you bear me any true affection, guide me now.*" He waited, certain that she would again refuse him.

But then his limbs began to tingle. Fatigue vanished, and an unnatural strength coursed through him. Somehow, Áine had joined herself to him. He felt it to his very marrow. Her magic arced along his nerves and rushed through his blood. Blue fire limned his body, but it did not burn his skin. Awash in wonder, he stared at the flames.

Why did he feel no fear? He'd always recoiled from anything having to do with the fae in the past. Yet now that he was engulfed in magic, he kent naught but relief. He was not alone. Hunter spurred his mount into a gallop certain that his fae ancestor would guide him.

Áine, in the guise of Madame Giselle, had spoken truly when last they'd met at the fair she'd conjured. She truly *did* care for him. Her maternal love swept through him in a surge so powerful he nearly wept. In his hour of greatest need, his ancestor had answered his plea, lending him but a small portion of her power to aid him. The soul-deep bond humbled him, and for the first time in his life, he let go of the constant control he held over himself. Meghan's life depended upon him, and he would not fail her.

The blue fire receded, whilst the strength remained. He reined Doireann in and searched the ground again for any sign of Cecil's passing. The rocky terrain gave nothing away. Hunter had no idea what direction Cecil might have taken once he'd ridden. His stallion veered to the south, and Hunter allowed him his head, sensing Áine held the reins.

Touching his spurs to his destrier's sides, he raced to reach Cecil, praying once again that Meghan would be protected from further harm. Once he found the two, 'twould be up to him to dispatch Cecil to hell, and oh, how he looked forward to the deed.

CHAPTER TWELVE

Disoriented, Meghan struggled to assess her situation as she came to. How had she come to be draped over somebody's horse—over a man's lap? Nausea roiled in her gut, and panic tightened her chest. Her head ached so badly she could hardly string a coherent thought together. Out of instinct, she pretended to remain unconscious. Clearly Hunter didn't have her, or she'd be held in his arms. So . . . who?

Opening one eye a mere slit, she took a peek. *Damn.* She recognized that boot and the bowlegged little weasel who wore it. *Cecil.* It all came back to her in a rush, and she had to swallow the groan rising in her throat. Cecil had come at her on his horse while she defended Hunter's back. The coward had hit her in the head with the pommel of his claymore. After that, everything went black.

Pinched as it was against the saddle, her right arm had gone to sleep. She shifted with the next bounce so the pressure point eased. A prickling tingle began at her shoulder and traced down to her hand. She flexed her fingers. Thank heavens the idiot hadn't tied her arms or legs. The hilts of her daggers bit into her midriff, so he hadn't disarmed her either. Did the arrogant jerk think his skills were superior to hers? He probably believed he could overpower her just by virtue of his gender. Dumbass.

Still, if he was convinced she was a witch or a faerie, binding her would've been useless. If that's what he thought, why risk having her cast a spell over him? Why take her at all? She didn't intend to stick around long enough to find out. She had to get away and soon, before Cecil took her farther from Hunter.

Oh God! How would she find her way back? What if Hunter . . . *No. Don't go there.* By the time she'd joined the battle, four of the MacKenzies had fallen. The MacKintosh must have won the skirmish. Of course they had. Tears stung at the back of her eyes. Hunter had to be all right, because she couldn't bring herself to touch upon any other possibility.

She inhaled slowly through her nose, gathered her reserves and pushed herself off the horse's back, slamming her elbow into Cecil's nose on the way. She landed on her feet and ran, taking one of her daggers from its sheath as she went. A muttered curse and the sound of hooves eating up the ground behind her spurred her on.

A hillock rose to her left, offering a defendable position. She altered her course and headed straight for the summit. A large rocky outcrop jutted up about fifteen feet at the center, surrounded by craggy shards of smaller broken boulders at the base. If she could manage to climb to the top, Cecil couldn't get near her with his sword. No way could he reach her before she had the chance to throw her blades.

Scrambling over the fragments of rock, she searched for footholds in the hard surface and inched her way up the side. Each movement sent jarring pain through her head. Her boot slipped on loose gravel. She fell to her knees and slid back a full yard before she could stop herself. Her hose tore, and both knees were raw and bloody where the skin had been scraped away.

"You canna escape, witch. I have you now," Cecil crowed. He

rested his forearm on the gullet of his saddle and stared up at her as if he had all the time in the world.

Meghan shoved her pain aside and clawed her way to the top of her stone perch. She stood on shaky legs, widened her stance and balanced herself on the smooth, slanted surface. "Seems to me I have the advantage, Cecil, but I'll play along." She flipped the dagger in her hand. Catching it by the blade, she readied herself to pitch it into his evil heart. "What do you want with me, now that you *have* me?" she asked in a mocking tone.

"Why, you will become my wife, of course." His horse pranced at the base of her island of safety. "Witch or fae, it matters no' to me. Either way, I will take advantage of whatever it may be that you can provide, or . . ." He shrugged. "You die."

"Sorry to disappoint." She shrugged back with all the indifference she could muster. "But I'm not a witch or a faerie. I'm just an ordinary human being—a regular lassie with mad skills when it comes to daggers and swords. Besides, if you are so certain I'm one or the other, why would you risk having me cast a spell? What if I decide to make you disappear into thin air like the fair?"

He fished a bundle out from under his shirt and waved it at her. "Think you I come to you unprepared? I had a ward made against such magic. There is naught you can do to me."

She caught a glimpse of movement in the distance. A rider crested the hill to the west, and she nearly fell to her skinned knees in relief. *Hunter.* He was alive, and he'd come after her. Oh man, did she love that stubborn, honorable, gorgeous idiot.

She blinked the sudden tears of relief away and brought her focus back to Cecil. Best keep him occupied and unaware that her champion was on his way. "I don't get it. You accuse me of being fae or a witch. You wanted to dispose of me the day we first met, and now you want to marry me. What changed?"

"The MacKenzies tell the tale of how the fae aided the Mac-Connell clan in years past. The association made the MacConnells powerful, undefeatable." He snorted. "I want that power for myself. I *will* have what aid you can provide to me, and with the wards I have in place, you canna harm me."

"I wouldn't marry you if you were the last bowlegged little weasel on earth. I sure hope you have a plan B."

"Ah, but you will become my wife." He snarled. "There are ways to force your compliance, my dear. I can always turn you over to the church for the heretic you are. Do you no' ken what will become of you then? You will be burned at the stake. Now be a good lass and come down, lest I am forced to lay siege until you grow too weak from hunger and thirst to refuse me."

He grabbed the waterskin from the cantle of his saddle and took a long drink. Smacking his lips when he was done, he held the skin out to her. "Come now, lass. Dinna be foolish. As my wife, you will be well provided for. Indeed, thanks to the new baron of DúnConnell, I will soon come into a holding of my own."

Her stomach lurched. What was he talking about? "I hate to be the one to break it to you, but you aren't the sharpest spear in the rack. I could kill you right now if I wanted to," she said, smirking back, "but I won't. I wouldn't want to deprive Hunter of the pleasure."

"Och, he's dead by now. Those wee daggers you carry will no' find their mark, no' when I can see clearly when you intend to throw them."

"We must agree to disagree on that point." She was sorely tempted to demonstrate. A blade in his thigh to distract him, followed by another right between the eyes. She reached for another dirk. Hunter's bellow stopped her hand.

Cecil's expression was priceless. Shock etched his face. His sword raised, he raced to meet Hunter. Doireann reared, striking out with his sharp hooves at the other horse's chest. Cecil's gelding screeched and backed away, putting space between him, the stallion and the very enraged baron—her knight without his shining armor. Meghan half scrambled, half slid down the granite slope, scraping the base of her thumb in the process. Adrenaline pumping through her veins was the only thing keeping her upright as she drew closer to the two knights. She took another dagger from her belt and stood at the ready, just in case Hunter needed her help.

"Are you all right, Meghan?" Hunter spared her a glance. "Did he hurt you, lass?"

"Skinned knees and a bump on the head, but otherwise I'm fine." She met his eyes and smiled. "I take it the MacKintosh defeated the MacKenzies?"

He nodded, and then he pointed his broadsword at Cecil. "What are you to the MacKenzies?" Hunter circled around the other horse and rider. Doireann snorted, tossed his head and laid his ears back. His front hooves minced the ground as if he wanted nothing more than to take another shot at the enemy. Hunter kept a tight rein on him.

"It makes no difference whether or no' you ken now, since you will soon be dead," Cecil boasted. "My sister is wed to their earl. One of the MacKenzie spies learned of the MacConnell clan's search for the old baron's grandson, an orphaned lad whose father disappeared afore he was born. The bairn's mother, a commoner, returned to her village on the shores of Loch Moigh. 'Twas *you* who handed me the information the MacKenzies sought." Cecil chortled.

"I passed along what I'd learned, and the earl granted me the task of keeping an eye on your whereabouts. 'Tis why I journeyed to Loch Moigh. Once you are dead, I have been promised a portion of *your* land, my lord. I *will* have your witch as well."

Hunter let out a roar and attacked. Seeing him handling his powerful stallion, battling the creep who had threatened them both—that did something to her insides. A gut-level, primitive exultation filled her—and pride followed fast in its wake. She didn't suffer a moment's doubt about the outcome. One-on-one there was no way Hunter could lose. Still, her heart pounded like a kettle drum.

Hunter's sheer physicality turned her insides to mush. The strict code of ethics and chivalry he lived by, the way his clan adored him . . . after this, how could she ever settle for less?

Since the day he'd dragged her through time, she'd never doubted she had his protection. Hunter had shared things with her he'd never shared with anyone else. She melted under his gray-eyed gaze and went weak in the knees whenever he turned his dimpled smile her way. She swallowed the lump in her throat and sheathed her daggers. She was hopelessly in love with an arrogant fifteenth-century Scottish lord.

He would be surrounded by treachery when he took his place at DúnConnell. Hadn't Cecil just told them the MacConnell clan was riddled with spies? Hunter needed her. She needed him. The only man she would ever love was too thickheaded to ask her to stay. Even if he did ask, she didn't know if she had the guts to leave her family, the fencing club or her century behind forever.

The battle was over quickly, and Cecil lay still on the ground. Hunter faced her, his expression a thunderous mask. He kicked Doireann's sides and cantered toward her. Leaning over in the saddle, he extended his hand. She ran to meet him, grasped his outstretched forearm and swung up behind him. He turned Doireann and spurred him into a gallop.

She put her arms around his waist and buried her face against his back. Judging by the tension emanating from him, he was still caught up in the adrenaline rush of battle. That or he was really pissed at her. *Or . . . both.* Yep. Probably both.

They continued on in silence for what seemed like forever. She glanced around his shoulder to see where they were heading, and then she checked the sun's position in the sky. How could it still be morning after so much had happened? The shimmer of water in the distance caught her eye. "Is that Loch Mór?"

"Aye." He veered to the right, following a narrow path into a forest of pine and yew. He reined Doireann to a stop in a small clearing at the north end of the lake.

Meghan sucked in a breath. The scent of pine permeated the air, and sunlight breaking through the canopy of evergreen boughs dappled the bed of reddish needles blanketing the forest floor. The stallion's sides heaved, and the sound of his breathing broke the stillness surrounding her.

Hunter swung his leg over Doireann's neck and dismounted. Turning an angry scowl her way, he dragged her from his horse by her upper arms. He held her aloft in his bruising grip with her feet dangling above the ground. Her face was close enough to his that the anger directed at her from his storm-gray eyes set off a cascade of shivers down her spine.

He shook her. "I *begged* you to hide in the hills until I came for you. I *begged* you to stay out of danger. Lass, *I* dinna *beg* anyone for *anything* anymore."

The contained anger edging his tone raised goose bumps at the back of her neck and down her arms. "I did . . . I—"

"Nay, you did *no*."

"Yes I did, I just didn't go very far."

"Dinna speak, woman." He shook her again. "Do you have *any* idea what your disobedience put me through?"

Her eyes went wide. "What *you* went through?" Anger chased the shivers away and brought hot tears to her eyes. "I saved your life. I had to stay close enough to watch over you, in case you needed me. I—"

"I nearly lost you." He set her down, and his gaze roamed over her in a frantic search. He touched the goose egg at her temple and growled at the sight of her torn hose and bloody knees. "Did I no' tell you I canna bear the thought of anything happening to you?" He dragged her into his arms with such force she couldn't breathe.

"I could ha' lost you," he rasped out again. "I canna lose you, lass. 'Twould be the death of me if aught were to happen to you." His Adam's apple bobbed. He stroked her hair and nuzzled the tender spot below her ear.

His ragged breathing turned her inside out. "I'm OK, Hunter. Cecil wasn't much of a threat. I could've taken him." She wrapped her arms around him, laying her cheek against his chest. He smelled like sweat and the outdoors, completely masculine. Intoxicating. "I couldn't let those bastards kill you. I can't bear the thought of anything happening to you either."

She tightened her hold. "Talk about heart-stopping moments." She was trembling now. "When I saw you surrounded by those three men trying their hardest to cut you into pieces, with that sword about to come down on your head . . . My heart stopped," she whispered.

Tilting her head back, she peered into his face. His wonderful gray eyes were so filled with emotion, the intensity heated her from the inside out. "I'm not even a little bit sorry I stayed close enough to help." Her stomach clenched. "That's the second time I've taken a life since I came here. Only this time, I knew without a doubt I did the right thing. If I had it to do over, I'd do exactly the same thing." She searched his face for . . . acceptance? Forgiveness? She wasn't sure which, but then his mouth found hers and nothing else mattered.

Desire ignited within her. Everything that had happened since he'd awakened her at dawn and everything she felt for him coalesced into a need so great, it stole her ability to think rationally. She wanted him, and she would not be denied. This time, she would not allow him to pull back from her—emotionally or physically.

Her tongue tangled with his, and she tugged at his shirt, pulling it from the belt around his waist. Once the linen came free, she ran her hands up his back, thrilling at the feel of bulging muscle under smooth, hot skin. Heat radiated between them, and her pulse soared. He groaned into her mouth, cupped her bottom and pulled her against him. The hardened ridge of his erection incited her. She went for his belt, desperate to free him from the wool he wore wrapped around his sculpted body. Hunter grabbed her hands, raised them in the air and drew her chain mail and tunic off over her head in a single motion. He tossed them to the ground, his eyes riveted on her. The sudden intake of his breath arced along her nerves, and liquid heat pooled between her thighs.

Tracing a finger along the edge of her lacy pink bra, he let out an appreciative moan. "What is this?"

"Victoria's Secret," she said on a sigh.

"Hmm? Why would Victoria give you this as her secret?"

"No, it's . . ." She went back to unfastening his belt. "I'll explain later."

His throaty chuckle struck a chord that resonated through to her soul. Somehow his clever fingers figured out how to unclasp the front of her bra, and his wonderful hands were on her. *Finally.*

His thumbs brushed across her nipples, hardening them into buds of tingling sensations that unfurled and fluttered all the way to her center. Aching with anticipation, she held her breath. He didn't disappoint. Hunter leaned over and took one of them into his mouth. He suckled and ran his tongue around her sensitized nipple, while lightly pinching the other. She nearly lost her legs. "Off. I want this off." She grasped his belt, too aroused to manage the buckle.

Her dad was going to be very disappointed with her, but she didn't care. She was going to give it up for Hunter, and the consequences be damned. That thought caused a painful wrench, but then, Hunter undid his belt and she forgot how to think. His kilt fell away. She tugged his shirt off over his head and stared. Oh yeah. Glorious, aroused and hers . . .

"Now you, *mo cridhe*," he said in a hoarse voice.

"Now me?" She couldn't take her eyes off of him to save her life. She reached out and ran her palm over his broad chest, eliciting a sexy growl. Nice. Stepping closer, she placed both palms against his bare skin. "You're like one of those Roman statues. Perfect." She glanced up, and her breath caught. His eyes were half-closed, molten and fixed on her. So sexy.

He put his large hands on her waist and drew her against him. His kiss started out as a bone-melting tender caress, turning quickly to a heated demand. His tongue took hers, dominating her response. His hands were everywhere.

He managed to get her out of her boots and hose, and set her away from him. He looked his fill. His chest rose and fell, as if he'd just run a marathon. Hooking a finger under the edge of her pink, lacy panties, he tugged at the elastic. "Another of Victoria's secrets?"

She throbbed with need at his touch. All she could manage was a nod and a gasp. His eyes flew to hers.

"You are so very lovely, Meghan." His hands dropped. He stepped back. "I dinna—"

"Oh, no you don't." She felt like screaming, or crying. "*Don't* do that retreat thing again. Do you have any idea what that does to me?"

He reached for the pile of wool at his feet. "Retreat thing?" Folding the kilt in half, he shook it out and laid it on a bed of pine needles. "None have ever accused me of *retreating*, lass." He held out his hand to her.

"Oh." Flustered, she stammered, "It's just that, in the past . . ."

He arched a brow. "Aye?"

When she didn't place her hand in his quickly enough, he strode toward her, scooped her up in his arms and carried her to the bed he'd made beneath the towering pines. "There will be no retreat this day, *mo anam*. I want you."

"OK," she whispered. "That's good, because I want you too." Oh man, did she want him. Every part of her ached and pulsed with wanting him. He laid her down, knelt beside her and skimmed his knuckles along her cheek, down the side of her neck and over a breast. Currents of heat sluiced through her at his touch.

"Are you certain, Beag Curaidh?" His gaze held passion—and vulnerability. "'Tis no' too late to say me nay. Though I warn you, doing so may cause me to beg for the second time in less than a day."

She held out her arms. "I'm sure."

He came to her, held her with reverent tenderness and showered her with kisses. Stroking her with his callused hands, he set her on fire.

"You are so soft, so beautiful." He drew back to look at her, tracing a finger from her chest to her navel. "Do you ken I've wanted you since first you stood victorious over me with my dirk in your hand?" His dimples appeared, and her breath seized. He tugged her panties off, and then he covered her mons with his large hand in a possessive gesture. "Och, lass, you've turned my life to chaos, one tumult after another."

Taking her bottom lip between his teeth, he teased at it. His fingers dipped, finding the sensitive nub between her folds, discovering just how hot and slick she was for him—only for him.

Her insides fluttered. Tingling shock waves of pleasure brought her hips off the ground to arch into him. She ran her hands over his back and down his very fine backside. With a moan, she reached around to touch him. Hot. Hard. He sucked in a breath, and his member twitched against her palm. Running her hand over his length, she reveled in the way he reacted, pressing himself into her palm.

Hunter made a purring sound deep in his throat. He deepened his kiss and stroked her until she cried out in helpless abandon. He covered her, bearing most of his weight on his forearms. His tongue mimicked the act of lovemaking as he nudged her knees apart. Moving to kiss her throat, he murmured something in Gaelic. She had no clue what he said, but the words were erotic to her ears. She wrapped her legs around his hips and urged him closer.

Reaching between their sweaty bodies, Hunter guided himself to her opening and teased her clit with the tip of his member. She was going to die if he didn't fill her soon. A spool of sensual tension wound tighter and tighter within her. She arched her hips up. He eased his way inside, the foreign fullness making her mindless. When he came up against the thin barrier, he pulled back. His heavy breathing filled her ears. "Och, Meghan. I—"

"Don't. Stop." She pulled him closer. One strong thrust, and he broke through. The tear stung, but only for a second. She shifted her weight, trying to get more comfortable.

He cradled her head with his hands and rested his forehead against hers. "I did no' mean to cause you pain." His hips moved slowly in an enticing circular motion. "Are you all right, Beag Curaidh?"

She stroked his cheeks. "I'm fine, Hunter." Drawing his face to hers, she kissed him. He moved against her. She met him halfway, and once again the tension built, climbing toward the peak of sexual ecstasy. They found their rhythm, rocking together in a dance as old as time.

"You're so tight, so perfect, *mo cridhe.* 'Tis as if . . ."

She would've asked him to complete his sentence, but she shattered into spasms of pleasure so pure and so all-consuming that speech was beyond her. He strained against her, his thrusts faster, erratic, until a pulse of heat exploded inside her as he climaxed.

He collapsed. She could hardly breathe from his weight, and yet she didn't want him anywhere else. His heart pounded next to hers, and his labored breathing against her neck sent a wave of emotion crashing over her. She wrapped her arms around him and stroked his back. Love. Longing. Babies, a home and hearth with him—she wanted it all, and she wanted it with Hunter. If he asked her to stay, she would.

He drew in a long breath and let it out on a sigh. "What am I to do with you, lass?" He lifted himself to peer at her. Tucking a strand of hair behind her ear, his eyes roamed over her face with a possessive glint. "Och, never have I been so torn in two."

She swallowed. "You could ask me to stay."

He rolled over to his back and covered his eyes with his arm. "Nay. I canna afford you."

"What do you mean? I don't eat *that* much, and—"

"'Tis no' your keep that concerns me, woman. 'Tis your safety." He lifted his arm to glower. "I'm riding into a war that has lasted a decade. I dinna ken who my enemies may be, or who I might call ally. You heard Cecil. My clan is corrupt with MacKenzie spies. If I kept you, there are those who would use you to get to me. I canna afford to be distracted by worry. I canna allow myself such vulnerability. Too many lives depend upon me now."

"A few minutes ago you said you couldn't *lose* me, and now—"

"To death. I canna lose you to death. In your own century, you'll be safe. Once you are returned to your kin, I will ken you live, that you are safe and far from harm. 'Tis best."

"You don't know that," she muttered. "I could be hit by a bus or something."

He got up and started gathering their clothing. "'Twould be foolish indeed to divide my attention between protecting you and executing my responsibilities as baron and laird to my clan. I vowed to do what is right. I swore to see you returned to your family. No matter how I wish things were otherwise, that is what I intend to do."

She shot up and snatched her undies from his hand. Her face burned with mortification. "Stupid, stubborn, horny, self-serving . . . *man*. It would've been nice if you'd mentioned all of this *before* we had sex."

"Whilst we were caught up in the throes of our passion? Would it ha' made a difference to the outcome?" He untangled and separated her chain mail from her tunic and handed them both to her. "I've ne'er made it a secret that I intend to see you home, lass. I vowed as much the day I took you through Madame Giselle's tent."

She glared. "Of course it would have made a difference. If you'd made that little speech before making your move, I wouldn't have given myself to you." *Liar.* Oh, how she wished her voice hadn't broken at the end of that last sentence. Such a fool.

"I . . ." She fought to control the tremor in her voice. "I'm going to the lake to wash." Embarrassment heated her face. Despair seized her heart.

Hunter pulled his shirt over his head, jammed his arms through the sleeves and grabbed his sword. "I'll go with you."

"No." She pointed a finger at him. "You won't. I don't *want* you anywhere near me." What she wanted was a few moments of privacy to muster her defenses. What she needed was a year or three to mend the rift in her soul.

"Meghan, you *own* my heart." He raked his fingers through his hair. "And I am no' pleased in the least. 'Tis a weakness."

He saw his feelings for her as a weakness? She owned his heart, and that gave him nothing but unhappiness. Her throat closed up. "I suppose you'll keep pestering Sky to marry you."

"Nay. That is done. To produce an heir, I must wed eventually, and I will do so out of duty. I ken you think me selfish, but what I do, I do to keep you safe. If you stayed and perished because of me, I would go mad. In your own time you are certain to live out your life as you were intended." He grunted. "Aye, 'twould be far more selfish of me to keep you here than to send you home."

"Don't kid yourself, Hunter," she gritted out between her clenched teeth. "What you do, you do to keep *yourself* safe." She pulled on her boots, grabbed her torn hose and headed for the lake—buck-naked.

"*You* are an ass—a delusional ass with an ego the size of the Grand Canyon," she shouted. "Thickheaded doesn't begin to describe you. I'm done beating my fists against your steel-plated armor. Done."

The tears started the second she left the clearing. Seething, she continued to mutter insults at the man all the way to the shoreline. Dumping her things on the ground, she waded into the frigid water. She washed her inner thighs, painfully aware of the soreness inside. "Stupid decision on my part."

She'd been under the influence of raging hormones and turned on by seeing Hunter in action as he defended her. She had mistaken relief and gratitude for something else. That's all there was to it. Lust and adrenaline were a deadly combination. A sob broke free, and she admitted the truth. It would take her a while to talk herself out of loving Hunter.

Once she finished washing, she dressed quickly and returned to the clearing. Why oh why hadn't they thought to bring Cecil's gelding with them? Riding so close to Hunter would be torture.

Dressed and ready to go, Hunter handed her a piece of jerky and half of an oatcake. "Eat, and then we'll be off. The rest of the men await us at Loch Dún Seilcheig."

Without a word, she accepted the food. It might've been cardboard for all she cared. Bite, chew, swallow and repeat. She ate until her stomach was filled and the food was gone.

Hunter took Doireann to the lake for a drink, and while he was gone, she surveyed the small clearing. She'd never see this place again, and that was a good thing. Losing her virginity was supposed to be special, not heartbreaking.

Her mother and father had told all three of their children over and over about the promises and commitment they'd made to each other before making love. They'd admonished her and her brothers not to take such a thing lightly, not to just give it away. She bit her lip. They'd be so disappointed.

Sadness settled over her, weighing her down like a pile of stones had been heaped onto her shoulders. Hunter rode back to the clearing. He took his foot out of the stirrup, and she clamored up behind him. Instead of putting her arms around his waist, she gripped the cantle at the back of his medieval saddle. Once more they were on the road, facing a long stretch of silence. She had nothing more to say and nothing more to give. Time to go home.

The sun had begun to set by the time she and Hunter rode into camp. Tieren and the others greeted them and asked what had become of Cecil. The campsite lay hidden behind a thick tangle of brush situated near the shore of yet another pristine lake. Exhausted, Meghan slid off Doireann's rump while Hunter related what had occurred. He bragged on her behalf, telling them all how she'd taken her stand atop a mighty boulder. She didn't want to be reminded.

"Aye," Hunter boasted. "I heard her taunt him. If I had no' gotten there when I had, 'tis sure Beag Curaidh would ha' slain the knave herself."

"'Twould ha' been her second kill this day," said one of the other soldiers, flashing her a grin. "She saved your life this morn, my lord. Did she no', lads?"

A round of ayes and nods were directed at her. She wanted to hide.

"Meghan." Tieren leaned over his pile of belongings and pulled something out. He approached with her sword and scabbard in his hands. "I found your scabbard with the packhorses and your sword on the ground."

"Oh, thank you." She blinked hard, took them from him and buckled the belt of her scabbard across her chest. "I had hoped someone would pick them up."

"Come. Sit by the fire." Tieren's gaze went to the bruise at her temple and then to her knees. "You look as if you could use a good rest, lass. Whilst we awaited your return, the lads and I did some fishing. Have some supper."

At the mention of rest, she yawned. She nodded and made her way to the campfire.

Hunter handed his horse off to George and followed behind her. "Were you able to rout the remaining MacKenzies, Tieren?"

The deep timbre of his voice brought a fresh ache to her chest. They hadn't spoken at all since they'd set out for camp.

"Aye, all but their commander." Tieren grunted. "I thought it best to let him escape. We want him to return to his master with news of their defeat, aye? I dinna think we will see more MacKenzies between here and Castle Inverness. I've seen no sign of the two we sent ahead. I fear they were slain."

"I thought the same during the battle. The MacKenzies will pay dearly," Hunter decreed. "For every man we lose, *they* shall lose ten."

The men shouted with bloodthirsty approval and pumped their fists in the air. She sighed and rolled her eyes. "Did anyone think to bring my horse along?"

"For certes, my lady," a burly redheaded soldier said, his expression incredulous. "Think you we'd leave something as valuable as a well-trained destrier behind?"

The others laughed, and she rose to move somewhere else. She wanted privacy. She was sick of men, especially kilted, bloodthirsty warrior types. A path led down a slight hill to the lake. She took it, wanting nothing more than to be alone.

Meghan found a secluded spot overlooking the lake. She sank to the ground, her bruised knees protesting the movement. Leaning back against the trunk of a pine, she closed her eyes and listened to the sound of the breeze whispering through the trees. Birds trilled from tree to tree, and their chittering sounds soothed her raw nerves.

Letting her mind wander, she relaxed each one of her sore muscles. She no longer wondered why she'd been brought to fifteenth-century Scotland. Her task had been to save Hunter's life. She'd done it, and now . . . Now she'd leave this place. So much had happened since the day Hunter had pulled her through Madame Giselle's tent. She rubbed her face. Good Lord, she'd killed two men!

She'd lost her virginity. No regrets. Hunter had said she owned his heart. He'd suffered so much loss as a child. She understood why he took the stance he did when it came to her, but that didn't make it hurt any less. He had things all wrong, of course, but it wasn't her job to straighten him out.

"Meg," Tieren said, appearing beside her. "I've brought you some supper." He lowered himself beside her, placing a large leaf holding a steaming piece of fish and some berries on her lap.

"Thanks." She fiddled with the edge of the leaf. "I'm not really hungry."

"What troubles you, lass?" He reached for her hand and took it between his. "Tell me, so that I might vanquish the sadness I see in your lovely eyes."

"Just tired." She took her hand back and broke off a piece of the fish. "It's been a busy day, what with getting conked on the head and kidnapped and all." She huffed out a breath.

"Rather than going after you myself, I sent Hunter. Because of his fae abilities, I kent he had the greater chance of finding you." His earnest gaze sought hers. "I wanted to be the one who came to your aid, Meg. You ken that, aye?"

She nodded.

"'Twas your safety I thought of first, lass. Never doubt that your safety comes first."

"Yeah. I get that. Both you and Hunter always put my safety first." Her tone sounded bitter, even to herself.

Tieren's eyes narrowed as he scrutinized her. "Something happened that has caused you grief. Tell me."

"Well, let's see." She canted her head. "We were ambushed this morning. Cecil, the bowlegged weasel, carried me off with the intention of forcing me to marry him so that I could make him powerful with my witchy or fae abilities." She popped a piece of fish into her mouth and took a minute to chew and swallow. "I killed a man. Again." She sighed. "That makes zero people I've killed in my own time and two in yours. My head aches. My knees hurt." She turned her palm over to show him the scrape at the base of her thumb. "This stings too. I'm exhausted." *And heartsick.*

"Och, you've had a time of it, my lady." He took her hand again, brought it to his lips and kissed the scrape she'd shown him. "We'll reach Castle Inverness on the morrow. You can rest there until you have recovered."

She grunted.

"Meg, I ken we have discussed this already, but . . . I fear the faerie will no' send you home. Doing so is no' how Giselle has acted in the past. 'Twas Haldor who returned Lady Erin to her century, no' Giselle."

Her heart raced. This was not the time for this conversation. She opened her mouth to ask him to stop, but he plowed on.

"I ken well where your heart lies, and I ken why you refused me. Indeed, you made yourself most clear on the point." He gripped her hand tighter. "But . . . do you no' see, lass? If you find yourself stranded here, you *must* marry. 'Tis the way of things. We get on well with one another. I would be a good husband to—"

"Meghan," Hunter's voice boomed. "I would prefer it if you returned to the safety of camp. Now."

"You don't get a say," Meghan snapped.

"As long as you are under my protection, I will have the final say in all matters pertaining to you," he roared. "Return to camp."

Tieren's scrutiny intensified. His glance flew from her to Hunter and back. "Think you I canna keep her safe, my lord?" He stood up and faced off with Hunter.

"I dinna doubt your skill, Tieren." Hunter held out his hand to her. "Come, Beag Curaidh. I want you where I can see you."

Oh brother. Hysteria, thy name is Meghan. A broken laugh escaped, and she clamped her mouth shut. "Of course, my lord." She took another bite of fish. "I shall return to camp—the minute *I* decide I want to, and not a second sooner."

She waved her hand in a shooing motion. "I have my sword, several daggers and a tree to guard my back. If I need either of *you*, I'll call out. Now, go away and leave me alone. *Both* of you." She waited, holding her breath, holding on to her sanity by a slender thread.

Hunter growled. Tieren raised an eyebrow at her. She closed her eyes, leaned her head back against the tree and ignored them. It worked. The two men stomped off. Several seconds of peace and quiet ensued.

Once she was sure they were gone, she stood up and hurled her supper as hard as she could. It flew through the air, hit a pine and tangled in its needles. Then she burst into tears. Too much. It was all too much. Being ripped from her home and family, only to fall for the single most stubborn man in the fifteenth century.

CHAPTER THIRTEEN

Castle Inverness dominated the horizon ahead, and the closer Hunter came to the imposing keep, the more agitated he became. The day had been dreary and damp, and the air now held the stillness of early eve. Fog rolled over the land from the sea, muffling the sounds of their passing.

'Twas Meghan who had talked him out of abandoning his role as baron to the MacConnells. Had she not done so, mayhap he would have set a new course for his life. The two of them could have wed. They might have spent the rest of their days in relative peace with the MacKintosh clan. Aye, this churning in his gut and the heaviness in his chest were all her fault.

He glanced at her out of the corner of his eye. Nay. 'Twas no good. He could not lie to himself. Giving up his inheritance had never been an option. He simply could not put Meghan in peril. He would not.

She sat upon Nevan's destrier, her posture straight and her head held high. Regal—so beautiful it pained him to look upon her. *Damnation.* She had torn his carefully laid plans asunder and rendered him defenseless. Mayhap she was a witch after all, for truly she had stolen his heart against his will. 'Twas pitiful the way he could not keep her out of his thoughts for even a moment's peace. Aye, and 'twas pathetic the way he could not keep from seeking her out every waking moment. He shook his head.

"Something on your mind, little brother?" Tieren smirked.

"There is much on my mind." He glowered. "And that's little brother, *my lord* to you."

Tieren laughed. "What would you have me do once we arrive at the keep, *my lord*?"

"Have your squire see to gathering our armor and gear. Tell George to make the armor ready for travel. We'll leave the tent and banners behind for now." His attention strayed once again to Meghan. She had ignored him since the morning he'd lain with her under the clear blue sky and evergreens. Even thinking of her naked made his tarse harden and throb.

God's blood, he'd never imagined being with a woman could transport him to such heights of ecstasy—or reduce him to such depths of misery. Overtaken by profound relief to find her alive, coupled with battle lust, he'd been too weak to turn away from the enticing temptation she'd presented. Battle sometimes did that to a man. 'Twas proof of life he'd sought in her arms—for them both.

He'd taken her maidenhead. Possessive satisfaction swept through him. He'd had it aright from the start. She had been formed solely for his pleasure. Then guilt rose like bile in his throat. He must be the lowest sort of churl to feel pride in light of what he'd taken from her. She was not his. "Have one of the lads make inquiries as to whether or no' Áine is still in residence."

"Áine?" Tieren's brow rose.

"Aye," Hunter said, lowering his voice. "I can no longer think of her as Madame Giselle, the old crone she pretends to be whilst amongst mortals. 'Twas Áine who warned me of the MacKenzie ambush, and she who guided me to Cecil after he took Meghan."

Hunter shuddered. "I tell you, Tieren, her magic filled me. She lent me her strength when I had none left. Had it no' been for her . . ." He let out a shaky breath. "The faerie is kin to me, and I will deny her no longer."

"'Tis just as well, Hunter. Though I dinna envy you, you may need her aid in the days to come." He shot him a questioning look. "Were you no' frightened?"

"Humbled, aye, but no' frightened. I ken now she would never harm me." His gaze slipped to Meghan once again. "Gratitude, more than aught else, is what filled me."

He and Tieren reached the portcullis, and the rest of their party trailed behind them. Hunter nodded to the guards who called out to him in greeting. He spurred Doireann into a canter and rode through the gate into the outer bailey. Several stable lads rushed forward. He dismounted and greeted the tallest. "Wallace, you were a mere lad the last time I laid eyes upon you." He slapped the lad's shoulder. "You've grown."

"Aye, Sir Hunter. I'm ten and six now." Wallace beamed as he took Doireann from him.

"Give Doireann a thorough rubdown, lad." Hunter gave Wallace's shoulder a final shake and let him go. "He'll want a measure of grain as well."

"I will, sir."

"You must call him lord now." Tieren handed the reins of his horse to the stable lad next to Wallace. "Sir Hunter is now the baron of DúnConnell."

"Och, my apologies, my lord." Wallace bowed. "I had no' heard ye'd come up in rank."

"No apology necessary. 'Tis a recent occurrence, and I've no' had time to send word." Hunter scratched at the stubble covering his chin. "That reminds me. I must send a missive to our king and another to Cecil's uncle, informing them of yesterday's events. 'Tis fortuitous for us the ambush took place on MacKintosh land. None can doubt we acted in defense. Tieren, instruct our guardsman to billet beneath the great hall with the rest of the castle's soldiers." His new commander nodded and went off to see his order carried out, and Hunter took his pack from Doireann's saddle.

Once their belongings and horses had been taken care of, he, Tieren and Meghan headed for the great hall of the keep. The lump at her temple had turned an ugly greenish-purple, and scabs had formed over both of her knees. A fierce wave of protectiveness swept through him. He wanted to snatch her up in his arms and shield her from any and all harm. As if she felt his perusal, she raised her eyes to his. He glimpsed a shadow of hurt before a flash of anger took its place, and she averted her gaze.

How could he leave it this way between them? 'Twas love for her that forced his hand, and he had to make her understand. Aye, he loved her more than life. He could no longer pretend otherwise. Even considering wedding any other soured his stomach, while the thought of another man touching her had him curling his hands into fists.

He took the stairs leading to the door to the keep, threw it open and strode inside. Rupert, the castle's steward, hurried to greet them, followed by Margaret, the keep's châtelaine.

"Sir Hunter, Sir Tieren, welcome! 'Tis good to have you back on Scottish soil, lads. All is well at Loch Moigh I trow?" Rupert snapped his fingers, and several servants appeared.

"All is well indeed, though I'm certain you received word of Robert's passing," Hunter said.

"Hunter is a baron now, Rupert. He's recently inherited his grandsire's title, baron of DúnConnell." Tieren puffed out his chest. "I command his garrison."

"We did hear of Lord Robert's passing. 'Twas grievous news indeed." Rupert turned to Hunter. "Well, well." He bowed low. "I am pleased to hear it, my lord. Sir Tieren, I am also quite pleased to hear of your appointment as his commander. Good news always follows bad, aye?"

"Mayhap you have it aright." Hunter smiled at the older man. He and Tieren had oft been scolded by Rupert for getting into some mischief or another as lads. 'Twas odd to think he'd gone from beggar to baron, and Tieren from the son of an alewife to his commander. The changes hadn't yet settled in his mind.

Margaret curtsied. "My lord, how long will you be with us this visit?"

"Only a night." Hunter gestured to Meghan to come forward. He took her elbow and presented her to the steward and châtelaine. "This is Lady McGladrey. Put her in the very best chamber we have to offer, and have a bath brought to her." He looked her over. She stiffened, but he ignored it. "Do you think you might find something suitable for her to wear whilst her garments are laundered and mended?"

"Aye. I'll see to it anon," Margaret said, calling forth a serving maid.

"Also see to it that my men are fed. We have six with us, and two more may yet join them this eve. 'Tis too late for them to take their meal with the keep's soldiers. Tieren, do you wish for a chamber above stairs, or would you prefer to stay below with the castle guards?"

Tieren grinned. "Och, a chamber would be most appreciated, my lord."

"I'll see one is prepared for ye, Sir Tieren." Margaret gave orders to a bevy of servants, and they scattered in all directions like wheat chaff in the wind. "Will you take your supper in your chamber, my lord, or would you prefer we bring refreshment for the three of you here to the hall?"

"If you don't mind, I would prefer to eat in my room." Meghan's voice sounded strained to his ears. "I'm really tired."

"If it pleases you, my lady." Margaret curtsied again. "I will take you there anon."

"Tieren and I will sup in the solar, Margaret. I've a few missives to write before I take my rest."

"Once the Lady McGladrey is settled, I'll see to it, my lord," Margaret said, leading Meghan to the stairs. "'Twill no' be long afore your bath is prepared, my lady. I've sent a maid to fetch a gown and night rail for ye as well. Sally will assist ye this eve."

"Thank you." Meghan followed the châtelaine up the stairs and out of sight.

Hunter didn't like having her out of his sight. Worry prickled at his senses, and he looked upon the stairs, longing to follow.

"My lord, would you like a bath brought to your chamber as well?" the steward asked, bringing Hunter's attention back to the hall.

"Aye, and I'll take my usual chamber, Rupert."

"Och, but 'tis no' fitting for one of your rank to be placed in such humble surroundings." Rupert frowned.

"Nonetheless, it is familiar and comfortable. I will sleep this night where I have always slept whilst visiting Castle Inverness."

The steward bowed. "As you wish." He gave instructions to several servants who scurried away to do his bidding. "If it pleases you, my lord, I will take my leave to see that all is prepared."

"My thanks, Rupert." Hunter turned to Tieren. "Once you see to the men, join me in the solar for our evening meal, aye?"

"Aye. I'll return by the time the kirk bells chime for Compline."

"Until then." Hunter took the stairs two at time. He reached the hall just in time to see Margaret usher Meghan through a door. Good. At least he kent where she would be. He turned toward the opposite direction. A servant was just leaving his chamber. 'Twas similar to the small room he had shared with his foster mother at Moigh Hall when first she came to the MacKintosh. He'd always preferred small and cozy to overlarge and grandiose. Smaller surroundings gave him a sense of safety. Would that change now that he was a noble?

"'Tis ready for you, my lord." The servant curtsied. "Lads will be up shortly with a tub and hot water."

"My thanks." He entered the small chamber and smiled. Recollections of his many stays here as a lad played through his mind. He'd oft shared the space with Tieren when they were both pages, following Malcolm everywhere he went. He'd thrived as Malcolm's page, then later as his squire. No lad could be luckier than he when it came to a mentor.

Once he'd bathed, shaved and dressed, Hunter sought the solar. There he selected three pieces of parchment, ink and fresh quills stripped of their feathers. He sat at a table and began the missives to King James and the earl of Glencairn, relating details of the ambush that had cost Cecil his life. The third he addressed to Edward at DúnConnell, alerting him that there were MacKenzie spies within their walls. He wrote briefly about the ambush and assured the older man that he'd emerged unharmed and victorious. By the time the kirk bells chimed Compline, his stomach rumbled with hunger.

Servants bearing food and drink entered, followed by Tieren. Hunter sealed the last missive with hot wax and affixed the seal from his signet ring. He stood up and stretched his cramped muscles. Sitting at a table and writing were no' for him. Mayhap he'd employ a scribe once he'd settled into his role as baron. He turned to one of the lads carrying their meal. "I've missives to send. Have the steward send someone for them anon."

"Aye, my lord." The lad set a pewter pitcher of ale and two mugs on the table.

"The guards upon the catwalk reported seeing two riders approaching. I trow it is our two guardsmen." Once their supper had been laid out, and the last of the servants had departed, Tieren took a seat and broke off a large chunk of bread. Then he reached for a thick slice of cold beef. "Áine is in Inverness."

Hunter nodded. The news should have brought him relief. It

didn't. He couldn't draw breath. His heart pounded, and his mouth went dry. He poured ale into the two goblets and handed one to Tieren.

The hunger that had plagued him but a moment ago had fled. The very thought of eating twisted his gut. Taking a long drink of ale to wet his mouth, he walked to the narrow window and stared out over the Moray Firth. He needed to lay eyes upon Meghan.

"Will you no' eat, Hunter?" Tieren asked.

"In a moment." He took another swallow of the ale, his mind in turmoil. "There's something I must do." He moved to the table and set down the half-finished ale.

Tieren's brows drew together. "What must you do at this hour?"

"I . . . Stay, Tieren. Eat." Hunter strode to the door. "We'll talk on the morrow."

His heart had climbed to his throat by the time he reached Meghan's chamber. He stood before her door. What could he say to make things right between them? Truth. He would tell her the truth, and she would forgive him. She would understand and see the rightness of his decision. He reached out with a trembling hand and knocked. God's blood! Facing his fiercest enemy was far easier than facing Meghan.

The door opened a crack, and she peered at him, a puzzled look upon her comely face. "Hunter. What brings you here?"

She didn't open the door any wider. She wore a night rail and a robe of midnight-blue velvet. Her hair, still damp from her bath, fell about her shoulders in a shining coppery veil. He had to swallow a time or two before he could find his voice. "I wish to talk."

"What about?"

"May I come in, Beag Curaidh?"

She looked over her shoulder at the chamber within, then back to him. "I don't think that's such a good idea."

"I wish only to talk." He rested his hand on the doorframe. "I dinna want to leave things as they are. It pains me that we might part without peace between us."

She sighed, backed up and opened the door. His heart took flight, and he crossed the threshold. Her sweet, clean scent wafted over him, and he drew it in. Two comfortable chairs were arranged near the hearth, and a small fire dispatched the slight chill and dampness of the night. He imagined what it would be like to sit in such a place each night with Meghan as his wife, sharing a quiet moment before retiring for the night. He gestured toward the hearth. "Will you sit, lass?"

She tightened the belt of her robe and walked over to take a seat. His palms sweating, he took the chair opposite, leaned forward and rested his elbows on his knees. He clasped his hands together to keep from reaching for her. His jaw clenched and unclenched, and uncertainty moistened his palms. "I wish to make my thinking clear."

Her brow rose, but she made no reply.

"That morning we . . . uh—"

"The morning we had sex?" She shrugged. "What about it?"

Did it mean so little to her that the mention warranted naught but a shrug? He straightened and ran his sweaty palms over the wool of his plaid. "I ken you think me selfish . . ."

"No." She shook her head. "I don't."

"You dinna?"

"No. Selfish isn't the right word. I prefer pea-brained or bull-headed."

"Bullheaded?" If his brow rose any higher, 'twould disappear into his scalp. He blinked. "Pea-brained? Nay, you dinna understand. I love you, Meghan. I love you more than life itself. 'Tis why I must make such a sacrifice. I mean only to see to your welfare before my own. Is that no' loving? Is that no' the very antithesis of selfishness?"

She made a strangled, chuffing sound and shook her head again. "Like I said . . . pea-brained."

"Why do you insist upon making such a fankle of my intentions? Do you think you ken better than I what my thoughts and feelings are on the matter?" He stood up and paced. "I am doing what is right. I am doing what is *honorable* on your behalf. You dinna understand, and I came here *hoping* to make it clear to you, so that there might be peace between us. 'Tis you who are being obstinate." She opened her mouth to retort, and he held up his hand to stop her. "Aye, 'tis true. You are being most difficult."

"*I'm* the one being difficult?" She snorted. "I make a *fankle* out of your intentions because you insist on deceiving yourself. That pisses me off."

He growled and came to loom over her. "Dinna presume deceit, Beag Curaidh. I, better than you, understand the dangers of my time."

She stood up, shoved him out of her way and strode over to the door. "OK. Thanks for your concern, Hunter. Now please go."

"No' until things are settled between us."

"Consider them settled."

"Nay, I willna until we have come to terms."

"Will you listen to what I have to say?"

"Aye, but I might no' agree."

She was silent for several seconds. "All right. I don't see the point, but I'll tell you what I think." She continued to stand by the door. "And then you go." She lifted her chin. "Deal?"

He swallowed against the boulder in his throat, managing a nod.

She sucked in a breath, leaned back against the oak and crossed her arms. "You lost your mother at such an early age, and then you lost your grandmother shortly after. You never knew your dad, and you faced life unable to hear and reduced to begging in order to survive." Her large brown eyes sought his. "That's way too much for a three- or four-year-old child to handle on his own. Way too much trauma for even the most well-adjusted, mature adult to face." She bit her lip for a second.

"Hunter, I can't even imagine how so much tragedy affected you." Her lovely face filled with heart-melting tenderness. "I do understand your thinking. It's far easier to send me away—where you can pretend that I will never die—than it is to risk building a life with me. I get it. When you say you can't bear the thought of anything happening to me, and then you push me away . . . I get it. Sending me away to places unseen feels safer to you than facing the possibility of yet another trauma—another loss."

His eyes stung, and he made a desperate effort to gain control over the uneasiness her words caused. Meghan pushed off the door and stepped closer. He fisted his hands at his sides. "Nonsense. What happened to me as a bairn a score of years ago does no' affect me as a man today."

"Don't kid yourself." She pushed her hair back over her shoulders. "Here's the thing, Hunter." Her voice was as soft as goose down against his skin. "No matter what you do or where I am, eventually I'm going to die. Everyone does. Stop fooling yourself. Your reasons for seeing me safely home are bogus." She let out a shaky breath. "If there is to be peace between us, let's be honest."

His jaw ached, and an iron band tightened around his chest. He studied the flames in the hearth. "I dinna ken what 'bogus' means."

"False."

"What of your family, Beag Curaidh?" He turned to glance at her. "Your father must hate me. I would hate him if the situation were reversed. 'Tis only right that I see you returned to him. I vowed—"

"You and your stupid vows." She huffed. "You might want to work on that a bit. Maybe *try* to refrain from uttering them impetuously, and keep it to one or two vows per year."

"A knight is only as good as his word, lass. I am bound by my honor, and—"

"Of course you are. I'm sure my dad is hurting—my mom and brothers too. I also think since my dad was taken from his time and place, he has a better understanding of what is going on. He's probably less worried about my actual well-being and more concerned with losing me to another century. If you and my father were ever to meet, I think the two of you would get along. You're a man worthy of my father's respect, Hunter. If he knew I had your protection, it would go a long way toward easing his worry."

She came to stand before him. "It's time you get real and stop rationalizing everything. I'm not about to try and change your mind where I'm concerned. I'm not going to ask you to keep me."

"Get real? How am I no' *real*, Meg?" Disappointment choked him. Had he wanted her to try and change his mind?

"In your case, it means facing your fears. I have a family and a life to get back to. Like I told you before, I'm done beating my fists against your armor." She rose up on her toes and brushed her lips against his. "There. We have peace and understanding between us. Now go."

He gripped her forearms and shook her. "By the holy rood, woman. You confound and besiege me until I dinna ken up from down." He drew her close and crushed his mouth to hers, his insides a quaking muddle of confusion, grief, lust and longing. She didn't kiss him back. He thrust her an arm's length away. "Let us leave it thus. You have your way of thinking, and I have mine."

"Exactly." She stepped out of his hold. "I would prefer it if Tieren escorts me to Madame Giselle's cottage tomorrow. I don't want you there." She walked to her door and swung it wide. "Good-bye, Hunter. Thanks for the memories."

He stormed out of the room and down the corridor to his chamber. He wanted to tear his hair and gnash his teeth. *Obstinate besom!* Nothing had been settled. There would be no peace. He would lose her on the morrow, and worst of all, she wanted *Tieren* to escort her.

Hunter rubbed the corners of his eyes with his thumb and forefinger. The early light of dawn streamed in through the narrow window of his chamber, and birdsong grated upon his nerves.

He hadn't slept.

His heart heavy, Hunter rose, washed and dressed. He also hadn't eaten since noon the previous day. How could he eat? He could scarce draw breath. His insides aquiver, he made his way to the great hall. Like him, Meghan was an early riser, and he could not face her. *Bloody hell.* He had far too much to do and far too much to worry about to be so disturbed.

To his profound relief, he found only Tieren, George and a few men he didn't recognize sitting at the table, breaking their fast. He approached, tapped Tieren on the shoulder, and once he had his commander's attention, he signed, *"Meghan wants you to take her to Áine's cottage. She does not want me there."*

"Aye?" Tieren frowned. "Why is that, do you suppose?"

"How should I ken how the woman's twisted mind works?" he snapped. He snatched up a piece of black bread and a slice of cheese and wolfed it down. The he reached for Tieren's ale to wash the tasteless mass down his throat. Slamming the goblet back on the table gave him a small measure of satisfaction. *"Once Meghan is in Áine's keeping, we leave,"* he signed. "Make the men ready. If you need me, I'll be in the lists. Come get me once 'tis done."

"Hunter—"

"Say naught." He strode toward the doors and gripped the hilt of the dirk at his waist. "We've a clan to protect and a war to fight. My mind is set upon *those* matters most needing my attention, and that is that." He threw the doors wide and took the steps two at a time.

God's blood, but he could not wait to beat his sword against another's. He jogged to the lists, warming up for the physical exertion to come. He came around the corner of the keep—and froze. *Meghan.*

She trained with a young soldier. She wore a different pair of hose and her leather tunic without the chain mail. He should have kent *she* would seek the same physical outlet as he. Transfixed, he watched. She had the advantage. Quick and nimble, she danced away from her opponent's blows, darting back in to make contact with her blade as effortlessly as a hummingbird darting in to take nectar from a rose. Seeing her thus brought back memories of the day he'd "rescued" her from her father—the day she had stood over him with his dagger at his throat.

His jaw clenched, and his eyes burned. Her opponent cried pax. Meghan wiped her brow with the palms of her hands, and then she sheathed her sword. His heart tumbled down to his knees, and he suspected 'twas only his boots that kept the organ from landing in the dirt. He couldn't avoid her without turning tail, and that he would not do. He forced his feet to move. "Good morn, Lady Meghan," he said with a bow. "You're in fine form this day. Would you care to indulge me in a bout?"

She startled. Her cheeks, already flushed with exertion, turned a deeper shade of red. "Good morning, my lord. No, thanks. I'm finished training. I'm going to go get something to eat before I . . ." Her lips compressed into a straight line, and she studied his boots.

Did she see his poor heart there? "Of course. Go. Break your fast."

"There's something you need to know before I leave." Her eyes caught and held his. "I love you, and I always will." Her eyes grew bright. "Have a good life," she muttered as she started out for the front of the keep. After a few paces, she turned to walk backward and shouted, "Oh yeah, and one more thing. *You* are an idiot."

With those parting words ringing in his ears, Meghan gave him her back and strode away, taking his beleaguered heart and soul with her. Scanning the field for the largest and fittest soldier, Hunter removed his scabbard and undraped the wool from over his shoulder to wrap around his waist and out of the way. Then he drew his shirt off over his head. "Oy, lad," he called once he'd selected whom to pummel. "Come train with a master swordsman—if you've the courage, that is."

The burly warrior grinned, eagerness lighting his countenance. "Master swordsman, ye say?" He rolled his shoulders, set his war club aside and drew his claymore. Sauntering toward Hunter, he challenged, "Let us see who the master might be, lad." With a growl, he charged.

Hunter met the challenge, pouring all of his frustration into his training. All morning he fought, always watching the sun rise higher in the sky and marking the bell's toll for Terce. Salty sweat stung his eyes. More dripped down his chest and back. His muscles grew fatigued, and he relished the burn. Finally Tieren approached. Hunter cried pax and stuck the tip of his sword into the dirt. "It is done?"

"It is."

"Good." All the air left his lungs. He propped himself up with his claymore as black spots danced before his eyes. "Good," he repeated as if trying to convince himself. "I'll jump into the river to cool off, and then let us depart."

"Aye, my lord." Tieren glared at him for a moment before turning on his heel and walking away.

Hunter returned to the outer bailey from the river. He shook the excess water from his hair and surveyed the assembly of men he would travel with. An additional packhorse carried the burden of their armor, and their two trailing guardsmen had joined them. Eight soldiers plus Tieren and himself.

He beckoned to George. He really did need to gain a squire or two once he reached DúnConnell. The image of Meghan's disgruntled expression when he suggested she serve him as squire flashed through his mind. "George, my pack is still in my chamber. Get it if you will."

"Aye, my lord." The squire rushed off to do his bidding.

Wallace led Doireann out of the stable. His horse's coat shone from the care the lad had given him. Another stable hand followed with Mìlidh saddled and bridled. *Meghan's horse.* Hunter's lungs seized. He grabbed the gullet of Doireann's saddle and held on. His head swam, and his heart thundered. George returned and handed Hunter the pack he'd gone to fetch.

Hunter swiped at the sweat beading his upper lip. He took the bundle from the squire's outstretched hands. "My thanks." He turned to the lad leading Nevan's destrier. "We will no' be needing the gelding. For the time being, return him to the stable." The stable lad bobbed his head and did as he was bid. Hunter tied his pack to the cantle and mounted, nudging his destrier toward the gate. His men fell into line, and he led them through the portcullis.

Tieren rode up beside him. "I see no way around it, my lord. We must travel through MacKenzie land to get to yours. I suggest taking the shortest route to Munro lands, then through to the earl of Ross's holdings and finally to the MacLeod's. All are allies to the MacKintosh, and 'twill take us closer to the Sutherlands, who are kin. We can call upon them for aid if need be. That will see us to the coast, where we can hire a ship to travel the rest of the way."

"I agree. I considered hiring a ship whilst here to take us 'round to the western coast, but 'twould take too long." Hunter spurred Doireann into a canter. "We must make haste."

Tieren kept pace with him. "Hunter, though you are now my liege lord, I feel I must speak."

"The deed is done, Tieren." Once again heart-pounding breathlessness plagued him. "Meghan is with her family. Safe." He glanced at his friend. "What is there to say?"

"Though I hate to admit defeat in matters of the heart, I will humble myself for your sake. Meghan loves *you*, Hunter. You. Do you ken how rare a jewel you gave up?" He grunted. "'Tis your greatest folly yet, and I worry about following a man in possession of such poor judgment."

"I ken she loves me, and I love her. She and I spoke of it. I ride to war, Tieren. To war." He spent the better part of the next hour explaining to his childhood friend why he had done what he'd done. "I did what was best for her."

"By God, man! You must be the biggest fool to ever walk upon Scottish soil." Tieren shook his head. "Who better than Meghan to stand by your side as your baroness? In all our travels together have we *ever* encountered a lass better able to defend herself? Have we ever encountered her like? Who better than she to guard your back and your bairns?"

Tieren glared at him. "Think you I dinna ken how it went between the two of you the day Cecil took Meghan?" he hissed out. "Mayhap the lass already carries your heir, ye wee *glaikit fouter*! Did you think on that before you sent her away?" The muscles at his jaw twitched, and a growl rumbled deep in Tieren's throat. "I swear, if you were no' my liege lord, I'd beat the shite out of you for that grievous wrong alone. And you, always smug in thinking yourself so bloody honorable." Tieren kicked his destrier's sides and galloped ahead, sending up a cloud of dust to clog Hunter's throat.

He hadn't thought of that. How had he failed to consider the consequences of his actions? What if his seed had taken root and Meghan already carried his bairn? The thought of her growing large with their son melted his heart. Tieren's words took bloody chunks out of his hide, and the farther they rode from Inverness, the greater the rending sensation grew in his soul. He'd been called a fool, an idiot, and by the two people who kent him best.

His breath left him, and once again his heart clawed its way up his throat. The truth nearly pitched him from the saddle. He'd oft felt this way before, during the years after he'd lost his hearing and his kin. The breathlessness and heart-pounding sensations were far too familiar to him. When he was a lad, and he kent he had no one to look after him, when he had no notion where his next meal might come from . . . the panic rose to swallow him whole. Aye, 'twas panic.

He reached into his sporran and drew out Meghan's silver spurs. He'd broken his vow to her and kept them. The first vow he'd ever broken, and all because he'd desperately needed something of hers to hold on to. He'd wanted something to remember her by in the desolate years without her to come. He studied the design of the engravings.

He had been deceiving himself. Meghan and Tieren had it aright, and he was a fool. *The love of a good woman is far greater than a fortune, land or a title—and I've thrown it away. I've cast my love aside like yesterday's soiled rushes.*

Hunter stuffed the spurs back into his sporran. He turned Doireann's head and kicked him into a gallop, heedless of whether or not his men followed. He would prostrate himself before Áine and beg her to bring Meghan back to him. If she would no', then he'd beg her to send him to her in the twenty-first century. God in heaven, he hoped against hope his fae ancestor would hear his plea.

CHAPTER FOURTEEN

Meghan pushed the uneaten bowl of stew away. "Thanks for lunch, Madame Giselle. It was very good; I'm just not very hungry." A broken heart did have a tendency to rob one of one's appetite. She glanced out the window. "Are you sure those three guys sleeping in your yard are all right?"

"I am quite certain Sir Nevan and his lads are well, but I am sure they would be grateful to learn of your concern." Amusement creased the corners of the old woman's eyes. "I would prefer it if you would call me by my given name, child. I am Áine, Hunter's grandmother many generations removed."

"Yeah, he told me." At the mention of Hunter's name, her insides gave a painful wrench. She sighed. "So . . . I wasn't really expecting a lunch date when Tieren dropped me off here. When are you going to send me home?" Áine's laughter coiled around her, sending shivers cascading down her spine.

"I will send you home if and when I am ready to do so, mortal, and not a moment sooner."

"OK. Good enough." She nodded, swallowing hard. Searching her mind for something to say, she blurted, "So . . . what's it like being a faerie? You're immortal, right? Does that get old? Living forever, I mean." *Shut up! For crying out loud, stop talking!* Oh, but her mouth didn't listen.

"What do you look like for real, Áine? What kind of magic does it take to make an entire fair disappear into thin air?" She slapped her hand over her runaway mouth to stifle the bubble of hysteria threatening to burst free. Her nerves were shot, that's all. She was exhausted and grieving. Considering everything she'd been through in the past couple of months, who could blame her for being so completely out of pocket?

Áine began to shimmer, and blue flame licked the surface of her skin, transforming her from an old lady into an ethereal being so beautiful, there was no way she could've come from this world. Her hair hung to her ankles, so blond it was almost white. And her eyes were an impossible clear aquamarine that glowed like neon.

"I am not a faerie, mortal." She smiled. "I am *Tuatha Dé Danann,* a direct descendant of the goddess Danu. Humans have named us fae, but 'tis not what we call ourselves. Does immortality get old? For some, mayhap, but not for me."

"Oh." What else could she say? Meghan wanted to ask where the *Tuatha* originated, but instead she nodded. "You're incredibly beautiful. Ethereal." More of the melodic laughter wrapped around her, only this time warmth washed over Meghan's skin in its wake.

"Why did you bring me to this century, Áine?" Tears sprang to her eyes. Mortification singed her. How could she be so out of control? *Because you're in the presence of a supernatural being, maybe?* "Were you the one who took my father from his time? Was I just a random weight you had to move from one side to the other in order to balance some kind of cosmic scale?" She ran her knuckles under her eyes to catch her tears. "Because I have to tell you, if that's the case . . . it really sucks. I miss my family, and once I go home, I'll miss Hunter for the rest of my life."

"The way you speak so freely in my presence is refreshing. I am greatly pleased that you do not fear me, child."

Áine reached out and stroked Meghan's hair as if she were a pet. Oddly enough, the being's touch soothed her.

"Yes. I am responsible for your father's journey to the future. Though, in my defense, 'twas accidental. I had no great plan for him. He simply came too close to the portal through time and was drawn in." She smiled, and light shone from her eyes. "He's done well for himself, has he not? He is content."

"Not right now he's not," Meghan huffed out. "I disappeared right before his eyes."

"If you wish, there are ways to dim recollection, erase memories altogether of your ever having existed. 'Twould make it easier for you and for your family."

"What?" Meghan leaped to her feet, adrenaline pumping alarm through her veins. "That sounded an awful lot like you don't plan to send me home."

Áine gave a slight shrug. "I am yet undecided. We will wait a bit and see what develops." She gestured to the seat. "Sit, child. Would you care for a mug of rosehip tea, or mayhap a calming chamomile?"

Her mind reeled. What would she do if Áine decided not to send her home? How would she live? The faerie had told Tieren she would return her to her family. Hadn't she? Come to think of it, Áine's response to his request had been kind of vague. She forced herself to slow her breathing. She'd return to Robley and Erin, where at least she knew she had a place to stay. Tears once again pricked at her eyes. "No tea. Thanks. Would you answer one more question?"

"I will if I am able, mortal. Ask."

"Hunter said he can't read my energy like he can with others. Why is that? Did you block me somehow?"

"'Tis a boon to you both, is it not? I made it so. That is all you need to know."

"I do appreciate it, though it hardly matters now." Meghan wandered around the interior of the cottage. She could train the men at Meikle Geddes. Robley might pay her. She'd be OK. "How long do you think it will take before you decide what to do with me?" Her voice sounded small. She was not small. She was a McGladrey knight, and a force to be reckoned with.

She sniffed. "Please don't take my memories away, or my family's. I don't want them to forget me. I don't want to forget them."

"As you wish."

The sound of pounding hoofbeats drew close. Áine rose from her place. "You will remain inside," she commanded. "Do you understand me, mortal? Do not fear."

The temperature inside the cottage took a sudden drop, and the air filled with electrical energy. Eyes wide, Meghan nodded. Were all the children of the goddess Danu so quick with the mood swings?

"Áine," a male voice shouted in the yard.

Oh God! Meghan's heart skipped a beat. *Hunter.* What was he doing here? She stepped toward the door, and a surge of energy shoved her into the corner by the small window. No matter how hard she fought, she couldn't move from the spot. She tried to call out to him, but her voice had also been bound up in the faerie's magic.

Áine glided to the door, waved her hand, and it opened. "Why do you bellow so at my door, Grandson? What is it you want?"

"I . . . I came to beg your forgiveness."

"Oh? What must I forgive?" Áine chuckled. "Tell me."

Meghan could just catch a glimpse of Hunter from her place by the window. He went down on one knee and bowed his head. A lump formed in her throat.

"I have been most arrogant," he rasped out. "I was wrong. Never again will I withhold from you the respect that is your due. I am eternally grateful for the aid you gave me in rescuing my love."

Meghan couldn't take her eyes from her humbled knight. He glanced at his ancestor, and even from where she stood, she could see the tears glistening in his eyes.

"And?"

Hunter's Adam's apple bobbed. "Granddam . . . I want her back," he said, his voice breaking. "Nay, I *need* Meghan back. I was so caught up in my fear and my pride that I . . . I turned her away. I distanced myself from her, stubbornly clinging to notions built upon my own foolish thinking. I was blind, and now she is gone. Please, Áine, Meghan has taken my heart with her. I beg of you, bring her back, or send me to her. I care naught which, so long as I can live my life by her side. Everything I believed I wanted and needed was . . . *bogus*. Meghan is all I need."

"Hmm. What makes you think she wants *you*, lad?" The faerie stepped out of the cottage to the yard. "What makes you think she'd give you another chance after the way you have dealt with her? You broke her heart."

I would. I will give him another chance! She struggled against the hold Áine exerted over her. Seeing her proud knight suffer twisted her into knots.

"I have no reason to think she wants me still. Nay, none at all, but she did love me once. I only ken that I *must* try to gain her love and trust once more." Hunter raised his pleading eyes to the faerie. "Meghan understands me better than I understand myself. Mayhap she will forgive me. Think you she might? I can only hope so, for I am lost without her."

More than anything, Meghan wanted to go to him. She wanted to wrap her arms around his broad shoulders and assure him that he was forgiven. She tried, she really did, but she couldn't free herself of the energy that held her fast.

"Do you realize I brought her to you as the perfect helpmate to rebuild our clan, Grandson?"

"I do now, aye," he murmured. "Meghan is perfect in every way, and I am a fool."

Meghan's heart melted.

"That you are, and I am not certain I wish to grant your request."

No! Her body might be bound, but her heart still leapfrogged around her chest in protest. What game was Áine playing?

"Surely there is something I can do or say to change your mind." Hunter's chin dropped to his chest. "Mayhap there's another wrong of old I might make right?"

Áine laughed. "You wish to right another wrong that in no way involved yourself in its inception?"

"Aye. If I must."

"Mayhap we can come to an agreement . . ."

"Whatever it might be, I will agree." Hunter's tone held a hint of hope. "What is it you wish of me?"

"A cottage near DúnConnell. Near enough that I might lay eyes upon you and your offspring when I wish it."

"Done." The word was out of his mouth before she'd finished the sentence.

"I will be welcome at your hearth, Hunter?" Áine asked. "Do you imagine I am unaware of your fear and repulsion of me?"

"I beg your pardon, Áine. You must also ken I dinna feel that way any longer." Hunter's voice softened. "I am open to you, Granddam. See for yourself."

One minute then another passed, and it felt like lifetimes to Meghan. Her family would miss her, and she would miss them, but Hunter was her future. The force holding her lifted, and the sudden freedom sent her pitching forward. She landed on her hands and sore knees. She pushed herself up and ran to the door. "Hunter!"

He rubbed his face, stared at her and blinked. She wanted to hurl herself into his arms, but he was still on one knee. He rose slowly, his eyes never leaving hers. "Meghan, love, I've come back for you. Can you ever forgive me for being such a pea-brained, obstinate idiot?"

"It depends." For his sake as well as hers, she had to hear the words. "Why have you come back for me? If it's just to tell me you're pea-brained, I already know."

"Nay. I've come to beg you to stay by my side for all the days we are granted upon this earth. Be my wife. Help me rebuild my clan." His eyes grew bright with tears. "I love you, *mo anam*."

This time she did hurl herself at him. He caught her, as she knew he would, and held her tight against his chest—her favorite place to be. "Yes, Hunter. I will stay with you."

"Oy, Hunter." Another male voice filled the clearing. "Where the devil am I?"

Hunter released her but kept her hand in his. "You're in Inverness, Nevan."

The two younger boys were sitting up, scratching their heads. "How did we get here, Sir Hunter?" the older of the two asked.

Meghan looked around. Áine had disappeared.

"'Tis a long story, lads. Come to the keep. There's to be a wedding." Hunter pulled her close to his side. "Nevan, on the morrow you and your lads can depart for your home, or you can travel with us to my holding."

"You have a holding?" Nevan muttered.

"Aye, I'm baron DúnConnell." Hunter's hand ran up and down her arm, and his eyes were fixed upon her. "Come. Make haste, Sir Nevan."

Nevan and the two boys rose on shaky legs. Hunter led her to his stallion and lifted her into the saddle. He swung up behind her. "Your horse and one of the lads' rouncies are here in Inverness, Nevan, along with you armor and gear. I'm afraid your fortune is still at Loch Moigh. Once you decide where you are going, we can have it sent to you."

"Och, my fortune is safe enough where 'tis. For the time being, I'll go with you to your holding." Nevan rubbed his face. "Last thing I remember is a fair . . ."

"Aye." Hunter grinned. "A fair where I found my love. Follow this path, lads. We'll await you in the keep." He kicked Doireann's sides.

Tieren and their guardsmen were waiting for them in the inner bailey. The castle's steward had joined them. Hunter dismounted and turned to help Meghan down.

"Rupert, send someone to tell the priest we will be at the kirk within the hour. Have him prepare for a wedding mass," Hunter commanded.

Tieren nodded at her, his expression resigned. "'Tis about time, little brother," he called.

"But . . . what of the banns?" Rupert asked. "And a feast must be prepared."

"We've no time. Have the kitchen lay out whatever they have on hand for our wedding feast. We must return to my keep as soon as possible." Hunter glanced at Meghan. "Do you mind overmuch, lass? We will spend the night here and depart in the morning."

"I don't mind at all." She smiled through the tears filling her eyes.

A bath, a change of clothes into a gown and an hour later she and Hunter walked to the church with Margaret and the soldiers in attendance. It seemed fitting. Perfect. Inverness's church was much more opulent than the one in Loch Moigh. This one had a lovely marble floor and stained-glass windows, not elaborate scenes, but geometric in design. Simple yet elegant.

Meghan's walk down the aisle was not what she'd imagined when she thought about getting married. Her gown, too short by a good two inches, was not white, but blue, and she held no bouquet. Her mother, father, brothers and grandparents were not sitting in the pews. She bit her lip and blinked against the sting in her eyes.

Hunter looped her arm through his. "I ken 'tis a hasty affair, love, but I dinna want to wait another moment to make you mine. We must ride for home on the morrow, and—"

"It's all right. I was just thinking of my family."

Hunter put his arm around her shoulders. "I am sorry for that, lass."

"I don't blame you for what happened. I never did." She laid her head on his shoulder for a second. "Áine brought us together."

They reached the altar where the priest awaited them. He lowered his brow and pursed his lips in disapproval. "This is highly irregular, my lord. No banns have been called, and I have no contract for marriage before me. Must I marry you in the back of the kirk? Is the lady, er . . ."

"Nay, Father," Hunter said. "We must travel in haste, and I think it best for the lady's honor if we say our vows before we leave. She will be unescorted by any other women on our journey."

Tieren stepped forward. "You will be well compensated for your trouble, Father."

The priest's brow rose a smidgen, and he spared her a glance. "Are ye being forced into this, my lady?"

"No." She looked into Hunter's beloved gray eyes. "I am more than willing."

"So be it. Kneel here." The priest moved behind the altar and began the mass.

"It's in Latin," she whispered. "I don't understand a thing he's saying."

Hunter leaned close. "No matter. I pledge to honor, cherish and protect you all the days of your life, Meg." He reached into his sporran and pulled out a band of gold.

"Where did you get the ring?"

"From the smithy. If it does no' fit, we'll have him fix it."

269

The priest cleared his throat and sent them both a stern look. Her heart fluttered away in her chest, and the priest droned on. She hardly noticed. Hunter knelt beside her, his eyes filled with love and tenderness as they met hers. They made the appropriate responses when the priest asked it of them, and Hunter slipped the ring on her finger when told to do so. Happiness filled her near to bursting. Never in a million years would she have guessed she'd be snatched from her time, only to find her love in the past.

Finally the mass ended. She was married. Her husband clasped her hand in his and led her out of the church. Amidst the congratulations, Margaret whispered that she'd had the same chamber Meghan had stayed in the night before prepared for their wedding night.

A small feast awaited them in the great hall. Food was the last thing on her mind. Hunter led her to the table on the dais and helped her settle into a chair, while servants poured wine and ale. Every moment she'd shared with Hunter since the day he'd snatched her from the exhibition with her father played through her mind. She smiled.

"What is it, *mo céile?*"

"I was just thinking about what led up to this point." She leaned against him, soaking up the warmth he radiated. "I will always miss my family, but I'm happy."

"It gladdens my heart to hear you say it. You were right all along, Meg. I was as blind as your grandmother's thirteen-year-old pug." He winked. "What is a pug, if you dinna mind my asking?"

She held her hands out to show him about how big most pugs were. "They are funny little dogs with pushed-in faces that make snoring noises when they breathe." She chuckled at his disgruntled expression. "I was frustrated with you when I said it."

"I imagine you were." He rubbed her palm with his thumb, his gaze filled with tenderness. "But you have forgiven me, aye?"

She nodded, and answering heat uncoiled within her. She couldn't wait to be alone with him. Meghan ate a few bites, had a goblet of very nice wine, and nudged her husband in the side. "How long do we have to stay here?"

"No' another moment." He rose and held out his hand to help her up. "My lady wife and I bid you all good eve. Our thanks for joining us to celebrate our wedding." He bowed to the small group of soldiers who were more than happy to stuff their faces and drink ale. The men cheered and stomped their feet.

"We're in the chamber I had last night, Hunter." She held on to his hand with both of hers.

"I would prefer to be with you under the sky and the pines like we were. That morning will always hold a place in my heart."

"We argued," she said, frowning up at him. Anticipation quickened her pulse, and a surge of desire swept through her.

"You gave yourself to me." He opened the chamber door and waited for her to enter. "I will never forget how sweet you were in my arms that morn."

The covers on the large four-poster bed had been turned down, and a nice fire burned in the hearth. Two goblets and a pitcher of wine sat on the table in the corner. Sunlight poured into the room from the window. Everything was perfect. She turned the ring on her finger. "Our wedding night is more like a wedding afternoon."

"Still, I propose we remain abed until morning, wife."

"I'm all for that, husband." She walked into his arms and tilted her head up for his kiss. He brushed his lips over hers and then nibbled at her bottom lip. Shivers of anticipation raced along her nerves. She put her arms around his neck and deepened the kiss, gratified when he groaned. Tugging and unbuckling, Meghan soon had him the way she wanted him—gloriously naked. Hunter returned the favor, and they held each other in the middle of the room.

"Dinna ever leave me, lass. Swear it."

"I would never leave you, Hunter, but—"

"Dinna say everyone dies. I ken as much." He stared intently into her eyes. "That's no' what I mean. I took you from your time. What if you get the chance to go back?"

"I'm right where I am meant to be." She tightened her arms around his waist. "I will stay with you forever. I swear it." Her family would always be with her in her heart, but deep in her bones she knew she belonged with Hunter, whatever the century might be.

"I ken my place now, Meg." He kissed her, stroking her skin with his callused hands, building the fire already smoldering between them. He nuzzled her neck and whispered, "In your arms, I am home. This is where I belong."

Hunter scooped her up and carried her to the bed, placing her in the center of the feather mattress. He stretched out next to her, and his heated gaze roamed over her. "Mine."

Meghan ran her palms over his muscled chest. Would she ever get used to how powerful he was? "Mine."

He chuckled and rolled over to cover her. Keeping his weight propped up on his elbows, he grinned down at her. "Beag Curaidh, 'tis true. I am yours."

His lovemaking was slow, tender and reverent. Passion flared, but her husband kept the fires banked. In this she was in perfect agreement. She wanted the sweet melding of their bodies and souls to last. Together they climbed to the peak of pleasure. Hunter called out her name when he came, and she fell apart in his strong arms.

Satisfied and happy, she lay in her husband's arms. "We're riding into a war at home."

"Aye." He tightened his arms around her. "With you by my side, I've no doubt of the outcome, lass. You are *almost* as skilled as I."

"*Almost?*" She pushed herself up to glare at him. He laughed, and his joy turned her insides to melted chocolate. He'd lost so much, gone through so much as a child, and seeing him so happy meant the world to her. "Any time, any place, consider the gauntlet tossed."

"Och, I only tease. You are every bit as skilled as . . . Allain."

She huffed out a disgruntled breath. He ran his hands up and down her arms, chuckling again.

"I would have you train our men in the mixed martial arts, Beag Curaidh. 'Twill give us another advantage against our enemies."

"I would love to train our men." She should tell him about gun powder, cannon and pistols. They would change things forever, and she wanted their clan to be prepared. Not now though. She didn't want to talk about wars and fighting when she had only loving him on her mind.

"That reminds me," he said as he got up and crossed the room to their pile of discarded clothing. He snatched up his sporran and opened it. Pulling out her spurs, he shot her a sheepish look. "I am ashamed to admit that I kept these." He padded back to the bed. "'Twas selfish, but I wanted something to remember you by, and these . . . Och, you are a knight in every sense of the word, and your spurs, more than anything else . . ." He placed them in her out-stretched hands. "Nothing could be more fitting to remind me of you. You will always be my Beag Curaidh. I will never forget how you saved Allain's life, or how you defeated me so easily the day I took you from your father."

Meghan held the spurs in her hands. Her father had given them to her when she'd passed all his tests of skill and strength. Her father had trained her. Had he suspected all along one of his children would travel back through time to balance the scales? Meghan set the spurs aside and held her arms out to Hunter. She was sure of one thing. She loved her pea-brained, obstinate knight, and her home was wherever he might be.

EPILOGUE

One Year Later

Hunter paced around his great hall. "Was it like this for you when Sky Elizabeth was born, Da? Did you make yourself ill with worry?" he asked, glancing at Malcolm where he sat by the hearth, his legs outstretched and an ale in his hands.

"Aye. What father to-be does no' worry?" Malcolm shot him a crooked smile.

"At least my Erin is with her, lad." Robley held up his mug of ale. "And Lady True. She could no' be in better hands."

"Aye, I ken as much, but . . . hasn't it gone on too long?" Hunter stared at the stairs leading to his chamber, where Meghan labored to give birth to their son. "I should go to her."

"Nay." Robley shook his head. "You should turn your mind to something else. The women will send someone with word should you be needed. Tell us how it goes with you and the MacKenzie clan?"

Malcolm straightened in his chair. "Aye, have there been any acts of aggression of late?"

Hunter stood before the hearth. "None for several months now. We are surrounded on all sides by MacKenzie land, but your lands border theirs to the east, and we've the Sutherlands to the north. For every croft they've raided, I've retaliated threefold. For every attack and ambush where they've taken a MacConnell life, I've taken ten of theirs." Hunter glanced up the stairs again. Did he only imagine he heard the cry of his newborn son? "The MacKenzies will trouble us no more, of that I am certain." He glanced at his foster father and Rob. "My thanks to you both for coming, and especially for bringing Erin and Ma with you."

"Och, we would no' have missed the birth of our first grandchild for anything, Hunter." Malcolm's voice was hoarse with emotion. "Your ma and I are gladdened to see you so content."

The doors to the great hall opened, and Áine entered, bringing the scent of a soft summer rain into the hall with her. She wore the guise of the old crone, of course. She always did whilst visiting.

"Shite." Malcolm shot up from his place and moved as far away from her as he could without leaving the hall.

Hunter grinned. "Áine, welcome." He gave his fae ancestor a hug. "You've come for news of our bairn?"

"I need no news." She patted his cheek. "Stop worrying, Grandson. Meghan and your heir are both fine." Turning to glance at Malcolm, she arched a brow. "You have no reason to fear me, Malcolm. Have I not told you oft enough? Must you cower in the corner so?"

"I dinna fear you, madam." Malcolm stayed where he was. "I simply find this corner of the great hall particularly comfortable."

True appeared at the top of the stairs and started down. "Hunter, come meet your son. He's perfect, and Meghan is well. She's asking for you."

He ran for the stairs, taking them three at a time, his heart thundering away in his chest.

Erin peered down the corridor at him. She held the door open. "Everything went well, Hunter. I'll leave you with your wife and son for a while, but I'll be back to check on her soon."

"My thanks, Erin." He gave her a quick hug. "We are so blessed to have you here." His eyes stung as he caught sight of his wife. She held their swaddled bairn to her breast, and she fair glowed with contentment and happiness. He swore his feet scarce touched the floorboards as he made his way to her side. She scooted over to make room for him, and he lowered himself to the bed beside her.

"Let me see our wee lad, my love." He put his arm around her just as their son's eyes closed.

Meghan placed their bairn on her lap and unwrapped him. "Isn't he beautiful, Hunter?"

He put his forefinger under his son's tiny hand, and the lad's fingers took hold. Hunter's heart turned over in his chest. "That he is, my love. Ne'er has there been such a perfect bairn, and he's ours." He drew her close and kissed her forehead. "What shall we call him? Did you decide between Connor or Mahon?" He touched his son's downy head. "May I hold him?"

"Of course you can hold him. He just ate, so you might want to pat his back a little." Meghan laid a folded piece of linen on his shoulder, and then she wrapped the blankets around their son again. "Remember to support his head."

"Aye, my love. I do have younger foster sisters and brothers, you ken. This willna be the first time I've held a bairn." He took his son from her. "You must be tired. Why don't you rest? I'll be right here to watch over you both." *Now and forever.* His chest filled with pride and love as he beheld the small circle of his family. Their circle would grow with time, but for now, he had more than enough. He wanted for nothing.

She yawned. "I hear footsteps in the hall. I'll rest once everyone has gotten a chance to meet Connor." She glanced at him. "I hope you're OK with the name. If we have another son, we'll call him Mahon after your father."

"Agreed." Their chamber door opened, and Malcolm and Robley entered.

"No more than two at a time can visit, and for no more than a few moments." Malcolm came to stand by their bed. "'Tis Erin's orders." He leaned close. "Let's have a look at him, my lad."

His foster father and Robley made a fuss over Connor for their allotted time, and then they left. Áine entered next. Her face lit with joy, and the corners of her birdlike eyes creased. He no longer had any trouble with her true appearance, but for the sake of their villagers, she came to them as Madame Giselle. Now that the old baron had passed, his clan no longer feared their fae heritage, and many, especially those who possessed fae abilities, suspected the old crone was more than she appeared to be.

"It's good to see you, Áine," Meghan said. "Would you like to meet the newest member of our family?"

"Aye, let me hold him." She held out her arms. "You are well, child?" she asked Meghan.

"I couldn't be better, thank you," Meghan said, beaming.

Hunter didn't hesitate, and rose with his son against his shoulder. Placing the bairn in her outstretched arms, he told her, "We're calling him Connor after Meghan's father."

"He's a fine lad," she said, rocking him gently and gazing at his face. "A fine lad indeed."

"I owe you my thanks, Granddam."

"Nonsense. You owe me nothing. Take care of your family, Hunter." She kissed Connor's forehead and handed him back. "I'll check in with you from time to time, but for now, I must leave."

For an instant, her appearance wavered and shimmered, and he caught a glimpse of her true being. "We will miss you, my lady. Dinna be gone for too long."

Áine's soft laughter filled their chamber and his heart.

"Time is relative, Grandson. A moment to me is a lifetime to you. If I wish, I can visit you as a wee lad, or as you will be in your dotage. Time does not stretch out in a line as you mortals think, but coils and bends over itself. It is a road with many stops along the way, both ahead and behind. Know this: you have my blessing and my protection in all things." Her eyes glowed blue. "I want only the best for you."

A nod was all he could manage. His heart was so full, speech was beyond him. His gaze went to his wife.

"We will miss you, Áine," Meghan said. "Don't be away from us for too long, whether in the past or the future."

As always, Meghan kent exactly what he felt and what to say. She was his center, his love, and he couldn't imagine his life without her. He nodded again, and Áine took her leave.

Hunter moved back to his place beside his wife. He placed their son on his lap, and they both watched as Connor slept. "I love you, Beag Curaidh."

"And I you," she whispered with a yawn.

"Sleep, lass. I have your back." His wife sighed and placed her head on his shoulder. He drew her close and rested his cheek on top of her head as she closed her lovely brown eyes. Content, he held his family in his arms, secure in his place and in his purpose.

ACKNOWLEDGMENTS

I wish to thank organizations like Romance Writers of America and Midwest Fiction Writers for nurturing and supporting authors like myself at every stage in our careers. I have learned so much and gained so much while in the company of other writers while attending the conferences and workshops.

I want to thank my fantastic critique partners, Tamara Hughes and Wyndemere Coffey, for your insights as well as for your friendship. To my wonderful agent, Nalini Akolekar, thank you for your belief in my stories. And to the amazing crew at Montlake Romance, I've said it before, and I'll say it again: I am so very fortunate to have the opportunity to work with such an amazing group of professionals! Thank you.

ABOUT THE AUTHOR

As a child, Barbara Longley moved frequently, learning early on how to entertain herself with stories. Adulthood didn't tame her peripatetic ways: she has lived on an Appalachian commune, taught on an Indian reservation, and traveled the country from coast to coast. After having children of her own, she decided to try staying put, choosing Minnesota as her home. By day, she puts her master's degree in special education to use teaching elementary school. By night, she explores all things mythical, paranormal, and newsworthy, channeling what she learns into her writing.

Ms. Longley loves to hear from readers and can be reached through her website, www.barbaralongley.com, Twitter @barbaralongley, or on Facebook facebook.com/barlongley.